Wisps of though flicked through Telzey's mind as the silent line of shadows moved deeper into the park with her.

They were curious; this was the first human mind which hadn't seemed deaf and silent to their form of communication. They'd been assured Telzey would have something of genuine importance to tell them; and there was some derision about that. But they were willing to wait a little, and find out.

"Tick-Tock?" she whispered, suddenly a little short of breath. A single up-and-down purring note replied from the bushes on her right. TT was still around, for whatever good that might do.

Then in the mental sensations washing about her, a special excitement rose suddenly, a surge of almost gleeful wildness that choked away her breath. Awareness followed of a pair of unseen malignant crimson eyes fastened on her, moving steadily closer—they'd turned her over to that red-eyed horror! She sat still, feeling mouse-sized.

Something came out with a crash from a thicket behind her. Her muscles went tight. But it was TT who rubbed a hard head against her shoulder, then stopped between Telzey and the bushes on their right, back rigid, neck fur erect, tail twisting. In the greenery something made a slow, heavy stir.

TT's lips peeled back from her teeth. Her head swung towards the motion, ears flattening, transformed to a split, snarling demon-mask. A long shriek ripped from her lungs, raw with fury, blood lust and challenge. . . .

# TELZEY AMBERDON

## The Complete Federation of the Hub

### Volume 1

## JAMES H. SCHMITZ

## EDITED BY ERIC FLINT

### co-edited by Guy Gordon

BAEN

TELZEY AMBERDON

This is a work of fiction. All the characters and events portrayed
in this book are fictional, and any resemblance to real people or
incidents is purely coincidental.

"Novice" © 1962, first appeared in *Analog*, June 1962; "Undercurrents" © 1964,
first appeared in *Analog*, May & June 1964; "Poltergeist" © 1971, first appeared
in *Analog*, July 1971; "Goblin Night" © 1965, first appeared in *Analog*, April
1965; "Sleep No More" © 1965, first appeared in *Analog*, August 1965; "The
Lion Game" © 1971, first appeared in *Analog*, August 1971; "Blood of Nalakia"
© 1953, first appeared under the title "The Vampirate" in *Science Fiction Plus*,
Dec. 1953; "The Star Hyacinths" © 1961, first appeared in *Amazing Stories*,
Dec. 1961; all copyright to the estate of James H. Schmitz.

Afterword © 2000 by Eric Flint; "A Short History of the Hub" © 2000 by
Guy Gordon.

A Baen Book

Baen Publishing Enterprises
P.O. Box 1403
Riverdale, NY 10471
www.baen.com

ISBN: 0-671-67851-0

Cover art by Bob Eggleton

First printing, March 2000
Second printing, November 2000
Third printing, February 2002

Distributed by Simon & Schuster
1230 Avenue of the Americas
New York, NY 10020

Production by Windhaven Press, Auburn, NH
Printed in the United States of America

# CONTENTS

# TELZEY

# I: Novice

There was, Telzey Amberdon thought, someone besides TT and herself in the garden. Not, of course, Aunt Halet, who was in the house waiting for an early visitor to arrive, and not one of the servants. Someone or something else must be concealed among the thickets of magnificently flowering native Jontarou shrubs about Telzey.

She could think of no other way to account for Tick-Tock's spooked behavior—nor, to be honest about it, for the manner her own nerves were acting up without visible cause this morning.

Telzey plucked a blade of grass, slipped the end between her lips and chewed it gently, her face puzzled and concerned. She wasn't ordinarily afflicted with nervousness. Fifteen years old, genius level, brown as a berry and not at all bad looking in her sunbriefs, she was the youngest member of one of Orado's most prominent families and a second-year law student at one of the most exclusive schools in the Federation of the Hub. Her physical, mental, and emotional health, she'd always been informed, were excellent. Aunt Halet's frequent cracks about the inherent instability of the genius level could be ignored; Halet's own stability seemed questionable at best.

But none of that made the present odd situation any less disagreeable . . .

The trouble might have begun, Telzey decided, during the night, within an hour after they arrived from the spaceport at the guesthouse Halet had rented in Port Nichay for their vacation on Jontarou. Telzey had retired at once to her second-story bedroom with Tick-Tock; but she barely got to sleep before something awakened her again. Turning over, she discovered TT reared up before the window, her forepaws on the sill, big cat-head outlined against the star-hazed night sky, staring fixedly down into the garden.

Telzey, only curious at that point, climbed out of bed and joined TT at the window. There was nothing in particular to be seen, and if the scents and minor night-sounds which came from the garden weren't exactly what they were used to, Jontarou was after all an unfamiliar planet. What else would one expect here?

But Tick-Tock's muscular back felt tense and rigid when Telzey laid her arm across it, and except for an absent-minded dig with her forehead against Telzey's shoulder, TT refused to let her attention be distracted from whatever had absorbed it. Now and then, a low, ominous rumble came from her furry throat, a half-angry, half-questioning sound. Telzey began to feel a little uncomfortable. She managed finally to coax Tick-Tock away from the window, but neither of them slept well the rest of the night. At breakfast, Aunt Halet made one of her typical nasty-sweet remarks.

"You look so fatigued, dear—as if you were under some severe mental strain . . . which, of course, you might be," Halet added musingly. With her gold-blond hair piled high on her head and her peaches and cream complexion, Halet looked fresh as a daisy herself . . . a malicious daisy. "Now wasn't I right in insisting to Jessamine that you needed a vacation away from that terribly intellectual school?" She smiled gently.

"Absolutely," Telzey agreed, restraining the impulse to fling a spoonful of egg yolk at her father's younger sister. Aunt Halet often inspired such impulses, but Telzey had promised her mother to avoid actual battles on the Jontarou trip, if possible. After breakfast, she went out into the back garden with Tick-Tock, who immediately walked into a thicket, camouflaged herself and vanished from sight. It seemed to add up to something. But what?

Telzey strolled about the garden a while, maintaining a pretense of nonchalant interest in Jontarou's flowers and colorful bug life. She experienced the most curious little chills of alarm from time to time, but discovered no signs of a lurking intruder, or of TT either. Then, for half an hour or more, she'd just sat cross-legged in the grass, waiting quietly for Tick-Tock to show up of her own accord. And the big lunkhead hadn't obliged.

Telzey scratched a tanned kneecap, scowling at Port Nichay's park trees beyond the garden wall. It seemed idiotic to feel scared when she couldn't even tell whether there was anything to be scared about! And, aside from that, another unreasonable feeling kept growing stronger by the minute now. This was to the effect that she should be doing some unstated but specific thing . . .

In fact, that Tick-Tock *wanted* her to do some specific thing!

Completely idiotic!

Abruptly, Telzey closed her eyes, thought sharply, "Tick-Tock?" and waited—suddenly very angry at herself for having given in to her fancies to this extent—for whatever might happen.

❖          ❖          ❖

She had never really established that she was able to tell, by a kind of symbolic mind-picture method, like a short waking dream, approximately what TT was thinking and feeling. Five years before, when she'd discovered Tick-Tock—an odd-looking and odder-behaved stray kitten then—in the woods near the Amberdons' summer home on Orado, Telzey had thought so. But it might never have been more than a colorful play of her imagination; and after she got into law school and grew increasingly absorbed in her studies, she almost forgot the matter again.

Today, perhaps because she was disturbed about Tick-Tock's behavior, the customary response was extraordinarily prompt. The warm glow of sunlight shining through her closed eyelids faded out quickly and was replaced by some inner darkness. In the darkness there appeared then an image of Tick-Tock sitting a little way off beside an open door in an old stone wall, green eyes fixed on Telzey. Telzey got the impression that TT was inviting her to go through the door, and, for some reason, the thought frightened her.

Again, there was an immediate reaction. The scene with Tick-Tock and the door vanished; and Telzey felt she was standing in a pitch-black room, knowing that if she moved even one step forwards, something that was waiting there silently would reach out and grab her.

Naturally, she recoiled . . . and at once found herself sitting, eyes still closed and the sunlight bathing her lids, in the grass of the guesthouse garden.

She opened her eyes, looked around. Her heart was thumping rapidly. The experience couldn't have lasted more than four or five seconds, but it had been extremely vivid, a whole, compact little nightmare. None of her earlier experiments at getting into mental communication with TT had been like that.

It served her right, Telzey thought, for trying such a childish stunt at the moment! What she should have done at once was to make a methodical search for the foolish beast—TT was bound to be *somewhere* nearby—locate her behind her camouflage, and hang on to her then until this nonsense in the garden was explained! Talented as Tick-Tock was at blotting herself out, it usually was possible to spot her if one directed one's attention to shadow patterns. Telzey began a surreptitious study of the flowering bushes about her.

Three minutes later, off to her right, where the ground was banked beneath a six-foot step in the garden's terraces, Tick-Tock's outline suddenly caught her eye. Flat on her belly, head lifted above her paws, quite motionless, TT seemed like a transparent wraith stretched out along the terrace, barely discernible even when stared at directly. It was a convincing illusion; but what seemed to be rocks, plant leaves, and sun-splotched earth seen through the wraith-outline was simply the camouflage pattern TT had printed for the moment on her hide. She could have changed it completely in an instant to conform to a different background.

Telzey pointed an accusing finger.

"See you!" she announced, feeling a surge of relief which seemed as unaccountable as the rest of it.

The wraith twitched one ear in acknowledgment, the head outlines shifting as the camouflaged face turned towards Telzey. Then the inwardly uncamouflaged, very substantial-looking mouth opened slowly, showing Tick-Tock's red tongue and curved white tusks. The mouth stretched in a wide yawn, snapped shut with a click of meshing teeth, became indistinguishable again. Next, a pair of camouflaged lids drew back from TT's round, brilliant-green eyes. The eyes stared across the lawn at Telzey.

Telzey said irritably, "Quit clowning around, TT!"

The eyes blinked, and Tick-Tock's natural bronze-brown color suddenly flowed over her head, down her neck and across her body into legs and tail. Against the side of the terrace, as if materializing into solidity at that moment, appeared two hundred pounds of supple, rangy, long-tailed cat . . . or catlike creature. TT's actual origin had never been established. The best guesses were that what Telzey had found playing around in the woods five years ago was either a bio-structural experiment which had got away from a private laboratory on Orado, or some spaceman's lost pet, brought to the capital planet from one of the remote colonies beyond the Hub. On top of TT's head was a large, fluffy pompom of white fur, which might have looked ridiculous on another animal, but didn't on her. Even as a fat kitten, hanging head down from the side of a wall by the broad sucker pads in her paws, TT had possessed enormous dignity.

Telzey studied her, the feeling of relief fading again. Tick-Tock, ordinarily the most restful and composed of companions, definitely was still tensed up about something. That big, lazy yawn a moment ago, the attitude of stretched-out relaxation . . . all pure sham!

"What *is* eating you?" she asked in exasperation.

The green eyes stared at her, solemn, watchful, seeming for that fleeting instant quite alien. And why, Telzey thought, should the old question of what Tick-Tock really was pass through her mind just now? After her rather alarming rate of growth began to taper off last year, nobody had cared any more.

For a moment, Telzey had the uncanny certainty of having had the answer to this situation almost in her grasp. An answer which appeared to involve the world of Jontarou, Tick-Tock, and of all unlikely factors—Aunt Halet.

She shook her head. TT's impassive green eyes blinked.

❖     ❖     ❖

Jontarou? The planet lay outside Telzey's sphere of personal interests, but she'd read up on it on the way here from Orado. Among all the worlds of the Hub, Jontarou was *the* paradise for zoologists and sportsmen, a gigantic animal preserve, its continents and seas swarming with magnificent game. Under Federation law, it was being retained deliberately in the primitive state in which it had been discovered. Port Nichay, the only city, actually the only inhabited point on Jontarou, was beautiful and quiet, a pattern of vast but elegantly slender towers, each separated from the others by four or five miles of rolling parkland and interconnected only by the threads of transparent skyways. Near the horizon, just visible from the garden, rose the tallest towers of all, the green and gold spires of the Shikaris' Club, a center of Federation affairs and of social activity. From the aircar which brought them across Port Nichay the evening before, Telzey had seen occasional strings of guesthouses, similar to the one Halet had rented, nestling along the park slopes.

Nothing very sinister about Port Nichay or green Jontarou, surely!

Halet? That blond, slinky, would-be Machiavelli? What could—?

Telzey's eyes narrowed reflectively. There'd been a minor occurrence—at least, it had seemed minor—just before the spaceliner docked last night. A young woman from one of the newscasting services had asked for an interview with the daughter of Federation Councilwoman Jessamine Amberdon. This happened occasionally; and Telzey had no objections until the newscaster's gossipy persistence in inquiring about the "unusual pet" she was bringing to Port Nichay with her began to be annoying. TT might be somewhat unusual, but that was not a matter of general interest; and Telzey said so. Then Halet moved smoothly into the act and held forth on Tick-Tock's appearance, habits, and mysterious antecedents, in considerable detail.

Telzey had assumed that Halet was simply going out of her way to be irritating, as usual. Looking back on the incident, however, it occurred to her that the chatter between her aunt and the newscast woman had sounded oddly stilted—almost like something the two might have rehearsed.

Rehearsed for what purpose? Tick-Tock . . . Jontarou.

Telzey chewed gently on her lower lip. A vacation on Jontarou for the two of them and TT had been Halet's idea, and Halet had enthused about it so much that Telzey's mother at last talked her into accepting. Halet, Jessamine explained privately to Telzey, had felt they were intruders in the Amberdon family, had bitterly resented Jessamine's political honors and, more recently, Telzey's own emerging promise of brilliance. This invitation was Halet's way of indicating a change of heart. Wouldn't Telzey oblige?

So Telzey had obliged, though she took very little stock in Halet's change of heart. She wasn't, in fact, putting it past her aunt to have some involved dirty trick up her sleeve with this trip to Jontarou. Halet's mind worked like that.

So far there had been no actual indications of purposeful mischief. But logic did seem to require a connection between the various puzzling events here . . . A newscaster's rather forced-looking interest in Tick-Tock—Halet could easily have paid for that interview. Then TT's disturbed behavior during their first night in Port Nichay, and Telzey's own formless anxieties and fancies in connection with the guesthouse garden.

The last remained hard to explain. But Tick-Tock . . . and Halet . . . might know something about Jontarou that she didn't know.

Her mind returned to the results of the half-serious attempt she'd made to find out whether there was something Tick-Tock "wanted her to do." An open door? A darkness where somebody waited to grab her if she took even one step forwards? It couldn't have had any significance. Or could it?

So you'd like to try magic, Telzey scoffed at herself. Baby games . . . How far would you have got at law school if you'd asked TT to help with your problems?

Then why had she been thinking about it again?

She shivered, because an eerie stillness seemed to settle on the garden. From the side of the terrace, TT's green eyes watched her.

Telzey had a feeling of sinking down slowly into a sunlit dream, into something very remote from law school problems.

"Should I go through the door?" she whispered.

The bronze cat-shape raised its head slowly. TT began to purr.

Tick-Tock's name had been derived in kittenhood from the manner in which she purred—a measured, oscillating sound, shifting from high to low, as comfortable and often as continuous as the unobtrusive pulse of an old clock. It was the first time, Telzey realized now, that she'd heard the sound since their arrival on Jontarou. It went on for a dozen seconds or so, then stopped. Tick-Tock continued to look at her.

It appeared to have been an expression of definite assent . . .

The dreamlike sensation increased, hazing over Telzey's thoughts. If there was nothing to this mind-communication thing, what harm could symbols do? This time, she wouldn't let them alarm her. And if they did mean something . . .

She closed her eyes.

The sunglow outside faded instantly. Telzey caught a fleeting picture of the door in the wall, and knew in the same moment that she'd already passed through it.

She was not in the dark room then, but poised at the edge of a brightness which seemed featureless and without limit, spread out around her with a feeling-tone like "sea" or "sky." But it was an unquiet place. There was a sense of unseen things on all sides watching her and waiting.

Was this another form of the dark room—a trap set up in her mind? Telzey's attention did a quick shift. She was seated in the grass again; the sunlight beyond her closed eyelids seemed to shine in quietly through rose-tinted curtains. Cautiously, she let her awareness return to the bright area; and it was still there. She had a moment of excited elation. She was controlling this! And why not, she asked herself. These things were happening in *her* mind, after all!

She would find out what they seemed to mean; but she would be in no rush to . . .

An impression as if, behind her, Tick-Tock had thought, "Now I can help again!"

Then a feeling of being swept swiftly, irresistibly forwards, thrust out and down. The brightness exploded in thundering colors around her. In fright, she made the effort to snap her eyes open, to be back in the garden; but now she couldn't make it work. The colors continued to roar about her, like a confusion of excited, laughing, triumphant voices. Telzey felt caught in the middle of it all, suspended in invisible spider webs. Tick-Tock seemed to be somewhere nearby, looking on. Faithless, treacherous TT!

Telzey's mind made another wrenching effort, and there was a change. She hadn't got back into the garden, but the noisy, swirling colors were gone and she had the feeling of reading a rapidly paging book now, though she didn't actually see the book.

The book, she realized, was another symbol for what was happening, a symbol easier for her to understand. There were voices, or what might be voices, around her; on the invisible book she seemed to be reading what they said.

A number of speakers, apparently involved in a fast, hot argument about what to do with her. Impressions flashed past . . .

Why waste time with her? It was clear that kitten-talk was all she was capable of! . . . Not necessarily; that was a normal first step. Give her a little time! . . . But what—exasperatedly—could *such* a small-bite *possibly* know that would be of significant value?

There was a slow, blurred, awkward-seeming interruption. Its content was not comprehensible to Telzey at all, but in some unmistakable manner it was defined as Tick-Tock's thought.

A pause as the circle of speakers stopped to consider whatever TT had thrown into the debate.

Then another impression . . . one that sent a shock of fear through Telzey as it rose heavily into her awareness. Its sheer intensity momentarily displaced the book-reading symbolism. A savage voice seemed to rumble:

"Toss the tender small-bite to *me*"—malevolent crimson eyes fixed on Telzey from somewhere not far away—"and let's be done here!"

Startled, stammering protest from Tick-Tock, accompanied by gusts of laughter from the circle. Great sense of humor these characters had, Telzey thought bitterly. That crimson-eyed thing wasn't joking at all!

More laughter as the circle caught her thought. Then a kind of majority opinion found sudden expression:

"Small-bite *is* learning! No harm to wait—We'll find out quickly—Let's . . ."

The book ended; the voices faded; the colors went blank. In whatever jumbled-up form she'd been getting the impressions at that point—Telzey couldn't have begun to describe it—the whole thing suddenly stopped.

✧     ✧     ✧

She found herself sitting in the grass, shaky, scared, eyes open. Tick-Tock stood beside the terrace, looking at her. An air of hazy unreality still hung about the garden.

She might have flipped! She didn't think so; but it certainly seemed possible! Otherwise . . . Telzey made an attempt to sort over what had happened.

Something *had* been in the garden! Something had been inside her mind. Something that was at home on Jontarou.

There'd been a feeling of perhaps fifty or sixty of these . . . well, beings. Alarming beings! Reckless, wild, hard . . . and that red-eyed nightmare! Telzey shuddered.

They'd contacted Tick-Tock first, during the night. TT understood them better than she could. Why? Telzey found no immediate answer.

Then Tick-Tock had tricked her into letting her mind be invaded by these beings. There must have been a very definite reason for that.

She looked over at Tick-Tock. TT looked back. Nothing stirred in Telzey's thoughts. Between *them* there was still no direct communication.

Then how had the beings been able to get through to her?

Telzey wrinkled her nose. Assuming this was real, it seemed clear that the game of symbols she'd made up between herself and TT had provided the opening. Her whole experience just now had been in the form of symbols, translating whatever occurred into something she could consciously grasp.

"Kitten-talk" was how the beings referred to the use of symbols; they seemed contemptuous of it. Never mind, Telzey told herself; they'd agreed she was learning.

The air over the grass appeared to flicker. Again she had the impression of reading words off a quickly moving, not quite visible book.

"You're being taught and you're learning," was what she seemed to read. "The question was whether you were capable of partial understanding as your friend insisted. Since you were, everything else that can be done will be accomplished very quickly."

A pause, then with a touch of approval, "You're a well-formed mind, small-bite! Odd and with incomprehensibilities, but well-formed—"

One of the beings, and a fairly friendly one—at least not unfriendly. Telzey framed a tentative mental question. "Who are you?"

"You'll know very soon." The flickering ended; she realized she and the question had been dismissed for the moment. She looked over at Tick-Tock again.

"Can't *you* talk to me now, TT?" she asked silently.

A feeling of hesitation.

"Kitten-talk!" was the impression that formed itself with difficulty then. It was awkward, searching; but it came unquestionably from TT. "Still learning, too, Telzey!" TT seemed half anxious, half angry. "We—"

A sharp buzz-note reached Telzey's ears, wiping out the groping thought-impression. She jumped a little, glanced down. Her wrist-talker was signaling. For a moment, she seemed poised uncertainly between a world where unseen, dangerous-sounding beings referred to one as small-bite and where TT was learning to talk, and the familiar other world where wrist-communicators buzzed periodically in a matter-of-fact manner. Settling back into the more familiar world, she switched on the talker.

"Yes?" she said. Her voice sounded husky.

"Telzey, dear," Halet murmured honey-sweet from the talker, "would you come back into the house, please? The living room—We have a visitor who very much wants to meet you."

Telzey hesitated, eyes narrowing. Halet's visitor wanted to meet *her*?

"Why?" she asked.

"He has something *very* interesting to tell you, dear." The edge of triumphant malice showed for an instant, vanished in murmuring sweetness again. "So please hurry!"

"All right." Telzey stood up. "I'm coming."

"Fine, dear!" The talker went dead.

Telzey switched off the instrument, noticed that Tick-Tock had chosen to disappear meanwhile.

Flipped? She wondered, starting up towards the house. It was clear Aunt Halet had prepared some unpleasant surprise to spring on her, which was hardly more than normal behavior for Halet. The other business? She couldn't be certain of anything there. Leaving out TT's strange actions—which might have a number of causes, after all—that entire string of events could have been created inside her head. There was no contradictory evidence so far.

But it could do no harm to take what *seemed* to have happened at face value. Some pretty grim event might be shaping up, in a very real way, around here . . .

"You reason logically!" The impression now was of a voice speaking to her, a voice that made no audible sound. It was the same being who'd addressed her a minute or two ago.

The two worlds between which Telzey had felt suspended seemed to glide slowly together and become one.

"I go to law school," she explained to the being, almost absently.

Amused agreement. "So we heard."

"What do you want of me?" Telzey inquired.

"You'll know soon enough."

"Why not tell me now?" Telzey urged. It seemed about to dismiss her again.

Quick impatience flared at her. "Kitten-pictures! Kitten-thoughts! Kitten-talk! Too slow, too slow! YOUR pictures—too much YOU! Wait till the . . ."

Circuits close . . . channels open . . . Obstructions clear? What *had* it said? There'd been only the blurred image of a finicky, delicate, but perfectly normal technical operation of some kind.

" . . . Minutes now!" the voice concluded. A pause, then another thought tossed carelessly at her. "This is more important to you, small-bite, than to *us*!" The voice impression ended as sharply as if a communicator had snapped off.

Not *too* friendly! Telzey walked on towards the house, a new fear growing inside her . . . a fear like the awareness of a storm gathered nearby, still quiet—deadly quiet, but ready to break.

"Kitten-pictures!" a voice seemed to jeer distantly, a whispering in the park trees beyond the garden wall.

Halet's cheeks were lightly pinked; her blue eyes sparkled. She looked downright stunning, which meant to anyone who knew her that the worst side of Halet's nature was champing at the bit again. On uninformed males it had a dazzling effect, however; and Telzey wasn't surprised to find their visitor wearing a tranced expression when she came into the living room. He was a tall, outdoorsy man with a tanned, bony face, a neatly trained black mustache, and a scar down one cheek which would have seemed dashing if it hadn't been for the stupefied look. Beside his chair stood a large, clumsy instrument which might have been some kind of telecamera.

Halet performed introductions. Their visitor was Dr. Droon, a zoologist. He had been tuned in on Telzey's newscast interview on the liner the night before, and wondered whether Telzey would care to discuss Tick-Tock with him.

"Frankly, no," Telzey said.

Dr. Droon came awake and gave Telzey a surprised look. Halet smiled easily.

"My niece doesn't intend to be discourteous, doctor," she explained.

"Of course not," the zoologist agreed doubtfully.

"It's just," Halet went on, "that Telzey is a little, oh, sensitive where Tick-Tock is concerned. In her own way, she's attached to the animal. Aren't you, dear?"

"Yes," Telzey said blandly.

"Well, we hope this isn't going to disturb you too much, dear." Halet glanced significantly at Dr. Droon. "Dr. Droon, you must understand, is simply doing . . . well, there is something very important he must tell you now."

Telzey transferred her gaze back to the zoologist. Dr. Droon cleared his throat. "I, ah, understand, Miss Amberdon, that you're unaware of what kind of creature your, ah, Tick-Tock is?"

Telzey started to speak, then checked herself, frowning. She had been about to state that she knew exactly what kind of creature TT was . . . but she didn't, of course!

Or did she? She . . .

She scowled absent-mindedly at Dr. Droon, biting her lip.

"Telzey!" Halet prompted gently.

"Huh?" Telzey said. "Oh . . . please go on, doctor!"

Dr. Droon steepled his fingers. "Well," he said, "she . . . your pet . . . is, ah, a young crest cat. Nearly full grown now, apparently, and—"

"Why, yes!" Telzey cried.

The zoologist looked at her. "You knew that—"

"Well, not really," Telzey admitted. "Or sort of." She laughed, her cheeks flushed. "This is the most . . . go ahead please! Sorry I interrupted." She stared at the wall beyond Dr. Droon with a rapt expression.

The zoologist and Halet exchanged glances. Then Dr. Droon resumed cautiously. The crest cats, he said, were a species native to Jontarou. Their existence had been known for only eight years. The species appeared to have had a somewhat limited range—the Baluit Mountains on the opposite side of the huge continent on which Port Nichay had been built . . .

Telzey barely heard him. A very curious thing was happening. For every sentence Dr. Droon uttered, a dozen other sentences appeared in her awareness. More accurately, it was as if an instantaneous smooth flow of information relevant to whatever he said arose continuously from what might have been almost her own memory, but wasn't. Within a minute or two, she knew more about the crest cats of Jontarou than Dr. Droon could have told her in hours . . . much more than he'd ever known.

She realized suddenly that he'd stopped talking, that he had asked her a question. "Miss Amberdon?" he repeated now, with a note of uncertainty.

"Yar-rrr-REE!" Telzey told him softly. "I'll drink your blood!"

"Eh?"

Telzey blinked, focused on Dr. Droon, wrenching her mind away from a splendid view of the misty-blue peaks of the Baluit range.

"Sorry," she said briskly. "Just a joke!" She smiled. "Now what were you saying?"

The zoologist looked at her in a rather odd manner for a moment. "I was inquiring," he said then, "whether you were familiar with the sporting rules established by the various hunting associations of the Hub in connection with the taking of game trophies?"

Telzey shook her head. "No, I never heard of them."

The rules, Dr. Droon explained, laid down the type of equipment . . . weapons, spotting and tracking instruments, number of assistants, and so forth . . . a sportsman could legitimately use in the pursuit of any specific type of game. "Before the end of the first year after their discovery," he went on, "the Baluit crest cats had been placed in the ultra-equipment class."

"What's ultra-equipment?" Telzey asked.

"Well," Dr. Droon said thoughtfully, "it doesn't quite involve the use of full battle armor . . . not quite! And, of course, even with that classification the sporting principle of mutual accessibility must be observed."

"Mutual . . . oh, I see!" Telzey paused as another wave of silent information rose into her awareness; went on, "So the game has to be able to get at the sportsman too, eh?"

"That's correct. Except in the pursuit of various classes of flying animals, a shikari would not, for example, be permitted the use of an aircar other than as a means of simple transportation. Under these conditions, it was soon established that crest cats were being obtained by sportsmen who went after them at a rather consistent one-to-one ratio."

Telzey's eyes widened. She'd gathered something similar from her other information source but hadn't quite believed it. "One hunter killed for each cat bagged?" she said. "That's pretty rough sport, isn't it?"

"Extremely rough sport!" Dr. Droon agreed dryly. "In fact, when the statistics were published, the sporting interest in winning a Baluit cat trophy appears to have suffered a sudden and sharp decline. On the other hand, a more scientific interest in these remarkable animals was coincidingly created, and many permits for their acquisition by the agents of museums, universities, public and private collections were issued. Sporting rules, of course, do not apply to that activity."

Telzey nodded absently. "I see! *They* used aircars, didn't they? A sort of heavy knockout gun—"

"Aircars, long-range detectors and stunguns are standard equipment in such work," Dr. Droon acknowledged. "Gas and poison are employed, of course, as circumstances dictate. The collectors were relatively successful for a while.

"And then a curious thing happened. Less than two years after their existence became known, the crest cats of the Baluit range were extinct! The inroads made on their numbers by man cannot begin to account for this, so it must be assumed that a sudden plague wiped them out. At any rate, not another living member of the species has been seen on Jontarou until you landed here with your pet last night."

Telzey sat silent for some seconds. Not because of what he had said, but because the other knowledge was still flowing into her mind. On one very important point that was at variance with what the zoologist had stated; and from there a coldly logical pattern was building up. Telzey didn't grasp the pattern in complete detail yet, but what she saw of it stirred her with a half incredulous dread.

She asked, shaping the words carefully but with only a small part of her attention on what she was really saying, "Just what does all that have to do with Tick-Tock, Dr. Droon?"

Dr. Droon glanced at Halet, and returned his gaze to Telzey. Looking very uncomfortable but quite determined, he told her, "Miss Amberdon, there is a Federation law which states that when a species is threatened with extinction, any available survivors must be transferred to the Life Banks of the University League, to insure their indefinite preservation. Under the circumstances, this law applies to, ah, Tick-Tock!"

So that had been Halet's trick. She'd found out about the crest cats, might have put in as much as a few months arranging to make the discovery of TT's origin on Jontarou seem a regrettable mischance— something no one could have foreseen or prevented.

In the Life Banks, from what Telzey had heard of them, TT would cease to exist as an individual awareness while scientists tinkered around with the possibilities of reconstructing her species.

Telzey studied her aunt's carefully sympathizing face for an instant, asked Dr. Droon, "What about the other crest cats you said were collected before they became extinct here? Wouldn't they be enough for what the Life Banks need?"

He shook his head. "Two immature male specimens are known to exist, and they are at present in the Life Banks. The others that were taken alive at the time have been destroyed . . . often under nearly disastrous circumstances. They are enormously cunning, enormously savage creatures, Miss Amberdon! The additional fact that they can conceal themselves to the point of being virtually indetectable except by the use of instruments makes them one of the most dangerous animals known. Since the young female which you raised as a pet has remained docile . . . so far . . . you may not really be able to appreciate that."

"Perhaps I can," Telzey said. She nodded at the heavy-looking instrument standing beside his chair. "And that's—?"

"It's a life detector combined with a stungun, Miss Amberdon. I have no intention of harming your pet, but we can't take chances with an animal of that type. The gun's charge will knock it unconscious for several minutes—just long enough to let me secure it with paralysis belts."

"You're a collector for the Life Banks, Dr. Droon?"

"That's correct."

"Dr. Droon," Halet remarked, "has obtained a permit from the Planetary Moderator, authorizing him to claim Tick-Tock for the University League and remove her from the planet, dear. So you see there is simply nothing we can do about the matter! Your mother wouldn't like us to attempt to obstruct the law, would she?" Halet paused. "The permit should have your signature, Telzey, but I can sign in your stead if necessary."

That was Halet's way of saying it would do no good to appeal to Jontarou's Planetary Moderator. She'd taken the precaution of getting his assent to the matter first.

"So now if you'll just call Tick-Tock, dear . . ." Halet went on.

Telzey barely heard the last words. She felt herself stiffening slowly, while the living room almost faded from her sight. Perhaps, in that instant, some additional new circuit had closed in her mind, or some additional new channel had opened, for TT's purpose in tricking her into contact with the reckless, mocking beings outside was suddenly and numbingly clear.

And what it meant immediately was that she'd have to get out of the house without being spotted at it, and go some place where she could be undisturbed for half an hour.

She realized that Halet and the zoologist were both staring at her.

"Are you ill, dear?"

"No." Telzey stood up. It would be worse than useless to try to tell these two anything! Her face must be pretty white at the moment—she could feel it—but they assumed, of course, that the shock of losing TT had just now sunk in on her.

"I'll have to check on that law you mentioned before I sign anything," she told Dr. Droon.

"Why, yes . . ." He started to get out of his chair. "I'm sure that can be arranged, Miss Amberdon!"

"Don't bother to call the Moderator's office," Telzey said. "I brought my law library along. I'll look it up myself." She turned to leave the room.

"My niece," Halet explained to Dr. Droon who was

beginning to look puzzled, "attends law school. She's always so absorbed in her studies . . . Telzey?"

"Yes, Halet?" Telzey paused at the door.

"I'm very glad you've decided to be sensible about this, dear. But don't take too long, will you? We don't want to waste Dr. Droon's time."

"It shouldn't take more than five or ten minutes," Telzey told her agreeably. She closed the door behind her, and went directly to her bedroom on the second floor. One of her two valises was still unpacked. She locked the door behind her, opened the unpacked valise, took out a pocket edition law library and sat down at the table with it.

She clicked on the library's view-screen, tapped the clearing and index buttons. Half a minute later, she was glancing over the legal section on which Dr. Droon had based his claim. The library confirmed what he had said.

Very neat of Halet, Telzey thought, very nasty . . . and pretty idiotic! Even a second-year law student could think immediately of two or three ways in which a case like that could have been dragged out in the Federation's courts for a couple of decades before the question of handing Tick-Tock over to the Life Banks became too acute.

Well, Halet simply wasn't really intelligent. And the plot to shanghai TT was hardly even a side issue now.

Telzey snapped the tiny library shut, fastened it to the belt of her sunsuit and went over to the open window. A two-foot ledge passed beneath the window, leading to the roof of a patio on the right. Fifty yards beyond the patio, the garden ended in a natural-stone wall. Behind it lay one of the big wooded park areas which formed most of the ground level of Port Nichay.

Tick-Tock wasn't in sight. A sound of voices came from ground-floor windows on the left. Halet had brought her maid and chauffeur along; and a chef had showed up in time to make breakfast this morning, as part of the city's guesthouse service. Telzey took the empty valise to the window, set it on end against the left side of the frame, and let the window slide down until its lower edge rested on the valise. She went back to the house guard-screen panel beside the door, put her finger against the lock button, and pushed.

The sound of voices from the lower floor was cut off as outer doors and windows slid silently shut all about the house. Telzey glanced back at the window. The valise had creaked a little as the guard field drove the frame down on it, but it was supporting the thrust. She returned to the window, wriggled feet foremost through the opening, twisted around and got a footing on the ledge.

A minute later, she was scrambling quietly down a vine-covered patio trellis to the ground. Even after they discovered she was gone, the guard screen would keep everybody in the house for some little while. They'd either have to disengage the screen's main mechanisms and start poking around in them, or force open the door to her bedroom and get the lock unset. Either approach would involve confusion, upset tempers, and generally delay any organized pursuit.

Telzey edged around the patio and started towards the wall, keeping close to the side of the house so she couldn't be seen from the windows. The shrubbery made minor rustling noises as she threaded her way through it . . . and then there was a different stirring which might have been no more than a slow, steady current of air moving among the bushes behind her. She shivered involuntarily but didn't look back.

She came to the wall, stood still, measuring its height, jumped and got an arm across it, swung up a knee and squirmed up and over. She came down on her feet with a small thump in the grass on the other side, glanced back once at the guest house, crossed a path and went on among the park trees.

❖          ❖          ❖

Within a few hundred yards, it became apparent
that she had an escort. She didn't look around for
them, but spread out to right and left like a skirmish
line, keeping abreast with her, occasional shadows slid
silently through patches of open, sunlit ground, disappeared again under the trees. Otherwise, there was
hardly anyone in sight. Port Nichay's human residents
appeared to make almost no personal use of the vast
parkland spread out beneath their tower apartments;
and its traffic moved over the airways, visible from
the ground only as rainbow-hued ribbons which bisec-
ted the sky between the upper tower levels. An
occasional private aircar went by overhead.

Wisps of thought which were not her own thoughts
flicked through Telzey's mind from moment to moment
as the silent line of shadows moved deeper into the
park with her. She realized she was being sized up,
judged, evaluated again. No more information was
coming through; they had given her as much information as she needed. In the main perhaps, they were
simply curious now. This was the first human mind
they'd been able to make heads or tails of, and that
hadn't seemed deaf and silent to their form of communication. They were taking time out to study it.
They'd been assured she would have something of
genuine importance to tell them; and there was some
derision about that. But they were willing to wait a
little, and find out. They were curious and they liked
games. At the moment, Telzey and what she might try
to do to change their plans was the game on which
their attention was fixed.

Twelve minutes passed before the talker on Telzey's
wrist began to buzz. It continued to signal off and
on for another few minutes, then stopped. Back in
the guesthouse they couldn't be sure yet whether she
wasn't simply locked inside her room and refusing to
answer them. But Telzey quickened her pace.

The park's trees gradually became more massive, reached higher above her, stood spaced more widely apart. She passed through the morning shadow of the residential tower nearest the guesthouse, and emerged from it presently on the shore of a small lake. On the other side of the lake, a number of dappled grazing animals like long-necked, tall horses lifted their heads to watch her. For some seconds they seemed only mildly interested, but then a breeze moved across the lake, crinkling the surface of the water; and as it touched the opposite shore, abrupt panic exploded among the grazers. They wheeled, went flashing away in effortless twenty-foot strides, and were gone among the trees.

Telzey felt a crawling along her spine. It was the first objective indication she'd had of the nature of the company she had brought to the lake, and while it hardly came as a surprise, for a moment her urge was to follow the example of the grazers.

"Tick-Tock?" she whispered, suddenly a little short of breath.

A single up-and-down purring note replied from the bushes on her right. TT was still around, for whatever good that might do. Not too much, Telzey thought, if it came to serious trouble. But the knowledge was somewhat reassuring . . . and this, meanwhile, appeared to be as far as she needed to get from the guesthouse. They'd be looking for her by aircar presently, but there was nothing to tell them in which direction to turn first.

She climbed the bank of the lake to a point where she was screened both by thick, green shrubbery and the top of a single immense tree from the sky, sat down on some dry, mossy growth, took the law library from her belt, opened it and placed it in her lap. Vague stirrings indicated that her escort was also settling down in an irregular circle about her; and apprehension shivered on Telzey's skin again. It wasn't that their attitude was hostile; they were simply overawing. And no one could predict what they might do next. Without looking up, she asked a question in her mind.

"Ready?"

Sense of multiple acknowledgments, variously tinged—sardonic; interestedly amused; attentive; doubtful. Impatience quivered through it too, only tentatively held in restraint, and Telzey's forehead was suddenly wet. Some of them seemed on the verge of expressing disapproval with what was being done here.

Her fingers quickly brought up the Federation law index, and the stir of feeling about her subsided, their attention captured again for the moment. Her thoughts became to some degree detached, ready to dissect another problem in the familiar ways and present the answers to it. Not a very involved problem essentially, but this time it wasn't a school exercise. Her company waited, withdrawn, silent, aloof once more, while the index searched the library. Within a minute and a half she had a dozen reference symbols. She called up the first reference, glanced over a few paragraphs, licked salty sweat from her lip, and said in her thoughts, emphasizing the meaning of each detail of the sentence so that there would be no misunderstanding, "This is the Federation law that applies to the situation which existed originally on this planet. . . ."

There were no interruptions, no commenting thoughts, no intrusions of any kind, as she went step by step through the section, turned to another one, and another. In perhaps twelve minutes she came to the end of the last one, and stopped. Instantly, argument exploded about her.

Telzey was not involved in the argument; in fact, she could grasp only scraps of it. Either they were excluding her deliberately, or the exchange was too swift, practiced and varied to allow her to keep up.

But their vehemence was not encouraging. And was it reasonable to assume that the Federation's laws would have any meaning for minds like these? Telzey snapped the library shut with fingers that had begun to tremble, and placed it on the ground. Then she stiffened. In the sensations washing about her, a special excitement rose suddenly, a surge of almost gleeful wildness that choked away her breath. Awareness followed of a pair of malignant crimson eyes fastened on her, moving steadily closer. A kind of nightmare paralysis seized Telzey—they'd turned her over to that red-eyed horror! She sat still, feeling mouse-sized.

Something came out with a crash from a thicket behind her. Her muscles went tight. But it was TT who rubbed a hard head against her shoulder, took another three stiff-legged steps forward and stopped between Telzey and the bushes on their right, back rigid, neck fur erect, tail twisting.

Expectant silence closed in about them. The circle was waiting. In the greenery on the right something made a slow, heavy stir.

TT's lips peeled back from her teeth. Her head swung towards the motion, ears flattening, transformed to a split, snarling demon-mask. A long shriek ripped from her lungs, raw with fury, blood lust and challenge.

The sound died away. For some seconds the tension about them held; then came a sense of gradual relaxation mingled with a partly amused approval. Telzey was shaking violently. It had been, she was telling herself, a deliberate test . . . not of herself, of course, but of TT. And Tick-Tock had passed with honors. That *her* nerves had been half ruined in the process would seem a matter of no consequence to this rugged crew . . .

She realized next that someone here was addressing her personally.

It took a few moments to steady her jittering thoughts enough to gain a more definite impression than that. This speaker, she discovered then, was a member of the circle of whom she hadn't been aware before. The thought-impressions came hard and cold as iron—a personage who was very evidently in the habit of making major decisions and seeing them carried out. The circle, its moment of sport over, was listening with more than a suggestion of deference. Tick-Tock, far from conciliated, green eyes still blazing, nevertheless was settling down to listen, too.

Telzey began to understand.

Her suggestions, Iron Thoughts informed her, might appear without value to a number of foolish minds here, but *he* intended to see they were given a fair trial. Did he perhaps hear, he inquired next of the circle, throwing in a casual but horridly vivid impression of snapping spines and slashed shaggy throats spouting blood, any objection to that?

Dead stillness all around. There was, definitely, no objection! Tick-Tock began to grin like a pleased kitten.

That point having been settled in an orderly manner now, Iron Thoughts went on coldly to Telzey, what specifically did she propose they should do?

Halet's long, pearl-gray sportscar showed up above the park trees twenty minutes later. Telzey, face turned down towards the open law library in her lap, watched the car from the corner of her eyes. She was in plain view, sitting beside the lake, apparently absorbed in legal research. Tick-Tock, camouflaged among the bushes thirty feet higher up the bank, had spotted the car an instant before she did and announced the fact with a three-second break in her purring. Neither of them made any other move.

The car was approaching the lake but still a good distance off. Its canopy was down, and Telzey could

just make out the heads of three people inside.
Delquos, Halet's chauffeur, would be flying the vehicle, while Halet and Dr. Droon looked around for
her from the sides. Three hundred yards away, the
aircar began a turn to the right. Delquos didn't like
his employer much; at a guess, he had just spotted Telzey and was trying to warn her off.

Telzey closed the library and put it down, picked
up a handful of pebbles and began flicking them idly,
one at a time, into the water. The aircar vanished to
her left.

Three minutes later, she watched its shadow glide
across the surface of the lake towards her. Her heart
began to thump almost audibly, but she didn't look up.
Tick-Tock's purring continued, on its regular, unhurried note. The car came to a stop almost directly overhead. After a couple of seconds, there was a clicking
noise. The purring ended abruptly.

Telzey climbed to her feet as Delquos brought the
car down to the bank of the lake. The chauffeur
grinned ruefully at her. A side door had been opened,
and Halet and Dr. Droon stood behind it. Halet
watched Telzey with a small smile while the naturalist
put the heavy life-detector-and-stungun device carefully down on the floorboards.

"If you're looking for Tick-Tock," Telzey said, "she
isn't here."

Halet just shook her head sorrowfully.

"There's no use lying to us, dear! Dr. Droon just
stunned her."

They found TT collapsed on her side among the
shrubs, wearing her natural color. Her eyes were shut;
her chest rose and fell in a slow breathing motion. Dr.
Droon, looking rather apologetic, pointed out to Telzey
that her pet was in no pain, that the stungun had simply put her comfortably to sleep. He also explained
the use of the two sets of webbed paralysis belts which

he fastened about TT's legs. The effect of the stun charge would wear off in a few minutes, and contact with the inner surfaces of the energized belts would then keep TT anesthetized and unable to move until the belts were removed. She would, he repeated, be suffering no pain throughout the process.

Telzey didn't comment. She watched Delquos raise TT's limp body above the level of the bushes with a gravity hoist belonging to Dr. Droon, and maneuver her back to the car, the others following. Delquos climbed into the car first, opened the big trunk compartment in the rear. TT was slid inside and the trunk compartment locked.

"Where are you taking her?" Telzey asked sullenly as Delquos lifted the car into the air.

"To the spaceport, dear," Halet said. "Dr. Droon and I both felt it would be better to spare your feelings by not prolonging the matter unnecessarily."

Telzey wrinkled her nose disdainfully, and walked up the aircar to stand behind Delquos's seat. She leaned against the back of the seat for an instant. Her legs felt shaky.

The chauffeur gave her a sober wink from the side.

"That's a dirty trick she's played on you, Miss Telzey!" he murmured. "I tried to warn you."

"I know." Telzey took a deep breath. "Look, Delquos, in just a minute something's going to happen! It'll look dangerous, but it won't be. Don't let it get you nervous . . . right?"

"Huh?" Delquos appeared startled, but kept his voice low. "Just *what's* going to happen?"

"No time to tell you. Remember what I said."

Telzey moved back a few steps from the driver's seat, turned around, said unsteadily, "Halet . . . Dr. Droon—"

Halet had been speaking quietly to Dr. Droon; they both looked up.

"If you don't move, and don't do anything stupid," Telzey said rapidly, "you won't get hurt. If you do . . . well, I don't know! You see, there's another crest cat in the car . . ." In her mind she added, "Now!"

It was impossible to tell in just what section of the car Iron Thoughts had been lurking. The carpeting near the rear passenger seats seemed to blur for an instant. Then he was there, camouflage dropped, sitting on the floorboards five feet from the naturalist and Halet.

Halet's mouth opened wide; she tried to scream but fainted instead. Dr. Droon's right hand started out quickly towards the big stungun device beside his seat. Then he checked himself and sat still, ashen-faced.

Telzey didn't blame him for changing his mind. She felt he must be a remarkably brave man to have moved at all. Iron Thoughts, twice as broad across the back as Tick-Tock, twice as massively muscled, looked like a devil-beast even to her. His dark-green marbled hide was criss-crossed with old scar patterns; half his tossing crimson crest appeared to have been ripped away. He reached out now in a fluid, silent motion, hooked a paw under the stungun and flicked upwards. The big instrument rose in an incredibly swift, steep arc eighty feet into the air, various parts flying away from it, before it started curving down towards the treetops below the car. Iron Thoughts lazily swung his head around and looked at Telzey with yellow fire-eyes.

"Miss Telzey! Miss Telzey!" Delquos was muttering behind her. "You're *sure* it won't . . ."

Telzey swallowed. At the moment, she felt barely mouse-sized again. "Just relax!" she told Delquos in a shaky voice. "He's really quite t-t-t-tame."

Iron Thoughts produced a harsh but not unamiable chuckle in her mind.

✧   ✧   ✧

The pearl-gray sportscar, covered now by its streamlining canopy, drifted down presently to a parking platform outside the suite of offices of Jontarou's Planetary Moderator, on the fourteenth floor of the Shikaris' Club Tower. An attendant waved it on into a vacant slot.

Inside the car, Delquos set the brakes, switched off the engine, asked, "Now what?"

"I think," Telzey said reflectively, "we'd better lock you in the trunk compartment with my aunt and Dr. Droon while I talk to the Moderator."

The chauffeur shrugged. He'd regained most of his aplomb during the unhurried trip across the parklands. Iron Thoughts had done nothing but sit in the center of the car, eyes half shut, looking like instant death enjoying a dignified nap and occasionally emitting a ripsawing noise which might have been either his style of purring or a snore. And Tick-Tock, when Delquos peeled the paralysis belts off her legs at Telzey's direction, had greeted him with her usual reserved affability. What the chauffeur was suffering from at the moment was intense curiosity, which Telzey had done nothing to relieve.

"Just as you say, Miss Telzey," he agreed. "I hate to miss whatever you're going to be doing here, but if you *don't* lock me up now, Miss Halet will figure I was helping you and fire me as soon as you let her out."

Telzey nodded, then cocked her head in the direction of the rear compartment. Faint sounds coming through the door indicated that Halet had regained consciousness and was having hysterics.

"You might tell her," Telzey suggested, "that there'll be a grown-up crest cat sitting outside the compartment door." This wasn't true, but neither Delquos nor Halet could know it. "If there's too much racket before I get back, it's likely to irritate him . . ."

A minute later, she set both car doors on lock and went outside, wishing she were less informally clothed. Sunbriefs and sandals tended to make her look juvenile.

The parking attendant appeared startled when she approached him with Tick-Tock striding alongside.

"They'll never let you into the offices with that thing, miss," he informed her. "Why, it doesn't even have a collar!"

"Don't worry about it," Telzey told him aloofly.

She dropped a two-credit piece she'd taken from Halet's purse into his hand, and continued on towards the building entrance. The attendant squinted after her, trying unsuccessfully to dispel an odd impression that the big catlike animal with the girl was throwing a double shadow.

The Moderator's chief receptionist also had some doubts about TT, and possibly about the sunbriefs, though she seemed impressed when Telzey's identification tag informed her she was speaking to the daughter of Federation Councilwoman Jessamine Amberdon.

"You feel you can discuss this . . . emergency . . . only with the Moderator himself, Miss Amberdon?" she repeated.

"Exactly," Telzey said firmly. A buzzer sounded as she spoke. The receptionist excused herself and picked up an earphone. She listened a moment, said blandly, "Yes . . . Of course . . . Yes, I understand," replaced the earphone and stood up, smiling at Telzey.

"Would you come with me, Miss Amberdon?" she said. "I think the Moderator will see you immediately . . ."

Telzey followed her, chewing thoughtfully at her lip. This was easier than she'd expected—in fact, too easy! Halet's work? Probably. A few comments to the effect of "A highly imaginative child . . . overexcitable," while Halet was arranging to have the Moderator's office authorize Tick-Tock's transfer to the Life Banks, along with the implication that Jessamine Amberdon would appreciate a discreet handling of any disturbance Telzey might create as a result.

It was the sort of notion that would appeal to Halet—

They passed through a series of elegantly equipped offices and hallways, Telzey grasping TT's neck-fur in lieu of a leash, their appearance creating a tactfully restrained wave of surprise among secretaries and clerks. And if somebody here and there was troubled by a fleeting, uncanny impression that not one large beast but two seemed to be trailing the Moderator's visitor down the aisles, no mention was made of what could have been only a momentary visual distortion. Finally, a pair of sliding doors opened ahead, and the receptionist ushered Telzey into a large, cool balcony garden on the shaded side of the great building. A tall, gray-haired man stood up from the desk at which he was working, and bowed to Telzey. The receptionist withdrew again.

"My pleasure, Miss Amberdon," Jontarou's Planetary Moderator said, "Be seated, please." He studied Tick-Tock with more than casual interest while Telzey was settling herself into a chair, added, "And what may I and my office do for you?"

Telzey hesitated. She'd observed his type on Orado in her mother's circle of acquaintances—a senior diplomat, a man not easy to impress. It was a safe bet that he'd had her brought out to his balcony office only to keep her occupied while Halet was quietly informed where the Amberdon problem child was and requested to come over and take charge.

What she had to tell him now would have sounded rather wild even if presented by a presumably responsible adult. She could provide proof, but until the

Moderator was already nearly sold on her story, that would be a very unsafe thing to do. Old Iron Thoughts was backing her up, but if it didn't look as if her plans were likely to succeed, he would be willing to ride herd on his devil's pack just so long . . .

Better start the ball rolling without any preliminaries, Telzey decided. The Moderator's picture of her must be that of a spoiled, neurotic brat in a stew about the threatened loss of a pet animal. He expected her to start arguing with him immediately about Tick-Tock.

She said, "Do you have a personal interest in keeping the Baluit crest cats from becoming extinct?"

Surprise flickered in his eyes for an instant. Then he smiled.

"I admit I do, Miss Amberdon," he said pleasantly. "I should like to see the species re-established. I count myself almost uniquely fortunate in having had the opportunity to bag two of the magnificent brutes before disease wiped them out on the planet."

The last seemed a less than fortunate statement just now. Telzey felt a sharp tingle of alarm, then sensed that in the minds which were drawing the meaning of the Moderator's speech from her mind there had been only a brief stir of interest.

She cleared her throat, said, "The point is that they weren't wiped out by disease."

He considered her quizzically, seemed to wonder what she was trying to lead up to. Telzey gathered her courage, plunged on, "Would you like to hear what did happen?"

"I should be much interested, Miss Amberdon," the Moderator said without change of expression. "But first, if you'll excuse me a moment . . ."

There had been some signal from his desk which Telzey hadn't noticed, because he picked up a small communicator now, said, "Yes?" After a few seconds, he resumed, "That's rather curious, isn't it? . . . Yes, I'd try that . . . No, that shouldn't be necessary . . . Yes, please do. Thank you." He replaced the communicator, his face very sober; then, his eyes flicking for an instant to TT, he drew one of the upper desk drawers open a few inches, and turned back to Telzey.

"Now, Miss Amberdon," he said affably, "you were about to say? About these crest cats . . ."

Telzey swallowed. She hadn't heard the other side of the conversation, but she could guess what it had been about. His office had called the guest house, had been told by Halet's maid that Halet, the chauffeur and Dr. Droon were out looking for Miss Telzey and her pet. The Moderator's office had then checked on the sportscar's communication number and attempted to call it. And, of course, there had been no response.

To the Moderator, considering what Halet would have told him, it must add up to the grim possibility that the young lunatic he was talking to had let her three-quarters-grown crest cat slaughter her aunt and the two men when they caught up with her! The office would be notifying the police now to conduct an immediate search for the missing aircar.

When it would occur to them to look for it on the Moderator's parking terrace was something Telzey couldn't know. But if Halet and Dr. Droon were released before the Moderator accepted her own version of what had occurred, and the two reported the presence of wild crest cats in Port Nichay, there would be almost no possibility of keeping the situation under control. Somebody was bound to make some idiotic move, and the fat would be in the fire . . .

Two things might be in her favor. The Moderator seemed to have the sort of steady nerve one would expect in a man who had bagged two Baluit crest cats. The partly opened desk drawer beside him must have a gun in it; apparently he considered that a sufficient precaution against an attack by TT. He wasn't likely to react in a panicky manner. And the mere fact that he suspected Telzey of homicidal tendencies would make him give the closest attention to what she said. Whether he believed her then was another matter, of course.

Slightly encouraged, Telzey began to talk. It did sound like a thoroughly wild story, but the Moderator listened with an appearance of intent interest. When she had told him as much as she felt he could be expected to swallow for a start, he said musingly, "So they weren't wiped out—they went into hiding! Do I understand you to say they did it to avoid being hunted?"

Telzey chewed her lip frowningly before replying. "There's something about that part I don't quite get," she admitted. "Of course I don't quite get either why you'd want to go hunting . . . twice . . . for something that's just as likely to bag you instead!"

"Well, those are, ah, merely the statistical odds," the Moderator explained. "If one has enough confidence, you see—"

"I don't really. But the crest cats seem to have felt the same way—at first. They were getting around one hunter for every cat that got shot. Humans were the most exciting game they'd ever run into."

"But then that ended, and the humans started knocking them out with stunguns from aircars where they couldn't be got at, and hauling them off while they were helpless. After it had gone on for a while, they decided to keep out of sight.

"But they're still around . . . thousands and thousands of them! Another thing nobody's known about them is that they weren't only in the Baluit Mountains. There were crest cats scattered all through the big forests along the other side of the continent."

"Very interesting," the Moderator commented. "Very interesting, indeed!" He glanced towards the communicator, then returned his gaze to Telzey, drumming his fingers lightly on the desktop.

She could tell nothing at all from his expression now, but she guessed he was thinking hard. There was supposed to be no native intelligent life in the legal sense on Jontarou, and she had been careful to say nothing so far to make the Baluit cats look like more than rather exceptionally intelligent animals. The next—rather large—question should be how she'd come by such information.

If the Moderator asked her that, Telzey thought, she could feel she'd made a beginning at getting him to buy the whole story.

"Well," he said abruptly, "if the crest cats are not extinct or threatened with extinction, the Life Banks obviously have no claim on your pet." He smiled confidingly at her. "And that's the reason you're here, isn't it?"

"Well, no," Telzey began, dismayed. "I—"

"Oh, it's quite all right, Miss Amberdon! I'll simply rescind the permit which was issued for the purpose. You need feel no further concern about that." He paused. "Now, just one question . . . do you happen to know where your aunt is at present?"

Telzey had a dead, sinking feeling. So he hadn't believed a word she said. He'd been stalling her along until the aircar could be found.

She took a deep breath. "You'd better listen to the rest of it."

"Why, is there more?" the Moderator asked politely.

"Yes. The important part! The kind of creatures they are, they wouldn't go into hiding indefinitely just because someone was after them."

Was there a flicker of something beyond watchfulness in his expression? "What would they do, Miss Amberdon?" he asked quietly.

"If they couldn't get at the men in the aircars and couldn't communicate with them"—the flicker again!—"they'd start looking for the place the men came from, wouldn't they? It might take them some years to work their way across the continent and locate us here in Port Nichay. But supposing they did it finally and a few thousand of them are sitting around in the parks down there right now? They could come up the side of these towers as easily as they go up the side of a mountain. And supposing they'd decided that the only way to handle the problem was to clean out the human beings in Port Nichay?"

The Moderator stared at her in silence a few seconds. "You're saying," he observed then, "that they're rational beings—above the Critical I.Q. level."

"Well," Telzey said, "legally they're rational. I checked on that. About as rational as we are, I suppose."

"Would you mind telling me now how you happen to know this?"

"They told me," Telzey said.

He was silent again, studying her face. "You mentioned, Miss Amberdon, that they have been unable to communicate with other human beings. This suggests then that you are a xenotelepath . . ."

"I am?" Telzey hadn't heard the term before. "If it means that I can tell what the cats are thinking, and they can tell what I'm thinking, I guess that's the word for it." She considered him, decided she had him almost on the ropes, went on quickly.

"I looked up the laws, and told them they could conclude a treaty with the Federation which would establish them as an Affiliated Species . . . and that would settle everything the way they would want it settled, without trouble. Some of them believed me. They decided to wait until I could talk to you. If it works out, fine! If it doesn't"—she felt her voice falter for an instant—"they're going to cut loose fast!"

The Moderator seemed undisturbed. "What am I supposed to do?"

"I told them you'd contact the Council of the Federation on Orado."

"Contact the Council?" he repeated coolly. "With no more proof for this story than your word, Miss Amberdon?"

Telzey felt a quick, angry stirring begin about her, felt her face whiten.

"All right," she said. "I'll give you proof! I'll have to now. But that'll be it. Once they've tipped their hand all the way, you'll have about thirty seconds left to make the right move. I hope you remember that!"

He cleared his throat. "I—"

"NOW!" Telzey said.

Along the walls of the balcony garden, beside the ornamental flower stands, against the edges of the rock pool, the crest cats appeared. Perhaps thirty of them. None quite as physically impressive as Iron Thoughts who stood closest to the Moderator; but none very far from it. Motionless as rocks, frightening as gargoyles, they waited, eyes glowing with hellish excitement.

"This is *their* council, you see," Telzey heard herself saying.

The Moderator's face had also paled. But he was, after all, an old shikari and a senior diplomat. He took an unhurried look around the circle, said quietly, "Accept my profound apologies for doubting you, Miss Amberdon!" and reached for the desk communicator.

Iron Thoughts swung his demon head in Telzey's direction. For an instant, she picked up the mental impression of a fierce yellow eye closing in an approving wink.

" . . . An open transmitter line to Orado," the Moderator was saying into the communicator. "The Council. And snap it up! Some very important visitors are waiting . . ."

The offices of Jontarou's Planetary Moderator became an extremely busy and interesting area then.

Quite two hours passed before it occurred to anyone to ask Telzey again whether she knew where her aunt was at present.

Telzey smote her forehead.

"Forgot all about that!" she admitted, fishing the sportscar's keys out of the pocket of her sunbriefs. "They're out on the parking platform . . ."

The preliminary treaty arrangements between the Federation of the Hub and the new Affiliated Species of the Planet of Jontarou were formally ratified two weeks later, the ceremony taking place on Jontarou, in the Champagne Hall of the Shikaris' Club.

Telzey was able to follow the event only by news viewer in her ship-cabin, she and Halet being on the return trip to Orado by then. She wasn't too interested in the treaty's details—they conformed almost exactly to what she had read out to Iron Thoughts and his co-chiefs and companions in the park. It was the smooth bridging of the wide language gap between the contracting parties by a row of interpreting machines and a handful of human xenotelepaths which held her attention.

As she switched off the viewer, Halet came wandering in from the adjoining cabin.

"I was watching it, too!" Halet observed. She smiled. "I was hoping to see dear Tick-Tock."

Telzey looked over at her. "Well, TT would hardly be likely to show up in Port Nichay," she said. "She's having too good a time now finding out what life in the Baluit range is like."

"I suppose so," Halet agreed doubtfully, sitting down on a hassock. "But I'm glad she promised to get in touch with us again in a few years. I'll miss her."

Telzey regarded her aunt with a reflective frown. Halet meant it quite sincerely, of course; she had undergone a profound change of heart during the past two weeks. But Telzey wasn't without some doubts about the actual value of a change of heart brought on by telepathic means. The learning process the crest cats had started in her mind appeared to have continued automatically several days longer than her rugged teachers had really intended; and Telzey had reason to believe that by the end of that time she'd developed associated latent abilities of which the crest cats had never heard. She'd barely begun to get it all sorted out yet, but . . . as an example . . . she'd found it remarkably easy to turn Halet's more obnoxious attitudes virtually upside down. It had taken her a couple of days to get the hang of her aunt's personal symbolism, but after that there had been no problem.

She was reasonably certain she'd broken no laws so far, though the sections in the law library covering the use and abuse of psionic abilities were veiled in such intricate and downright obscuring phrasing—deliberately, Telzey suspected—that it was really difficult to say what they did mean. But even aside from that, there were a number of arguments in favor of exercising great caution.

Jessamine, for one thing, was bound to start worrying about her sister-in-law's health if Halet turned up on Orado in her present state of mind, even though it would make for a far more agreeable atmosphere in the Amberdon household.

"Halet," Telzey inquired mentally, "do you remember what an all-out stinker you used to be?"

"Of course, dear," Halet said aloud. "I can hardly wait to tell dear Jessamine how much I regret the many times I . . ."

"Well," Telzey went on, still verbalizing it silently, "I think you'd really enjoy life more if you were, let's say, about halfway between your old nasty self and the sort of sickening-good kind you are now."

"Why, Telzey!" Halet cried out with dopey amiability. "What a delightful idea!"

"Let's try it," Telzey said.

There was silence in the cabin for some twenty minutes then, while she went painstakingly about remolding a number of Halet's character traits for the second time. She still felt some misgiving about it; but if it became necessary, she probably could always restore the old Halet *in toto*.

These, she told herself, definitely were powers one should treat with respect! Better rattle through law school first; then, with that out of the way, she could start hunting around to see who in the Federation was qualified to instruct a genius-level novice in the proper handling of psionics . . .

# II: Undercurrents

## Chapter 1

At the Orado City Space Terminal, the Customs and Public Health machine was smoothly checking through passengers disembarking from a liner from Jontarou. A psionic computer of awesome dimensions, the machine formed one side of a great hall along which the stream of travelers moved towards the city exits and their previously cleared luggage. Unseen behind the base of the wall—armored, as were the housings of all Federation psionic machines in public use—its technicians sat in rows of cubicles, eyes fixed on dials and indicators, hands ready to throw pinpointing switches at the quiver of a blip.

The computer's sensors were simultaneously searching for contraband and dutiable articles, and confirming the medical clearance given passengers before an interstellar ship reached Orado's atmosphere. Suggestions of inimical or unregistered organisms, dormant or

active, would be a signal to quarantine attendants at
the end of the slideways to shepherd somebody politely
to a detention ward for further examination. Customs
agents were waiting for the other type of signal.

It was a dependable, unobtrusive procedure, causing no unnecessary inconvenience or delay, and so
generally established now at major spaceports in the
Federation of the Hub that sophisticated travelers
simply took it for granted. However, the machine had
features of which neither Customs nor Health were
aware. In a room across the spaceport, two men sat
watchfully before another set of instruments connected to the computer's scanners. Above these instruments was a wide teleview of the Customs hall.
Nothing appeared to be happening in the room until
approximately a third of the passengers from Jontarou
had moved through the computer's field. Then the
instruments were suddenly active, and a personality
identification chart popped out of a table slot before
the man on the left.

He glanced at the chart, said, "Telzey Amberdon.
It's our pigeon. Fix on her!"

The man on the right grunted, eyes on the screen
where the teleview pickup had shifted abruptly to a
point a few yards ahead of and above a girl who had
just walked into the hall. Smartly dressed and carrying a small handbag, she was a slim and dewy
teenager, tanned, blue-eyed, and brown-haired. As the
pickup began to move along the slideway with her,
the man on the right closed a switch, placed his hand
on a plunger.

Simultaneously, two things occurred in the hall.
Along the ceiling a string of nearly microscopic ports
opened, extruding needle paralyzers pointed at the girl;
and one of the floating ambulances moored tactfully
out of sight near the exits rose, shifted forward twenty
feet and stopped again. If the girl collapsed, she would
be on her way out of the hall in a matter of seconds,

the event almost unnoticed except by the passengers nearest her.

"If you want her, we have her," said the man on the right.

"We'll see." The first observer slipped the identification chart into one of his instruments, and slowly depressed a calibrated stud, watching the girl's face in the teleview.

Surprise briefly widened her eyes; then her expression changed to sharp interest. After a moment, the observer experienced a sense of question in himself, an alert, searching feeling.

Words abruptly formed in his mind.

"Is somebody there? Did somebody speak just now?"

The man on the right grinned.

"A lamb!"

"Maybe." The first observer looked thoughtful. "Don't relax just yet. The response was Class Two."

He waited while the sense of question lingered, strengthened for a few seconds, then faded. He selected a second stud on the instrument, edged it down.

This time, the girl's mobile features showed no reaction, and nothing touched his mind. The observer shifted his eyes to a dial pointer, upright and unmoving before him, watched it while a minute ticked past, released the stud. Sliding the identification pattern chart out of the instrument, he checked over the new factors coded into it, and returned it to the table slot.

Forty-two miles off in Orado City, in the headquarters complex of the Federation's Psychology Service, another slot opened, and a copy of the chart slid out on a desk. Somebody picked it up.

"Hooked and tagged and never knew it," the first observer was remarking. "You can call off the fix." He added, "Fifteen years old. She was spotted for the first time two weeks ago. . . ."

In the Customs hall the tiny ports along the ceiling sealed themselves and the waiting ambulance slid slowly back to its mooring points.

The visiting high Federation official was speaking in guardedly even tones.

"I, as has everyone else," he said, "have been led to believe that the inspection machines provided by the Psychology Service for Health and Customs respected the anonymity of the public."

He paused. "Obviously, this can't be reconciled with the ability—displayed just now—of identifying individuals by their coded charts!"

Boddo, director of the Psychology Service's Department Eighty-four, laid the identification chart marked with the name of Telzey Amberdon down before him. He looked at it for a moment without speaking, his long, bony face and slanted thick brows giving him a somewhat satanic appearance. The visitor recently had been appointed to a Federation position which made it necessary to provide him with ordinarily unavailable information regarding the Psychology Service's means and methods of operation. He had spent two days being provided with it, in department after department of the Service, and was showing symptoms, not unusual on such occasions, of accumulated shock.

The policy in these cases was based on the assumption that the visitor possessed considerable intelligence, or he would not have been there. He should be given ample time to work out the shock and revise various established opinions. If he failed to do this, his mind would be delicately doctored before he left Headquarters, with the result that he would forget most of what he had learned and presently discover good reason for taking another job—specifically one which did not involve intimate contacts with the Psychology Service.

Boddo, not an unkind man, decided to do what he could to help this unwitting probationer over the hump.

"The Customs computer isn't supposed to be able to identify individuals," he agreed. "But I believe you already know that many of the psionic machines we put out aren't limited to the obvious functions they perform."

"I understand, of course, that complete candor can't always be demanded of a government agency." The visitor indicated the one-way screen through which they had looked in on the room at the spaceport. "But this is deliberate, planned deception. If I understood correctly what happened just now, the so-called Customs machine—supposedly there simply to expedite traffic and safeguard the health of this world—not only identifies unsuspecting persons for you but actually reads their minds."

"The last to a rather limited extent," Boddo said. "It's far from being the best all-around device for that purpose. In practice a vanishingly small fraction of the public is affected. I couldn't care less about having the thoughts of the average man or woman invaded; and if I wanted to, I wouldn't have the time. Department Eighty-four is the branch of the Service's intelligence which investigates, registers, records and reports on psis, and real or apparent psionic manifestations outside the Service. This office coordinates such information. We aren't interested in anything else.

"I imagine," Boddo went on, "you've been told of the overall program to have advanced psionic machines in general use throughout the Hub in the not too distant future?"

"Yes, and I don't like it," the visitor said. "The clandestine uses to which these machines are being put today certainly are undesirable enough. What is to insure that the further spread of your devices won't lead to the transformation of the Federation into a police state with an utterly unbreakable hold on the minds of the population? The temptation . . . the possibility . . . will always be there.

"And if *that* doesn't happen," he said, "in a few decades the situation will be as bad, or worse. Inevitably, the machines will multiply the tremendous problems already presented by organized crime, by power politics, by greed, stupidity and ignorance."

"As I've understood it," Boddo replied, "the gradual, orderly introduction of psionic machines is expected to solve the problems you've mentioned progressively as the program unfolds."

"I don't see how that will happen," said the visitor. "Unless that's the reason you track down these so-called human psis. A clever campaign to divert the public's concern to such people might very well leave the psionic *machines* looking innocuous by comparison."

"Um . . ." Boddo pursed his lips, frowning. "As it happens," he observed, "the purpose of this office is almost the reverse of what you suggest."

"I don't follow that," the visitor said shortly.

Boddo said, "The last thing in the world we'd want is to bring the information this office gathers to the public's attention. The Service, of course, is conducting a continuous campaign on many fronts to reduce uneasiness and hostility about psionic machines. *Our* specific assignment is to prevent occurrences—arising from the activities of human psis—which might strengthen that feeling. Or, if they can't be prevented, to provide harmless explanations for them, and to make sure they aren't repeated—at least not by the psi in question."

The official scowled. "I still don't see . . . What occurrences?"

"We are not," Boddo said patiently, "in the least worried about what dowsers, professional mind-readers and fortune-tellers might do. Not at all. The public's familiar with them and regards them on the whole as harmlessly freakish. When the performance of such a person is sufficiently dependable, we call him or her a Class One psi. Class One falls into rather neat categories—eighteen, to be exact—and functions in a stereotyped manner. The Class One, in fact, is almost defined by his limitations."

"Then . . ."

"Yes," Boddo said, "there's another type. The Class Two. A rare bird, as he apparently always has been. But recent breakthroughs in psionic theory and practice make it easier to identify him. We feel that the most desirable place for a Class Two at present is in the Psychology Service. I'll introduce you presently to a few of them."

"I . . . what kind of people are they?"

Boddo shrugged. "Not too remarkable—except for their talents. If you met the average Class Two, you'd see a normal, perhaps somewhat unusually healthy human being. As for the talents, anything a Class One can do, the Class Two who has developed the same line does better; and he's almost never restricted to a specialty, or even to two or three specialties. In that respect, his talent corresponds more closely to normal human faculties and acquired skills. It can be explored, directed, trained and developed."

"Developed to what extent?" the official asked.

"It depends on the individual. You mentioned mind-reading. In the Class Two who has the faculty, it may appear as anything from a Class One's general impressions or sensing of scattered specific details on up. Up to the almost literal reading of minds." Boddo looked thoughtfully at the visitor. "A very few can tell what's passing through any mind they direct their attention on as readily and accurately as if they were reading a book. The existence of such people is one of the things we prefer not to have publicized at present. It might produce unfavorable reactions."

Doubt and uneasiness were showing in the visitor's face. "That would not be surprising. Such abnormal powers leave the ordinary man at a severe disadvantage."

"True enough," Boddo said. "But the ordinary man is under a similar disadvantage whenever he confronts someone who is considerably more intelligent or more experienced than himself, or who simply points a gun at him. And he's much more likely to run into difficulties like that. It's extremely improbable that he would come to the attention of a capable Class Two mind-reader even once in his lifetime. If he did, the probability is again that the mind-reader would have no interest in him. But if he did happen to take an interest in our ordinary man, there's still no reason to assume it would be for any malevolent purpose."

The visitor cleared his throat. "But there are criminal psis?"

"Of course there are," Boddo said.

"And your office takes steps to protect the public against them?"

Boddo shook his head.

"Don't misunderstand me," he said. "It isn't my business to look out for the public. I believe you know that the only category of crimes with which the Psychology Service concerns itself directly are those against the Federation or against humanity. That applies also where psis are involved. What a Class Two does becomes of interest to us only when it might have an adverse effect on the psionic program. Then it doesn't matter whether he's actually committing crimes or not. We close down on him very quickly. Indirectly, of course, that does protect the public.

"Ordinarily, it isn't a question of malice. A Class Two may get careless, or he begins to engage in horse play at the expense of his neighbors. He's amusing himself. But as a result, he draws attention. Bizarre things have happened which seemingly can't be explained by ordinary reasoning. At other times, such incidents would cause some speculation and then be generally forgotten. At present, they can have more serious repercussions. So we try to prevent them. If necessary, we provide cover explanations and do what is necessary to bring the offending psi under control."

"In what way do you control these people?" the visitor asked.

Boddo picked up the personal identification chart of Telzey Amberdon.

"Let's consider the case of the young psi who came through the space terminal a short while ago," he said. "It will illustrate our general methods satisfactorily." He blinked at the codings on the chart for a moment, turned it over, thrust one end into a small glowing desk receptacle marked *For Occasional Observation*, withdrew it and dropped it into a filing slot.

"We knew this psi would be arriving on Orado today," he went on. "We'd had no previous contact with her, and only one earlier report which indicated she had acted as a xenotelepath—that is, she had been in mental communication with members of a telepathic nonhuman race. That particular ability appears in a relatively small number of psis, but its possessor is more often than not a Class One who fails to develop any associated talents.

"The check made at the spaceport showed immediately that this youngster is not Class One. She is beginning to learn to read human minds, with limitations perhaps due chiefly to a lack of experience, and she has discovered the art of telephypnosis, which is a misnamed process quite unrelated to ordinary hypnotic methods, though it produces similar general effects. These developments have all taken place within the past few weeks."

The visitor gave him a startled look. "You make that child sound rather dangerous!"

Boddo shrugged. "As far as this office is concerned, she is at present simply a Class Two, with a quite good though still largely latent potential. She picked up a scrambled telepathic impulse directed deliberately at her, but was not aware then that her mind was being scanned by our machine. A really accomplished Class Two would sense that. Neither did she realize that the machine was planting a compulsion in her mind."

"A compulsion?" the official repeated.

Boddo considered, said, "In effect, she's now provided with an artificial conscience regarding her paranormal talents which suggests, among other things, that she should seek proper authorization in using them. That's the standard procedure we follow after identifying a Class Two."

"It prevents them from using their abilities?"

"Not necessarily. It does tend to keep them out of minor mischief, but if they're sufficiently self-willed and motivated, they're quite likely to override the compulsion. That's particularly true if they discover what's happened, as some of them do. Still, it places a degree of restraint on them, and eventually leads a good number to the Psychology Service . . . which, of course, is what we want."

The visitor reflected. "What would you have done if the girl had realized the Customs machine was investigating her mind?"

Boddo smiled briefly. "Depending on her reactions, the procedure might have become a little more involved at that point. The ultimate result would have been about the same—the compulsion would have been installed."

There was a pause. The official looked thoughtful. He said finally, "You feel then that the Service's method of supervising psis is adequate?"

"It appears to keep the Class Two psis from causing trouble well enough," Boddo said. "Naturally, it isn't completely effective. For one thing, we can't expect to get a record of all of them. Then there's a divergent group called the unpredictables. Essentially they're just that. You might say the one thing they show in common is a highly erratic development of psionic ability."

"What do you do about them?"

Boddo said, "We have no formula for handling unpredictables. It wouldn't be worth the trouble to try to devise one which was flexible enough to meet every possibility. They're very rarely encountered."

"So rarely that there's no reason to worry about them?"

Boddo scratched his cheek, observed, "The Service doesn't regard an unpredictable as a cause for serious concern."

## Chapter 2

Scowling with concentration, Telzey Amberdon sat, eyes closed, knees drawn up and arms locked about them, on the couch-bed in her side of duplex bungalow 18-19, Student Court Ninety-two, of Pehanron College. When she'd looked over at the rose-glowing pointers of a wall clock on the opposite side of the room, they had told her there wasn't much more than an hour left before Orado's sun would rise. That meant she had been awake all night, though she was only now beginning to feel waves of drowsiness.

Except for the glow from the clock, the room was dark, its windows shielded. She had thought of turning on lights, but there was a chance that a spot check by the college's automatic monitors would record the fact; and then Miss Eulate, the Senior Counselor of Section Ninety-two, was likely to show up during the morning to remind Telzey that a fifteen-year-old girl, even if she happened to be a privileged Star Honor Student, simply must get in her full and regular sleep periods.

It would be inconvenient just now if such an admonishment was accompanied by a suspension of honor student privileges. So the lights stayed out. Light, after all, wasn't a requirement in sitting there and probing about in an unsuspecting fellow-creature's mind, which was what Telzey had been engaged in during the night.

If the mind being probed had known what was going on, it might have agreed with Miss Eulate. But it didn't. It was the mind of a very large dog named Chomir, owned by Gonwil Lodis who occupied the other side of the duplex and was Telzey's best college friend, though her senior by almost four years.

Both Gonwil and Chomir were asleep, but Chomir slept fitfully. He was not given to prolonged concentration on any one subject, and for hours Telzey had kept him wearily half dreaming, over and over, about certain disturbing events which he hadn't really grasped when they occurred. He passed most of the night in a state of vague irritation, though his inquisitor was careful not to let the feeling become acute enough to bring him awake.

It wasn't pleasant for Telzey either. Investigating that section of Chomir's mind resembled plodding about in a dark swamp agitated by violent convulsions and covered by a smothering fog. From time to time, it became downright nerve-wracking as blasts of bewildered fury were transmitted to her with first-hand vividness out of the animal's memories. The frustrating side of it, however, was that the specific bits of information for which she searched remained obscured by the blurry, sporadic, nightmarish reliving which seemed to be the only form in which those memories could be made to show up just now. And it was extremely important to get the information because she suspected Chomir's experiences might mean that somebody was planning the deliberate murder of Gonwil Lodis.

She had got into the investigation almost by accident. Gonwil was one of the very few persons to whom Telzey had mentioned anything about her recently acquired ability to pry into other minds, and she had been on a walk with Chomir in the wooded hills above Pehanron College during the afternoon. Without apparent cause, Chomir suddenly had become angry, stared and sniffed about for a moment, then plunged bristling and snarling into the bushes. His mistress sprinted after him in high alarm, calling out a warning to anyone within earshot, because Chomir, though ordinarily a very well-mannered beast, was physically capable of taking a human being or somebody else's pet dog apart in extremely short order. But she caught up with him within a few hundred yards and discovered that his anger appeared to have spent itself as quickly as it had developed. Instead, he was acting now in an oddly confused and worried manner.

Gonwil thought he might have scented a wild animal. But his behavior remained a puzzle—Chomir had always treated any form of local wildlife they encountered as being beneath his notice. Half seriously, since she wasn't entirely convinced of Telzey's mind-reading ability, Gonwil suggested she might use it to find out what had disturbed him; and Telzey promised to try it after lights-out when Chomir had settled down to sleep. It would be her first attempt to study a canine mind, and it might be interesting.

Chomir turned out to be readily accessible to a probe, much more so than the half-dozen non-telepathic human minds Telzey had looked into so far, where many preliminary hours of search had been needed to pick up an individual's thought patterns and get latched solidly into them. With Chomir she was there in around thirty minutes. For a while, most of what she encountered appeared grotesquely distorted and incomprehensible; then something like a translating machine in Telzey's brain, which was the xenotelepathic ability, suddenly clicked in, and she found herself beginning to change the dog's sleep impressions into terms which had a definite meaning to her. It was a little like discovering the key to the operation of an unfamiliar machine. She spent an hour investigating and experimenting with a number of its mechanisms; then, deciding she could control Chomir satisfactorily for her purpose, she shifted his thoughts in the direction of what had happened that afternoon.

Around an hour or so later again, she stopped to give them both a rest.

The event in the hills didn't look any less mystifying now, but it had begun to acquire definitely sinister overtones. If Chomir had known of the concept of unreality, he might have applied it to what had occurred. He had realized suddenly and with a blaze of rage that somewhere nearby was a man whom he remembered from a previous meeting as representing a great danger to Gonwil. He had rushed into the woods with every intention of tearing off the man's head, but then the fellow suddenly was gone again.

That was what had left Chomir in a muddled and apprehensive frame of mind. The man had both been there, and somehow not been there. Chomir felt approximately as a human being might have felt after an encounter with a menacing phantom which faded into thin air almost as soon as it was noticed. Telzey then tried to bring the earlier meeting with the mysterious stranger into view; but here she ran into so much confusion and fury that she got no clear details. There were occasional impressions of white walls—perhaps a large, white-walled room—and of a narrow-faced man, who somehow managed to stay beyond the reach of Chomir's teeth.

By that time, Telzey felt somewhat disturbed. Something out of the ordinary clearly had happened. And supposing the narrow-faced stranger did spell danger to Gonwil . . .

Gonwil had told her, laughing, not believing a word of it, a story she'd been hearing herself since she was a child; how on Tayun, the planet from which she had come to Orado to be a student at Pehanron, there were people who had been responsible for the death of her parents when she was less than a year old, and who intended eventually to kill Gonwil as the final act of revenge for some wrong her father supposedly had done.

Tayun appeared to have a well-established vendetta tradition, so the story might not be completely impossible. But as Gonwil told it, it did seem very unlikely.

On the other hand, who else could have any possible reason for wanting to harm Gonwil?

The instant she asked herself the question, Telzey felt a flick of alarmed shock. Because now that the possibility had occurred to her, she could answer the question immediately. She knew a group of people who might very well want to harm Gonwil, not as an act of vendetta but for the simple and logical reason that it would be very much to their material benefit if Gonwil died within the next few months.

She sat still a while, barely retaining her contacts with Chomir while she turned the thought around, considered it and let it develop. If she was right, this was an extremely ugly thing, and she could see nothing to indicate she was wrong.

Late last summer she had been invited to spend a few days with Gonwil as house guests of a lady who

was Gonwil's closest living relative and a very dear
friend, and who would be on Orado with her family for a short stay before returning to Tayun. Socially
speaking, the visit was not a complete success, though
Gonwil remained unaware of it. Telzey and the Parlin
family—father, mother, and son—formed strong feelings of mutual dislike almost at sight, but stayed polite
about it. Malrue Parlin was a handsome, energetic
woman, who completely overshadowed her husband
and son. She'd been almost excessively affectionate
towards Gonwil.

It was Malrue, from what Telzey had heard, who
had always been deeply concerned that the hypotheti-
cal vendettists might catch up with Gonwil some
day . . .

When his parents left, Parlin Junior remained on
Orado with the avowed intention of winning Gonwil
over to the idea of becoming his bride. Gonwil,
though moderately fond of Junior, didn't care for the
idea. But, more from fear of hurting Malrue's feelings than his, she'd been unable to bring herself to
brush Junior off with sufficient firmness. At least, he'd
kept returning.

And the thing, Telzey thought, it never had
occurred to Gonwil, or to her, to speculate about was
that Gonwil had inherited a huge financial fortune
which Malrue Parlin was effectively controlling at
present, and which she would go on controlling if
Junior's suit was successful . . . or again if Gonwil
happened to die before she came of age, which she
would in just three months time.

In spite of Gonwil's diffidence in handling Junior,
it must have become clear to both Junior and his
mother some while ago that the marriage plan had
fizzled.

One somehow didn't consider that people one had
met, even if one hadn't liked them, might be planning murder. It seemed too unnatural. But murder

was in fact the most common of major crimes anywhere in the Hub, and it was general knowledge that the more sophisticated murderers quite regularly escaped retribution. The Federation's legal code made no more than a gesture of attempting to cope with them. It was a structure of compromises in everything but its essentials, with the primary purpose of keeping six hundred billion human beings living in more than a thousand semi-autonomous sun systems away from wholesale conflicts, while the area of generally accepted lawful procedure and precedent was slowly but steadily extended. In that, it was surprisingly effective. But meanwhile individual citizens could suddenly find themselves in situations where Federation Law told them in effect that it could do nothing and advised them to look out for themselves.

Murder, aside from its more primitive forms, frequently provided such a situation. There was a legal term for it, with a number of semilegal implications. It was "private war."

Telzey's impulse was to wake up Gonwil and tell her what had occurred to her. But she rejected the idea. She had only her report of Chomir's experiences to add to things Gonwil already knew; and so far those experiences proved nothing even if Gonwil didn't assume they existed in Telzey's imagination rather than in Chomir's memory. She would be incapable of accepting, even theoretically, that Malrue might want her dead; and in attempting to disprove it, she might very well do something that would precipitate the danger.

The thing to go for first was more convincing evidence of danger. Telzey returned her attention to Chomir.

Near morning, she acknowledged to herself she would get no further with the dog. He was responding

more and more sluggishly and vaguely to her prods.
She'd caught glimpses enough meanwhile to know his
memory did hold evidence that wickedness of some
kind was being brewed, but that was all. The animal
mind couldn't cooperate any longer.

She should let Chomir rest for some hours at least.
After he was fresh again, she might get at what she
wanted without much trouble.

She eased off her contacts with his mind, drew
away from it, felt it fade from her awareness. She
opened her eyes again, yawned, sighed, reached over
to the end of the couch and poked at the window
control shielding. The room's windows appeared in
the far wall, the shrubbery of the tiny bungalow
garden swaying softly in the predawn quiet of the
student court. Telzey turned bleary eyes towards the
wall clock.

In an hour and a half, her father would be at his
office in Orado City. The city was just under an hour
away by aircar, and she'd have to get his advice and
assistance in this matter at once. If Gonwil's death
was planned, the time set for it probably wasn't many
days away. Malrue and her husband were supposed
to be on their way back to Orado for another of their
annual visits, and Chomir's hated acquaintance had
turned up again yesterday. The danger period could
be expected to begin with Malrue's arrival.

By the time she'd showered, dressed and break-
fasted, she found herself waking up again. Sunshine
had begun to edge into the court. Telzey glanced at
her watch, grabbed her personal communicator,
clipped her scintillating Star Honor Student pass to
her hat, and poked at the duplex's interphone buzzer.

After some seconds, Gonwil's voice came drows-
ily from the instrument. "Uh . . . who . . ."

"Me."

"Oh . . . Whyya up so early?"

"It's broad daylight," Telzey said. "Listen, I'm flying

in to Orado City to see my father. I'm starting right
now. If anyone is interested, tell them I'll be back
for lunch, or I'll call in."

"Right." Gonwil yawned audibly.

"I was wondering," Telzey went on. "When did you
say Mr. and Mrs. Parlin are due to land?"

"Day after tomorrow . . . last I heard from Junior.
Why?"

"Got anything planned for the first part of the
holidays?"

"Well, just to stay away from Sonny somehow. He
heard about the holidays."

"I've thought of something that will do it," Telzey
said.

"Fine!" Gonwil said heartily. "What?"

"Tell you when I get back. You're free to leave after
lunch, aren't you?"

Gonwil clucked doubtfully. "There's six more test
chips I'll have to clean up, and Finance Eleven is a
living stinker! I think I can do it. I'll get at it right
away. . . . Hey, wait a minute! Did you find out anything about . . . uh, well, yesterday?"

"We're started on it," Telzey said. "But I didn't
really find out much."

In the carport back of the duplex, she eased herself into the driver's seat of a tiny Cloudsplitter and
turned it into an enclosed ground traffic lane. The
Star Honor Student pass got her through one of
Pehanron's guard-screen exits without question; and
a minute later the little car was airborne, streaking
off towards the east.

Twenty miles on, Telzey checked the time again,
set the Cloudsplitter to home in on one of Orado
City's major traffic arteries, and released its controls.
Her father should be about ready to leave his hotel
by now. She dialed his call number on the car's
communicator and tapped in her personal symbol.

Gilas Amberdon responded promptly. He had been, he acknowledged, about ready to leave; and yes, he would be happy to see her at his office in around forty-five minutes. What was it about?

"Something to do with xenotelepathy," Telzey said.

"Let's hear it." His voice had changed tone slightly.

"That would take a little time, Gilas."

"I can spare the time."

He listened without comment while she told him about her attempt to explore Chomir's memories, what she seemed to have found, and what she was concluding from it. It would be easy to persuade Gonwil to keep out of sight for a day or two, with the idea of avoiding Junior; after that, her loyalty to Malrue might create additional problems.

Gilas remained silent for a little after she finished. Then he said, "I'll do two things immediately, Telzey."

"Yes?"

"I'll have the Kyth Agency send over an operator to discuss the matter—Dasinger, if he's available. If your mysterious stranger is remaining in the vicinity of Pehanron College, the agency should be able to establish who he is and what he's up to. Finding him might not be the most important thing, of course."

Telzey felt a surge of relief. "You do think Malrue Parlin . . ."

"We should have some idea about that rather soon. The fact is simply that if the situation between Gonwil and the Parlins is as you've described it in respect to the disposal of her holdings in case of death, it demands a close investigation in itself. Mrs. Parlin, while she isn't in the big leagues yet, is considered one of the sharper financial operators on Tayun."

"Gonwil says she's really brilliant."

"She might be," Gilas said. "In any case, we'll have a check started to determine whether there have been previous suggestions of criminality connected with her

operations. We'll act meanwhile on the assumption that
the danger exists and is imminent. Your thought of
getting Gonwil away from the college for a couple of
days, or until we see the situation more clearly, is a
very good one. We'll discuss it when you get here."

"All right."

"I don't quite see," Gilas went on, "how we're going
to explain what we want done, in the matter of the
man the dog's run into twice, without revealing something of your methods of investigation."

"No. I thought of that."

He hesitated. "Well, Dasinger's agency is commend-
ably close-mouthed about its clients' affairs. The
information shouldn't go any further. Are you coming in your own car?"

"Yes."

"Set it down on my private flange then. Ravia will
take you through to the office."


# Chapter 3


Switching off the communicator, Telzey glanced
at her watch. For the next thirty minutes, the Cloudsplitter would continue on automatic towards one
of the ingoing Orado City air lanes. After it swung
into the lane, she would make better time by taking over the controls. Meanwhile, she could catch
up on some of the sleep she'd lost.

She settled back comfortably in the driver's seat
and closed her eyes.

At once a figure which gave the impression of huge-
ness began to appear in her mind. Telzey flinched
irritably. It had been over a week since the Psionic Cop
last came climbing out of her unconscious to lecture

her; she'd begun to hope she was finally rid of him. But he was back, a giant with a stern metallic face, looking halfway between one of the less friendly Orado City air patrolmen and the humanized type of robot. In a moment, he'd start warning her again that she was engaging in activities which could lead only to serious trouble. . . .

She opened her eyes abruptly and the Cop was gone. But she might as well give up the idea of a nap just now. The compulsion against using telepathy somebody had thoughtfully stuck her with was weakening progressively; but the long session with Chomir could have stirred it up enough to produce another series of nightmares in which the Psionic Cop chased her around to place her under arrest. Half an hour of nightmares wouldn't leave her refreshed for the meeting with Gilas's detectives.

Telzey straightened up, sat frowning at the horizon. There had been no way of foreseeing complications like the Psionic Cop when the telepathic natives of Jontarou nudged her dormant talent into action, a little over eight weeks ago. The prospects of life as a psi had looked rather intriguing. But hardly had she stepped out of the ship at Orado City when her problems began.

First, there'd been the touch of something very much like a strong other-mind impulse in the Customs Hall. Some seconds after it faded, Telzey realized it hadn't been structured enough to be some other telepath's purposeful thought. But she'd had no immediate suspicions. The Customs people used a psionically powered inspection machine, and she was within its field at the moment. Undoubtedly, she'd picked up a brief burst of meaningless psionic noise coming from the machine.

She forgot about that incident then, because her mother met her at the spaceport. Federation Councilwoman Jessamine Amberdon had been informed of the events on Jontarou, and appeared somewhat agitated about them. Telzey found herself whisked off promptly to be put through a series of psychological tests, to make sure she had come to no harm. Only when the tests indicated no alarming changes in her mental condition, in fact no detectable changes at all, did Jessamine seem reassured.

"Your father took immediate steps to have your part in the Jontarou matter hushed up," she informed Telzey. "And . . . well, xenotelepathy hardly seems very important! You're not too likely to run into telepathic aliens again." She smiled. "I admit I've been worried, but it seems no harm has been done. We can just forget the whole business now."

Telzey wasn't too surprised. Jessamine was a sweet and understanding woman, but she had the streak of conservatism which tended to characterize junior members of the Grand Council of the Federation. And discreet opinion-sampling on shipboard already had told Telzey that conservative levels of Hub society regarded skills like telepathy as being in questionable taste, if indeed, they were not simply a popular fiction. Jessamine must feel it could do nothing to further the brilliant career she foresaw for her daughter if it was rumored that Telzey had become a freak.

It clearly was not the right time to admit that additional talents of the kind had begun to burgeon in her on the trip home. Jessamine was due to depart from Orado with the Federation's austere Hace Committee within a few days, and might be absent for several months. It wouldn't do to get her upset all over again.

With Telzey's father, it was a different matter. Gilas Amberdon, executive officer of Orado City's Bank of Rienne, could, when he chose, adopt a manner conservative enough to make the entire Hace Committee look frivolous. But this had never fooled his daughter much, and Gilas didn't disappoint her.

"You appear," he observed in the course of their

first private talk after her return, "to have grasped
the principle that it rarely pays to give the impression of being too unusual."

"It looks that way," Telzey admitted.

"And of course," Gilas continued, "if one does happen to be quite unusual, there might eventually be
positive advantages to having played the thing down."

"Yes," Telzey agreed. "I've thought of that."

Gilas tilted his chair back and laced his fingers
behind his neck. It was his customary lecture position, though there appeared to be no lecture impend-
ing at the moment.

"What are your plans?" he asked.

"I want to finish law school first," Telzey said. "I
think I can be out of Pehanron in about two years—
but not if I get too involved in something else."

He nodded. "Then?"

"Then I might study telepathy and psionics generally. It looks as if it could be very interesting."

"Not a bad program," Gilas observed absently. He
brought his chair back down to the floor, reached for
a cigarette and lit it, eyes reflective.

"Psionics," he stated, "is a subject of which I know
almost nothing. In that I'm not unique. Whatever
research worthy of the name is being done on it has
been going on behind locked doors for some time.
Significant data are not released."

Telzey frowned slightly. "How do you know?"

"As soon as I learned of your curious adventures
on Jontarou, I began a private investigation. A fact-
finding agency is at present assembling all available
information on psionics, sorting and classifying it.
Because of the general aroma of secrecy in that area,
they haven't been told for whom they're working. The
results they obtain are forwarded to me through the
nondirect mailing system."

Oh, very good! He couldn't have arranged things
better if she'd told him just what she wanted.

"How useful the material we get in that manner will be remains to be seen," Gilas concluded. "But we have two years to consider what other approaches are indicated."

Telzey took a selection of the chips already forwarded to the bank by the fact-finding agency back to college with her. It had begun to be apparent on the return trip from Jontarou, when she was checking through the space liner's library, that there was something distinctly enigmatic about the subject of psis in the Hub. It expressed itself in the lack of information. She discovered a good deal on the government-controlled psionic machines, but what it all added up to was that they were billion-credit gadgets with mystery-shrouded circuits, which no private organization appeared able to build as yet, though a variety of them had been in public service for years.

About human psis, there was nothing worth the trouble of digging it out.

In her rooms at Pehanron that evening, she went over the fact-finding agency's chips. Again there was nothing really new. The reflection that all this could hardly be accidental crossed her mind a number of times.

Later in the night, Telzey had her first dream of the Psionic Cop. He came tramping after her, booming something about having received complaints about her; and for some reason it scared her silly. She woke up with her heart pounding wildly and found herself demonstrating other symptoms of anxiety. After getting a glass of water, she lay down again to think about it.

It had been a rather ridiculous dream, but she still felt shaky. She almost never had nightmares. But in Psych Two she'd learned that a dream, in particular a nightmare, always symbolized something of significance to the dreamer, and there had been instructions in various self-help methods which could be used in tracking a disturbing dream down to its source.

It took around an hour to uncover the source which had produced the dream-symbol of the Psionic Cop.

There was no real question about its nature. She'd been given a set of suggestions, cunningly interwoven with various aspects of her mental life, and anchored to emotional disturbance points. When she acted against the suggestions, the disturbances were aroused. The result had been a menacing dream.

She dug at the planted thoughts for a while, then decided to leave them alone. If the Psych texts were right, nothing in her mind that she had taken a really thorough look at was going to bother her too much again.

The question was who had been interested in giving her such instructions. Who didn't want her to experiment with psionics on her own or get too curious about it?

From there on, the details began to fall into place. . . .

The odd burst of psionic noise as she came through the Customs hall at the space terminal in Orado City—Telzey considered it with a sense of apprehensive discovery.

The Customs machine certainly wasn't supposed to be able to affect human minds. But it belonged to the same family as the psionic devices of the rehabilitation centers and mental therapy institutions, which did read, manipulate, and reshape human minds. The difference, supposedly, was simply that the Customs machine was designed to do other kinds of work.

But the authority which designed, constructed and maintained all psionic machines, the Federation's Psychology Service, was at present keeping the details of design and construction a carefully guarded secret. The reason given for this was that experimentation with the machines must be carried further before such details could be offered safely to the public. Which meant that whatever the Psychology Service happened to want built into any of its machines could be built into it. And that might include something which transmitted to the mind of psis an order to either enter the Psychology Service or stop putting their special abilities to use.

That was roughly what the suggestions they'd put into *her* mind amounted to.

But what was the purpose?

She couldn't know immediately—and, probably, she was not supposed to be wondering. The dream had led her to discover their trick, and that had brought her to the edge of something they wouldn't want known.

It wasn't a comfortable reflection. Telzey had listened to enough political shop talk among her mother's colleagues to know that the Federation could act in very decisive, ruthless ways in a matter of sufficient importance. And here was something, some plan or policy in connection with psis and psionics, apparently important enough to remain unknown even to junior members of the Federation's Grand Council! Jessamine would have expressed a very different kind of concern if she'd had any inkling that a branch of Federation government was interested in her daughter's experience with xenotelepathy.

Telzey rubbed her neck pensively. She could keep such thoughts to herself, but she couldn't very well help having them. And if the Psychology Service looked into her mind again, they might not like at all what she'd been thinking.

So what should she do?

The whole thing was connected, of course, with their top-secret psionic machines. There was one of those—a supposedly very advanced type of mind-reader, as a matter of fact—about which she could get detailed first-hand information without going farther than the Bank of Rienne. And she might learn something from that which would fill in the picture for her.

The machine was used by Transcluster Finance, the giant central bank which regulated the activities of major financial houses on more than half the Federation's worlds, and wielded more actual power than any dozen planetary governments. In the field of financial ethics, Transcluster made and enforced its own laws. Huge sums of money were frequently at stake in disputes among its associates, and machines of presumably more than human incorruptibility and accuracy were therefore employed to help settle conflicting charges and claims.

Two members of the Bank of Rienne's legal staff who specialized in ethics hearings were pleased to learn of Telzey's scholarly interest in their subject. They explained the proceedings in which the psionic Verifier was involved at considerable length. In operation, the giant telepath could draw any information pertinent to a hearing from a human mind within minutes. A participant who wished to submit his statements to verification was left alone in a heavily shielded chamber. He sensed nothing, but his mind became for a time a part of the machine's circuits. He was then released from the chamber, and the Verifier reported what it had found to the adjudicators of the hearing. The report was accepted as absolute evidence; it could not be questioned.

Rienne's attorneys felt that the introduction of psionic verification had in fact brought about a noticeable improvement in ethical standards throughout Transcluster's vast finance web. Of course it was possible to circumvent the machines. No one was obliged to make use of them; and in most cases, they were instructed to investigate only specific details of thought and memory indicated to them to confirm a particular claim. This sometimes resulted in a hearing decision going to the side which most skillfully presented the evidence in its favor for verification, rather than to the one which happened to be in the right. A Verifier was, after all, a machine and ignored whatever was not covered by its instructions, even when the mind it was scanning contained additional information with a direct and obvious bearing on the case. This had been so invariably demonstrated in practice that no reasonable person could retain the slightest qualms on the point. To further reassure those who might otherwise hesitate to permit a mind-reading machine to come into contact with them, all records of a hearing were erased from the Verifier's memory as soon as the case was closed.

And that, Telzey thought, did in a way fill in the picture. There was no evidence that Transcluster's Verifiers operated in the way they were assumed to be operating—except that for fifteen years, through innumerable hearings, they had consistently presented the appearance of being able to operate in no other manner. But the descriptions she'd been given indicated they were vaster and presumably far more complex instruments than the Customs machine at the Orado City space terminal; and from that machine—supposedly no telepath at all—an imperceptible psionic finger had flicked out, as she passed, to plant a knot of compulsive suggestions in her mind.

So what were the Verifiers doing?

One of them was set up, not at all far away, in the heart of Hub finance, a key point of the Federation. Every moment of the day, enormously important information was coming in to it from a thousand worlds—flowing through the vicinity of the Psychology Service's mind-reading device.

Could it really be restricted to scanning specific minute sections of the minds brought into contact with it in the ethics hearings?

Telzey wondered what the two amiable attorneys would say if she told them what she thought about that.

But, of course, she didn't.

It was like having wandered off-stage, accidentally and without realizing it, and suddenly finding one-self looking at something that went on behind the scenery.

Whatever the purpose of the something was, chance observers weren't likely to be welcome.

She could tiptoe away, but so long as the Psychology Service was theoretically capable of looking inside her head at any moment to see what she had been up to, that didn't change anything. Sooner or later they'd take that look. And then they'd interfere with her again, probably in a more serious manner.

So far, there seemed to be no way of getting around the advantage they had in being able to probe minds. Of course, there were such things as mind-blocks. But even if she'd known how to go about finding somebody who would be willing to equip her with one, mind-blocks were supposed to become dangerous to one's mental health when they were retained indefinitely. And if she had one, she would have to retain it indefinitely. Mind-blocks weren't the answer she wanted.

On occasion, in the days following her conversation with the ethics hearing specialists, Telzey had a very odd feeling that the answer she wanted wasn't far away. But nothing else would happen; and the feeling faded quickly. The Psionic Cop popped up in her dreams now and then, each time with less effect than before; or more rarely, he'd come briefly into her awareness after she'd been concentrated on study for a few hours. On the whole, the Cop was a minor nuisance. It looked as if the underlying compulsion had been badly shaken up by the digging around she'd done when she discovered it, and was gradually coming apart.

But that again might simply prompt the Psychology Service to take much more effective measures the next time. . . .

That was how matters stood around the beginning of the third week after Telzey's return from Jontarou. Then, one afternoon, she met an alien who was native to a non-oxygen world humans listed by a cosmographic code symbol, and who possessed a well-developed psionic talent of his own.

She had spent several hours that day in one of Orado City's major universities to gather data for a new study assignment and, on her way out, came through a hall containing a dozen or so live habitat scenes from wildly contrasting worlds. The alien was in one of the enclosures, which was about a thousand cubic yards in size and showed an encrusted jumble of rocks lifting about the surface of an oily yellow liquid. The creature was sprawled across the rocks like a great irregular mass of translucent green jelly, with a number of variously shaped, slowly moving crimson blotches scattered through its interior.

Strange as it appeared, she was in a hurry and wouldn't have done more than glance at it through the sealing energy field which formed the transparent front wall if she hadn't caught a momentary telepathic impulse from within the enclosure as she passed. This wasn't so unusual in itself; there was, when one gave close attention to it, frequently a diffused psionic murmuring of human or animal origin or both around, but as a rule it was unaware and vague as the sound somebody might make in breathing.

The pulse that came from the alien thing seemed quite different. It could have been almost a softly whispered question, the meaningful probe of an intelligent telepath.

Telzey checked, electrified, to peer in at it. It lay motionless, and the impulse wasn't repeated. She might have been mistaken.

She shaped a thought herself, a light, unalarming "Hello, who are you?" sort of thought, and directed it gently at the green-jelly mass on the rocks.

A slow shudder ran over the thing; and then suddenly something smashed *through* her with numbing force. She felt herself stagger backwards, had an instant's impression of another blow coming, and of raising her arm to ward it off. Then she was somehow seated on a bench at the far end of the hall, and a uniformed attendant was asking her concernedly how she felt. It appeared she had fainted for the first time in her life. He'd picked her up off the floor and carried her to the bench.

Telzey still felt dazed, but not nearly dazed enough to tell him the truth. At the moment, she wasn't sure just what had happened back there, but it definitely was something to keep to herself. She told him the first thing to come to her mind, which was that she had skipped lunch and suddenly began to feel dizzy. That was all she remembered.

He looked somewhat relieved. "There's a cafeteria upstairs."

Telzey smiled, nodded. "I'll eat something and then I'll be all right!" She stood up.

The attendant didn't let her get away so easily. He accompanied her to the cafeteria, guiding her along by an elbow as if she were an infirm old lady. After he'd settled her at a table, he asked what she would like, and brought it to her. Then he sat down across from her.

"You do seem all right again!" he remarked at last. His anxious look wasn't quite gone. "The reason this has sort of spooked me, miss," he went on, "is something that happened around half a year ago."

"Oh? What was that?" Telzey asked carefully,

sipping at the foamy chocolate-colored drink he had got for her. She wasn't at all hungry, but he obviously intended to hang around until she downed it.

There had been this other visitor, the attendant said, a well-dressed gentleman standing almost exactly where Telzey had been standing. The attendant happened to be glancing towards him when the gentleman suddenly began to stagger around, making moaning and screeching sounds, and dropped to the floor. "Only that time," the attendant said, "he was dead before we got there. And, ugh, his face . . . well, excuse me! I don't want to spoil your appetite. But it was a bad affair all around."

Telzey kept her eyes on her drink. "Did they find out what was wrong with him?"

"Something to do with his heart, they told me." The attendant looked at her doubtfully. "Well, I suppose it *must* have been his heart. It's just that those are very peculiar creatures they keep in that hall. It can make you nervous working around them."

"What kind of creatures are they?" Telzey asked.

He shook his head, said they didn't have names. Federation expeditions brought them back from one place and another, and they were maintained here, each in its made-to-order environment, so the scientists from the university could study them. In his opinion, they were such unnatural beasts that the public should be barred from the hall; but he didn't make the rules. Of course, there was actually no way they could hurt anybody from inside the habitat tanks, not through those force fields. But it had unnerved him today to see another visitor topple over before that one particular tank. . . .

He returned to his duties finally, and Telzey pushed her empty glass aside and considered the situation.

By now, every detail of what happened there had returned to her memory. The green-jelly creature definitely did hurt people through the energy screens

around its enclosure . . . if the people happened to
be telepaths. In them it found mental channels
through which it could send savage surges of psi
force. So the unfortunate earlier visitor had been
a psi, who responded as unsuspectingly as she did
to the alien's probing whisper, and then met quick
death.

She'd fallen into the same trap, but escaped. In
the first instant of stunned confusion, already losing
consciousness, she'd had a picture of herself raising
her arm to block the creature's blows. She hadn't done
it, of course; the blows weren't physical ones, and
couldn't be blocked in that manner. But in the same
reflexive, immediate manner, she'd done something
else, not even knowing what she did, but doing it
simply because it was the only possible defensive
move she could have made at that instant, and in that
particular situation.

Now she knew what the move had been. Something that seemed as fragile as a soap bubble was
stretched about her mind. But it wasn't fragile. It was
a curtain of psi energy she'd brought into instant
existence to check the creature's psi attacks as her
senses blacked out.

It was still there, being maintained by a small part
of her consciousness. She felt certain she could drop
it, then raise it again at will—though she had no
intention of doing that until she was a good, long
distance away from the hostile mind in the habitat
tank downstairs.

Although it needn't be, Telzey thought, a particularly hostile creature. Perhaps it had simply acted as
it would have done on its own world where other
telepathic creatures might be a natural prey, to be
tricked into revealing themselves as they came near,
and then struck down.

In a public park, ten minutes later, she sat down
in a quiet place where she could make an undisturbed

investigation of her psi bubble and its properties. After an hour or so, she decided she had learned enough about it for the moment, and went back to the hall of the live habitat scenes. There was a different attendant on duty now, and half-a-dozen other people were peering in at the occupant of one of the other tanks.

Telzey settled down on a bench opposite the enclosure of the green-jelly alien. He lay unmoving on his rocks and gave no indication of being aware of her return. She opened a section of the bubble, and sent him a sharp "You, there!" thought. A definitely unfriendly thought.

At once, he slammed back at her with a violence which seemed to shake the hall all around her. But the bubble was closed again, and there were no other effects. The attendant and the people farther down the hall obviously hadn't sensed anything. This was a matter strictly between psis.

Telzey let a minute or so pass before she gave the creature another prodding thought. This time, he was slower to react, and when he did, it was with rather less enthusiasm. He mightn't have liked the experience of having his thrusts bounced back by the bubble.

He had killed a human psi and tried to kill her, but she felt no real animosity towards him. He was simply too different for that. She could, however, develop a hate-thought if she worked at it, and she did. Then she opened the bubble and shot it at him.

The outworld thing shuddered. He struck back savagely and futilely. She lashed him with hate again, and he shuddered again.

Minutes later, he suddenly went squirming and flowing down the rocks and into the oily yellow liquid that washed around them. He was attempting panicky flight, and there was nowhere to go. Telzey stood up carefully and went over to the enclosure, where

she could see him bunched up against the far side
beneath the surface. He gave the impression of being
very anxious to avoid further trouble with her. She
opened the bubble wider than before, though still
with some caution, picked out his telepathic channels and followed them into his mind. There was no
resistance, but she flinched a little. The impression
she had—translated very roughly into human terms—
was of terrified, helpless sobbing. The creature was
waiting to be killed.

She studied the strange mind a few minutes longer,
then drew away from it, and left the habitat hall. It
wouldn't be necessary to do anything else about the
green-jelly alien. He wasn't very intelligent, but he
had an excellent memory.

And never, never, *never*, would he attempt to attack
one of the terrible human psis again.

Telzey had a curious feeling about the bubble. It
was something with which she had seemed immediately more than half familiar. Letting it flick into being
and out again soon was as automatic as opening and
closing her eyes. And in tracing out the delicate
manipulations by which its wispiest sections could be
controlled and shifted, she had the impression of
merely needing to refresh her memory about details
already known. . . . *This*, of course, was the way to
go about *that*! That was how it worked. . . .

There had been that other tantalizing feeling
recently. Of being very close to an answer to her problems with the Psychology Service, but not quite able
to see it. Perhaps the bubble had begun to form in
response to her need for an answer and the awareness of it would have come to her gradually if the
alien's attack hadn't brought it out to be put to instant
emergency use. It was a fluid pattern, drawing the
psi energy that sustained it from unknown sources,
as if there were an invisible ocean of psi nearby to

which she had put out a tap. She had heard of soft-bodied, vulnerable creatures which survived by fitting themselves into the discarded hard shells of other creatures and trudging about in them. The bubble was a little like that, though the other way around—something she had shaped to fit her; not a part of herself, but a marvelously delicate and adjustable apparatus which should have many uses beyond turning into a solid suit of psi armor in emergencies.

At the moment, for example, it might be used to prepare a deceptive image of herself to offer to future Psychology Service investigators. . . .

That took several days. Then, so far as Telzey could tell, any significant thinking she did about psionics, or the Psychology Service and its machines, would produce only the blurriest of faint traces under a telepathic probe. The same for her memories on the subject, back to the night when she'd been scared out of sleep by her first dream of the Psionic Cop. And the explanation was that the Cop had scared her so that she'd lost her interest in the practice of telepathy then and there.

Since their suggestion had been to do just that, they might buy it. On the other hand, if they took a really careful look into her mind, the thought-camouflage might not fool them long, or even for an instant. But they'd have to start searching around then to find out what really had been going on; and if they touched any part of the bubble block, she should know it. She had made other preparations for that.

In a rented deposit vault of the nondirect mailing system in Orado City there was a stack of addressed and arrival-dated microchips, all with an identical content; and on Telzey's personal communicator two tiny control buttons were keyed to the vault. Five minutes after she pressed down the first button, the chips would be launched into the automatic mazes of the nondirect system, where nothing could intercept or identify them until they reached their individual destinations. She could stop the process by depressing the second button before the five minutes were up, but in no other manner. The chips contained the thinking she'd done about the psionic machines. It might be only approximately correct, but it still was a kind of thinking the Psychology Service would not want to see broadcast at random to the news media of the Hub.

It wasn't a wholly satisfactory solution for a number of reasons, including the one that she couldn't know just what she might start by pushing the button. But it would have to do until she thought of something better. If there were indications of trouble, simply revealing that she could push it should make everybody quite careful for the moment. And after completing her preparations, she hadn't actually been expecting trouble, at least not for some while. She was behaving in a very innocuous manner, mainly busy with her legitimate studies; and that checked with the picture presented by the thought-camouflage. She'd talked about telepathy only to Gilas and Gonwil, telling Gonwil just enough to make sure she wouldn't mention the esoteric chips Telzey occasionally immersed herself in to somebody else.

Now, of course, that might change to some extent. As Gilas had implied, they couldn't risk holding back information from the detectives he was employing because what they withheld might turn out to have been exactly the information the detectives had needed. If they were as discreet as Gilas thought, it probably wouldn't matter much.

Telzey twisted her mouth doubtfully, staring at the thin, smoky lines of air traffic converging far ahead on Orado City. . . .

*Probably*, it wouldn't!

# Chapter 4

Several hours after Telzey's departure, Pehanron College's buildings and grounds, spreading up the sunsoaked hills above the residential town of Beale, were still unusually quiet.

Almost half the student body was struggling with mid-summer examinations, and a good proportion of those who had finished had obtained permission to get off to an early start for the holidays. The carports extending along the backs of the student courts showed a correspondingly large number of vacancies, though enough gleaming vehicles remained to have supplied the exhibits for the average aircar show, a fair percentage running up into the price ranges of small interstellar freighters. Pehanron sometimes was accused of opening its lists only to the sons and daughters of millionaires; and while this wasn't strictly true, the college did scout assiduously for such of them as might be expected to maintain the pace of its rugged curriculum. Pehanron liked to consider itself a select hatchery from which sprang a continuous line of leaders in many fields of achievement, and as a matter of fact, it did turn out more than its share of imposing names.

There was no one in sight in Court Ninety-two when Senior Counselor Eulate turned into it, arriving from the direction of the managerial offices. Miss Eulate was a plump, brisk little woman whose normal expression when she felt unobserved was a vaguely worried frown. The frown was somewhat pronounced at the moment.

At the gate of the duplex bungalow marked 18-19, the counselor came to an abrupt stop. In the center of the short garden path, head and pointed wolf ears turned in her direction, lay a giant white dog of the type known as Askanam arena hounds—a breed regarded, so Miss Eulate had been told, as the ultimate in reckless canine ferocity and destructiveness when aroused.

The appearance of Chomir—a yellow-eyed, extravagantly muscled hundred-and-fifty-pounder—always brought this information only too vividly back to Miss Eulate's mind. Not wishing to arouse the silently staring monster now, she continued to hesitate at the gate. Then, hearing the intermittent typing from beyond the open door at the end of the path, she called out in a carefully moderate tone. "Gonwil?"

The typing stopped. Gonwil's voice replied, "Yes . . . is that you, Miss Eulate?"

"It is. Please keep an eye on Chomir while I come in."

"Oh, for goodness sake!" Gonwil appeared laughing in the door. She was eighteen; a good-looking, limber-bodied, sunny-tempered blonde. "Now you know Chomir won't hurt you! He *likes* you!"

Miss Eulate's reply was a skeptical silence. But she proceeded up the path now, giving the giant hound a wary four feet of clearance as she went by. To her relief Chomir didn't move until she was past; then he merely placed his massive head back on his forelegs and half closed his eyes. Airily ignoring Gonwil's amused smile, Miss Eulate indicated the closed entrance door on the other side of the duplex as she came up. "Telzey isn't still asleep?"

"No, she left early. Did you want to see her?"

Miss Eulate shook her head.

"This concerns you," she said. "It would be better if we went inside."

In Gonwil's study, she brought a note pad and a small depth photo from her pocket. She held out the pad. "Do these names mean anything to you?"

Gonwil took the pad curiously. After a moment, she shook her head.

"No. Should they?"

Looking as stern as her chubby features permitted, Miss Eulate handed her the photo. "Then do you know these two people?"

Gonwil studied the two figures briefly, said, "To the best of my knowledge, I've never seen either of them, Miss Eulate. What is this about?"

"The Tayun consulate in Orado City had the picture transmitted to us a short while ago," Miss Eulate said. "The two persons in it—giving the names I showed you—called the consulate earlier in the morning and inquired about you."

"What did they want?"

"They said they had learned you were on Orado and would like to know where you could be found. They implied they were personal friends of yours from Tayun."

The girl shook her head. "They may be from Tayun, but we aren't even casually acquainted. I . . ."

"The consulate," Miss Eulate said grimly, "suspected as much! They secretly recorded the screen images of the callers, who were then requested to come to the consulate to be satisfactorily identified while your wishes in the matter were determined. The callers agreed but have failed to show up. The consulate feels this may indicate criminal intentions. I understand you have been placed on record there as being involved in a private war on Tayun, and . . ."

"Oh, no!" Gonwil wrinkled her nose in sudden dismay. "Not that nonsense again! Not just *now*!"

"Please don't feel alarmed!" Miss Eulate told her, not without a trace of guilty relish. The counselor took a strong vicarious interest in the personal affairs of her young charges, and to find one of them touched by the dangerous glamour of a private war was undeniably exciting. "Nobody can harm you here," she went on. "Pehanron maintains a very dependable security system to safeguard its students."

"I'm sure it does," Gonwil said. "But frankly, Miss Eulate, I don't need to be safeguarded and I'm not at all alarmed."

"You aren't?" Miss Eulate asked, surprised.

"No. Whatever reason these people had for pretending to be friends of mine . . . I can think of several perfectly harmless ones . . . they aren't vendettists."

"Vendettists?"

Gonwil smiled. "Commercial vendetta. An old custom on Tayun—a special kind of private war. A couple of generations ago it was considered good form to kill off your business competitors if you could. It isn't being done so much any more, but the practice hasn't entirely died out."

Miss Eulate's eyebrows rose. "But then . . ."

"Well, the point is," Gonwil said, "that *I'm* not involved in any vendetta or private war! And I never have been, except in Cousin Malrue's imagination."

"I don't understand," the counselor said. "Cousin Malrue . . . you're referring to Mrs. Parlin?"

"Yes. She isn't exactly a cousin but she's the closest relative I have. In fact, the only one. And I'm very fond of her. I practically grew up in the Parlin family . . . and of course they've more or less expected that Junior and I would eventually get married."

Miss Eulate nodded. "Rodel Parlin the Twelfth. Yes, I know." She had met the young man several times on his visits to the college to see Gonwil and gained an excellent impression of him. It looked like an eminently suitable match, one of which Pehanron would certainly have approved; but regrettably Gonwil had not returned Rodel Parlin the Twelfth's very evident affection in kind.

"Now, Cousin Malrue," Gonwil went on, "has always been afraid that one or the other of my father's old business enemies on Tayun was going to try to have me killed before I came of age. My parents and my uncle—my father's brother—founded Lodis Associates and made a pretty big splash in Tayun's financial world right from the start. Malrue and her husband joined the concern before I was born, and then, when I was about a year and a half old, my parents and my uncle were killed in two separate accidents. Cousin Malrue was convinced it was vendetta action. . . ."

"Mightn't it have been?" Miss Eulate asked.

Gonwil shrugged. "She had some reason for suspecting it at the time. My parents and uncle apparently had been rather ruthless in the methods they used to build up Lodis Associates, and no doubt they had plenty of enemies. The authorities who investigated the matter said very definitely that the deaths had been accidental, but Malrue didn't accept that.

"Then, after the directors of a Tayun bank had been appointed my guardians, some crank sent them a message. It said my parents had died as a result of the evil they'd done, and that their daughter would never live to handle the money they had robbed from better people than themselves. You can imagine what effect that had on Cousin Malrue!"

"Yes, I believe I can."

"And that," Gonwil said, "is really the whole story. Since then, every time it's looked as if I might have come close to being in an accident or getting harmed in some way, Cousin Malrue has taken it for granted that vendettists were behind it. The thing has simply preyed on her mind!"

Miss Eulate looked doubtful, asked, "Isn't it possible that you are taking the matter too lightly, Gonwil? As you may remember, I met Mrs. Parlin on one occasion here. We had quite an extensive conversation, and she impressed me as being a very intelligent and levelheaded person."

"Oh, she is," Gonwil said. "Don't misunderstand me. Cousin Malrue is in fact the most intelligent woman I've ever known. She's been running Lodis

Associates almost single-handedly for the past fifteen years, and the firm's done very well in that time.

"No, it's just that one subject on which she isn't reasonable. Nobody can argue her out of the idea that vendettists are lurking for me. It's very unfortunate that those mysterious strangers, whoever they were, should have showed up just now. By Tayun's laws I'll become a responsible adult on the day I'm nineteen, and that's only three months away."

Miss Eulate considered, nodded. "I see! You will then be able to handle the money left to you by your parents. So if the vendettists want to make good on their threat, they would have to, uh, eliminate you before that day!"

"Uh-huh," Gonwil said. "Actually, of course, most of the money stays in Lodis Associates, but from then on I'll have a direct voice in the concern's affairs. The Parlin family and I own about seventy per cent of the stock between us. I suppose those nonexistent vendettists would consider that the same thing as handling my parents' money."

Miss Eulate was silent a moment. "If the people who called the consulate were not the vendettists," she said, "why should they have behaved in such a suspicious manner?"

Gonwil laughed ruefully.

"Miss Eulate, I do believe you could become almost as bad as Cousin Malrue about this! Why, they might have had any number of reasons for acting as they did. If they were from Tayun, they could know I'd soon be of age and they might have some business they'd like me to put money in. Or perhaps they just didn't express themselves clearly enough, and they're actually friends of some friends of mine who asked them to look me up on Orado. Or they could be from a Tayun news agency, looking for a story on the last member of the Lodis family. You see?"

"Well, there are such possibilities, of course," the

counselor conceded. "However, I fail to understand then why you appear to be concerned about Mrs. Parlin's reactions. If nothing comes of the matter, isn't it quite unlikely that she'll ever learn that somebody has inquired about you?"

"Ordinarily, it would be," Gonwil said glumly. "But she and Rodel the Twelfth are due to arrive on Orado at almost any moment. I'd been expecting them the day after tomorrow, but Junior called an hour ago to say the schedule had changed, and they'd be here today. Malrue is bound to find out what happened, and, to put it mildly, she's going to be extremely upset!"

"Yes, no doubt." Miss Eulate hesitated, went on. "I dislike to tell you this, but it's been decided that until a satisfactory explanation for the appearance of the two strangers at the consulate has been obtained, certain steps will have to be taken to insure your personal safety. You understand that the college has a contractual obligation to your guardians to see that no harm comes to you while you are a student."

Gonwil looked at her, asked, "Meaning I'm restricted to the campus?"

"I'm afraid we'll have to go a little further than that. We are assigning guards to see to it that no un-authorized persons enter bungalow 18-19, and I must instruct you not to leave it for the next day or two."

"Oh, dear! And all because . . ." Gonwil shook her blonde head. "Cousin Malrue will have kittens when she hears *that*!"

The counselor looked surprised.

"But why should Mrs. Parlin have, uh, kittens?" she inquired. "Surely she will see that the college is acting only to keep you out of possible danger!"

"She simply won't believe I'm not in danger here, Miss Eulate! When my guardians enrolled me at Pehanron, she didn't at all like the idea of my com-ing to Orado by myself. That's why the college has had to put up with that monster Chomir for the past two years! My guardians thought it would calm Malrue down if I kept one of the famous Askanam arena hounds around as a bodyguard. They sent all the way there to get one of the best."

Miss Eulate nodded. "I see. I . . ." Her voice died in her throat.

Moving with ghostly quiet, Chomir had appeared suddenly in the doorway to the garden. He stood there, yellow eyes fixed on them.

"He heard me use his name and came to see if I'd called him," Gonwil said apologetically. "I'll send him back out till we're finished."

"No," the counselor said with some firmness, "tell him to come in. I shouldn't allow him to frighten me, and I know it. Now is as good a time as any to overcome that weakness!"

Gonwil looked pleased. "Come on in, boy!"

The Askanam came forward, moving lightly and easily in spite of his size. In the patch of sunlight from the door, an ivory brindle pattern was faintly visible in the short white hair of his hide, the massive cables of surface muscle shifting and sliding beneath it. Miss Eulate, for all her brave words just now, felt her mouth go parched. Ordinarily she liked dogs, and Chomir was a magnificent dog. But there were those stories about his breed—merciless killers developed by painstaking geneticists to perform in the bloody arenas of Askanam and to provide the ruling nobility of that colorful and tempestuous world with the most incorruptible and savage of guards. . . .

"I imagine," the counselor observed uncomfortably, "that Chomir would, in fact, be an excellent protector for you if it became necessary."

"No doubt about that," Gonwil agreed. "And I very much hope it never becomes necessary. It would be a fearful mess! Have I told you what happened when they were going to teach him how to defend me?"

"No, you haven't," Miss Eulate acknowledged, wishing she hadn't brought up the subject.

"It was just before I left for Orado. My guardians had hired an Askanam dog trainer. Chomir wasn't much more than a pup then, but when they're training arena dogs on Askanam, they don't use human beings to simulate an attacker. They use special robots which look and move and smell like human beings.

"I found out why! They turned two of those poor machines loose on me, and Chomir shook both of them to pieces before I could shout, 'Stop!' The trainer told me that when he's really clamping his jaws down on something, he slams on close to two thousand pounds of pressure."

"Good heavens!" Miss Eulate said faintly.

"Anyway," Gonwil went on, unaware of the effect she was creating, "everyone decided right then that one thing Chomir didn't need was attack training!" She prodded the dog's hard flank affectionately with a shoe tip. "Of course, he does have a terrific pedigree to account for it. His sire was a famous arena dog who killed thirty-two men and all kinds of fighting animals. He must have been a pretty horrible beast! And on his dam's side . . ."

She broke off, having finally caught Miss Eulate's expression, went on after a moment, "I don't really mind so much being confined to quarters. But I'm hoping the mystery at the consulate will be solved before the Parlins arrive. There's no possible way I could avoid seeing Malrue, and . . ."

She checked herself for the second time, added in a different tone, "That's Junior calling again now!"

"Eh?" Miss Eulate asked. Then, following Gonwil's gaze, she became aware of a faint, silvery tinkling from the table. A tiny, jewel-bright device stood there, out of which the sound evidently came. On closer inspection, it appeared to be a beautifully inlaid powder compact. Miss Eulate looked puzzledly back at the girl.

"A personalized communicator," Gonwil explained wryly. "A gift from Junior which came in the mail this morning. He has the twin to it, and the only use for the set is that Junior and I can talk together wherever either of us happens to be on Orado." She gave Miss Eulate a small smile, added, "Junior is very difficult to discourage!"

The miniature communicator stopped its tinkling for a few seconds, then began again. Gonwil still made no move towards it. Miss Eulate asked, "Aren't you going to answer him?"

"No. If I don't switch it on, he'll think I'm not around."

Miss Eulate sighed and arose.

"Well," she said, "I should get back to the office. We'll trust this has been as you feel, a false alarm. But until we're quite certain of it, we must take whatever precautions seem indicated."

Gonwil grimaced resignedly.

The counselor went on, "And since the Bank of Rienne is acting as your guardians on Orado, I'm also obliged to see to it that they are informed of the occurrence."

At that, Gonwil's face suddenly brightened.

"Miss Eulate," she said, "when you make that call . . . and please make it at once . . . would you have it put through directly to Mr. Amberdon?"

"Why, yes, I can do that. But why specifically Mr. Amberdon?"

"He may be able to do something. Besides, Telzey's gone to see him. She should be with him just about this time—and she can usually think of a way out of anything."

"I'm quite aware of it," Miss Eulate said, rather shortly. Privately she regarded Telzey, in spite of her unquestioned scholastic brilliance, as something of a college problem. She added, "Well, I'll see what can be done."

# Chapter 5

There had been enough general activity during the past two hours to leave Telzey unaware, except for a fleeting moment now and then, that she had begun to feel some physical effects of having passed up the night's sleep.

She couldn't, she thought, have complained that her warning wasn't taken seriously! Of course, the fact that Gonwil was a temporary ward of the bank would have required that it be given attention, even without the backing of the personal interest of Rienne's executive officer and his daughter.

A query regarding the internal structure of the Tayun concern of Lodis Associates had gone to Transcluster Finance Central almost immediately after her call to Gilas, and she had barely arrived at the bank when a reply came back.

Transcluster's records confirmed in every particular what she had gathered in casual talk with Gonwil from time to time and failed to give its proper significance. Lodis Associates basically had been set up in a manner which tended to leave control of the concern with the founding associates and their heirs. Shares could be sold only after being offered to all other associates at the original value. Since the original value had been approximately a twentieth of the present one, current sales to outsiders were in effect blocked. If a deceased associate left no natural heirs, his stock was distributed among the surviving associates in proportion to their holdings.

Which meant that Gonwil's death would in fact place the Parlin family in control of the concern . . .

And that seemed enough to convince both Gilas and Wellan Dasinger, the chief of the Kyth Detective

Agency, who had arrived before Telzey, that the danger was real. It puzzled her because it hardly looked like conclusive proof of anything, but she decided they were aware of possibilities in situations of that kind which she couldn't know about. Within an hour, the Bank of Rienne and the Kyth Agency had initiated cluster-spanning activities on behalf of the bank's temporary ward which would have stunned Gonwil if she'd been told about them.

So much action should have been reassuring. But her father and Dasinger still looked worried; and presently Gilas appeared to realize again that she was around, and explained. It was a delicate situation. As Gonwil's appointed local guardian, the bank could act with a certain amount of authority; but that advantage was based on a technicality which could be shattered in an instant by her guardians on Tayun. "And they're aware, of course—at least in a general way—of Mrs. Parlin's plans."

Telzey gave him a startled look. "Why should . . ."

"Since Gonwil was a minor," Gilas said, "her guardians could have taken legal steps to nullify the condition that her death would benefit the other members of Lodis Associates. And considering that business practices on Tayun remain close to the level of tribal warfare, they *would* have done it—automatically on assuming guardianship—unless it was to their own benefit to be a little negligent about the matter."

"Her own guardians would help Malrue kill Gonwil?" Telzey said incredulously.

"Probably not directly. And of course if Gonwil had decided to marry the son, no one would have had any reason to kill her. But as it stands, we must expect that her guardians will try to hamper any obvious efforts now to protect her against Malrue Parlin. So we have to be very careful not to reveal our suspicions at present. Until we can get Gonwil's formal request to represent her in the matter, we'll be on very shaky legal ground if we're challenged from Tayun. And from what I know of Gonwil, it's going to be difficult for her to accept that she might be in danger from Mrs. Parlin."

Telzey nodded. "We'll almost have to prove it first."

Dasinger put in, "Supposing—this is a theoretical question—but supposing this turned into a situation where Miss Lodis saw that in order to stay alive herself it might be necessary to have Mrs. Parlin killed. Knowing her as you do, do you think she could be brought to agree to the action?"

Telzey stared at the detective, realized with some shock that he had been speaking seriously, that it wasn't a theoretical question at all.

She said carefully, "I can't imagine her agreeing to any such thing, Mr. Dasinger! She just isn't a—a violent person. I don't think she's ever intentionally hurt anybody."

"And of course," the detective said, "the Parlin family, having known her since infancy, is quite aware of that."

"Yes . . . I suppose so." It was another disturbing line of thought.

Gilas said quickly, smiling, "Well, we don't intend to let it come to that. In a general way though, Telzey, Gonwil's attitudes are likely to be a handicap here. We'll see how well we can work around them for now."

She didn't answer. There was, of course—as Gilas knew—a way to change Gonwil's attitudes. But it didn't seem necessary to mention that immediately.

Wellan Dasinger, who might be Gilas's junior by seven or eight years, had an easy tone and manner and didn't seem too athletically built. But somehow one gradually got the impression that he was the sort of man who would start off each day with forty push-ups and a cold needle shower as a matter of course. Telzey didn't know what his reaction had been when

Gilas told him she'd been getting information from the mind of a dog, but he discussed it with her as if it were perfectly normal procedure. Kyth operatives had been dispatched to Beale to look around for the mysterious stranger of Chomir's memories; and Dasinger, unhurriedly and thoughtfully, went over every detail she had obtained, then questioned her at length about Gonwil's relationship to the Parlins, the vendetta stories, the maneuvering to get Gonwil married to Junior.

There seemed to be no question of Dasinger's competence. And it was clear he didn't like the situation.

Information began flowing back from Tayun over interstellar transmitters from various contacts of the bank and Dasinger's agency. One item seemed to provide all the evidence needed to indicate that caution was advisable in dealing with the Parlin family. During the past two decades, the number of shareholders in Lodis Associates had diminished by almost fifty per cent. The last three to go had dropped out simultaneously after transferring their holdings to Malrue Parlin, following a disagreement with her on a matter of company policy. Some of the others had taken the same route, but rather more had died in one way or another. There had never been any investigation of the deaths. The remaining associates appeared to be uniformly staunch supporters of Mrs. Parlin's policies.

Dasinger didn't like that either.

"Leaving out crude measures like counterviolence," he told Telzey, "there probably are going to be just two methods to make sure your friend gets a chance to enjoy a normal life span. One of them is to route Mrs. Parlin into Rehabilitation. If she's tamed down, the rest of the clique shouldn't be very dangerous. She's obviously the organizer."

Telzey asked uncertainly, "What's the other method?"

"Have Miss Lodis hand over her stock to Mrs.

Parlin for whatever she's willing to pay. I doubt it would be safe to argue too strongly about the price."

Telzey was silent a moment. "Supposing," she said finally, "that Gonwil did agree to . . . well, counterviolence. That would be a private war—"

"Yes, we'd have to register to make it legitimate."

"You—your agency—handles private wars?"

"Occasionally we'll handle one," Dasinger said. "It depends on the client and the circumstances. I'd say this is such an occasion."

She looked at him. "Isn't that pretty risky work?"

The detective pursed his lips judiciously.

"No, not too risky. It would be expensive and messy. Mrs. Parlin appears to be an old hand at this, but we'd restrict the main action to Orado. If she imported her own talent, they'd be at a severe disadvantage here. And the better local boys wouldn't want any part of it after we got word around that the Kyth Agency was representing the other side. We should have the thing settled, without placing Miss Lodis in jeopardy, in about six months, even if we had to finish up on Tayun. But it appears Miss Lodis has a prejudice against such methods."

"Yes, she does," Telzey said. After a moment, she added, "So do I."

"I don't know about your friend, Miss Amberdon," Dasinger said pleasantly, "but I expect you'll grow out of it. At the moment though, it seems our line should be to try to manipulate Mrs. Parlin into Rehabilitation. We should know inside an hour about how good a chance we'll have to do it. I'm waiting for a call."

The call came in ten minutes later. It was from the Kyth Agency.

There appeared to be much Pehanron's law courses hadn't mentioned about the practical aspects of mindblocks.

The Tayun connection's report to the agency was that the Parlin family had been for years on the official list of those who were provided with mind-blocks for general commercial reasons. These, Dasinger explained, were expensive, high-precision jobs which ordinarily did not restrict their possessor in any noticeable way. But when specific levels of stress or fatigue were developed, the block automatically cut in to prevent the divulging of information from the areas it was set to cover.

"You see how it works," Dasinger said. "You have the block installed, have its presence officially confirmed, and have the fact published. Thereafter, nobody who's bothered to check the list will attempt to extort the information from you, because they know you can't give it. The Rehabilitation machines supposedly can take down any block, but they might need a year. Otherwise, nothing I've ever heard of can get much through a solidly installed block—continuous questioning, drugs, mind-probes, threats, torture, enforced sleeplessness, hypnotics. All that can be accomplished is to kill the blocked person eventually, and if that's your goal there're easier ways of going about it."

Apparently, too, the fancier type of block did not bring on the mental deterioration she'd heard about. Malrue Parlin's faculties obviously hadn't been impaired.

"A commercial block of that nature," Gilas said slowly, "presumably would cover plans to murder a business associate for profit in any case." He looked as if he'd bitten into something sour. "When it comes to the Parlins, we can be sure it would cover them. There've been a number of occasions when Mrs. Parlin must have banked on that for protection if an investigation should catch up with her."

"Getting rid of unwanted fellow associates was a business matter, so the block would automatically cover any action to that end," Dasinger agreed.

Gilas rubbed his chin, took out a cigarette, lit it. He scowled absently at Telzey.

"Then circumstantial evidence isn't going to get us anywhere against the lady," he said. "Either in Federation court or in a Transcluster hearing. It's too bad, because in a few hours this morning we've accumulated almost enough evidence to force the Parlins to clear themselves through a subjective probe. After we've sorted it over, we might find we have enough. But a subjective probe would simply confirm that they're equipped with blocks. Tampering with a recognized block is legally equivalent to manslaughter. That would end our case." He looked at the detective. "So what do you suggest?"

"A trap," Dasinger said. "Now, before they find out they're suspected. Later on they wouldn't be likely to fall for it."

"And how do we go about it?"

"My boys are trying to locate Junior. We're not sure he's in Orado City; at any rate, he hasn't checked in at his hotel. But they should have his rooms tapped for view and sound by now, and when they find him, they'll keep watch on him around the clock.

"Two days from now, when his parents arrive, we should be able to have them under observation before they leave the spaceport. There's no reason to think they'll be taking extraordinary precautions at that time, so we should very shortly pick up enough of the conversation between them and Junior to know what their plans are.

"If the plans include the immediate murder of Miss Lodis, we'll go along with it. And with a little luck, we'll catch either the Parlins themselves or somebody who can be proved to be their agent in the actual attempt to commit murder. If they're to wind up in Rehabilitation, we shouldn't try to settle for anything less definite."

He turned to Telzey. "Naturally, Miss Lodis won't be the bait for our trap. We'll have a decoy, someone who can impersonate her to the extent required.

But meanwhile we may have a difficult problem in keeping her out of the way without tipping our hand—unless, of course, something can be done immediately to weaken her trust in Mrs. Parlin."

He'd said it very casually. But he might know more about what a psi could accomplish in that direction than he'd indicated. And she could do it. It would take some time; she had found making the initial contact with the mind of a nonpsi human an involved and rather difficult process—something very different from getting into an exchange with other telepaths, and more involved by a good bit than the same proceeding had been with Chomir. But then Gonwil wouldn't realize she was being influenced in any way while her lifelong feelings about Cousin Malrue began to change. . . .

Telzey said, "I arranged with Gonwil that we'd start out on a holiday trip together after I get back to the college today. We'll take Chomir along. If we can find some place where there isn't too much disturbance—"

Dasinger smiled, nodded. "We'll take care of that."

"Then," Telzey said, "I think I could talk Gonwil into cooperating with us—before Mr. and Mrs. Parlin get here."

"That would be very helpful! And now the dog . . . you mentioned that you should be able to find out exactly why the dog considers that unidentified stranger to be an enemy."

"Yes," Telzey said. Unless she was mistaken, Dasinger had a very fair picture of what she intended to do about Gonwil; and that explained, of course, why he'd accepted her account of Chomir's adventures without question. He did know something about psis. "I think I could get that from him in another couple of hours," she said. "We'd come pretty close to it before I had to stop this morning."

She left the office area a few minutes later to pick

up the Cloudsplitter and start back to Pehanron. She
had a plan of her own, but it would be best to wait
until they had Gonwil under cover before mention-
ing it. Gilas mightn't like it; but she'd talk to Dasinger
first to find out if it might be feasible to plant her
somewhere in the immediate vicinity of the Parlins
after they arrived. Gonwil would be cooperating by
that time; and while she didn't know whether she
could get into a mind that was guarded by a block,
it would be worth trying it if she could remain unobserved around Malrue long enough to carry out the
preliminary work.

Because if she could do it, they'd do better than
find out what the murder plans were. Without knowing why, Malrue would quietly give up her evil intentions towards Gonwil within a few hours, and remain
incapable of developing them again or permitting her
husband and son to carry on. And that would settle
the whole matter in the simplest possible way.

She was approaching the exits to the upper level
parking strip where she had left the Cloudsplitter
when somebody addressed her.

"Miss Amberdon! One moment, please!"

It was one of the bank guards. Telzey stopped.
"Yes?"

"Mr. Amberdon's secretary notified us just now to
watch for you here," the guard explained. "There's
an open line to her office in this combooth. She said
to tell you a very important matter had come up, and
you should hear about it before leaving the building."

Telzey slipped into the booth, frowning. Gilas could
have reached her through her personal communicator while she was in the bank . . . perhaps he didn't
want to chance being overheard by some stray beam-
tapper. The door closed automatically behind her as
she touched the ComWeb's button, and Ravia, Gilas's
blue-haired, highly glamorous and highly efficient
secretary, appeared in the screen.

"I thought they might still catch you," she said, smiling. "Your father would like to speak to you on a shielded line, Telzey. You're on one now, and I'll connect you with him."

Her image faded. Gilas came on, said briskly, "There you are! There's been a change of schedule. Take your car down to the general parking area. You'll find two of Dasinger's men waiting for you with a carrier. They'll load on your car and take you back to Pehanron with them. We'll brief you on the way."

"What's happened?" she asked, startled.

"We've had a very unpleasant surprise. You'd barely left when two items of information came in. The first was that Mr. and Mrs. Parlin were found listed among the passengers of a ship which berthed at the space terminal something over an hour ago. We're having the Orado City hotels checked, but we don't know where the pair is at present. And Junior hasn't been found yet."

Telzey swallowed.

"Then," Gilas went on, "I had a call from Pehanron College. I'll give you the details on that a little later. What it seems to amount to is that the Parlins have succeeded in creating an atmosphere of alarm and confusion regarding Gonwil's safety, which should serve to keep suspicions turned well away from them if something actually happens to her. One result is that special measures will be needed now to get Gonwil away from Pehanron without dangerous delays. You probably could handle that part of it better than any outsider. Do you want to try it?"

"Yes, of course," she said.

Telzey discovered the hand that rested on the screen button was trembling a little.

"All right." Gilas gave her a brief smile. "I'll tell you the rest of it after you're in the carrier."

The screen went blank.

"And all I've been trying to do all morning,"

Gonwil exclaimed, somewhere between laughter and dismay, "was to settle down quietly without interruptions to get those grisly Finance Eleven chips cleaned up! You'd think everybody had gone out of their minds!"

Telzey looked sympathetic. Gonwil's lunch had been delivered to her in the duplex, on Miss Eulate's instructions; and a few college guards in civilian clothes loafed around outside, trying to look as if they'd just happened to wander into the area and weren't really much interested in anything here. Gonwil filled Telzey in on the morning's events while she ate the lunch and Telzey thoughtfully sipped a mug of milk. The first thing Malrue Parlin and her husband had done after landing at Orado City's spaceport was to check in at the Tayun consulate. The first thing the consul general there, an old acquaintance, had done was to tell them about the ominous strangers who had inquired about Gonwil Lodis early in the day. And the fat was in the fire.

"Cousin Malrue went into a howling tizzy!" Gonwil reported, shuddering. "She said she'd always known it was too risky for me to be studying on Orado. So she wanted to get me away from here now, with the Parlin family, where I'd be safe. Naturally, Pehanron said, 'No!'—and am I glad! Old Eulate's bad enough about this, but Malrue . . . !"

"Think she might pop in on you here?"

Gonwil nodded. "The whole family plans to show up at Pehanron this evening. Malrue will be battling with Eulate—and I'll be in the middle! And there's no way I can stop it."

"You wouldn't be in the middle," Telzey observed, "if you weren't here."

"If I weren't . . ." Gonwil glanced sharply over at her, lowered her voice to a whisper. "How . . . when Eulate's got those people staring at my front and back doors? I'm confined to quarters."

"First step," Telzey whispered back, "we move your chips and stuff to my side. Eulate said under the circumstances it'd be all right if I helped you a little on the tests."

"They can see *your* front and back doors too, dopey!" Gonwil pointed out. "What good will that do?"

"They can't see inside my carport."

"Huh? No!" Gonwil grinned. "The shower window . . ." She looked doubtfully at Chomir. "Can we boost Musclehead through it?"

"We can try. Want to?"

"Ha! When?"

"Right now. Before Eulate realizes you've got a loophole left."

"I should leave her a note," Gonwil remarked. "Something reassuring. I simply *had* to get away for a few days—or suffer a nervous breakdown. . . ."

"Sounds fine," Telzey approved.

"Then, perhaps I should call Malrue and tell her, so . . ."

"Are *you* out of your mind?"

Gonwil looked reluctant. "You're right. Me being at Pehanron is bad, but going off by myself would be worse. If we didn't agree to wait till she could pick us up outside, she'd be perfectly capable of tipping off Eulate!"

Some minutes later, Telzey came out the back door on her side of the bungalow, dressed for a town trip again. The two Pehanron guards stationed across the traffic lane eyed her as she started towards the enclosed carport, but made no move. They hadn't been instructed to keep watch on Telzey.

Inside the stall and out of their sight, she slid behind the Cloudsplitter's hood, roared the main engine experimentally a few times, glanced up. The shower window already stood open. Chomir's big white head appeared in it now, pointed ears tipped questioningly forwards, broad brow wrinkled in concentration. He had grasped that something unusual was required of him—but what? To look out of Telzey's shower window?

Telzey beckoned.

"Down here, Brainless!"

She couldn't hear Gonwil's voice above the noise of the engine, but Chomir's air of well-meaning bewilderment increased. Why, his eyes inquired of Telzey, was Gonwil shoving around at his rear? Then his forepaws came into view, resting on the window sill. Telzey gestured violently, pointing at the ground below the window.

Urged on from in front and behind, Chomir suddenly got the picture. He grinned, lolled out his tongue, sank back, came up and out in a flowing, graceful leap, clearing the window frame by a scant half-inch on all sides. He landed and waved his tail cheerfully at Telzey.

She caught his collar and patted him, while Gonwil, red-faced from her effort to lift more than her own weight in dog straight up, came wriggling through the shower window after him with an overnight bag containing the Finance Eleven chips and her library. Telzey slid open the Cloudsplitter's luggage compartment.

A minute later, she turned the little car out into the traffic lane. She had barely been able to shove the luggage compartment's door shut on her two passengers; but they were safely out of sight. The two guards stared thoughtfully after the car as it went gliding down the lane. They could hear the music of a newsviewer program within the duplex. It might be a good half-hour before they got the first proddings of suspicion about Telzey and her aircar.

Coming up to the force-screen exit she'd used in the morning, Telzey snapped the Star Honor Student pass back on her hat. The guards were screening incoming visitors with unusual care today, but students going out were a different matter. They glanced at the pass, at her, waved her through.

As she lifted the car over the crest of the wooded hills north of the college area, a big green airvan veered out of the direction in which it was headed and turned north ahead of her, picking up speed. Fifteen miles on and a few minutes later, Telzey followed the van down to the side of an isolated farm building. En route, there had been a few cautiously questioning knocks from the inside of the luggage compartment. But Telzey ignored them and Gonwil, puzzled, no doubt, about the delay in being let out but trustful as ever, had subsided again.

In the shadow of the farm building, Telzey set the Cloudsplitter down behind the van. Gilas Amberdon clambered out of the front section of the big vehicle and met her beyond hearing range of the luggage compartment.

"Any problems?"

"Not so far," Telzey said. "They're both inside. Has the Kyth Agency found out where the Parlins are?"

"No," Gilas said. "The calls they've made were routed through Orado City but apparently didn't originate there. The chances are they aren't hiding deliberately and will disclose their whereabouts as soon as they hear Gonwil has disappeared from the college."

He studied her a moment. "I realize we're working you a little hard, Telzey. If you take six hours off and catch up on some sleep after we get to the Kyth hideout, it shouldn't make any difference."

She shook her head. "I don't feel particularly tired. And I want to finish up with Chomir. I've got a hunch what he knows will be really important when we get it figured out."

Gilas considered. "All right. Dasinger would like to have that. We'll be there shortly. You'll get separate quarters as you specified—close enough to Gonwil and Chomir to let you work your mental witchcraft on them. And you'll be completely undisturbed."

"That will be fine," Telzey said.

Her father smiled. "Then let's go!"

He started towards the front of the van. Telzey walked back to the Cloudsplitter and slipped into her seat. Half a minute later, the end of the van opened out. She slid the car up and inside and shut off its engine. Benches lined this section of the vehicle. Aside from that, it was empty.

The loading door slammed shut again and the section lights came on overhead. Telzey waited until she felt the van lift creakily into the air. Then she opened the luggage compartment and let her rumpled passengers emerge.

"What in the world," Gonwil inquired bewilderedly, straightening up and staring around as Chomir eased himself out of the Cloudsplitter behind her, "are we doing in this thing?"

"Being scooted off to a safe hiding place," Telzey said. "That was all arranged for in advance."

"Arranged for—safe . . ." Gonwil's voice was strained. "Telzey! Whose idea was this?"

"The Bank of Rienne's."

The room they'd put her in here, Gonwil acknowledged, was, though not very large, comfortable and attractively furnished. If, nevertheless, it gave her a somewhat oppressive feeling of being imprisoned, that could be attributed to the fact that it was windowless and lacked means of outside communication.

The only way to leave would be to go through a short corridor and open a door at the far end, which let into an office where a number of people were working. So she couldn't have slipped away unnoticed, but there was no reason to think the people in the office would try to detain her if she did decide to leave. She'd simply been asked to stay here long enough to let the Bank of Rienne determine whether there could be any sinister significance to the appearance of the inquisitive strangers at the Tayun consulate that morning.

During the brief ride in the airvan, Telzey had explained that the bank felt its investigation would be greatly simplified if it could be carried out in complete secrecy. Pehanron College did not seem a safe place to leave Gonwil if somebody did intend to harm her; and to avoid revealing that it was taking a hand in the matter, the bank had called on Telzey, through her father, to spirit Gonwil quietly away from the campus.

Allowing for the fact that, at the moment, everybody appeared obsessed by the notion that Tayun vendettists were after her, it wasn't an unreasonable explanation. The Bank of Rienne did have some grounds to consider itself responsible for her here. "But why," Gonwil had asked, "didn't you tell me all this before we left?"

"Would you have come along if I had?" Telzey said.

Gonwil reflected and admitted that she probably wouldn't have come along. She didn't want to appear ungrateful; and she had now begun to feel the first touches of apprehension. When so many people, including Telzey's eminently practical father, were indicating concern for her safety, the possibility couldn't be denied that there was more to the old vendettist stories than she'd been willing to believe. Cousin Malrue, after all, was no fool; perhaps she had done Malrue an inexcusable injustice in belittling her warnings! Gonwil had only a vague idea of the methods a capable murderer might use to reach his victim; but it was generally accepted that he had a frightening array of weapons to choose from, and that every precaution must be taken in such situations.

At any rate, she was perfectly safe here. The door to the room was locked; she had one key to it, Gilas

Amberdon another. She was to let no one but Telzey in, and to make sure that no one else attempted to enter, Chomir was on guard in the corridor outside. It was comfortable to remember now that if Chomir was no shining light when it came to the standard doggy tricks, the protection of a human being was as solidly stamped into his nature as the gory skills of the arena. While he could move, only Gonwil or Telzey would open that door until one of them convinced him he could stop being a watchdog again.

And now that she was alone, Gonwil thought, there was something she should take care of promptly.

Opening the overnight bag she had taken from the college, she arranged her study materials on a desk shelf, then brought out the miniature camouflaged communicator which had come with the mail in the morning. She had dropped Junior's unwanted token of affection in with the library and other items, intending to show it to Telzey later on.

She studied the tiny instrument a moment, pensively biting her lip. There had been no opportunity to tell Telzey about it, so no one here knew she had the thing. The lack of communicators among the room furnishings might mean that they'd rather she didn't send messages outside. But they hadn't said so.

And it seemed only fair to send Malrue a reassuring word through Junior now. There would be no need to mention the Bank of Rienne's investigation. She could tell Junior a very harmless story, one designed only to keep his mother from becoming completely distraught when she heard from Pehanron College that Gonwil had chosen to disappear.

Gonwil glanced back a moment at the door. Then she placed the communicator in the palm of her left hand, and shifted the emerald arrowhead in its cover design a quarter turn to the right. That, according to the instructions which had come with it, made it ready for use. She placed it on the desk shelf, and pressed down with a fingertip on the golden pinhead stud in the center of the cover.

A slender fan of golden light sprang up and out from around the rim of the communicator, trembled, widened, and held steady. It was perhaps three feet across, not much over two high, slightly concave. This was the vision screen.

Now, if she turned the little arrowhead to the third notch, and Junior's communicator was set to receive, he should hear her signal.

Some ten or twelve seconds passed. Then Rodel Parlin the Twelfth's handsome, narrow face was suddenly there in the fan-shaped golden light screen before her.

"Well, *at last!*" he exclaimed. "I've been trying to call you but . . ."

"I didn't switch it on until just now," Gonwil admitted.

"Busy as all that with your tests?" Junior's gaze shifted past her, went around the room. "What's this?" he inquired. "Did Pehanron actually change your quarters because of the vendettist scare?"

So the Parlins hadn't been told she was gone. Gonwil smiled.

"Pehanron didn't!" she said. "I did. The fuss was getting too much for my nerves, so I sneaked out!"

For a moment, Junior looked startled. "You've left the college?"

"Uh-huh."

"Well, I . . . where are you now?"

"I'm not telling anybody," she said. "I've gone underground, so to speak, and I intend to stay out of sight until the thing blows over."

"Well, uh, Malrue . . ."

"I know. That's why I called the first chance I had. I don't want Malrue to worry unnecessarily, so you tell her I'm in a perfectly safe place. Nobody here knows me, so nobody—including vendettists—can find out where I've gone. Tell Malrue I'm being very careful, and whenever you all decide there's no more danger, I'll come out again."

Junior studied her, frowning doubtfully.

"Malrue," he observed, "isn't going to like that very much!"

"Yes, I . . . just a moment!" Gonwil turned towards the door. Sounds of scratching came from it, then a deep whine. "That's Chomir! He heard us talking, and I'd better let him in before he arouses the neighborhood. It's difficult enough to be inconspicuous with *him* around!"

"I can imagine."

Gonwil unlocked the door and opened it partly, glancing up the hall as Chomir slid through into the room, ears pricked. The door at the far end of the corridor was closed; he hadn't been heard in the office. She locked the door quietly again. Chomir stared for an instant at the image in the view-field, took a sniff at the air to confirm that while he'd heard Junior's voice, Junior was not physically present. Chomir was familiar with the phenomenon of communicator screens and the ghosts that periodically appeared in them. Satisfied, he sat down beside the door.

"I was wondering whether you'd left him behind," Junior remarked as Gonwil came back.

"Oh, I wouldn't do that to Chomir! About Malrue . . ."

He grinned. "I know! She does carry on rather badly at times like this! I'll be tactful in what I tell her."

"Thanks," Gonwil said gratefully. "I wouldn't want her to feel that I'm avoiding her in particular. But would you please not tell her about sending me a personal communicator? Say I was just using a regular ComWeb in making this call. Otherwise, she'd want to argue me out of this, and I'd hate to have to refuse her."

"You can depend on me. When will you call again?"

"Sometime early tomorrow?"

"I'll be waiting." He turned his head to the left, appeared to listen. Then he looked back at her.

"I believe I hear Malrue coming," he said quietly. "Goodbye, Gonwil!"

"'By, Junior!"

His face vanished. Still smiling, Gonwil bent over the communicator, searching for the pinhead stud. Junior had been on his best behavior this time; she was very glad she'd decided to make the call.

She pushed down the stud, and the light screen disappeared.

From the far end of the corridor outside came the sound of a violently slammed door.

Startled, Gonwil swung about. Footsteps were pounding up the short corridor now, but she wasn't aware of them. She stood dead-still, staring.

The white shape crouched across the room, ears back and down, huge teeth bared, could hardly be recognized as Chomir. He might have been listening to the approaching steps. But then the snarling head moved. The eyes found Gonwil, and instantly he was coming towards her in a flat, long spring, jaws wide.

As she watched Chomir move off beside Gonwil through the entrance tunnel to the Kyth hideout where the airvan had stopped, Telzey put out a tentative probe towards him.

This time, she was inside the dog's mind at once and so definitely that she could sense him striding along and the touch of the hard flooring beneath his pads. Satisfied, she withdrew. The contacts established during the night's work hadn't faded; she could resume her investigation immediately.

Left alone in the room reserved for her, less than fifty feet from the one to which they had conducted Gonwil, Telzey settled into an armchair and closed her eyes. Chomir still seemed to be moving about, but that made no difference. At this stage, she could work below his awareness without disturbing him or interfering with his activities.

She picked up the familiar memory chains within seconds, and then hesitated. Something had changed here. There was a sense of being drawn quietly away from the memories towards another area of mind.

She didn't know what it meant. But since psi seemed sometimes to work independently on problems in which one was involved, this might turn out to be a short-cut to the information for which she had been digging throughout the night. Telzey let herself shift in the indicated direction. There was a momentary odd feeling of sinking, then of having made a transition, of being somewhere else.

And it had been a short-cut. This was an aspect of mind she hadn't explored before, but it wasn't difficult to understand. A computer's processes might have presented a somewhat similar pattern: impersonal, unaware, enormously detailed and busy. Its universe was the living animal body that generated it, and its function was essentially to see to it that its universe remained physically in good operating condition. As Telzey grasped that, her attention shifted once more—now to a disturbance point in the Chomir universe. Something was wrong there. The body-mind knew it was wrong but was unable to do anything about it.

Telzey studied the disturbance point absorbedly. Suddenly its meaning became clear; and then she knew this was the information she had come to find. And it was very ugly and disturbing information.

She opened her eyes. Her thoughts seemed sluggish, and for some seconds the room looked hazy and blurred about her. Then, as the body-mind patterns faded from her awareness, she discovered she was back in the ordinary sort of contact with Chomir—

very clear, strong contact. She had a feeling of catching Gonwil's voice impressions through him.

The voice impressions ended. There was a moment's pause. A sharp surge of uneasiness passed through Chomir.

What did that . . .

Telzey felt the blood drain from her face as she scrambled abruptly out of the chair, reaching for the room communicator. Then her breath caught. She stopped in mid-motion, stood swaying. Electric shivers were racing over her skin. The air seemed to tingle. Psi energy was building up swiftly, oppressively; and she was its focal point.

Fury swept towards her, mindless, elemental, like a roaring wind. She seemed to move, and the room flickered out of existence. Something raged, and about her spun a disk of noise, of shock-distorted faces, of monstrously straining muscles. She moved again, and everything was still and clear.

She was looking into another room, a day-bright room where a man in a yellow suit stood beside a window, studying the small device he held in one hand. Beyond the window, sunlit parkland stretched away in long, rising slopes; and in the far distance, high on the slopes, was the glassy glitter of a familiar cluster of buildings. Pehanron College.

Something appeared to startle the man. His face turned quickly towards her; and as she registered the details of the sharp features and wispy blond mustache, his eyes became round, white-rimmed holes of intense fright.

The room vanished. Then there was one more sensation, remarkably like being slammed several times on top of the head by a giant fist; and a wave of blackness rolled over Telzey and swept her down. . . .

# Chapter 6

"Oh, he's admitted it, all right!" Dasinger said, frowning at the solidopic of the man with the thin blond mustache. "In fact, as soon as he was told why he'd been picked up, he became anxious to spill everything he knew. But his confession isn't going to be of much use against the Parlins."

"Why not?" Telzey asked.

"Because one thing he didn't know was who his employers were." The detective nodded at the chip-viewer he'd put on the table before her. "You can get the details from the report faster than I could give them to you. I have some questions myself, by the way."

"What about, Mr. Dasinger?"

"It seems," Dasinger said, "that when you sensed the dog was turning on Miss Lodis, you did three things almost simultaneously. You pinned the animal down in some manner . . ."

Telzey nodded. "I kept locking his muscles on him. That's what it felt like."

"That's what it looked like," Dasinger agreed. "When we got into the room, he was twisting around on the floor and seemed unable to open his jaws. Even so, he gave us one of the most startling demonstrations of animal athletics I've seen. It was a good half minute before somebody could line up on him long enough to feed him a stunner! Besides keeping Miss Lodis from getting killed in there, you've probably also saved the lives of three or four of my men . . . a detail which the Kyth Agency will remember. Now, as you clamped down on the dog, you also blasted a telepathic warning to your father to let us know Miss Lodis needed immediate help."

"Uh-huh. I didn't realize till afterwards I'd done it though."

"Meanwhile again," Dasinger said, indicating the solidopic, "you were putting in a personal appearance in the city of Beale, a good thousand miles away, in the room where this gentleman was operating the instrument which was supposed to be accomplishing the murder of Miss Lodis."

Telzey hesitated, said "I *seemed* to be there, for just a few moments. He looked scared to death, and I was wondering if he could see me."

"He saw something," the detective said, "and he's described it. The description fits you. The fellow hadn't been told who the intended victim was, and up to that moment he hadn't particularly cared. But his conclusion was that the accusing wraith of the person he'd just helped murder had appeared in the room. That left his nerves in pitiable condition, I'm happy to say, and has made him very easy to handle.

"On the other hand, of course, this experience, again limits his usefulness to us. We don't want him to talk about it, because we don't want to start speculations about you personally."

"No, I see."

"I'm assuming," Dasinger went on, "that it was also a rather unusual experience as far as you were concerned. If you could do that kind of thing regularly, you obviously wouldn't need assistance in solving Miss Lodis's problems."

Telzey hesitated. It seemed to her there had been, in that instant, a completely improbable combination of factors, resulting in something like a psychic explosion. The fury pouring out of the dog's mind might have set it off; and she'd been simply involved in it then, doing what she urgently wished to do, but not at all controlling the fact that she was doing it, or how it was done.

It had worked out very well; Gonwil and some

other people and Chomir would be dead now if it hadn't happened in just that way. But she wasn't eager for another experience of the kind. The next time it might as easily work out very badly.

She explained it to Dasinger as well as she could. He listened attentively, frowning now and then. At last he said, "Perhaps you'd better look over the report on Mrs. Parlin's hired assassin. Then I'll explain what the situation seems to be now."

Whether or not she'd actually gone to Beale in any physical sense during those few seconds, she hadn't relaxed her mental hold on Chomir while she was doing it. And while that had saved lives, it had one drawback. When someone finally poured a stunblast into the big dog, the connection between them was strong enough to transmit echoes of the pounding shock to her brain. It knocked her out, but since she hadn't absorbed the stunner physically the Kyth operatives brought her around again within minutes.

Then, after she'd barely finished giving them the description of the man in Beale, along with the information that Pehanron College could be seen at a certain angle, roughly five miles away, from the window of the room he was in, some well-meaning character slipped her a sedative in a glass of water without stopping to inquire whether she wanted one. Conceivably, she appeared a little feverish and wild-eyed, as who wouldn't under such circumstances? At any rate, she was unconscious again before she knew what had occurred.

The next time she awoke, eighteen hours had passed and she was in one of the cabins of the spacecruiser maintained by the Bank of Rienne for Gilas Amberdon's use. They were in space, though not far from Orado; she was in bed, and a large woman in a nurse's uniform was sitting next to the bed. The large woman informed her firmly that she would remain in bed until Mr. Amberdon's physician had come out from the planet to examine her again. Telzey, with equal firmness, dismissed the nurse from the cabin, got dressed, and went out to learn what had taken place meanwhile.

In the passage she encountered Dasinger, looking harried. The Kyth chief told her Gilas and Gonwil were in the communications cabin, involved in a ship-to-planet conference with Rienne's legal department, and offered to bring her up-to-date.

It appeared that the Kyth operatives dispatched to Beale early yesterday to look for Chomir's menacing stranger had picked up their quarry very shortly after receiving Telzey's description of him and of the area where he could be found. It had been a lucky break; he was on his way to the nearest spaceport by then. They learned his name was Vingar, that he was a native of Askanam where he had some reputation as a trainer of arena animals; and that he had received an extremely attractive financial offer to come to Orado and apply for work in a high-priced veterinarian establishment in the town of Beale, where he presently would carry out a specific assignment. The vet's was the place where Gonwil left Chomir regularly for his check-up and shots.

In due time, acting on instructions, Vingar drugged the big dog and planted a device in his brain, of a type sometimes used on Askanam fighting animals when the betting was heavy. Essentially, it was a telecontrolled miniature instrument which produced at will anything from a brief surge of anger to sustained insane fury. Animals so manipulated rarely lost a fight in which they were otherwise evenly matched, and cheating was almost impossible to prove because the instrument dissolved itself after fulfilling its function, leaving only microscopic scars in the brain tissue. After arousing Chomir from his drugged sleep, Vingar tested his device and found it in good working order.

Some months passed without further action. Then Vingar received instructions to check the dog's response again at the first available opportunity. He had done this from an aircar while Gonwil and Chomir were on one of their customary hikes in the hills. Following his report that the dog had reacted satisfactorily to minimum stimulus, he was told to wait for a signal which would be his cue to employ the instrument at full output for a period of five minutes, after which it was to be destroyed in the usual manner. This would conclude the services for which he had been hired.

Vingar had no real doubt that at least one person would be slaughtered by the white hound during those five minutes—that this was calculated murder. But he was being paid well enough to tell himself that what happened when he pushed down the control plunger was not his responsibility but that of his employers. And a few hours later, he would be on his way back to Askanam, and need never hear what the result of his action had been.

The vendettist scare at the Tayun consulate followed. Professionally, Dasinger regarded it as an unnecessary touch; the authorities investigating Gonwil's death were certain to conclude that her giant pet had gone berserk and destroyed her with the savagery that could be expected of a fierce fighting breed. But the Parlins evidently preferred to have an alternate explanation ready if there were any questions. When Junior established that Gonwil was for the moment alone in a locked room with the dog, the signal was flashed to Vingar to carry out his orders.

It was a complete picture, except for the unfortunate fact mentioned by Dasinger; the man from Askanam simply did not have the faintest notion who had hired him or from what source his pay had come. He did not know the Parlins, had never seen one of them or heard their voices. He had been told what to do through the impersonal medium of a telewriter. The Kyth Agency would keep him under wraps; but there seemed to be no practical possibility of using him as a witness.

Telzey asked, "Does Malrue know it didn't work . . . That Gonwil didn't get killed or hurt?"

"She knows she couldn't have been hurt seriously enough to incapacitate her," Dasinger said. "She also knows we're aware it was attempted murder, and who was behind it."

"Oh . . . how did she find out?"

"Indirectly, from us. It couldn't very well be avoided. Miss Lodis responded in a very level-headed manner after the situation had been explained to her and she was over the first feeling of shock about it. Junior's call immediately before the dog's attack fitted in too well with the rest of it to let her retain doubts about Mrs. Parlin's guilt. She agreed at once to apply to become the legal ward of the Bank of Rienne. That made it possible for us to act freely on her behalf; but when her guardians on Tayun were notified of the move, it told them, of course, that Mrs. Parlin's plans had miscarried and that they themselves were suspected of complicity. They must have warned the Parlins immediately."

"They didn't argue about the bank becoming Gonwil's guardian?" Telzey asked.

"No. The thing had come into the open, and they realized it. Which is why we're in space. It's one way to make sure Miss Lodis is safe for the moment."

Telzey had a sinking feeling. "For the moment? You don't think the Parlins might give up?"

The detective shook his head. "Not after what we've learned about Mrs. Parlin. She's playing for high stakes here. She's planned for years to get Miss Lodis's share of the company in her hands, and she won't stop now simply because it can't be done quietly any more. It's reasonable to suppose she won't be involved in future murder attempts herself, since that might get her into trouble. But all she has to do is set enough price on your friend's head to attract professional sharpshooters. From now on, that's what we'll have to look for."

"But then . . ." Telzey paused. "Then what are we going to do?"

"At present," Dasinger said, "the matter is in the hands of Rienne's attorneys. They'll investigate all legal possibilities. That may take some days. That the Parlins are anticipating moves in that area is indicated by the fact that they've assembled a legal staff of their own. But I don't think they're greatly worried by that approach."

He considered, added, "We'll see what develops. I haven't, of course, suggested to Miss Lodis that we might turn the situation into a registered private war. She's still pretty badly shaken up by the treachery of the Parlin family, and particularly of Mrs. Parlin."

"You're waiting to let her find out there's nothing else she can do?" Telzey asked.

"Perhaps I am."

Telzey shook her head.

"She still won't do it," she said. "Not if it means killing Malrue Parlin."

"It would mean that," Dasinger said. "We might simply frighten the lady into backing off. But it wouldn't settle anything. Miss Lodis would never be safe from her again. Unless, of course, she simply turned her stock over to Mrs. Parlin, on Mrs. Parlin's terms."

"She'd sooner do that," Telzey said. Her skin was crawling.

"Would you like to see it happen?"

"No," Telzey admitted.

"Well, let's let it rest there," Dasinger said. "The

lawyers may come up with something. Incidentally, you might see what you can do about Chomir, Miss Amberdon. He's in rather bad shape."

"I thought he was all right again!" Telzey said, startled.

"Oh, the stunner didn't harm him, of course. I'll take you there, and we'll see what you think. If it weren't ridiculous, I'd say he was suffering from a psychotic collapse, brought on by guilt. When Miss Lodis tries to talk to him, he looks away and pretends she isn't there."

Dasinger's diagnosis was accurate enough. Telzey found Chomir lost in a black stew of despondency. His memory of what had occurred after the rage stimulus began to blaze through his brain was a horrid muddle of impressions; but he knew the evil stranger had been nearby in his insubstantial way, and that he, Chomir, had done dreadful things. And the stranger had again escaped. Chomir felt miserably unable to face Gonwil. . . .

It might be possible actually to delete unpleasant memories from a mind, but Telzey hadn't found out how to do it. However, it wasn't difficult to blur out some remembered event until it was barely discernible, and then to shift over other little chunks of memory and imagination from here and there and work them together until, so far as the owner of the mind was concerned, a completely new memory had been created in place of the obscured one.

After about an hour and a half, Chomir wasn't even aware that he had been glooming about something a short while ago. When Gonwil showed up, having heard that Telzey had awakened and was with the dog, he was plainly back to normal behavior.

Other problems, unfortunately, weren't going to be as simple to solve. Gonwil felt that after the first round of conferences with the Bank of Rienne's legal department the lawyers' initial attitude of cautious optimism was beginning to fade. The possibility of bringing charges against the Parlin family in Federation court had been ruled out almost at once. A conviction could be obtained against Vingar; but not—while their mind-blocks protected them from subjective probes—against the Parlins. And there was, of course, no point in prosecuting Vingar alone. It would be preferable to leave the Parlins unaware for the present of what had happened to their hireling from Askanam.

Rienne's attorneys regarded the prospects of a Transcluster Finance ethics hearing as somewhat more promising, though one would have to give detailed consideration to the evidence which might be presented for verification before forming a definite conclusion. If it could be shown in an ethics hearing that the Parlins had planned the murder of a business associate for profit, the results would be almost as satisfactory as a court conviction. Transcluster's adjudicators could not route them through Rehabilitation, but they could order the confiscation of their holdings in Lodis Associates and block them for life from again playing an open role in the Hub's financial world.

The alternative—not infrequently chosen in such cases—was voluntary Rehabilitation. Rienne's attorneys' hope was that some connection could be established between the Parlin family and the death of various other members of Lodis Associates who had been known to be in opposition to them. Added to evidence obtained from the attempted murder of Gonwil Lodis, it might give them a case, though a most difficult one to prepare. The Verifier gave no consideration to probabilities and did not evaluate evidence aside from reporting that the mental information made available to it had showed a specific claim to be true or false, or had failed to show either its truth or falsity. Any facts obtained must therefore be carefully arranged into a pattern which would condemn the Parlins when confirmed by the mind-machine. And that would take time.

The truth of the matter probably was, Telzey thought, that a Verifier, or its operators, was capable of sizing up the merits of a case almost as soon as an ethics hearing began—if her calculations about the function and potential of the Psychology Service's machines had come anywhere near the mark. But in dealing with them it could make no practical difference, because they wouldn't admit to seeing more than they were supposed to see, even if it meant letting a hearing end in favor of someone like Malrue Parlin. Of course, they couldn't have maintained their big secret otherwise. But it seemed very unlikely that the lawyers were going to dig up something in Malrue's past which could coax a damaging report out of the machine. Malrue would have been as cautious about leaving no direct evidence of earlier murderous activities as she had been in her plans for Gonwil.

The lawyers obviously weren't counting on it either. Another matter they would investigate was the possibility of breaking the clause which effectively prevented Gonwil from selling her stock in Lodis Associates to anyone but another associate. If the Bank of Rienne acquired the stock, it would put an end to Malrue's maneuverings. At the moment, however, it looked as if six or eight years of wrangling in Tayun courts might be required to force a favorable decision on that point.

All in all, Telzey reflected, Dasinger's pessimism was beginning to appear justified. And the mere fact that they were at present confined to the spacecruiser was an intimation of what it could be like to live for years on guard against some unknown assassin's stroke, or hiding somewhere, shut off from normal existence. Dasinger might, as a matter of fact, have arranged the temporary retreat from Orado in part to demonstrate just that.

When they gathered for dinner, she learned that Pehanron College, after being privately briefed by Rienne officials on the current state of affairs, had sent word it was cooperating by placing both Gonwil and Telzey on technical sick leave for as long as might be necessary.

That seemed somehow the most decisive move of the day.

After dinner, she retired early to her cabin. It was possible, as Dasinger had suggested, that the attorneys would still come up with a practical solution. But one clearly couldn't depend on it.

She sent out a thread of thought for Chomir, located him in the cruiser's lounge with Gonwil and Gilas, and slipped back into his mind. It was as easy now as walking into a house to which one owned the key. When ship-night was sounded an hour or so later, she was with him as he followed Gonwil to her cabin. And quite a little later again, she knew Gonwil finally had found troubled sleep.

Telzey withdrew from Chomir and put out the drifting telepathic probe which by and by would touch one of Gonwil's sleeping thoughts and through it establish the first insubstantial bridge between their minds. Then, in a day or two, she would be in control of Gonwil's mental activities, in the same unsuspected and untraceable way and as completely, as she was of Chomir's.

She felt uncomfortable about it. It hadn't disturbed her at all to tap the minds of strangers, just to see what was in there and to experiment a little. Intruding on the private thoughts of a friend, secretly and uninvited, somehow seemed a very different matter.

But the way things appeared to be going made it necessary now.

❖   ❖   ❖

It was a week before the subject of registering for a private war came up again; and now it wasn't Dasinger's suggestion. The bank's attorneys recommended the move, though with obvious reluctance, to Gilas and Gonwil, as an apparently necessary one if Mrs. Parlin's designs on Gonwil's share in Lodis Associates were to be checked.

By then, nobody, including Gonwil, was really surprised to hear of it. It had been a frustrating week for the legal staff. While they felt they weren't at the end of their resources, it was clear that Malrue Parlin had been prepared for years to face a day of reckoning. The investigators on Tayun reported many suspicious circumstances about her activities, but produced no scrap of legal evidence to connect the Parlins to them. Malrue had few allies with whom she had worked directly; and all of them had protected themselves as carefully as she did.

Other approaches had brought equally negative results. The rule barring members of Lodis Associates from selling shares to outsiders before their fellows were given an opportunity to purchase them at a prohibitively low price was found to be backed in full by Tayun law. While Gonwil was still a child, the rule could have been set aside with relative ease, but there appeared to be no way around it now that she would be a legally responsible adult within a few months. The minor shareholders in the concern had declined offers of her stock at something approximating its present value, and indicated they would have no interest in it at any price. They clearly didn't intend to get into Malrue Parlin's game.

The Parlins were still on Orado, equipped with a formidable bodyguard and an equally formidable corps of lawyers, both imports from Tayun who evidently had preceded Malrue and her husband here, to be brought into action if needed. But Malrue had made no immediate moves. She might be satisfied to let

Gonwil's supporters find out for themselves that her legal position was unassailable.

Telzey had remained a detached observer of these developments, realizing they were running uncomfortably close to Dasinger's predictions. She was giving most of her time to Gonwil. Her previous investigations of human minds had been brief and directed as a rule to specific details, but she felt there was reason to be very careful here.

What was going on inside Gonwil's blond head nowadays wasn't good. Harm had been done, and Telzey was afraid to tamper with the results, to attempt the role of healer. It wasn't a simple matter of patching up a few memories as with Chomir; there was too much she didn't understand. Gonwil would have to do her own healing, at least at the start, and to an extent she was doing it. During the first day or two, her thoughts had a numbed quality to them. Outwardly she acquiesced in everything, was polite, smiled occasionally. But something had been shattered; and she was waiting to see what the people about her would do, how they intended to put all the pieces together again. When she thought of Cousin Malrue's treachery, it was in a puzzled, childish manner.

Then, gradually, she began to understand that the pieces weren't simply going to be put together again now. This ugliness could go on indefinitely, excluding her meanwhile from normal human life.

The realization woke Gonwil up. Until then, most of the details of the situation about her had been blurred and without much meaning. Now she started to look them over carefully, and they became obvious enough.

The efforts of Rienne's lawyers to find a satisfactory solution had begun to bog down because this was a matter which the Federation's laws did not adequately cover. She had been one of the Hub's favored and pampered children, but in part that was now the reason she was being forced towards the edge of a no man's land where survival depended on oneself and one's friends. Unless something quite unexpected happened, she would soon have to decide what the future would be like.

The thought startled her, but she accepted it. There was a boy in the Federation Navy, a cadet she'd met the previous summer, who played a part in her considerations. So did Telzey, and Dasinger and his agency, and Malrue and her husband and Junior, and the group of professional gunmen they'd brought in from Tayun to be their bodyguards. All of them would be affected in one way or another by what she agreed to. She must be very careful to make no mistakes.

Gonwil, seen directly in her reflections and shifts of feeling now that she'd snapped out of the numbed shock, seemed more likable than ever to Telzey. But she didn't like at all what was almost surely coming.

It came. Mainly perhaps for the purpose of having it on record, Rienne's legal department had notified the Parlins' lawyers in Orado City that Miss Lodis desired to dispose of her stock in Lodis Associates. A reply two days later stated that Malrue Parlin, though painfully affected by Miss Lodis's estrangement from herself and her family, was willing to take over the stock. She was not unmindful of her right to purchase at the original value, but would pay twice that, solely to accommodate Miss Lodis.

In Telzey's opinion, the legal department flipped when it read the reply. It had, of course, been putting up with a good deal during the week. It called promptly for a planet-to-ship general conference, and pointed out that the sum Malrue offered was approximately a tenth of the real value of Gonwil's share in the concern. In view of the fact that an attempt to murder Miss Lodis already had been made, Mrs.

Parlin's reply must be considered not a bona fide offer but a form of extortion. A threat was implied.

However, Mrs. Parlin might be showing more confidence than she felt. If violence again entered the picture, she was now not invulnerable. To some extent, at least, she was bluffing. To counter the bluff, she should be shown unmistakably that Miss Lodis was determined to defend herself and her interests by whatever means were necessary.

The legal department's advice at this point must be to have Miss Lodis register the fact that against her wishes she had become involved in a private war with the Parlin family, and that she was appointing the Kyth Agency to act as her agent in this affair. The events and investigations of the past week provided more than sufficient grounds for the registration, and its purpose would go beyond making it clear to the Parlins that from now on they would be in jeopardy no less than Miss Lodis. It had been discovered that while the rule which prevented the sale of Lodis Associates stock outside the concern could not be broken in court, it could be rescinded by a two-thirds majority vote of the shareholders, and Miss Lodis and the Parlin family between them controlled more than two thirds of the stock. No doubt, forcible means would be required to persuade the Parlins to agree to the action, but the agreement would be valid if obtained in that manner under the necessities of a registered private war. Miss Lodis could then sell her shares at full value to the Bank of Rienne or a similar institution, which would end the Parlins' efforts to obtain them, and take her out of danger.

Registration, the legal department added, was a serious matter, of course, and Miss Lodis should give it sufficient thought before deciding to sign the application they had prepared. On the other hand, it might be best not to delay more than a day or two.

The Parlins' attitude showed she would be safe only so long as they did not know where she was.

"Has she discussed it with you?" Dasinger asked.

Telzey looked at him irritably. Her nerves had been on edge since the conference ended. Things had taken a very unsatisfactory turn. If Malrue Parlin would only drop dead!

She shook her head. "She's been in her room. We haven't talked about it yet."

Dasinger studied her face. "Your father and I," he remarked, "aren't entirely happy about having her register for a private war."

"Why not? I thought you . . ."

He nodded. "I know. But in view of what you said, I've been watching her, and I'm inclined to agree now that she might be too civilized for such methods. It's a pleasant trait, though it's been known to be a suicidal one."

He hesitated, went on. "Aside from that, a private war is simply the only practical answer now. And it would be best to act at once while the Parlin family is together and on Orado. If we wait till they scatter, it will be the devil's own job roping them in again. I think I can guarantee that none of the three will be physically injured. As for Miss Lodis's feelings about it, we—your father and I—assume that your ability to handle emotional disturbances isn't limited to animals."

Telzey shifted uneasily in her chair. Her skull felt tight; she might be getting a headache. She wondered why she didn't tell the detective to stop worrying. Gonwil had found her own solution before the conference was over. She wouldn't authorize a private war for any purpose. No matter how expertly it was handled, somebody was going to get killed when two bands of armed men came into conflict, and she didn't want the responsibility for it.

Neither did she want to run and hide for years to keep Malrue from having her killed. The money wasn't worth it.

So the logical answer was to accept Malrue's offer and let her have the stock and control of Lodis Associates. Gonwil could get along very well without it. And she wouldn't have consented to someone's death to keep it.

Gonwil didn't know why she hadn't told them that at the conference, though Telzey did. Gonwil had intended to speak, then suddenly forgotten her intention. Another few hours, Telzey had thought, to make sure there wasn't some answer as logical as surrender but more satisfactory. A private war didn't happen to be it.

She realized she'd said something because Dasinger was continuing. Malrue Parlin appeared to have played into their hands through overconfidence. . . .

That, Telzey thought, was where they were wrong. The past few days had showed her things about Gonwil which had remained partly unrevealed in two years of friendship. But a shrewd and purposeful observer like Malrue Parlin, knowing Gonwil since her year of birth, would be aware of them.

Gonwil didn't simply have a prejudice against violence; she was incapable of it. Malrue knew it. It would have suited her best if Gonwil died in a manner which didn't look like murder, or at least didn't turn suspicion on the Parlins. But she needn't feel any concern because she had failed in that. The shock of knowing that murder had been tried, of realizing that more of that kind of thing would be necessary if Malrue was to be stopped, would be enough. It wasn't so much fear as revulsion—a need to draw away from the ugly business. Gonwil would give in.

Cousin Malrue hadn't been overconfident. She'd simply known exactly what would happen.

Anger was an uncomfortable thing. Telzey's skin crawled with it. Dasinger asked a question, and she said something which must have made sense because he smiled briefly and nodded, and went on talking. But she didn't remember then what the question had been or what she had replied. For a moment, her vision blurred and the room seemed to rock. It was almost as if she'd heard Malrue Parlin laughing nearby, already savoring her victory, sure she'd placed herself beyond reprisal.

Malrue winning out over Gonwil like that was a thing that couldn't be accepted; and she'd prevented Gonwil from admitting it. But she was unable to do what Gilas and Dasinger expected now—change Gonwil's opinions around until she agreed cheerfully to whatever arrangements they made. And if people got killed during her private war, well, that would be too bad but it had been made inevitable by the Parlins' criminal greed and the Federation's sloppy laws, hadn't it.

It was quite possible to do, but not by changing a few of Gonwil's civilized though unrealistic attitudes. It could be done only by twisting and distorting whatever was Gonwil. And that wouldn't ever be undone again.

Malrue laughed once more, mocking and triumphant, and it was like pulling a trigger. Dasinger still seemed to be talking somewhere, but the room had shifted and disappeared. She was in a darkness where laughter echoed and black electric gusts swirled heavily around her, looking out at a tall, handsome woman in a group of people. Behind Telzey, something rose swiftly, black and towering like a wave about to break, curving over towards the woman.

Then there was a violent, wrenching effort of some sort.

❖          ❖          ❖

She was back in her chair, shaking, her face wet with sweat, with a sense of having stopped at the last possible instant. The room swam past her eyes and it seemed, as something she half-recalled, that Dasinger had just left, closing the door behind him, still unaware that anything out of the ordinary was going on with Telzey. But she wasn't completely alone. A miniature figure of the Psionic Cop hovered before her face, gesticulating and mouthing inaudible protests. He looked ridiculous, Telzey thought. She made a giggling noise at him, shaking her head, and he vanished.

She got out a handkerchief and dabbed at her face. She felt giddy and weak. Dasinger had noticed nothing, so she hadn't really gone anywhere physically, even for a second or two. Nevertheless, on Orado half a million miles away, Malrue Parlin, laughing and confident in a group of friends or guests, had been only moments from invisible, untraceable death. If that wave of silent energy had reached her, she would have groaned and staggered and fallen, while her companions stared, sensing nothing.

What created the wave? She hadn't done it consciously—but it would be a good thing to remember not to let hot, foggy anger become mixed with a psi impulse again! She wasn't Gonwil, but to put somebody to death in that manner would be rather horrid. And the weakness in her suggested that it mightn't be healthy for the psi who did it, unless he had something like the equipment of that alien in the university's habitat museum.

At any rate, her anger had spent itself now. The necessity of doing something to prevent Gonwil's surrender remained.

And then it occurred to Telzey how it might be done.

She considered a minute or two, and put out a search-thought for Chomir, touched his mind and slipped into it. Groping about briefly, she picked up the artificial memory section she'd installed to cover the disturbing events in the Kyth Agency's hideout.

She had worked the section in rather carefully. Even if Chomir had been a fairly introspective and alert human being, he might very well have accepted it as what had happened. But it wasn't likely that an intruding telepath who studied the section at all closely would be fooled. She certainly wouldn't be. It seemed a practical impossibility to invest artificial memories with the multitudinous, interconnected, coherent detail which characterized actual events. Neither was the buried original memory really buried when one began to search for it. It could be brought out and developed again.

And if such constructions couldn't fool her, could they fool a high-powered psionic mind-reading device, built for the specific purpose of finding out what somebody really thought, believed and remembered . . . such as Transcluster Finance's verifying machines?

They couldn't of course.

Telzey sat still again a while, biting her lip, frowning, mentally checking over a number of things. Then she went to look for Gilas.

"It's a completely outrageous notion!" her father said a short while later, his tone still somewhat incredulous. He glanced over at Dasinger, who had been listening intently, cleared his throat. "However, let's look at it again. You say you can manufacture 'memories' in the dog's mind which can't be distinguished from things he actually remembers?"

Telzey nodded.

"I can't tell any difference," she said. "And I don't see how a Verifier could."

"Possibly it couldn't," Gilas said. "But we don't really know what such a machine is doing."

"Well, we know what it does in an ethics hearing,"

Telzey said. "Supposing it did see they were fake memories. What would happen?"

Gilas hesitated, said slowly, "The Verifier would report that it had found nothing to show that the Parlins were connected in any way with the attempt to use Chomir to commit murder. It would report nothing else. It can produce relevant evidence, including visual and auditory effects, to substantiate a claim it has accepted. But it can't explain or show why it is rejecting a claim. To do that would violate the conditions under which it operates."

Dasinger said quietly, "That's it. We can't lose anything. And if it works, we'd have them! Vingar is the only one who can prove the Parlins never came near his device. But we're keeping him out of sight, and the Parlins can't admit they know he exists without damning themselves! And they can't obtain verification for their own claims of innocence—"

"Because of their mind-blocks!" Gilas concluded. His mouth quirked for an instant; then his face was sober again. "We will, of course, consider every decision. Telzey, go and get Gonwil. We want her in on it, and no one else." He looked at Dasinger. "What will we tell the lawyers?"

Dasinger considered. "That we feel an ethics hearing should be on the record to justify declaring a private war," he said. "They won't like it, of course. They know it isn't necessary."

"No," Gilas agreed, "but it's a good enough excuse. And if they set it up for that purpose, it will cover the steps we'll have to take."

# Chapter 7

"The statements made by this witness have been neither confirmed nor disproved by verification."

The expressionless face of the chief adjudicator of the Transcluster ethics hearing disappeared from the wall screen of the little observer's cubicle before Telzey as he ended his brief announcement. She frowned, turned her right hand over, palm up, glanced at the slender face of her timepiece.

It had taken less than two minutes for Transcluster's verification machine to establish that it could find nothing in the mind of Rodel Parlin the Twelfth relevant to the subject matter it had been instructed to investigate, and to signal this information to the hearing adjudicators. Junior, visible in the Verifier's contact chamber which showed in the far left section of the screen, had not reacted noticeably to the announcement. It could hardly have been a surprise to him. His parents had preceded him individually to the chamber to have their claims of being innocent of homicidal intentions towards Gonwil Lodis submitted to test, with identical results. Only the stereotyped wording of the report indicated in each case that the machine had encountered mental blocks which made verification impossible. From the Parlins' point of view, that was good enough. The burden of proof rested with their accusers; and they simply had no proof. The demand for an ethics hearing had been a bluff, an attempt perhaps to get a better price for Gonwil's capitulation. If so, it had failed.

The central screen view was shifting back to the hexagonal hall where the Verifier was housed. It appeared almost empty. A technician sat at the single control console near the center, while the machine itself was concealed behind the walls. When he brought it into operation, the far end of the hall came alive with a day-bright blur of shifting radiance, darkening to a sullen red glow as he shut the machine off again. So far, that and the reports of the chief adjudicator had been the only evidence of the Verifier's function; and the play of lights might be merely window dressing, designed to make the proceedings more impressive. It had to be that, Telzey thought, if her speculations about the machine were right. It wasn't really being switched on and off here, but working round the clock, absorbing uncensored information constantly from hundreds or thousands of minds, and passing it on.

But watching the hall darken again as the technician turned away from the console and began to talk into a communicator, Telzey acknowledged to herself that she felt a shade less certain now of the purpose for which the Psychology Service was quietly distributing its psionic machines about the Hub. Gilas was in the observation cubicle next to hers, with two of Rienne's attorneys; while Gonwil waited with Dasinger and a few Kyth men in some other section of the great Transcluster Finance complex for a summons from the adjudicators to take Chomir to the contact chamber. The hearing had been under way for a little over an hour.

That was the puzzling point. She had come in nervously ready for an indication that the Verifier and the human minds behind it knew what she had been up to before the hearing even began. Her own thoughts were camouflaged; but Gonwil, Gilas and Dasinger were unconsciously broadcasting the information that she was a psi who had manipulated the memories of a hearing witness in a manner calculated to trick the verification machine into making a false report.

While it was the only way left to get at Malrue, the Psychology Service certainly must consider it as flagrant a violation of their rules against the independent use of psionics as could be imagined. But, so far as Telzey could tell, nothing happened then . . . nothing, at any rate, that didn't conform in every detail to what was generally assumed to happen at an ethics hearing.

The hearing got off to an unhurried and rather dull start. One of Rienne's attorneys formally presented the general charge against the Parlins—they had planned and attempted to carry out the murder of Gonwil Lodis for financial gain. He brought out background data on Lodis Associates to show the motive, displayed the device used to throw Chomir into a killing rage, explained the purpose for which similar instruments were employed on Askanam. A description of the occurrence in the Kyth Agency's hideout followed, including Gonwil's preceding conversation with Junior by the personalized communicator he had sent her, though naturally excluding Telzey's role in checking the dog's attack until a guard had been able to stun him.

Then the specific charge was made. The Parlins had caused the demonstrated device to be used on the dog at a moment when they could assume it would result in Gonwil Lodis's death, leaving no indication that her death had been planned.

From what Telzey had heard, it was the standard sort of introduction. An ethics hearing developed like a game of skill, unfolding from formalized beginnings, and it wasn't until after a few moves and countermoves had been made that significant revelations could be expected. On this occasion, however, the Parlins' attorneys evidently felt they could afford to skip such cautious preliminaries. It was clear now that Vingar had been captured before he could leave Orado and had talked; but while he presumably would appear as a witness, nothing he knew could endanger the Parlins' position. The attorneys announced that their three principals denied the charges and wished to testify to their innocence under verification if the commercial mind-blocks they employed would permit this.

Having demonstrated then that the mind-blocks, as a matter of fact, did not permit it, the Parlins had retired to wait out the rest of the hearing unchallenged.

Which meant that the next witness up should be Chomir . . .

❖      ❖      ❖

The use of an animal as a verification witness had been cleared in advance with the adjudicators. It was not without precedent; Chomir would be admitted even if, for some reason, the opposing attorneys objected, and objections weren't expected. The Verifier would be instructed only to establish whether anything could be found in the dog's memory to show the Parlin family had been directly responsible for the murder device planted in his brain.

It was what she had planned. But she had expected to have some intimation by now of what the Verifier's reaction to their doctored witness would be. And there'd been nothing. . . .

Telzey leaned forward suddenly and switched off the central screen and voice transmitters. It might still be several minutes before Chomir was taken to the contact chamber. They'd been told he would be doped first to keep him quiet while the machine carried out its work.

She shifted in the chair, laid her hands, palms down, on the armrests, and closed her eyes. The psi bubble about her mind opened. Her awareness expanded out cautiously into the Transcluster complex.

It wasn't quiet there. Psi whispered, murmured, muttered, in an incessant meaningless trickling from the swarms of humanity which crowded the vast Central. But that seemed to be all. The unaware insect buzz of thousands of minds faded, swelled, faded monotonously; and nothing else happened. She could detect no slightest hint of an active telepath, mechanical or human, nearby.

She didn't know what it meant. She opened her eyes again, nerves on edge, and as the psi whisperings receded from her awareness, the side screen showed her Chomir already standing in the contact chamber, looking sleepy and bored. She reached out quickly, switched the center screen back on.

Pitch-blackness appeared before her, gleaming with a suggestion of black glass. After a puzzled instant, Telzey realized she must be looking at the projection field within which the Verifier sometimes produced impressions connected with the search it was conducting. The field hadn't come into action when the Parlins were in the chamber; there had been nothing to show. Its appearance in the screen now indicated the machine had begun its work on the dog.

Too late to stop it; she could give Gilas no plausible reason for interrupting the hearing at this point. She watched the screen, waiting, her hands gripping the chair.

There was a sudden strong impression of somebody looking at her. Automatically, Telzey glanced around at the blank wall of the cubicle. No one was there, but the feeling persisted.

Then she knew Transcluster's Verifier had found her.

Her left hand made a panicky flick to her communicator, jabbed down a tiny button. Why had she imagined it would be similar to a human mind, the mind of any living being? This was like being stared at by the sea. And like a vast, cold sea wave it was coming towards her. The bubble snapped tight.

Ordinarily, it might give only a splinter of its attention to the ethics hearings for which it was supposedly here, and to the relatively unimportant people involved in them; so perhaps it wasn't until this moment that it had become aware some telepathic meddler had been at work on the animal mind it was to investigate . . . and that the meddler was present at the hearing. In any event, it was after the meddler now.

The cold psi wave reached the bubble, rolled over it, receded, came again. An unprotected mind must have been flooded in an instant. As it was, Telzey stayed untouched. It closed over the bubble again, and now it remained.

It might have lasted only for seconds. There was a sense of weight building up, of slow, monstrous pressures, shifting, purposely applied. Then the pressures relaxed and withdrew.

The machine mind was still there, watching. She had the feeling that others watched through it.

She brought out the thought record she had prepared for them, and flicked the bubble shielding away from it. And if that let them see she had never been so scared in her life, the thought record still spoke for itself.

"Take a good look!" she invited.

Almost instantly, she was alone.

Her eyes fastened, somewhat blurrily, on the projection field in the screen. Colors were boiling up in it. Then there was a jarring sensation of opening alien eyes and looking out from them.

How it was done Telzey couldn't imagine. But she, and presumably everyone else watching the verification field at that moment, was suddenly aware of being inside Chomir's head. There came a reddish flash, then a wave of rage building up swiftly to blazing fury. The fury receded again.

A picture came into being, in glimpsed fragments and scraps of almost nightmarish vividness, of the white-walled room in which Chomir had found himself when he awoke with the microscopic Askanam device freshly inserted in his brain. As he had done then, he was pacing swiftly and irritably about the room, the walls and a semi-transparent energy barrier at one end flowing past him in the projection field.

Again came the red flash, followed by the surge of rage. The dog stopped in mid-stride, head swinging towards the barrier. A figure moved vaguely behind the barrier. He hurled himself at it. The barrier flung him back, once, twice. As he came smashing up against it for the third time, the scene suddenly froze.

At this distance, only inches away, the energy field was completely transparent. Three people stood in the section of the room beyond. Rodel Parlin the Twelfth a few feet ahead of his parents, right hand holding an instrument, a small but readily recognizable one. His thumb was on a plunger of the instrument, pressing it down. All three stared at the dog.

The projection field went blank.

For a second, Telzey had the feeling of somebody's screams echoing through her thoughts. It was gone immediately, so she couldn't be sure. But precisely how Malrue Parlin was reacting to what she had just seen in the Verifier's projection field was obviously of no particular importance now.

Telzey put the tip of her left forefinger on the second of the two little buttons she'd had programmed recently in her communicator, and pushed it gently down.


A ComWeb chimed persistently. Half awake, Telzey frowned. She had been dreaming, and there seemed to have been something important about the dream because she was trying to hang on to it. But it faded from her awareness like a puff of thin smoke, and she couldn't recall what it had been. She woke up all the way just as the ComWeb went silent.

And where was she? Couch in the semi-dark of a big, comfortable room, rustic type, with the smell of pine trees . . . The far wall was a single window and it was night outside. Moving pinpoints of light and a steadier radiance glittered through a pale, ghostly swirling. . . .

Tor Heights . . .

Of course! Tor Heights, the mountain sports resort . . . in starshine with a snowstorm moving past. With the hearing over, Gilas had suggested she go ahead with Chomir and rent a cabin here, so she and Gonwil could relax from recent stresses for a few days before returning to Pehanron College. He and Gonwil would stay on until the posthearing arrangements with the Transcluster adjudicators and the Parlins' attorneys had been concluded, and then follow. After she'd secured the cabin and fed Chomir, she found herself getting sleepy and curled up for a nap.

That might have been a couple of hours ago.

As she climbed off the couch, the ComWeb began chiming again in the adjoining room. This time the summons was accompanied by Chomir's attention-requesting rumble. Glancing at her watch, Telzey ran to take the call. She switched on the instrument, and Gonwil's face appeared in the screen, eyes big and sober.

"Hi!" she said. "Your father and I are leaving Draise in about twenty minutes, Telzey. Thought I'd let you know."

"Everything over?" Telzey asked.

"Not quite. They still have a lot of details to settle, but they don't need us around for that. What made it all very simple was that Malrue and Rodel Senior signed up for voluntary Rehabilitation, rather than take Transcluster's penalties." She hesitated. "I almost feel sorry for them now."

"Don't be an idiot," Telzey said thoughtfully. "They've had it coming for years."

"I know. But still . . . well, *I* couldn't have done it! Not to keep from losing the money."

Telzey admitted she couldn't have done it either. "What about Junior?"

Gonwil smiled briefly. "He wasn't having any! He told the adjudicators that losing his Lodis holdings still would leave him enough to be a playboy the rest of his life, and he couldn't care less about getting placed on Transcluster's black list. The adjudicators said he was practically frothing! Apparently, they were all in a severe state of shock when the hearing ended."

"Glad to hear it," Telzey said. She didn't find herself feeling in the least sorry for the Parlins. "How will you like having Malrue back in Lodis Associates after they let her out of Rehabilitation?"

"I don't know just how I would feel about it," Gonwil said, "but I won't be there when she comes back. That ruling's been canceled, and I'm selling to the Bank of Rienne. I decided I'm not really cut out to be a Tayun financier. Besides, I've . . . oh, started to develop other interests."

"Like in the Federation Navy?" Telzey asked.

Gonwil colored slightly. "Perhaps."

After she had switched off, Telzey found and pushed the button which started the big fireplace in the main room going, then another button which let the sound of the soft, roaring rush of the storm pass through the cabin. She got a glass of milk and sat down reflectively with it before the fire.

Of course, the Parlins had realized they'd lost the hearing as soon as they saw themselves in the projection field. They must have nearly gone out of their minds for a while. But they couldn't prove they'd never been in such a room with Chomir, and to dispute a Verifier's report was useless. What had happened seemed impossible! But they were trapped, and they knew it.

Nevertheless, Telzey thought, it was very unlikely the senior Parlins would have preferred rehabilitation to losing their Lodis stock—if it had been left up to them. That was what had jolted Gonwil: she knew such a decision didn't really go with the kind of people they were. But it couldn't be explained to her, or to anybody else, that the decision hadn't been their own.

Telzey sipped meditatively at her milk. Clear and obvious in the thought record she'd displayed to the Verifier, and to whatever Psychology Service agents were studying her through their machine, was the information that unless a certain thing was done and certain other things were not done, vast numbers of copies of a report she'd deposited in a nondirect mailing vault would be dumped into the nondirect system within minutes, tagged with randomly selected delivery dates extending up to fifteen years in the future.

On any day, during that fifteen-year period, there might show up at some of the Hub's more prominent news services a concise statement, with data appended, of every significant fact she had deduced or suspected concerning psis and psionics in the Hub, and particularly of the role the Psychology Service and its psionic machines appeared to be playing. The first such missive to reach its destination should make quite a splash throughout the Hub. . . .

So she'd blackmailed a department of the Over-government, and while they mightn't relish it much, frankly, it felt good. Among the things they weren't to do was to try to take control of her, mentally or physically. And the thing to be done, of course, was to see to it that the Parlins were found guilty at the ethics hearing of the crime they'd planned, even though the methods of convicting them might be open to question.

Considering the Verifier's ability to scan minds at large, they must have been aware by then that the Parlins were guilty, though they wouldn't have lifted a finger to help out Gonwil if they hadn't been forced to it. Being forced to it, they turned in a fast, artistic job, using Telzey's fabrication but adding a number of lifelike touches she couldn't have provided, and presenting it in a convincing dramatic manner.

Then they'd had to take immediate additional action to keep the stunned Parlins from wailing loudly enough to raise doubts about the infallibility of the ethics hearing procedures. As she knew from experience, the psionic machines were very good at installing on-the-spot compulsions.

So Malrue and her husband had applied for rehabilitation. The machines in the rehabilitation center would take it from there. The Psychology Service might have exempted Junior as being too much of a lightweight to worry about, but they certainly had seen to it that he wouldn't do any talking.

So far, so good, Telzey thought. She put down the glass of milk and slipped off her shoes. Chomir had strolled in from the next room and settled himself in front of her, and she placed her feet on his back now, kneading the thick, hard slabs of muscle with toes and heels. He grunted comfortably.

Gonwil's difficulties were over. And now where did she stand with the Psychology Service?

She considered it a while. Essentially, they seemed to be practical people, so they shouldn't be inclined to hold grudges. But she would look like a problem to them.

She'd reduced the problem as much as possible. Letting somebody look into sections of your mind was a good deal more satisfactory than making promises when you were out to create an atmosphere of confidence. If they had seen what you really intended, they didn't worry about cheating.

The Psychology Service knew now she wouldn't give away any of their secrets unless they forced her to it— which again was a practical decision on her part. She couldn't talk about them to Gonwil or her parents or Dasinger because their minds would be an open book any time they came near a psionic machine, and if she had told them too much, they might be in trouble then.

And in her own interest, she had no intention of telling people in general what she knew about psis— not, at least, until she understood a great deal more of what she'd be talking about.

Again, so far, so good.

Then there was the matter of having threatened to use the nondirect mailing system to expose them. She hadn't let them see whether she intended to give up that arrangement or not. As a matter of fact, the package of prepared reports had been destroyed shortly before she set off for Tor Heights, because of the risk of something going wrong accidentally and, not inconceivably, changing the course of Federation history as a result. They probably had expected her to do it, but they couldn't be sure. And even if they were, they didn't know what else she might have cooked up.

So the probability was they would decide it was wisest to leave her alone as long as she didn't disturb their plans. For her part, she would be very happy to leave them alone providing they didn't start trying to run her life again. No doubt, they could have taught her what she wanted to know about psionics; but their price looked like more than she was willing to pay. And she didn't seem to be doing too badly at teaching herself.

The Federation of the Hub was a vast area, after all. Aside from occasional contacts with their mechanized spy network, there was no real reason, Telzey concluded, why she and the Psychology Service should ever run into each other again.

Satisfied, she reached around for a couch cushion, placed it behind her neck, wriggled into a different position, laid her head back and closed her eyes. Might as well go on napping until Gilas and Gonwil arrived. On checking in here, she'd been told that float-ski conditions were perfect, so tomorrow should be a strenuous day....

# III: Poltergeist

Late summer had faded into fall in that region of Orado, and though the afternoon sun was still warm, the season was over at the mountain resort lake. No more than a dozen boats could be seen drifting slowly about its placid surface.

The solitude suited Telzey fine. The last three weeks at college had been packed; the weeks to come were going to be at least as demanding. For this one weekend she was cutting out of the pressure. They were to be two totally unambitious days, dedicated to mental and physical loafing, separated by relaxed nightlong sleep. Then, some time tomorrow evening, refreshed and renewed, she'd head south to Pehanron College and dive back into her study schedule.

The little kayak she'd rented went gliding across the green-blue lake toward the distant banks opposite the quiet resort village. Great cliffs rose there, broken by numerous narrow bays where trees crowded down to the edge of the water. If she came across some interesting looking spot, she might get out and do a little leisurely exploring.

She pressed a fingertip against the acceleration

button on the console before her. A paddle was fastened along the side of the kayak, but it hadn't touched water this afternoon, and wouldn't. Exercise definitely wasn't on the program. Telzey clasped her hands behind her head, settled against the cushioned backrest, steering rod held lightly between tanned knees.

Her eyebrows lifted.

What was *that*?

It came again. A faint quivering tingle, not of the nerves, but of mind . . . a light momentary touch of psi energy. Interest stirred briefly. She was a psi of some months' standing, a telepath—still a beginner and aware of it. So far, there hadn't been as much opportunity to practice her newly discovered abilities as she'd have liked. The college workload was too heavy at present, and she'd learned quickly that investigating the possibilities of a burgeoning psi talent was no casual undertaking. It was full of surprises, not always pleasant ones. She'd have more leisure for that kind of thing by and by.

As for those ripples of energy, they hadn't necessarily been generated in the vicinity of the lake. Chance could have brought them echoing into her awareness from some other area of the planet. In any case, she didn't intend to break her restful mood now by trying to determine their source.

Eyes half shut, knees occasionally nudging the kayak's steering rod a little to one side or the other, Telzey watched the tall gray cliffs along the lake front drift slowly closer. She sensed no more psi touches and the momentary experience soon sank to the back of her thoughts. There was a government department called the Psychology Service which demonstrated a paternalistically restrictive attitude toward psis who weren't members of its organization and not inclined to join up. Not long after her telepathic ability began to manifest, she'd discovered that the Service had tagged her, put restraints on her use of psi. She'd worked free of the restraints and maneuvered the Service then into accepting the fact that it would be best all around if she were left alone. It wasn't impossible though that they still had an eye on her, that those psi whispers had been bait designed to draw some reaction from her the Service could study.

Telzey decided not to worry about it. If it had been bait, she hadn't accepted it. Some other day she might, just to see what would happen.

Nobody seemed to be living along the water inlets among the cliffs. Campers might be there in summer. Tall trees stood gathered above the shelving rocks, and there were indications of animal life. They were pleasant, peaceful nooks. The kayak circled through each in turn, emerged, glided on along the cliffs to the next. So far, Telzey hadn't seen one that evoked the urge to explore.

But this she thought might be it.

Cup-shaped and considerably larger than most, the bay was enclosed by great steep rock walls on both sides. Trees rose above a sandy shore ahead, their ranks stretching far back into a cleft in the mountain. It would be easy to beach the kayak here and get out.

She saw someone lying on the sand then, not far above the water. A motionless figure, face down, feet turned toward her. There was no boat in sight, but an aircar might be parked back among the trees. What seemed immediately wrong was that the man wasn't dressed for a sprawl on the sand. He was wearing city clothes, an orange and white business suit. She had the impression he might be sick or dead—or stoned and sleeping it off.

She sent the kayak gliding closer to shore. Thirty feet away, she stopped, called out to the figure, "Hello there! Are you all right?"

He wasn't dead, at any rate. At the sound of her voice, his body jerked; then he was up on hands and knees, staring around at the trees clustered along the bank above him.

"I'm out here!" Telzey called.

He turned his head, saw her, got to his feet. Brushing sand from his coat, he started down toward the water's edge. Telzey saw his mouth working silently. Something certainly was wrong with that man!

"Are you sick?" she asked him. "You were lying there so quietly."

He looked distressed. But he shook his head, tried to smile.

"No," he said. "I'm quite all right. Thank you very much for your concern. It's good of you. But . . . well, I'd rather be by myself." He tried to smile again.

Telzey hesitated. His voice indicated he was neither drunk nor doped. "You're sure you're all right?" she said. "You don't look well."

"No, I'm perfectly all right. Please do go now! This isn't . . . well, it simply isn't a good place for a young girl to be."

Scared, she decided suddenly. Badly scared. Of what? She glanced over toward the silent trees, said, "Why don't you come with me then? The kayak will carry two."

"No, I can't. I—"

Great electric surges all about and through her— a violent burst of psi. And a rushing, grinding noise overhead. Something struck the water with a heavy splash ten feet away. Telzey jammed the acceleration button full down, swung the steering rod far over. The kayak darted forward, curving to the left. Another splash beside the boat. This time Telzey was drenched with water, momentarily blinded by it.

The bulk of the rockslide hit the surface of the bay instants later. She was clear of it by then, rushing along parallel to the shore. She shook water from her eyes, stabbed the brake button.

The kayak slammed against something just beneath

the surface, spun sideways with a rending sound, over-
turned, pitching her into the water.

The kayak was a total loss. Face submerged, she
could see it from the shifting surface, twenty feet
down in the clear dark depth of the bay where it had
slid after tearing itself open almost from bow to stern
along a projecting ledge of rock. Feeling weak with
shock, she lifted her head, stroked through angrily
tossing water toward the shore where the man stood
watching her. Presently she found a sloping sand bar
underfoot, waded out.

"I'm so sorry!" he said, white-faced. "You aren't
hurt, are you?"

Telzey's legs were trembling. She said, not too
steadily, "Just scared to death."

"I would have come to your help—but I can't
swim." He looked haggard enough but must be considerably younger than he'd seemed from the kayak,
probably not much over thirty.

"Well, I can," Telzey said. "So that was all right."
She gave him a brief reassuring smile, wondering a
good deal about him now. Then she looked up at the
cliff on her right, saw the fresh scar there in the
overhanging wall a hundred and fifty feet up.

"That was a mess of rock that came down," she
remarked, pushing her hands back over her hair,
squeezing water out of it.

"It was terrible. Terrible!" The man sighed heavily.
"I . . . well, I have towels and clothing articles back
there. Perhaps you could find something you could
use if you'd like to dry and change."

"No, thanks," Telzey said. "My clothes are water-
proofed. I'll be dry again in no time. You don't
happen to have a boat around, do you? Or an aircar?"

He shook his head. "I'm afraid not. Neither."

She considered it, and him. "You live here?"

He said hesitantly, "No. Not exactly. But I'd

planned to stay here a while." He paused. "The truth
is, I did use a boat to come across the lake from the
village this morning. But after I'd unloaded my supplies and equipment, I destroyed the boat. I didn't
want to be tempted to leave too quickly again—"

He cleared his throat, looking as if he badly wanted
to go on but couldn't quite bring himself to it.

"Well," Telzey said blandly, "it doesn't really matter.
If I'm not back with the kayak by dark, the resort
people will figure I'm having a problem and start
looking for me."

The man seemed to reach a decision. "I don't want
to alarm you, Miss—"

"I'm Telzey Amberdon."

He said his name was Dal Axwen. "There's something I must tell you. While you're here, we'll have
to be very careful. Or something may happen to you."

She said cautiously, "What might happen to me?"

He grimaced. "I haven't the faintest idea—that's
what makes it so difficult. I do know you're in danger." He cleared his throat again. "I'm sure this will
sound as if I'm out of my mind. But the fact is—I'm
being haunted."

Something shivered over Telzey's skin. "Haunted
by what?" she asked.

Dal Axwen shook his head. "I can't say. I don't
know who he is. Or what he is."

Telzey said after a moment, "You don't think that
rock fall was an accident?"

"No," he said. "It wasn't an accident. I didn't think
he would go that far, but you can see why I wanted
you to go away immediately."

Telzey said, "He wasn't trying to get at you with
the rocks?"

Axwen shook his head. "He intends to destroy me.
Everything indicates it. But not directly—not physi-
cally. If he wanted that, he'd have done it by now.
There's nothing I could have done to prevent it."

❖     ❖     ❖

Telzey was silent. At the instant she'd felt that eruption of energy, a tight protective screen of psi force had closed about her mind. While Axwen was talking she'd lightened it carefully, gradually. And now that she was looking for indications of that kind, she could tell there was something around on the psi level. A mentality. She had the impression it was aware of her, though it wasn't reacting in any way to the thinning of her screen. Otherwise, she couldn't make out much about it as yet.

She looked at Axwen. He was watching her with a kind of anxious intentness.

"You say you don't know what he is?" she asked. "Haven't you seen him?"

Axwen hesitated, then said wonderingly, "Why, I think you believe me."

"Oh, I believe you, all right," Telzey said. "Those rocks were up there, part of the mountain, a long, long time. It really seems more likely something started them down on purpose at the moment I was under them than that it just happened."

"Perhaps it's because you're still almost a child," Axwen said nodding. "But it's a relief in itself to find someone who accepts my explanation for these occurrences." He looked up at the cliff and shivered. "He's never done anything so completely terrifying before. But it's been bad enough."

"You've no idea at all who's doing it?" Telzey asked.

"He's something that can't be seen," Axwen said earnestly. "An evil spirit! I don't know what drew him to me, but he's selected me as his victim. I've given up any hope of ever being free of him again."

An electric tingling began about Telzey's screen. The psi mentality was active again, though on a relatively minor level. Her gaze shifted past Axwen's shoulder. Thirty feet farther along the shore, sand swirled up and about silently as if more and more of it were being flung high into the air by shifting violent blasts of wind in this wind-still bay. Then the sand cloud collapsed. Falling, it seemed to outline for a moment a squat ugly figure moving toward them. Then it was gone.

*All right, I'm already scared,* Telzey told the psi awareness mentally. *You don't have to work at it.*

She sensed no response, no reaction whatever.

Couldn't it hear her?

She moistened her lips, puzzled, looked up at Dal Axwen's worried, sad face.

"Let's walk around in the open a bit while I dry off," she suggested. "How did all this get started?"

Axwen couldn't say precisely when his troubles had begun. There'd been scattered occurrences in the past few years which in retrospect indicated it was developing during that period. He was an attorney; and sometimes at his office, sometimes at home, he'd discover small articles had been displaced, were lying where he hadn't left them. It seemed inexplicable, particularly when they happened to be objects he'd been handling perhaps only moments before. Once he found a stack of papers strewn about the carpet as if by a sudden gust of wind, in a room into which no wind could have penetrated.

"It was mystifying, of course," he said. "But those events were quite infrequent, and I didn't really think too much about them. They didn't seem important enough. Then one night a door started slamming in my home. That was half a year ago."

That was the first of a series of events. There were periods in which nothing happened, but he never knew when a previously solid chair might collapse, or other even more disconcerting things would occur. He began to wake up at night to hear somebody walking heavily about the room. When he turned on the light, the footsteps stopped and no one was there. He took to sleeping with every part of the house well illuminated, but assorted manifestations continued. His office staff presently came in for its share of mystifying and alarming experiences and deserted him. Replacements didn't last long. It didn't really seem to matter. By then his business was almost nonexistent.

"Last night at my home there was a continuing series of disturbances—enough to make it impossible for me to get to sleep. It was as if he'd decided to drive me out of my mind. Finally I drugged myself heavily and fell asleep almost at once. I slept for a full twelve hours and woke up more refreshed than I'd been in weeks. There were no indications that my persecutor was around. That's when it occurred to me that if I went far away and hid for a while, I might be able to rid myself of him permanently. I acted on the thought at once, picked out this resort at random from a listing, flew up here, bought a boat in the village, loaded it up with camping equipment and supplies, and set out across the lake. This bay seemed ideal for my purpose. Then, when I was beginning to feel almost certain that I was free of him at last, he let me know he'd found me again."

"How did he do that?" Telzey asked.

"I had set up my shelter and was reaching for one of the food containers. It exploded just as I touched it. I wasn't hurt in the least. But I knew what it meant. I could almost hear him laughing at me."

Axwen added, looking dolefully at Telzey, "I don't remember very well what happened most of the rest of the day. I was in a state of total despair and fear. I remember lying here on the sand, thinking I might never get up again. Finally I heard you call me."

Some time passed—

Axwen stirred suddenly, lifted his head, and observed in a startled voice, "It seems to be getting dark very quickly."

Telzey glanced over at him. They were sitting on the sand now, a few feet apart, looking toward the lake beyond the bay. She felt tired and tense. Her face was filmed with sweat. She'd been working around inside Axwen's mind for some while, investigating, probing. Naturally she hadn't let him become aware of what she did.

It had been instructive. She knew by now what manner of entity haunted Axwen, and why he was being haunted. The haunter wasn't far away, and eager, terribly eager, to destroy her, the psi who seemed to stand between itself and its prey. It had appalling power; she couldn't match it on that direct level. So far, she'd been holding it off with a variety of stratagems. But it was beginning to understand what she did and to discover how to undo the stratagems. It couldn't be too long before she'd find she'd run out of workable defenses.

She didn't know just when the moment would come. So she'd decided to bring Dal Axwen awake again. She had to try to get his help while it was still possible.

Axwen then had come awake and made his puzzled comment on the apparent shortness of the day.

Telzey said, "I guess it's just turning evening at the normal time for this latitude and season."

Axwen looked at his watch. "You're right," he admitted. "Strange—the last two hours seem to have passed like a dream. I recall almost nothing of what we said and did." He shook his head. "So I seem to be losing my memory, too. Well, at least there've been no further manifestations." He glanced at Telzey in sudden question. "Or have there been?"

"No," Telzey said.

Axwen yawned comfortably, gazing over at her.

"It's curious," he remarked. "I feel very calm now, quite undisturbed. I'm aware of my predicament and really see no way out. And I'm concerned that you may come to harm before you're away from here. At the same time, I seem almost completely detached from those problems."

Telzey nodded. "You try to never get angry at anyone, don't you?"

Axwen shook his head. "No, I don't approve of anger. When I feel such an impulse, which isn't often, I'm almost always able to overcome it. If I can't overcome it, then at least I won't express it or act on it."

Telzey nodded again. "You're someone who has about the average amount of human meanness in him. He knows it's not good, and he's trained himself, much more carefully than the average man, not to let it show in what he says or does. In fact, he's trained himself to the point where he usually doesn't even feel it."

Axwen said uncertainly, "This discussion is beginning to be rather confusing."

"A couple of things happened when you were ten years old," Telzey said. She went on talking a minute or two. Axwen's face grew strained as he listened. She said then, "I might have hypnotized you a while ago, or given you a spray of dope and asked you questions and told you to forget them again. But you'd better believe I know what I just told you because I read your mind. It isn't all I've done either. You've felt calm and detached till now because that's how I arranged it. I've been keeping you calm and detached. I don't want you to get any more upset than we can help." She added, "I'm afraid you're going to be pretty upset anyway."

Axwen stared at her. "About what?"

"The fact that you have a kind of second personality," Telzey said.

His eyelids flickered for a moment, and his jaw muscles went tight. He said nothing.

"Let me tell you about him," Telzey went on. "He's the things you haven't wanted to be consciously. That's about it. The way most people would look at it, it didn't make him very evil. But he's known what he is for quite a time, and he knows about you. You're the controlling personality. He's been locked away, unable to do anything except watch what you do. And he wasn't even always able to do that. He hasn't liked it, and he doesn't like you. You're his jailer. He's wanted to be the controlling personality and have it the other way around."

Axwen sighed. "Please don't talk like that," he said. He considered, added, "However, if I did have such a secondary personality as a result of having purged myself of characteristics of which I couldn't approve, I agree that I'd keep it locked away. The baser side of our nature, whatever form it takes, shouldn't be permitted to emerge while we can prevent it."

"Well, things have been changing there," Telzey said. "You see, Mr. Axwen, you're a psi, too."

He was silent a moment, eyes fixed on her. Then he shook his head slowly.

"You don't believe you're a psi?" Telzey said.

"I'm afraid I don't." Axwen half smiled. "I'll admit that for a moment you almost had me believing you were one."

Telzey nodded. "That's how the real trouble started," she said. "You didn't want to believe it. You should have realized a few years ago that you were beginning to develop psi abilities and could control them. But it frightened you. So that was something else you pushed out of awareness." She added, "These last few months I've noticed other people doing the same thing. Usually it doesn't matter—there isn't enough ability there anyway to make much difference."

"Then why should it make any difference to me?" Axwen said gently.

Telzey didn't reply immediately. That gentleness overlay a mental rigidity strained to the breaking point. Axwen could hardly have avoided having uneasy intimations by now of what she was leading him to. But he still wouldn't let himself see it; and if the barriers against understanding he'd developed over the years were to be broken down, he'd have to do it himself—immediately. His personality was too brittle, too near collapse under pressure as it was, to be tampered with at this point by a psi—certainly by a psi whose experience was no more extensive than her own.

Just now, in any case, she'd have no time at all for doubtful experiments.

"I never heard of a psi with anything like your potential in some areas, Mr. Axwen," she told him. "I didn't know it was possible. You've shoved control of all that power over to your other personality. He's been learning how to use it."

Axwen made a sudden ragged breathing noise.

"So he's who has been haunting you this past half year," she went on. "Really, of course, you've been haunting yourself."

If it hadn't been for the careful preliminary work she'd done on him, Axwen's reaction, when it finally came, might have been shattering. As it was, she was able to handle it well enough. Some five minutes later, he said dully, "Why would he do such a thing to me?"

It was progress. He'd accepted one part of the situation. He might now be willing to accept the remaining, all-important part. "You said you thought he was trying to drive you out of your mind," Telzey said. "He is, in a way. After he's reduced you down to where you can barely think, *he'll* be the controlling personality."

Axwen said, in desperation, "Then he'll succeed! I can't hope to stand up against his persecution much longer!"

"You won't have to," Telzey told him.

He looked at her. "What do you mean?"

Telzey said, "I've checked this very carefully. You can take psi control away from him if you'll do it at once. I can show you how to do it and help you do it. I know people I could send you to who could help you better than I, but we haven't nearly enough time left for that. And we can do it. Then—"

Axwen's jaw had begun to tremble; his eyes rolled like those of a frightened animal. "I will not associate myself with whatever that creature has become," he said hoarsely. "I deny that he's part of me!"

"Mr. Axwen," she said, "let me tell you some more about him, about the situation. I'll talk about him as if he weren't really you. He's one kind of psi; I'm another. In a way, he's much stronger than I am. I couldn't begin to tap the kind of energies he's been handling here, and if I could, they'd kill me.

Telzey pushed her palm across her forehead, wiped away sweat.

"There's a lot he doesn't understand. I'm the first psi he met—he didn't know there were others. He thought I was dangerous to him, so he tried to kill me, his way.

"I can't do any of the things he does. What I've done mainly when I had the time was study minds. What they're like, what you can do with them. Like I studied you today—and him. He didn't know I was doing it for a while, and when he knew that he didn't know how to stop me. He's been trying to do things that will kill me. But each time I confuse him, or make him forget what he wants to do, or how to do it. Sometimes he even forgets for a while that we're here, or what he is. I'm holding him down in a lot of different ways.

"But he keeps on trying to get away—and he is tremendously strong. If I lose control of him completely, he'll kill me at once. He's drawn in much more energy to use against me than he can handle safely—he still doesn't know enough about things like that. He's trying to find out how I'm holding him, and he's catching on. I can't talk to him because he can't hear me. If I had the time, I think I could get him to understand, but I won't have the time. I simply can't hold him that long. Mr. Axwen, don't you see that you must take control? I'll help you, and you can do it—I promise you that!"

"No." There was the flat finality of despair in the word. "But there is something I can do . . ."

Axwen started climbing to his feet, dropped awkwardly back again.

"That would be stupid," Telzey said.

He stared at her. "You stopped me!"

"I'm not letting you dive into the bay and drown yourself!"

"What else is left?" He was still staring at her, face chalk-white. His eyes widened then, slowly and enormously. *"You—"*

Telzey clamped down on the new horror exploding in him.

"No, I'm *not* some supernatural thing!" she said quickly. "I haven't come here to trick you into spiritual destruction. I'm *not* what's been haunting you!"

Something else slipped partly from her control then. Far back in the forested cleft behind them, high up between the cliffs, there was a sound like an echoing crash of thunder. Electric currents whirled about her.

"What's that?" Axwen gasped.

"He's got away." Telzey drew a long unsteady breath. "He doesn't know exactly where we are, but he's looking for us."

She blotted consciousness from Axwen's mind. He slumped over, lay on his side, knees drawn up toward his chest.

She couldn't blot consciousness so easily from the other personality. Nor could she restore the controls it had broken. The crashing sounds moved down through the cleft toward them. There was one thing left she could do, if she still had time for it.

She drew a blur of forgetfulness across its awareness of her, across its purpose. The noise stopped. For the moment, the personality was checked. Not for long—it knew what was being done to it in that respect now and would start forcing its way out of the mental fog.

Psi slashed delicately at its structure. It was an attack it could have blocked with a fraction of the power available to it. But it didn't know how to block it, or, as yet, that it was being attacked. Something separated. A small part of the personality vanished. A small part of its swollen stores of psi vanished with it.

She went on destructuring Dal Axwen's other personality. It wasn't pleasant work. Sometimes it didn't know what was happening. Sometimes it knew and struggled with horrid tenacity against further disintegration. She worked very quickly because, for a while, it still could have killed her easily if it had discovered in this emergency one of the ways to do it. Then, presently, she was past that point. Its remnants went unwillingly, still clinging to shreds of awareness, but no longer trying to resist otherwise. That seemed to make it worse.

It took perhaps half an hour in all. The last of Axwen's buried personality was gone then, and the last of the psi energy it had drawn into itself had drained harmlessly away. Telzey checked carefully to make sure of it. Then she swallowed twice, and was sick. Afterwards, she rinsed her mouth at the water's edge, came back and brought Axwen awake.

❖    ❖    ❖

A search boat from the resort village picked them up an hour later. The resort had considerable experience in locating guests who went off on the lake by themselves and got into difficulties. Shortly before midnight, Telzey was in her aircar, on the way back to Pehanron College. All inclination to spend the rest of the weekend at the lake had left her.

The past hours had brought her an abrupt new understanding of the people of the Psychology Service and their ways. Dal Axwen was a psi who should have been kept under observation and restraint while specialists dissolved the rigid blocks which prevented him from giving sane consideration to his emerging talent. If the Service people had discovered him in time, they could have saved him intact, as she'd been unable to do. And there might be many more psi personalities than she'd assumed who could be serious problems to themselves and others unless given guidance—with or without their consent.

It seemed then that in a society in which psis were a factor, something like the Psychology Service was necessary. Their procedures weren't as arbitrary as they'd appeared to her. She'd keep her independence of them; she'd earned that by establishing she could maintain it. But it would be foolish to turn her back completely on the vast stores of knowledge and experience represented by the Service . . .

Her reflections kept returning unwillingly to Dal Axwen's reactions. He'd been enormously, incredulously grateful after she restored him to consciousness. He'd laughed and cried. He'd kept trying to explain how free, relaxed and light he felt after the months of growing nightmare oppression, how safe he knew he was now from further uncanny problems of the kind. Forgetting she still was able to read his mind, knew exactly how he felt—

Telzey shook her head. She'd killed half a unique

human being, destroyed a human psi potential greater than she'd suspected existed.

And Axwen—foolish, emptied Axwen—had thanked her with happy tears streaming from his eyes for doing it to him!

# IV: Goblin Night

There was a quivering of psi force. Then a sudden, vivid sense of running and hiding, in horrible fear of a pursuer from whom there was no escape—

Telzey's breath caught in her throat. A psi screen had flicked into instant existence about her mind, blocking out incoming impulses. The mental picture, the feeling of pursuit, already was gone, had touched her only a moment; but she stayed motionless seconds longer, eyes shut, pulses hammering out a roll of primitive alarms. She'd been dozing uneasily for the past hour, aware in a vague way of the mind-traces of a multitude of wildlife activities in the miles of parkland around. And perhaps she'd simply fallen asleep, begun to dream . . .

Perhaps, she thought—but it wasn't very likely. She hadn't been relaxed enough to be touching the fringes of sleep and dream-stuff. The probability was that, for an instant, she'd picked up the reflection of a real event, that somebody not very far from here had encountered death in some grisly form at that moment.

She hesitated, then thinned the blocking screen to let her awareness spread again through the area, simultaneously extended a quick, probing thread of thought with a memory-replica of the pattern she'd caught. If it touched the mind that had produced the pattern originally, it might bring a momentary flash of echoing details and further information . . . assuming the mind was still alive, still capable of responding.

She didn't really believe it would still be alive. The impression she'd had in that instant was that death was only seconds away.

The general murmur of mind-noise began to grow up about her again, a varying pulse of life and psi energies, diminishing gradually with distance, arising from her companions, from animals on plain and mountain, with an undernote of the dimmer emanations of plants. But no suggestion came now of the vividly disturbing sensations of a moment ago.

Telzey opened her eyes, glanced around at the others sitting about the campfire in the mouth of Cil Chasm. There were eleven of them, a group of third and fourth year students of Pehanron College who had decided to spend the fall holidays in Melna Park. The oldest was twenty-two; she herself was the youngest—Telzey Amberdon, age fifteen. There was also a huge white dog named Chomir, not in view at the moment, the property of one of her friends who had preferred to go on a spacecruise with a very special date over the holidays. Chomir would have been a little in the way in an IP cruiser, so Telzey had brought him along to the park instead.

In the early part of the evening, they had built their fire where the great Cil canyon opened on the rolling plain below. The canyon walls rose to either side of the camp, smothered with evergreen growth; and the Cil River, a quick, nervous stream, spilled over a series of rocky ledges a hundred feet away. The boys had set up a translucent green tent canopy, and sleeping bags were arranged beneath it. But Gikkes and two of the other girls already had announced that when they got ready to sleep, they were going to take up one of the aircars and settle down in it for the night a good thirty feet above the ground.

The park rangers had assured them such measures weren't necessary. Melna Park was full of Orado's native wildlife—that, after all, was why it had been established—but none of the animals were at all likely to become aggressive towards visitors. As for human marauders, the park was safer than the planet's cities. Overflights weren't permitted; visitors came in at ground level through one of the various entrance stations where their aircars were equipped with sealed engine locks, limiting them to contour altitudes of a hundred and fifty feet and to a speed of thirty miles an hour. Only the rangers' cars were not restricted, and only the rangers carried weapons.

It made Melna Park sound like an oasis of sylvan tranquility. But as it turned towards evening, the stars of the great cluster about Orado brightened to awesomely burning splendor in the sky. Some of them, like Gikkes, weren't used to the starblaze, had rarely spent a night outside the cities where nightscreens came on gradually at the end of the day to meet the old racial preference for a dark sleep period.

Here night remained at an uncertain twilight stage until a wind began moaning up in the canyon and black storm clouds started to drift over the mountains and out across the plain. Now there were quick shifts between twilight and darkness, and eyes began to wander uneasily. There was the restless chatter of the river nearby. The wind made odd sounds in the canyon; they could hear sudden cracklings in bushes and trees, occasional animal voices.

"You get the feeling," Gikkes remarked, twisting her neck around to stare up Cil Chasm, "that something like a lullbear or spook might come trotting out of there any minute!"

Some of the others laughed uncertainly. Valia said, "Don't be silly! There haven't been animals like that in Melna Park for fifty years." She looked over at the group about Telzey. "Isn't that right, Pollard?"

Pollard was the oldest boy here. He was majoring in biology, which might make him Valia's authority on the subject of lullbears and spooks. He nodded, said, "You can still find them in the bigger game preserves up north. But naturally they don't keep anything in public parks that makes a practice of chewing up the public. Anything you meet around here, Gikkes, will be as ready to run from you as you are from it."

"That's saying a lot!" Rish added cheerfully. The others laughed again, and Gikkes looked annoyed.

Telzey had been giving only part of her attention to the talk. She felt shut down, temporarily detached from her companions. It had taken all afternoon to come across the wooded plains from the entrance station, winding slowly above the rolling ground in the three aircars which had brought them here. Then, after they reached Cil Chasm where they intended to stay, she and Rish and Dunker, two charter members of her personal fan club at Pehanron, had spent an hour fishing along the little river, up into the canyon and back down again. They had a great deal of excitement and caught enough to provide supper for everyone; but it involved arduous scrambling over slippery rocks, wading in cold, rushing water, and occasional tumbles, in one of which Telzey knocked her wrist-talker out of commission for the duration of the trip.

Drowsiness wasn't surprising after all the exercise. The surprising part was that, in spite of it, she didn't seem able to relax completely. As a rule, she felt at home wherever she happened to be outdoors. But something about this place was beginning to bother her. She hadn't noticed it at first, she had laughed at Gikkes with the others when Gikkes began to express apprehensions. But when she settled down after supper, feeling a comfortable muscular fatigue begin to claim her, she grew aware of a vague disturbance. The atmosphere of Melna Park seemed to change slowly. A hint of cruelty and savagery crept into it, of hidden terrors. Mentally, Telzey felt herself glancing over her shoulder towards dark places under the trees, as if something like a lullbear or spook actually was lurking there.

And then, in that uneasy, half-awake condition, there suddenly had been this other thing, like a dream-flash in which somebody desperately ran and hid from a mocking pursuer. To the terrified human quarry, the pursuer appeared as a glimpsed animalic shape in the twilight, big and moving swiftly, but showing no other details.

And there had been the flickering of psi energy about the scene . . .

Telzey shifted uncomfortably, running her tongue tip over her lips. The experience had been chillingly vivid; but if something of the sort really had occurred, the victim had died moments later. In that respect, there was no reason to force herself to quick decisions now. And it might, after all, have been a dream, drifting up in her mind, created by the mood of the place. She realized she would like to believe it was a dream.

But in that case, what was creating the mood of the place?

Gikkes? It wasn't impossible. She had decided some time ago that personal acquaintances should be off limits to telepathic prowling, but when someone was around at all frequently, scraps of information were likely to filter through. So she knew Gikkes also had much more extensively developed telepathic awareness than the average person. Gikkes didn't know it and couldn't have put it to use anyway. In her, it was an erratic, unreliable quality which might have kept her in a badly confused state of mind if she had been more conscious of its effects.

But the general uneasiness Telzey had sensed and that brief psi surge—if that was what it was—fragmentary but carrying a complete horrid little story with it, could have come to her from Gikkes. Most people, even when they thought they were wide awake, appeared to be manufacturing dreams much of the time in an area of their minds they didn't know about; and Gikkes seemed nervous enough this evening to be manufacturing unconscious nightmares and broadcasting them.

But again—what made Gikkes so nervous here? The unfamiliar environment, the frozen beauty of the starblaze overhanging the sloping plain like a tent of fire, might account for it. But it didn't rule out a more specific source of disturbance.

She could make sure, Telzey thought, by probing into Gikkes's mind and finding out what was going on in there. Gikkes wouldn't know it was happening. But it took many hours, as a rule, to develop adequate contact unless the other mind was also that of a functioning telepath. Gikkes was borderline—a telepath, but not functional, or only partly so—and if she began probing around in those complexities without the experience to tell her just how to go about it, she might wind up doing Gikkes some harm.

She looked over at Gikkes. Gikkes met her eyes, said, "Shouldn't you start worrying about that dog of Gonwil's? He hasn't been in sight for the past half-hour."

"Chomir's all right," Telzey said. "He's still checking over the area."

Chomir was, in fact, only a few hundred yards

away, moving along the Cil River up in the canyon.
She'd been touching the big dog's mind lightly from
time to time during the evening to see what he was
doing. Gikkes couldn't know that, of course—nobody
in this group suspected Telzey of psionic talents. But
she had done a great deal of experimenting with
Chomir, and nowadays she could, if she liked, almost
see with his eyes, smell with his nose, and listen
through his ears. At this instant, he was watching half
a dozen animals large enough to have alarmed Gikkes
acutely. Chomir's interest in Melna Park's wildlife
didn't go beyond casual curiosity. He was an Askanam
hound, a breed developed to fight man or beast in
pit and arena, too big and powerful to be apprehensive about other creatures and not inclined to chase
strange animals about without purpose as a lesser dog
might do.

"Well," Gikkes said, "if I were responsible for
somebody else's dog, if I'd brought him here, I'd be
making sure he didn't run off and get lost—"

Telzey didn't answer. It took no mind-reading to
know that Gikkes was annoyed because Pollard had
attached himself to Telzey's fan club after supper and
settled down beside her. Gikkes had invited Pollard
to come along on the outing; he was president of various organizations and generally important at Pehanron
College. Gikkes, the glamour girl, didn't like it at all
that he'd drifted over to Telzey's group, and while
Telzey had no designs on him, she couldn't very well
inform Gikkes of that without ruffling her further.

"I," Gikkes concluded, "would go look for him."

Pollard stood up. "It would be too bad if he strayed
off, wouldn't it?" he agreed. He gave Telzey a lazy
smile. "Why don't you and I look around a little
together?"

Well, that was not exactly what Gikkes had
intended. Rish and Dunker didn't think much of it

either. They were already climbing to their feet, gazing sternly at Pollard.

Telzey glanced at them, checked the watch Dunker had loaned her after she smashed the one in her wrist-talker on the fishing excursion.

"Let's wait another five minutes," she suggested. "If he isn't back by then, we can all start looking."

As they settled down again, she sent a come-here thought to Chomir. She didn't yet know what steps she might have to take in the other matter, but she didn't want to be distracted by problems with Gikkes and the boys.

She felt Chomir's response. He turned, got his bearings instantly with nose, ears, and—though he wasn't aware of that—by the direct touch of their minds, went bounding down into the river, and splashed noisily through the shallow water. He was taking what seemed to him a short cut to the camp. But that route would lead him high up the opposite bank of the twisting Cil, to the far side of the canyon.

"Not that way, stupid!" Telzey thought, verbalizing it for emphasis. "Turn around—go back!"

And then, as she felt the dog pause comprehendingly, a voice, edged with the shock of surprise—perhaps of fear—exclaimed in her mind, *"Who are you? Who said that?"*

There had been a number of occasions since she became aware of her abilities when she'd picked up the thought-forms of another telepath. She hadn't tried to develop such contacts, feeling in no hurry to strike up an acquaintanceship on the psionic level. That was part of a world with laws and conditions of its own which should be studied thoroughly if she was to avoid creating problems for herself and others, and at present she simply didn't have the time for thorough study.

Even with the tentative exploration she'd been doing, problems arose. One became aware of a situation of which others weren't aware, and then it wasn't always possible to ignore the situation, to act as if it didn't exist. But depending on circumstances, it could be extremely difficult to do something effective about it, particularly when one didn't care to announce publicly that one was a psi.

The thing that appeared to have happened in Melna Park tonight had seemed likely to present just such problems. Then this voice spoke to her suddenly, coming out of the night, out of nowhere. Another telepath was in the area, to whom the encounter was as unexpected as it was to her. There was no immediate way of knowing whether that was going to help with the problem or complicate it further, but she had no inclination to reply at once. Whoever the stranger was, the fact that he—there had been a strong male tinge to the thoughts—was also a psi didn't necessarily make him a brother. She knew he was human; alien minds had other flavors. His questions had come in the sharply defined forms of a verbalization; he might have been speaking aloud in addressing her. There was something else about them she hadn't noticed in previous telepathic contacts—an odd, filtered quality as though his thoughts passed through a distorting medium before reaching her.

She waited, wondering about it. While she wasn't strongly drawn to this stranger, she felt no particular concern about him. He had picked up her own verbalized instructions to Chomir, had been startled by them, and, therefore, hadn't been aware of anything she was thinking previously. She'd now tightened the veil of psi energy about her mind a little, enough to dampen out the drifting threads of subconscious thought by which an unguarded mind was most easily found and reached. Tightened further, as it could be in an instant, it had stopped genuine

experts in mind-probing in their tracks. This psi was
no expert; an expert wouldn't have flung surprised
questions at her. She didn't verbalize her thinking as
a rule, and wouldn't do it now until she felt like it.
And she wouldn't reach out for him. She decided the
situation was sufficiently in hand.

The silence between them lengthened. He might
be equally wary now, regretting his brief outburst.

Telzey relaxed her screen, flicked out a search-
thought to Chomir, felt him approaching the camp
in his easy, loping run, closed the screen again. She
waited a few seconds. There was no indication of
interest apparently, even when he had his attention
on her, he was able to sense only her verbalized
thoughts. That simplified the matter.

She lightened the screen again. "Who are *you*?"
she asked.

The reply came instantly. "So I wasn't dreaming!
For a moment, I thought . . . Are there two of you?"

"No. I was talking to my dog." There was something odd about the quality of his thoughts. He might
be using a shield or screen of some kind, not of the
same type as hers but perhaps equally effective.

"Your dog? I see. It's been over a year," the voice
said, "since I've spoken to others like this." It paused.
"You're a woman . . . young . . . a girl . . ."

There was no reason to tell him she was fifteen.
What Telzey wanted to know just now was whether
he also had been aware of a disturbance in Melna
Park. She asked, "Where are you?"

He didn't hesitate. "At my home. Twelve miles
south of Cil Chasm across the plain, at the edge of
the forest. The house is easy to see from the air."

He might be a park official. They'd noticed such
a house on their way here this afternoon and specu-
lated about who could be living there. Permission to
make one's residence in a Federation Park was supposedly almost impossible to obtain.

"Does that tell you anything?" the voice went on.

"Yes," Telzey said. "I'm in the park with some friends. I think I've seen your house."

"My name," the bodiless voice told her, "is Robane. You're being careful. I don't blame you. There are certain risks connected with being a psi, as you seem to understand. If we were in a city, I'm not sure I would reveal myself. But out here . . . Somebody built a fire this evening where the Cil River leaves the Chasm. I'm a cripple and spend much of my time studying the park with scanners. Is that your fire?"

Telzey hesitated a moment. "Yes."

"Your friends," Robane's voice went on, "they're aware you and I . . . they know you're a telepath?"

"No."

"Would you be able to come to see me for a while without letting them know where you're going?"

"Why should I do that?" Telzey asked.

"Can't you imagine? I'd like to talk to a psi again."

"We *are* talking," she said.

Silence for a moment.

"Let me tell you a little about myself," Robane said then. "I'm approaching middle age—from your point I might even seem rather old. I live here alone except for a well-meaning but rather stupid housekeeper named Feddler. Feddler seems old from my point of view. Four years ago, I was employed in one of the Federation's science departments. I am . . . was . . . considered to be among the best in my line of work. It wasn't very dangerous work so long as certain precautions were observed. But one day a fool made a mistake. His mistake killed two of my colleagues. It didn't quite kill me, but since that day I've been intimately associated with a machine which has the responsibility of keeping me alive from minute to minute. I'd die almost immediately if I were removed from it.

"So my working days are over. And I no longer want to live in cities. There are too many foolish people there to remind me of the one particular fool I'd prefer to forget. Because of the position I'd held and the work I'd done, the Federation permitted me to make my home in Melna Park where I could be by myself . . ."

The voice stopped abruptly but Telzey had the impression Robane was still talking, unaware that something had dimmed the thread of psi between them. His own screen perhaps? She waited, alert and quiet. It might be deliberate interference, the manifestation of another active psionic field in the area— a disturbing and malicious one.

" . . . On the whole, I like it here." Robane's voice suddenly was back, and it was evident he didn't realize there had been an interruption. "A psi need never be really bored, and I've installed instruments to offset the disadvantages of being a cripple. I watch the park through scanners and study the minds of animals . . . Do you like animal minds?"

That, Telzey thought, hadn't been at all a casual question. "Sometimes," she told Robane carefully. "Some of them."

"Sometimes? Some of them? I wonder . . . Solitude on occasion appears to invite the uncanny. One may notice things that seem out of place, that are disquieting. This evening . . . during the past hour perhaps, have you . . . were there suggestions of activities . . ." He paused. "I find I don't quite know how to say this."

"There was something," she said. "For a moment, I wasn't sure I wasn't dreaming."

"You mean something ugly . . ."

"Yes."

"Fear," Robane's voice said in her mind. "Fear, pain, death. Savage cruelty. So you caught it, too. Very strange! Perhaps an echo from the past touched our minds in that moment, from the time when creatures who hated man still haunted this country.

"But—well, this is one of the rare occasions when I feel lonely here. And then to hear another psi, you see ... Perhaps I'm even a little afraid to be alone in the night just now. I'd like to speak to you, but not in this way—not in any great detail. One can never be sure who else is listening ... I think there are many things two psis might discuss to their advantage."

The voice ended on that. He'd expressed himself guardedly, and apparently he didn't expect an immediate reply to his invitation. Telzey bit her lip. Chomir had come trotting up, had been welcomed by her and settled down. Gikkes was making cooing sounds and snapping her fingers at him. Chomir ignored the overtures. Ordinarily, Gikkes claimed to find him alarming; but here in Melna Park at night, the idea of having an oversized dog near her evidently had acquired a sudden appeal—

So Robane, too, had received the impression of unusual and unpleasant events this evening ... events he didn't care to discuss openly. The indication that he felt frightened probably needn't be taken too seriously. He was in his house, after all; and so isolated a house must have guard-screens. The house of a crippled, wealthy recluse, who was avoiding the ordinary run of humanity, would have very effective guard-screens. If something did try to get at Robane, he could put in a call to the nearest park station and have an armed ranger car hovering about his roof in a matter of minutes. That suggestion had been intended to arouse her sympathy for a shut-in fellow psi, help coax her over to the house.

But he had noticed something. Something, to judge from his cautious description, quite similar to what she had felt. Telzey looked at Chomir, stretched out on the sandy ground between her and the fire, at the big, wolfish head, the wedge of powerful jaws. Chomir was not exactly an intellectual giant but he had the excellent sensory equipment and alertness of a breed of fighting animals. If there had been a disturbance of that nature in the immediate vicinity, he would have known about it, and she would have known about it through him.

The disturbance, however, might very well have occurred somewhere along the twelve-mile stretch between the point where Cil Chasm split the mountains and Robane's house across the plain. Her impression had been that it was uncomfortably close to her. Robane appeared to have sensed it as uncomfortably close to him. He had showed no inclination to do anything about it, and there was, as a matter of fact, no easy way to handle the matter. Robane clearly was no more anxious than she was to reveal himself as a psi; and, in any case, the park authorities would be understandably reluctant to launch a search for a vicious but not otherwise identified man-hunting beast on no better evidence than reported telepathic impressions—at least, until somebody was reported missing.

It didn't seem a good idea to wait for that. For one thing, Telzey thought, the killer might show up at their fire before morning . . .

She grimaced uneasily, sent a troubled glance around the group. She hadn't been willing to admit it but she'd really known for minutes now that she was going to have to go look for the creature. In an aircar, she thought, even an aircar throttled down to thirty miles an hour and a contour altitude of a hundred and fifty feet, she would be in no danger from an animal on the ground if she didn't take very stupid chances. The flavor of psi about the event she didn't like. That was still unexplained. But she was a psi herself, and she would be careful.

She ran over the possibilities in her mind. The best

approach should be to start out towards Robane's house and scout the surrounding wildlands mentally along that route. If she picked up traces of the killer-thing, she could pinpoint its position, call the park rangers from the car, and give them a story that would get them there in a hurry. They could do the rest. If she found nothing, she could consult with Robane about the next moves to make. Even if he didn't want to take a direct part in the search, he might be willing to give her some help with it.

Chomir would remain here as sentinel. She'd plant a trace of uneasiness in his mind, just enough to make sure he remained extremely vigilant while she was gone. At the first hint from him that anything dangerous was approaching the area, she'd use the car's communicator to have everybody pile into the other two aircars and get off the ground. Gikkes was putting them in the right frame of mind to respond very promptly if they were given a real alarm.

Telzey hesitated a moment longer but there seemed to be nothing wrong with the plan. She told herself she'd better start at once. If she waited, the situation, whatever it was, conceivably could take an immediately dangerous turn. Besides, the longer she debated about it, the more unpleasant the prospect was going to look.

She glanced down at Dunker's watch on her wrist. "Robane?" she asked in her mind.

The response came quickly. "Yes?"

"I'll start over to your house now," Telzey said. "Would you watch for my car? If there is something around that doesn't like people, I'd sooner not be standing outside your door."

"The door will be open the instant you come down," Robane's voice assured her. "Until then, I'm keeping it locked. I've turned on the scanners and will be waiting . . ." A moment's pause. "Do you have additional reason to believe—"

"Not so far," Telzey said. "But there are some things I'd like to talk about—after I get there . . ." She didn't really intend to go walking into Robane's house until she had more information about him. There were too many uncertainties floating around in the night to be making social calls. But he'd be alert now, waiting for her to arrive, and might notice things she didn't.

The aircar was her own, a fast little Cloudsplitter. No one objected when she announced she was setting off for an hour's roam in the starblaze by herself. The fan club looked wistful but was well trained, and Pollard had allowed himself to be reclaimed by Gikkes. Gikkes clearly regarded Telzey's solo excursion as a fine idea . . .

She lifted the Cloudsplitter out of the mouth of Cil Chasm. At a hundred and fifty feet, as the sealed engine lock clicked in, the little car automatically stopped its ascent. Telzey turned to the right, along the forested walls of the mountain, then swung out across the plain.

It should take her about twenty minutes to get to Robane's house if she went there in a straight line; and if nothing else happened, she intended to go there in a straight line. What the park maps called a plain was a series of sloping plateaus, broken by low hills, descending gradually to the south. It was mainly brush country, dotted with small woods which blended here and there into patches of forest. Scattered herds of native animals moved about in the open ground, showing no interest in the aircar passing through the clusterlight overhead.

Everything looked peaceful enough. Robane had taken her hint and remained quiet. The intangible bubble of the psi screen about Telzey's mind thinned, opened wide. Her awareness went searching ahead, to all sides . . .

Man-killer, where are you?

❖          ❖          ❖

Perhaps ten minutes passed before she picked up the first trace. By then, she could see a tiny, steady spark of orange light ahead against the dark line of the forest. That would be Robane's house, still five or six miles away.

Robane hadn't spoken again. There had been numerous fleeting contacts with animal minds savage enough in their own way, deadly to one another. But the thing that hunted man should have a special quality, one she would recognize when she touched it.

She touched it suddenly—a blur of alert malignance, gone almost at once. She was prepared for it, but it still sent a thrill of alarm through her. She moistened her lips, told herself again she was safe in the car. The creature definitely had not been far away. Telzey slipped over for a moment into Chomir's mind. The big dog stood a little beyond the circle of firelight, probing the land to the south. He was unquiet but no more than she had intended him to be. His senses had found nothing of unusual significance. The menace wasn't there.

It was around here, ahead, or to left or right. Telzey let the car move on slowly. After a while, she caught the blur for a moment again, lost it again . . .

She approached Robane's house gradually. Presently she could make it out well enough in the clusterlight, a sizable structure, set in a garden of its own which ended where the forest began. Part of the building was two-storied, with a balcony running around the upper story. The light came from there, dark-orange light glowing through screened windows.

The second fleeting pulse of that aura of malevolence had come from this general direction; she was sure of it. If the creature was in the forest back of the house, perhaps watching the house, Robane's apprehensions might have some cause, after all. She had brought the Cloudsplitter almost to a stop some five hundred yards north of the house; now she began moving to the left, then shifted in towards the forest, beginning to circle the house as she waited for another indication. Robane should be watching her through the telescanners, and she was grateful that he hadn't broken the silence. Perhaps he had realized what she was trying to do.

For long minutes now, she had been intensely keyed up, sharply aware of the infinite mingling of life detail below. It was as if the plain had come alight in all directions about her, a shifting glimmer of sparks, glowing emanations of life-force, printed in constant change on her awareness. To distinguish among it all the specific pattern which she had touched briefly twice might not be an easy matter. But then, within seconds, she made two significant discoveries.

She had brought the Cloudsplitter nearly to a stop again. She was now to the left of Robane's house, no more than two hundred yards from it. Close enough to see a flock of small, birdlike creatures flutter about indistinctly in the garden shrubbery. Physical vision seemed to overlap and blend with her inner awareness, and among the uncomplicated emanations of small animal life in the garden, there was now a center of mental emanation which was of more interest.

It was inside the house, and it was human. It seemed to Telzey it was Robane she was sensing. That was curious, because if his mind was screened as well as she'd believed, she should not be able to sense him in this manner. But, of course, it might not be. She had simply assumed he had developed measures against being read as adequate as her own.

Probably it was Robane. Then where, Telzey thought, was that elderly, rather stupid housekeeper named Feddler he'd told her about? Feddler's presence, her mind unscreened in any way, should be at least equally obvious now.

With the thought, she caught a second strong glow. That was not the mind of some stupid old woman, or of anything human. It was still blurred, but it was the mind for which she had been searching. The mind of some baleful, intelligent tiger-thing. And it was very close.

She checked again, carefully. Then she knew. It was not back in the forest, and not hidden somewhere on the plain nearby.

It was inside Robane's house.

For a moment, shock held her motionless. Then she swung the Cloudsplitter smoothly to the left, started moving off along the edge of the forest.

"Where are you going?" Robane's voice asked in her mind.

Telzey didn't answer. The car already was gliding along at the thirty miles an hour its throttled-down engine allowed it to go. Her forefinger was flicking out the call number of Rish's aircar back at the camp on the Cloudsplitter's communicator.

There'd been a trap set for her here. She didn't yet know what kind of a trap, or whether she could get out of it by herself. But the best thing she could do at the moment was to let other people know immediately where she was—

A dragging, leaden heaviness sank through her. She saw her hand drop from the communicator dial, felt herself slump to the left, head sagging down on the side rest, face turned half up. She felt the Cloudsplitter's engines go dead. The trap had snapped shut.

The car was dropping, its forward momentum gone. Telzey made a straining effort to sit back up, lift her hands to the controls, and nothing happened. She realized then that nothing could have happened if she had reached the controls. If it hadn't been for the countergravity materials worked into its structure, the Cloudsplitter would have plunged to the ground like a rock. As it was, it settled gradually down through the air, swaying from side to side.

She watched the fiery night sky shift above with the swaying of the car, sickened by the conviction that she was dropping towards death, trying to keep the confusion of terror from exploding through her . . .

"I'm curious to know," Robane's voice said, "what made you decide at the last moment to decline my invitation and attempt to leave."

She wrenched her attention away from terror, reached for the voice and Robane.

There was the crackling of psi, open telepathic channels through which her awareness flowed in a flash. For an instant, she was inside his mind. Then psi static crashed, and she was away from it again. Her awareness dimmed, momentarily blurred out. She'd absorbed almost too much. It was as if she'd made a photograph of a section of Robane's mind— a pitiful and horrible mind.

She felt the car touch the ground, stop moving. The slight jolt tilted her over farther, her head lolling on the side rest. She was breathing; her eyelids blinked. But her conscious efforts weren't affecting a muscle of her body.

The dazed blurriness began to lift from her thoughts. She found herself still very much frightened but no longer accepting in the least that she would die here. She should have a chance against Robane. She discovered he was speaking again, utterly unaware of what had just occurred.

"I'm not a psi," his voice said. "But I'm a gadgeteer—and, you see, I happen to be highly intelligent. I've used my intelligence to provide myself with instruments which guard me and serve my wishes here. Some give me abilities equivalent to those of a psi. Others, as you've just experienced, can be used to neutralize power devices or to paralyze the human voluntary muscular system within as much as half a mile of this room.

"I was amused by your cautious hesitation and attempted flight just now. I'd already caught you. If I'd let you use the communicator, you would have found it dead. I shut it off as soon as your aircar was in range . . ."

Robane not a psi? For an instant, there was a burbling of lunatic, silent laughter in Telzey's head. In that moment of full contact between them, she'd sensed a telepathic system functional in every respect except that he wasn't aware of it. Psi energy flared about his words as he spoke. That came from one of the machines, but only a telepath could have operated such a machine.

Robane had never considered that possibility. If the machine static hadn't caught her off guard, broken the contact before she could secure it, he would be much more vulnerable in his unawareness now than an ordinary nonpsi human.

She'd reached for him again as he was speaking, along the verbalized thought-forms directed at her. But the words were projected through a machine. Following them back, she wound up at the machine and another jarring blast of psi static. She would have to wait for a moment when she found an opening to his mind again, when the machines didn't happen to be covering him. He was silent now. He intended to kill her as he had others before her, and he might very well be able to do it before an opening was there. But he would make no further moves until he felt certain she hadn't been able to summon help in a manner his machines hadn't detected. What he had done so far he could explain—he had forced an aircar prowling about his house to the ground without harming its occupant. There was no proof of anything else he had done except the proof in Telzey's mind, and Robane didn't know about that.

It gave her a few minutes to act without interference from him.


"What's the matter with that dog?" Gikkes asked nervously. "He's behaving like . . . like he thinks there's something around."

The chatter stopped for a moment. Eyes swung over to Chomir. He stood looking out from the canyon ledge over the plain, making a rumbling noise in his throat.

"Don't be silly," Valia said. "He's just wondering where Telzey's gone." She looked at Rish. "How long has she been gone?"

"Twenty-seven minutes," Rish said.

"Well, that's nothing to worry about, is it?" Valia checked herself, added, "Now look at that, will you!" Chomir had swung around, moved over to Rish's aircar, stopped beside it, staring at them with yellow eyes. He made the rumbling noise again.

Gikkes said, watching him fascinatedly, "Maybe something's happened to Telzey."

"Don't talk like that," Valia said. "What could happen to her?"

Rish got to his feet. "Well—it can't hurt to give her a call . . ." He grinned at Valia to show he wasn't in the least concerned, went to the aircar, opened the door.

Chomir moved silently past him into the car.

Rish frowned, glanced back at Valia and Dunker coming up behind him, started to say something, shook his head, slid into the car, and turned on the communicator.

Valia inquired, her eyes uneasily on Chomir, "Know her number?"

"Uh-huh." They watched as he flicked the number out on the dial, then stood waiting.

Presently Valia cleared her throat. "She's probably got out of the car and is walking around somewhere."

"Of course she's walking," Rish said shortly.

"Keep buzzing anyway," Dunker said.

"I am." Rish glanced at Chomir again. "If she's anywhere near the car, she'll be answering in a moment . . ."

"Why don't you answer me?" Robane's voice asked, sharp with impatience. "It would be very foolish of you to make me angry."

Telzey made no response. Her eyes blinked slowly at the starblaze. Her awareness groped, prowled, patiently, like a hungry cat, for anything, the slightest wisp of escaping unconscious thought, emotion, that wasn't filtered through the blocking machines, that might give her another opening to the telepathic levels of Robane's mind. In the minutes she'd been lying paralyzed across the seat of the aircar, she had arranged and comprehended the multi-detailed glimpse she'd had of it. She understood Robane very thoroughly now.

The instrument room of the house was his living area. A big room centered about an island of immaculate precision machines. Robane rarely was away from it. She knew what he looked like, from mirror images, glimpses in shining instrument surfaces, his thoughts about himself. A half-man, enclosed from the waist down in a floating, mobile machine like a tiny aircar, which carried him and kept him alive. The little machine was efficient; the half-body protruding from it was vigorous and strong. Robane in his isolation gave fastidious attention to his appearance. The coat which covered him down to the machine was tailored to Orado City's latest fashion; his thick hair was carefully groomed.

He had led a full life as scientist, sportsman, and man of the world, before the disaster which left him bound to his machine. To make the man responsible for the disaster pay for his blunder in full became

Robane's obsession and he laid his plans with all the care of the trophy hunter he had been. His work for the Federation had been connected with the further development of devices permitting the direct transmission of sensations from one living brain to another and their adaptation to various new uses. In his retirement in Melna Park, Robane patiently refined such devices for his own purposes and succeeded beyond his expectations, never suspecting that the success was due in part to the latent psionic abilities he was stimulating with his experiments.

Meanwhile, he had prepared for the remaining moves in his plan, installed automatic machinery to take the place of his housekeeper, and dismissed the old woman from his service. A smuggling ring provided him with a specimen of a savage natural predator native to the continent for which he had set up quarters beneath the house. Robane trained the beast and himself, perfecting his skill in the use of the instruments, sent the conditioned animal out at night to hunt, brought it back after it had made the kill in which he had shared through its mind. There was sharper excitement in that alone than he had found in any previous hunting experience. There was further excitement in treating trapped animals with the drug that exposed their sensations to his instruments when he released them and set the killer on their trail. He could be hunter or hunted, alternately and simultaneously, following each chase to the end, withdrawing from the downed quarry only when its numbing death impulses began to reach him.

When it seemed he had no more to learn, he had his underworld connections deliver his enemy to the house. That night, he awakened the man from his stupor, told him what to expect, and turned him out under the starblaze to run for his life. An hour later, Robane and his savage deputy made a human kill, the instruments fingering the victim's drug-drenched nervous system throughout and faithfully transmitting his terrors and final torment.

With that, Robane had accomplished his revenge. But he had no intention now of giving up the exquisite excitements of the new sport he had developed in the process. He became almost completely absorbed by it, as absorbed as the beast he had formed into an extension of himself. They went out by night to stalk and harry, run down and kill. They grew alike in cunning, stealth, and savage audacity, were skillful enough to create no unusual disturbance among the park animals with their sport. By morning, they were back in Robane's house to spend most of the day in sleep. Unsuspecting human visitors who came through the area saw no traces of their nocturnal activities.

Robane barely noticed how completely he had slipped into this new way of living. Ordinarily, it was enough. But he had almost no fear of detection now, and sometimes he remembered there had been a special savor in driving a human being to his death. Then his contacts would bring another shipment of "supplies" to the house, and that night he hunted human game. Healthy young game which did its desperate best to escape but never got far. It was something humanity owed him.

For a while, there was one lingering concern. During his work for the Overgovernment, he'd had several contacts with a telepath called in to assist in a number of experiments. Robane had found out what he could about such people and believed his instruments would shield him against being detected and investigated by them. He was not entirely sure of it, but in the two years he had been pursuing his pleasures undisturbed in Melna Park his uneasiness on that point had almost faded away.

Telzey's voice, following closely on his latest human

kill, startled him profoundly. But when he realized that
it was a chance contact, that she was here by accident,
it occurred to him that this was an opportunity to find
out whether a telepathic mind could be dangerous to
him. She seemed young and inexperienced—he could
handle her through his instruments with the slightest
risk to himself.

Rish and Dunker were in Rish's aircar with Chomir,
Telzey thought, and a third person, who seemed to be
Valia, was sitting behind them. The car was aloft and
moving, so they had started looking for her. It would
be nice if they were feeling nervous enough to have
the park rangers looking for her, too; but that was very
unlikely. She had to handle Chomir with great caution
here. If he'd sensed any fear in her, he would have
raced off immediately in her general direction to protect her, which would have been of no use at all.

As it was, he was following instructions he didn't
know he was getting. He was aware which way the
car should go, and he would make that quite clear
to Rish and the others if it turned off in any other
direction. Since they had no idea where to look for
her themselves, they would probably decide to rely
on Chomir's intuition.

That would bring them presently to this area. If
she was outside the half-mile range of Robane's energy
shut-off device by then, they could pick her up safely.
If she wasn't, she'd have to turn them away through
Chomir again or she'd simply be drawing them into
danger with her. Robane, however, wouldn't attempt
to harm them unless he was forced to it. Telzey's
disappearance in the wildlands of the park could be
put down as an unexplained accident; he wasn't risking
much there. But a very intensive investigation would
get under way if three other students of Pehanron
College vanished simultaneously along with a large
dog. Robane couldn't afford that.

*"Why don't you answer?"*

There was an edge of frustrated rage in Robane's projected voice. The paralysis field which immobilized her also made her unreachable to him. He was like an animal balked for the moment by a glass wall. He'd said he had a weapon trained on her which could kill her in an instant as she lay in the car, and Telzey knew it was true from what she had seen in his mind. For that matter, he probably only had to change the setting of the paralysis field to stop her heartbeat or her breathing.

But such actions wouldn't answer the questions he had about psis. She'd frightened him tonight; and now he had to run her to her death, terrified and helpless as any other human quarry, before he could feel secure again.

"Do you think I'm afraid to kill you?" he asked, seeming almost plaintively puzzled. "Believe me, if I pull the trigger my finger is touching, I won't even be questioned about your disappearance. The park authorities have been instructed by our grateful government to show me every consideration, in view of my past invaluable contributions to humanity, and in view of my present disability. No one would think to disturb me here because some foolish girl is reported lost in Melna Park . . ."

The thought-voice went on, its fury and bafflement filtered through a machine, sometimes oddly suggestive even of a ranting, angry machine. Now and then it blurred out completely, like a bad connection, resumed seconds later. Telzey drew her attention away from it. It was a distraction in her waiting for another open subconscious bridge to Robane's mind. Attempts to reach him more directly remained worse than useless. The machines also handled mind-stuff, but mechanically channeled, focused, and projected; the result was a shifting, flickering, nightmarish distortion of emanations in which Robane and his instruments seemed to blend in constantly changing patterns. She'd tried to force through it, had drawn back quickly, dazed and jolted again . . .

Every minute she gained here had improved her chances of escape, but she thought she wouldn't be able to stall him much longer. The possibility that a ranger patrol or somebody else might happen by just now, see her Cloudsplitter parked near the house, and come over to investigate, was probably slight, but Robane wouldn't be happy about it. If she seemed to remain intractable, he'd decide at some point to dispose of her at once.

So she mustn't seem too intractable. Since she wasn't replying, he would try something else to find out if she could be controlled. When he did, she would act frightened silly—which she was in a way, except that it didn't seem to affect her ability to think now— and do whatever he said except for one thing. After he turned off the paralysis field, he would order her to come to the house. She couldn't do that. Behind the entry door was a lock chamber. If she stepped inside, the door would close; and with the next breath she took she would have absorbed a full dose of the drug that let Robane's mind-instruments settle into contact with her. She didn't know what effect that would have. It might nullify her ability to maintain her psi screen and reveal her thoughts to Robane. If he knew what she had in mind, he would kill her on the spot. Or the drug might distort her on the telepathic level and end her chances of getting him under control.

"It's occurred to me," Robane's voice said, "that you may not be deliberately refusing to answer me. It's possible that you are unable to do it either because of the effect of the paralysis field or simply because of fear."

Telzey had been wondering when it would occur to him. She waited, new tensions growing up in her.

"I'll release you from the field in a moment," the

voice went on. "What happens then depends on how
well you carry out the instructions given you. If you
try any tricks, little psi, you'll be dead. I'm quite aware
you'll be able to move normally seconds after the field
is off. Make no move you aren't told to make. Do
exactly what you are told to do, and do it without
hesitation. Remember those two things. Your life
depends on them."

He paused, added, "The field is now off . . ."

Telzey felt a surge of strength and lightness all
through her. Her heart began to race. She refrained
carefully from stirring. After a moment, Robane's voice
said, "Touch nothing in the car you don't need to
touch. Keep your hands in sight. Get out of the car,
walk twenty feet away from it, and stop. Then face
the house."

Telzey climbed out of the car. She was shaky
throughout; but it wasn't as bad as she'd thought it
would be when she first moved again. It wasn't bad
at all. She walked on to the left, stopped, and looked
up at the orange-lit, screened windows in the upper
part of the house.

"Watch your car," Robane's voice told her.

She looked over at the Cloudsplitter. He'd turned
off the power neutralizer and the car was already
moving. It lifted vertically from the ground, began
gliding forward thirty feet up, headed in the direction of the forest beyond the house. It picked up
speed, disappeared over the trees.

"It will begin to change course when it reaches the
mountains," Robane's voice said. "It may start circling
and still be within the park when it is found. More
probably, it will be hundreds of miles away. Various
explanations will be offered for your disappearance
from it, apparently in midair, which needn't concern
us now . . . Raise your arms before you, little psi.
Spread them farther apart. Stand still."

Telzey lifted her arms, stood waiting. After an

instant, she gave a jerk of surprise. Her hands and arms, Dunker's watch on her wrist, the edges of the short sleeves of her shirt suddenly glowed white.

"Don't move!" Robane's voice said sharply. "This is a search-beam. It won't hurt you."

She stood still again, shifted her gaze downwards. What she saw of herself and her clothes and of a small patch of ground about her feet all showed the same cold, white glow, like fluorescing plastic. There was an eerie suggestion of translucence. She glanced back at her hands, saw the fine bones showing faintly as more definite lines of white in the glow. She felt nothing and the beam wasn't affecting her vision, but it was an efficient device. Sparks of heatless light began stabbing from her clothing here and there; within moments, Robane located half a dozen minor items in her pockets and instructed her to throw them away one by one, along with the watch. He wasn't taking chances on fashionably camouflaged communicators, perhaps suspected even this or that might be a weapon. Then the beam went off and he told her to lower her arms again.

"Now a reminder," his voice went on. "Perhaps you're unable to speak to me. And perhaps you could speak but think it's clever to remain silent in this situation. That isn't too important. But let me show you something. It will help you keep in mind that it isn't at all advisable to be too clever in dealing with me . . ."

Something suddenly was taking shape twenty yards away, between Telzey and the house; and fright flicked through her like fire and ice in the instant before she saw it was a projection placed a few inches above the ground. It was an image of Robane's killer, a big, bulky creature which looked bulkier because of the coat of fluffy, almost feathery fur covering most of it like a cloak. It was half crouched, a pair of powerful forelimbs stretched out through the cloak of fur. Ears like upturned horns projected from the sides of the head, and big, round, dark eyes, the eyes of a star-night hunter, were set in front above the sharply curved, serrated cutting beak.

The image faded within seconds. She knew what the creature was. The spooks had been, at one time, almost the dominant life form on this continent; the early human settlers hated and feared them for their unqualified liking for human flesh, made them a legend which haunted Orado's forests long after they had, in fact, been driven out of most of their territory. Even in captivity, from behind separating force fields, their flat, dark stares, their size, goblin appearance, and monkey quickness disturbed impressionable people.

"My hunting partner," Robane's voice said. "My other self. It is not pleasant, not at all pleasant, to know this is the shape that is following your trail at night in Melna Park. You had a suggestion of it this evening. Be careful not to make me angry again. Be quick to do what I tell you. Now come forward to the house."

Telzey saw the entry door in the garden slide open. Her heart began to beat heavily. She didn't move.

"Come to the house!" Robane repeated.

Something accompanied the words, a gush of heavy, subconscious excitement, somebody reaching for a craved drug . . . but Robane's drug was death. As she touched the excitement, it vanished. It was what she had waited for, a line to the unguarded levels of his mind. If it came again and she could hold it even for seconds—

It didn't come again. There was a long pause before Robane spoke.

"This is curious," his voice said slowly. "You refuse. You know you are helpless. You know what I can do. Yet you refuse. I wonder . . ."

He went silent. He was suspicious now, very. For a moment, she could almost feel him finger the trigger of his weapon. But the drug was there, in his reach. She was cheating him out of some of it. He wouldn't let her cheat him out of everything . . .

"Very well," the voice said. "I'm tired of you. I was interested in seeing how a psi would act in such a situation. I've seen. You're so afraid you can barely think. So run along. Run as fast as you can, little psi. Because I'll soon be following."

Telzey stared up at the windows. Let him believe she could barely think.

"Run!"

She whipped around, as if shocked into motion by the command, and ran, away from Robane's house, back in the direction of the plain to the north.

"I'll give you a warning," Robane's voice said, seeming to move along with her. "Don't try to climb a tree. We catch the ones who do that immediately. We can climb better than you can, and if the tree is big enough we'll come up after you. If the tree's too light to hold us, or if you go out where the branches are too thin, we'll simply shake you down. So keep running."

She glanced back as she came up to the first group of trees. The orange windows of the house seemed to be staring after her. She went in among the trees, out the other side, and now the house was no longer in sight.

"Be clever now," Robane's voice said. "We like the clever ones. You have a chance, you know. Perhaps somebody will see you before you're caught. Or you may think of some way to throw us off your track. Perhaps you'll be the lucky one who gets away. We'll be very, very sorry then, won't we? So do your best, little psi. Do your best. Give us a good run."

She flicked out a search-thought, touched Chomir's

mind briefly. The aircar was still coming, still on course, still too far away to do her any immediate good . . .

She ran. She was in as good condition as a fifteen-year-old who liked a large variety of sports and played hard at them was likely to get. But she had to cover five hundred yards to get beyond the range of Robane's house weapons, and on this broken ground it began to seem a long, long stretch. How much time would he give her? Some of those he'd hunted had been allowed a start of thirty minutes or more . . .

She began to count her steps. Robane remained silent. When she thought she was approaching the end of five hundred yards, there were trees ahead again. She remembered crossing over a small stream followed by a straggling line of trees as she came up to the house. That must be it. And in that case, she was beyond the five-hundred-yard boundary.

A hungry excitement swirled about her and was gone. She'd lashed at the feeling quickly, got nothing. Robane's voice was there an instant later.

"We're starting now . . ."

So soon? She felt shocked. He wasn't giving her even the pretense of a chance to escape. Dismay sent a wave of weakness through her as she ran splashing down into the creek. Some large animals burst out of the water on the far side, crashed through the bushes along the bank, and pounded away. Telzey hardly noticed them. Turn to the left, downstream, she thought. It was a fast little stream. The spook must be following by scent and the running water should wipe out her trail before it got here . . .

But others it had followed would have decided to turn downstream when they reached the creek. If it didn't pick up the trail on the far bank and found no human scent in the water coming down, it only had to go along the bank to the left until it either heard her in the water or reached the place where she'd left it.

They'd expect her, she told herself, to leave the water on the far side of the creek, not to angle back in the direction of Robane's house. Or would they? It seemed the best thing to try.

She went downstream as quickly as she could, splashing, stumbling on slippery rock, careless of noise for the moment. It would be a greater danger to lose time trying to be quiet. A hundred yards on, stout tree branches swayed low over the water. She could catch them, swing up, scramble on up into the trees.

Others would have tried that, too. Robane and his beast knew such spots, would check each to make sure it wasn't what she had done.

She ducked, gasping, under the low-hanging branches, hurried on. Against the starblaze a considerable distance ahead, a thicker cluster of trees loomed darkly. It looked like a sizable little wood surrounding the watercourse. It might be a good place to hide.

Others, fighting for breath after the first hard run, legs beginning to falter, would have had that thought.

Robane's voice said abruptly in her mind, "So you've taken to the water. It was your best move . . ."

The voice stopped. Telzey felt the first stab of panic. The creek curved sharply ahead. The bank on the left was steep, not the best place to get out. She followed it with her eyes. Roots sprouted out of the bare earth a little ahead. She came up to them, jumped to catch them, pulled herself up, and scrambled over the edge of the bank. She climbed to her feet, hurried back in the general direction of Robane's house, dropped into a cluster of tall grass. Turning, flattened out on her stomach, she lifted her head to stare back in the direction of the creek. There was an opening in the bushes on the other bank, with the clusterlight of the skyline showing through it. She watched that, breathing as softly as she could. It occurred to her that if a breeze was moving the wrong way, the spook might catch her scent on the air. But she didn't feel any breeze.

Perhaps a minute passed—certainly no more. Then a dark silhouette passed lightly and swiftly through the opening in the bushes she was watching, went on downstream. It was larger than she'd thought it would be when she saw its projected image; and that something so big should move in so effortless a manner, seeming to drift along the ground, somehow was jolting in itself. For a moment, Telzey had distinguished, or imagined she had distinguished, the big, round head held high, the pointed ears like horns. *Goblin,* her nerves screamed. A feeling of heavy dread flowed through her, seemed to drain away her strength. This was how the others had felt when they ran and crouched in hiding, knowing there was no escape from such a pursuer . . .

She made herself count off a hundred seconds, got to her feet, and started back on a slant towards the creek, to a point a hundred yards above the one where she had climbed from it. If the thing returned along this side of the watercourse and picked up her trail, it might decide she had tried to escape upstream. She got down quietly into the creek, turned downstream again, presently saw in the distance the wood which had looked like a good place to hide. The spook should be prowling among the trees there now, searching for her. She passed the curve where she had pulled herself up on the bank, waded on another hundred steps, trying to make no noise at all, almost certain from moment to moment she could hear or glimpse the spook on its way back. Then she climbed the bank on the right, pushed carefully through the hedges of bushes that lined it, and ran off into the open plain sloping up to the north.

❖         ❖         ❖

After perhaps a hundred yards, her legs began to lose the rubbery weakness of held-in terror. She was breathing evenly. The aircar was closer again and in not too many more minutes she might find herself out of danger. She didn't look back. If the spook was coming up behind her, she couldn't outrun it, and it wouldn't help to feed her fears by watching for shadows on her trail.

She shifted her attention to signs from Robane. He might be growing concerned by now and resort to his telescanners to look for her and guide his creature after her. There was nothing she could do about that. Now and then she seemed to have a brief awareness of him, but there had been no definite contact since he had spoken.

She reached a rustling grove, walked and trotted through it. As she came out the other side, a herd of graceful deer-like animals turned from her and sped with shadowy quickness across the plain and out of her range of vision. She remembered suddenly having heard that hunted creatures sometimes covered their trail by mingling with other groups of animals . . .

A few minutes later, she wasn't sure how well that was working. Other herds were around; sometimes she saw shadowy motion ahead or to right or left; then there would be whistles of alarm, the stamp of hoofs, and they'd vanish like drifting smoke, leaving the section of plain about her empty again. This was Robane's hunting ground; the animals here might be more alert and nervous than in other sections of the park. And perhaps, Telzey thought, they sensed she was the quarry tonight and was drawing danger towards them. Whatever the reason, they kept well out of her way. But she'd heard fleeing herds cross behind her a number of times, so they might in fact be breaking up her trail enough to make it more difficult to follow. She kept

scanning the skyline above the slope ahead, looking for the intermittent green flash of a moving
aircar or the sweep of its search-beam along the
ground. They couldn't be too far away.

She slowed to a walk again. Her legs and lungs
hadn't given out, but she could tell she was tapping
the final reserves of strength. She sent a thought to
Chomir's mind, touched it instantly and, at the same
moment, caught a glimpse of a pulsing green spark
against the starblaze, crossing down through a dip in
the slopes, disappearing beyond the wooded ground
ahead of her. She went hot with hope, swung to the
right, began running towards the point where the car
should show again.

They'd arrived. Now to catch their attention . . .

"Here!" she said sharply in the dog's mind.

It meant: "Here I am! Look for me! Come to me!"
No more than that. Chomir was keyed up enough
without knowing why. Any actual suggestion that she
was in trouble might throw him out of control.

She almost heard the deep, whining half-growl with
which he responded. It should be enough. Chomir
knew now she was somewhere nearby, and Rish and
the others would see it immediately in the way he
behaved. When the aircar reappeared, its search-beam
should be swinging about, fingering the ground to
locate her.

Telzey jumped down into a little gully, felt, with
a shock of surprise, her knees go soft with fatigue
as she landed, and clambered shakily out the other
side. She took a few running steps forward, came to
a sudden complete stop.

*Robane!* She felt him about, a thick, ugly excitement. It seemed the chance moment of contact for
which she'd been waiting, his mind open, unguarded.

She looked carefully around. Something lay beside
a cluster of bushes thirty feet ahead. It appeared to
be a big pile of wind-blown dry leaves and grass, but

its surface stirred with a curious softness in the
breeze. Then a wisp of acrid animal odor touched
Telzey's nostrils and she felt the hot-ice surge of deep
fright.

The spook lifted its head slowly out of its fluffed,
mottled mane and looked at her. Then it moved from
its crouched position ... a soundless shift a good
fifteen feet to the right, light as the tumbling of a
big ball of moss. It rose on its hind legs, the long
fur settling loosely about it like a cloak, and made
a chuckling sound of pleasure.

The plain seemed to explode about Telzey.

The explosion was in her mind. Tensions held too
long, too hard, lashed back through her in seething confusion at a moment when too much needed to be done
at once. Her physical vision went black; Robane's beast
and the starlit slope vanished. She was sweeping
through a topsy-turvy series of mental pictures and sensations. Rish's face appeared, wide-eyed, distorted with
alarm, the aircar skimming almost at ground level along
the top of a grassy rise, a wood suddenly ahead. *"Now!"*
Telzey thought. Shouts, and the car swerved up again.
Then a brief, thudding, jarring sensation underfoot ...

That was done.

She swung about to Robane's waiting excitement,
slipped through it into his mind. In an instant, her
awareness poured through a net of subconscious psi
channels that became half familiar as she touched
them. Machine static clattered, too late to dislodge
her. She was there. Robane, unsuspecting, looked out
through his creature's eyes at her shape on the plain,
hands locked hard on the instruments through which
he lived, experienced, murdered.

In minutes, Telzey thought, in minutes, if she was
alive minutes from now, she would have this mind—
unaware, unresistant, wide open to her—under control. But she wasn't certain she could check the spook

then through Robane. He had never attempted to
hold it back moments away from its kill.

Vision cleared. She stood on the slope, tight tendrils of thought still linking her to every significant
section of Robane's mind. The spook stared, hook-
beak lifted above its gaping mouth, showing the thick,
twisting tongue inside. Still upright, it began to move,
seemed to glide across the ground towards her. One
of its forelimbs came through the thick cloak of fur,
four-fingered paw raised, slashing retractile claws
extended, reaching out almost playfully.

Telzey backed slowly off from the advancing goblin
shape. For an instant, another picture slipped through
her thoughts . . . a blur of motion. She gave it no
attention. There was nothing she could do there now.

The goblin dropped lightly to a crouch. Telzey saw
it begin its spring as she turned and ran.

She heard the gurgling chuckle a few feet
behind her, but no other sound. She ran headlong
up the slope with all the strength she had left. In
another world, on another level of existence, she
moved quickly through Robane's mind, tracing out
the control lines, gathering them in. But her
thoughts were beginning to blur with fatigue. Bushy
shrubbery dotted the slope ahead. She could see
nothing else.

The spook passed her like something blown by the
wind through the grass. It swung around before her,
twenty feet ahead; and as she turned to the right, it
was suddenly behind her again, coming up quickly,
went by. Something nicked the back of her calf as it
passed—a scratch, not much deeper than a dozen or
so she'd picked up pushing through thorny growth
tonight. But this hadn't been a thorn. She turned left,
and it followed, herding her; dodged right, and it was
there, going past. Its touch seemed the lightest flick
again, but an instant later there was a hot, wet line
of pain down her arm. She felt panic gather in her

throat as it came up behind her once more. She stopped, turning to face it.

It stopped in the same instant, fifteen feet away, rose slowly to its full height, dark eyes staring, hooked beak open as if in silent laughter. Telzey watched it, gasping for breath. Streaks of foggy darkness seemed to float between them. Robane felt far away, beginning to slip from her reach. If she took another step, she thought, she would stumble and fall; then the thing would be on her.

The spook's head swung about. Its beak closed with a clack. The horn-ears went erect.

The white shape racing silently down the slope seemed unreal for a moment, something she imagined. She knew Chomir was approaching; she hadn't realized he was so near. She couldn't see the aircar's lights in the starblaze above, but it might be there. If they had followed the dog after he plunged out of the car, if they hadn't lost . . .

Chomir could circle Robane's beast, threaten it, perhaps draw it away from her, keep it occupied for minutes. She drove a command at him—another, quickly and anxiously, because he hadn't checked in the least; tried to slip into his mind and knew suddenly that Chomir, coming in silent fury, wasn't going to be checked or slowed or controlled by anything she did. The goblin uttered a monstrous, squalling scream of astounded rage as the strange white animal closed the last twenty yards between them; then it leaped aside with its horrid ease. Sick with dismay, Telzey saw the great forelimb flash from the cloak, strike with spread talons. The thudding blow caught Chomir, spun him around, sent him rolling over the ground. The spook sprang again to come down on its reckless assailant. But the dog was on his feet and away.

It was Chomir's first serious fight. But he came of generations of ancestors who had fought one another

and other animals and armed men in the arenas of
Askanam. Their battle cunning was stamped into his
genes. He had made one mistake, a very nearly fatal
one, in hurtling in at a dead run on an unknown
opponent. Almost within seconds, it became apparent that he was making no further mistakes.

Telzey saw it through a shifting blur of exhaustion.
As big a dog as Chomir was, the squalling goblin must
weigh nearly five times as much, looked ten times
larger with its fur-mane bristling about it. Its kind had
been forest horrors to the early settlers. Its forelimbs
were tipped with claws longer than her hands and
the curved beak could shear through muscle and bone
like a sword. Its uncanny speed . . .

Now somehow it seemed slow. As it sprang, slashing down, something white and low flowed around
and about it with silent purpose. Telzey understood
it then. The spook was a natural killer, developed by
nature to deal efficiently with its prey. Chomir's breed
were killers developed by man to deal efficiently with
other killers.

He seemed locked to the beast for an instant, high
on its shoulder, and she saw the wide, dark stain on
his flank where the spook's talons had struck. He
shook himself savagely. There was an ugly, snapping
sound. The spook screeched like a huge bird. She saw
the two animals locked together again, then the spook
rolling over the ground, the white shape rolling with
it, slipping away, slipping back. There was another
screech. The spook rolled into a cluster of bushes.
Chomir followed it in.

A white circle of light settled on the thrashing
vegetation, shifted over to her. She looked up, saw
Rish's car gliding down through the air, heard voices
calling her name—

She followed her contact thoughts back to Robane's
mind, spread out through it, sensing at once the
frantic grip of his hands on the instrument controls.

For Robane, time was running out quickly. He had been trying to turn his beast away from the dog, force it to destroy the human being who could expose him. He had been unable to do it. He was in terrible fear. But he could accomplish no more through the spook. She felt his sudden decision to break mind-contact with the animal to avoid the one experience he had always shunned—going down with another mind into the shuddering agony of death.

His right hand released the control it was clutching, reached towards a switch.

"No," Telzey said softly to the reaching hand.

It dropped to the instrument board. After a moment, it knotted, twisted about, began to lift again.

"No."

Now it lay still. She considered. There was time enough.

Robane believed he would die with the spook if he couldn't get away from it in time. She thought he might be right; she wouldn't want to be in his mind when it happened, if it came to that.

There were things she needed to learn from Robane. The identity of the gang which had supplied him with human game was one; she wanted that very much. Then she should look at the telepathic level of his mind in detail, find out what was wrong in there, why he hadn't been able to use it . . . some day, she might be able to do something with a half-psi like Gikkes. And the mind-machines—if Robane had been able to work with them, not really understanding what he did, she should be able to employ similar devices much more effectively. Yes, she had to carefully study his machines—

She released Robane's hand. It leaped to the switch, pulled it back. He gave a great gasp of relief.

For a moment, Telzey was busy. A needle of psi energy flicked knowingly up and down channels, touching here, there, shriveling, cutting, blocking . . . Then it was done. Robane, half his mind gone in an instant, unaware of it, smiled blankly at the instrument panel in front of him. He'd live on here, dimmed and harmless, cared for by machines, unwitting custodian of other machines, of memories that had to be investigated, of a talent he'd never known he had.

"I'll be back," Telzey told the smiling, dull thing, and left it.

She found herself standing on the slope. It had taken only a moment, after all. Dunker and Valia were running towards her. Rish had just climbed out of the aircar settled forty feet away, its search-beam fixed on the thicket where the spook's body jerked back and forth as Chomir, jaws locked on its crushed neck, shook the last vestiges of life from it with methodical fury.

# V: Sleep No More

Three weeks passed before Telzey returned to Robane's house.

Her encounter with the spook created very little stir. She'd asked her companions not to talk about it, on the ground that it would upset her family if they learned she'd been in danger. Some of the group felt it was a shame to keep so thrilling an adventure a secret, but they'd agreed. The park officials wanted no publicity either. The only news mention of the incident was that a spook, which somehow had found its way from one of the northern wildlife preserves into Melna Park, had been killed there by a visitor's guard dog, and that the park was being carefully scanned to make sure no more of the dangerous animals had strayed in. Telzey's story to her friends was that there'd been a malfunction in the Cloud-splitter. The car had settled inertly to the ground, and when she got out to do something about it, the malfunction apparently cut out again, and the Cloud-splitter floated up out of her reach before she could stop it and drifted away. She'd started walking back to Cil Canyon, and presently found the spook on her trail. The Cloudsplitter was located by a police car next day, fifty miles beyond the park borders, and restored to its owner. Before leaving the park, Telzey quietly recovered Dunker's watch and the other articles Robane had made her discard at the house.

The only people who could see a connection between the dead spook and Robane were the smugglers who'd provided him with an animal of that kind, and they'd have no interest in the fact that it was dead. If anyone who might be associated with Robane in his general work with psi machines became aware of his present condition, the mental damage would be attributed to a miscalculated experiment. Psi machines were considered uncertain devices in that respect. In any case, there was nothing to link Telzey to him. Nor was there really any reason why she couldn't go quietly back to Melna Park at any time to conclude her investigation. She wouldn't need to come within half a mile of the house for that.

She kept putting it off. She wasn't quite sure why. When the weekend came around, she simply found herself unwilling to make the trip. Robane was unfinished business. It wasn't usually her way at all to leave unfinished business lying around. But she told herself she'd take care of it the following week.

One night then she had a dream. It was an uncomfortable, sweaty, nightmarish sort of dream, though nothing much really happened. It seemed to go on for some time. She appeared to be floating in the air near Robane's house, watching it from various angles, aware that Robane watched her in turn, hating her for what she'd done to him and waiting for a chance to destroy her. In the dream, Telzey reminded herself quite reasonably that it wasn't possible—Robane couldn't remember what she'd done or anything about her; he wouldn't recognize her if she were standing before him. Then she realized suddenly that it wasn't Robane but the house itself which watched her with such spiteful malice, and that something was about to happen to her. She woke up with a start of fright.

That settled it. She lay awake a while, considering. A weekend was coming up again. She could fly to Melna Park after her last scheduled lecture in the afternoon, and register at a park hotel. She'd have two full days if necessary to wind up matters at Robane's house. That certainly would be time enough. She'd extract the remaining information she wanted from him, then see to it that somebody among the park authorities discovered a good reason to pay the recluse a visit at his home. When they saw the condition he was in, they'd transfer him to an institution; and Robane shouldn't be disturbing her sleep again.

He did, however, that night in her room at the park hotel. Or something did. She'd retired soon after dinner, wanting to get off to an early start, found then that she wasn't at all sleepy, tuned in somnomusic, switched on the window screen, and went over to it in the darkened room. She stood there a while, looking out. In the cluster light, Melna Park sloped away, dim and vast, toward the northern mountains. Robane's house lay behind a fold of the mountains. At the restricted pace possible in the park, it would take her almost four hours to get to the house from the hotel tomorrow—twice the time she'd spent crossing half a continent from Pehanron College in the evening.

The music was producing drowsiness in her, but tensions seemed to fight it. It was almost an hour before she got to bed and fell asleep, and it turned then into an uncomfortable night. There were periods of disagreeable dreaming, of which she could recall only scraps when she woke up. For the most part, she napped fitfully; kept coming awake. Something in her simply didn't want to relax; and as she began to go to sleep and her mental screens loosened normally, it drew them abruptly tight, bringing her back to weary alertness. She was up at daybreak at last, heavy-lidded and irritable. But a cold shower opened her eyes, and after she'd had breakfast, she seemed reasonably refreshed.

Ten minutes later, she was on her way to Robane's house through a breezy late-autumn morning. Melna Park was famed for varied and spectacular color changes in its vegetation as winter approached, and the tourist traffic was much heavier now than three weeks ago. Almost everywhere Telzey looked, aircars floated past, following the rolling contours of the ground. The Cloudsplitter moved along at the steady thirty miles an hour to which it was restricted. She'd slipped the canopy down; sun warmth seeped through her, while a chilled wind intermittently whipped her hair about her cheeks. Nighttime tensions grew vague and unreal. The relaxation which had eluded Telzey at the hotel came to her, and she was tempted to ground the car and settle down for an hour's nap in the sunshine before going on. But she wanted to reach the house early enough to be finished with Robane before evening.

Near noon, she reached the series of mile-wide plateaus dropping from the point where Cil Canyon cut through the mountains to the southern forests where Robane's house stood. She circled in toward the house, brought it presently into the car's viewscreen. It looked precisely as she remembered seeing it in the cluster light, neat, trim, quiet. A maintenance robot moved slowly about in the garden.

She considered relaxing her screens and directing a probing thought to Robane's mind from where she was. But she had most of the day left, and a remnant of uneasiness made her wary. She dropped the car behind a rise which hid Robane's house from her, moved on back of the rise for about a mile and settled to the ground at the edge of a stand of trees. Carrying a pocket telscreen, she walked to the top of the rise and across it, threading her way among the trees until she came to a point from where she could watch the house without being picked up in scanning devices from there.

She kept the house area in the telscreen for about ten minutes. The only sign of life was the tending machine in the garden. That was out of sight in some shrubbery for a while, then emerged and began moving back and forth across one of the lawns while a silvery mist arising from the shrubbery indicated a watering system had been turned on. Finally the robot trundled to the side of the house and paused before it. A wide door slid open in the wall, and the machine rolled inside.

Telzey put the telscreen down. She'd had a look through the door before it closed. A large aircar stood behind it. Robane, as was to be expected in his present state, should be at home.

And now, she decided, a light—a very light—probe. Just enough to make quite sure Robane was, in fact, as she'd left him, that there'd been no unforeseen developments of any kind around here.

Leaning against the sun-warm trunk of a tall tree she closed her eyes and thinned the screens about her mind, let them open out. She felt a sudden tug of anxiety resistance, but the screens stayed open. The blended whispers of life currents about her began to flow into her awareness.

Everything seemed normal . . . She flicked a thread of thought down to the forest then, to Robane's house, touched for a moment the patterns she remembered.

Something like a shout flashed through her mind. Not words, nothing even partly verbalized; nevertheless, it was a clear sharp command, accompanied by a gust of hate like a curse. The hate was directed at her. The command—

In the split instant of shock as her screens contracted into a tight hard shield, she'd seemed aware of a blurred dark image rushing toward her. Then the image, the command-and-hate impressions, the touch of Robane's mind, were blocked off together by the shield.

Telzey opened her eyes, glanced about. For long seconds, she remained motionless. The trees stirred above as a breeze rustled past. Here in the world of material reality, nothing seemed changed or different. But what had she run into at Robane's house?

A sound reached her . . . the rolling thunder of explosion. It faded away, echoing across the plain.

It seemed to have come from the forest to the south. Telzey listened a moment, moved forward until she could look out from behind the trees.

An ugly rolling cloud of yellow smoke partly concealed the area where the house had stood. But it was clear that house and garden had been violently obliterated.

And that, Telzey thought numbly, was in part her answer.

By the time she got back to the Cloudsplitter and lifted it from the ground, tourist aircars were gliding in cautiously toward the site of the explosion. A ranger car screamed down out of the sky, passed above her and vanished. Telzey remained behind the rise and continued to move to the west. She was almost certain that whoever had blown up Robane in his house wasn't physically in the area. But there was no need to expose herself any more than she'd already done.

Robane had been used as bait—bait to trap a psi. The fact that he'd been destroyed then indicated that whoever set the trap believed the psi for whom it was intended had been caught. And there must be a reason for that belief. In whatever she did now, she'd better be extremely careful.

She brought the thought impressions she'd recorded back into awareness, examined them closely.

They were brief but strong and vivid. She began to distinguish details she hadn't consciously noted in the instant of sensing them. This psi was human, must be; and yet the flavor of the thought forms suggested almost an alien species. They were heavy with arrogance as if the psi himself felt he was different from and superior to human beings. The thrust of hard power carrying the impressions had been as startling to her as the sudden angry roar of an animal nearby. She recalled feeling that a curse was being pronounced on her.

And blended in was a communication—not intended for her, and not too clear. It was, Telzey thought, the sort of mental shortcode which developed among associated telepaths: a flick of psi which might transmit an involved meaning. She could guess the basic meaning here. Success! The quarry was snared! He'd had one or more companions. His own kind, whatever it was.

Finally, the third part, the least clear section of the thought structure. It had death in it. Her death. It was a command; and she was almost certain it had been directed at the indistinct shape she'd seemed to glimpse rushing toward her. Something that might have been a large animal.

Her death . . . how? Telzey swallowed uncomfortably. They might have been involved with the ring which had catered to Robane's criminal inclinations—minds like that would have no objection to delivering one human being to another, to be hunted down and killed for sport. But psis would have recognized a special value in Robane. He was a precision instrument that could provide them with machines to extend and amplify their powers. His inventive genius had been at the disposal of a telepath who'd set him problems and left him to work them out, not knowing why he did it, or for whose benefit, in the solitude of Melna Park.

She'd put an end to Robane's usefulness and might presently have come on clues pointing to them in the unconscious recesses of his mind if they hadn't discovered what had been done. They knew it was the work of another psi. She'd sealed most of Robane's memories away but left them intact; and that told them she planned to return to look for more information. They could have destroyed Robane at once, but they wanted to dispose of the unidentified meddler. So they'd set up the trap with Robane's mind as the bait. The psi who touched that mind again would spring the trap. And, some twenty minutes ago, cautious and light as her touch had been, she'd sprung it.

Immediately afterwards, she'd locked her screens. In doing it, she might have escaped whatever was planned for her. But she had to accept the probability that she still was in the trap—and she didn't yet know what it was.

The Cloudsplitter went gliding at its thirty miles an hour across the upper plateaus of the plain, a hundred feet above the ground. The southern forest where the house had stood had sunk out of sight. The flanks of the mountains curved away ahead. Telzey turned the car in farther toward them. Another car slipped past at the edge of her vision, half a mile to the left. She had an impulse to follow it, to remain near other people. But she kept the Cloudsplitter on its course. The company of others would bring her no safety, and mingling with them might distract her attention dangerously.

She set the car on automatic control, sat gazing at the mountains through the windshield. The other impression at the moment of touching Robane's mind—the shape like an animal's—it might have been a hallucination, her own mind's symbol of some death energy directed at her. Psi could kill swiftly, could be used as a weapon by minds which understood its use for that purpose and could handle the forces they turned on another. But if that had been the trap, it seemed to her she would have interpreted it differently—not as a moving shadow, a half-glimpsed animal shape, an image darting toward her.

What else could it be? Telzey shook her bead. She didn't know, and she couldn't guess. She could find out; eventually she'd have to find out. But not yet.

She glanced at the car clock. Give it another hour. Evidently they hadn't identified her physically; but it could do no harm to place more physical distance between herself and the area of Robane's house before she made any revealing moves. Mentally, she should have seemed to vanish for them as her shield closed. The difficulty was that the shield couldn't stay closed indefinitely.

An hour later, the effects of having passed a night with very little sleep were becoming noticeable. There were moments of reduced wakefulness and physical lassitude of which she'd grow suddenly aware. The nearest ranger car would have provided her with a stimulant if she'd put out a communicator call for one, but her enemies might have means of monitoring events in the park she didn't know about. It didn't seem at all advisable to draw attention to herself in that way, or in any other way. She'd simply have to remain alert long enough to get this situation worked out.

The test she intended was a simple one. The psi shield would flash open, instantly be closed again. During that moment, her perceptions, fully extended, would be set to receive two impressions: thought patterns of the telepath who'd laid a trap for her, and the animal shape involved with the trap. If either was still in her mental vicinity, some trace would he obtained, however faintly. If neither was there, she could begin to believe she'd eluded them. Not indefinitely; psis could determine who had destroyed

Robane's effectiveness if they put in enough work on it. But that would be another problem. Unless they were as intently prepared as she was to detect some sign from her now, the momentary exposure of her mind should pass unnoticed.

The shield flicked open, flicked shut, as her sensitized perceptions made their recording. Telzey sat still for a moment then, feeling the heavy drumming of fear.

Slowly, like an afterimage, she let the recorded picture form again in awareness.

A dark beast shape. What kind of beast she didn't know. Something like a great uncouth baboon—a big heavy head, strong body supported on four huge hand-paws.

As the shield opened, she had the feeling of seeing it near her, three-dimensional, every detail clearly etched though it stood in a vague nothingness. The small red eyes stared in her direction. And short as the moment of exposure was, she was certain she'd seen it start in recognition, begin moving toward her, before it vanished beyond the shield again.

What was it? A projection insinuated into her mind by the other telepath in the instant of contact between them—something she was supposed to develop to her own destruction now?

She didn't think so. It seemed too real, too alertly, menacingly, alive. In some way she'd seen what was there—the vague animal shape she'd glimpsed—nearby and no longer vague. In physical space, it might be hundreds of miles away; or perhaps it was nowhere in that sense at present. In the other reality they shared, she hadn't drawn away from it. After its attention was turned on her, it had waited while she was concealed by her shield, moved closer at the brief new impression it received of her mind. . . . What would happen when, in its manner, it reached her, touched her?

She didn't know the answer to that. She let the image fade, began searching for traces of the telepathic mind associated with it. After long seconds, she knew nothing had been recorded in her perceptions there. The psi was gone. He'd prepared the trap, set the creature on her; then apparently turned away—as if confident he'd done all that needed to be done to dispose of her.

The thought was briefly more chilling than the waiting beast image. But if it was only an animal she had to deal with, Telzey told herself, escape might be an easier matter than it would have been if minds like the one she had encountered had remained on her trail.

The animal still seemed bad enough. She'd never heard of a creature which tracked down prey by sensing mental emanations, as this one evidently did. It might be a native of some unrecorded world, brought to the Hub for the specific purpose of turning it into a hunter of human psis—psis who could make trouble for its masters. It knew about mind shields. Either it had dealt with such defenses in its natural state, or it had been trained to handle them. At any rate, it seemed quite aware that it need only wait with a predator's alert patience until the quarry's shield relaxed. As hers would eventually. She couldn't stay awake indefinitely; and asleep she didn't have enough control to keep so steady and relentless a watcher from detecting mental activity.

It had been a trap in several ways then. If she'd entered Robane's house, she would have vanished in the explosion with him. Since she'd checked first, they'd turned this thing on her. It was either to destroy her outright or force her into behavior that would identify her to its masters—and she had to get rid of it before the need to sleep brought down her defenses.

She felt the psi bolt begin to assemble itself. No ordinary brief sharp slash of psi was likely to serve here. She'd turn the heaviest torrent of energy she could channel on her uncanny pursuer. Something like a black electric swirling about her was sending ripples over her skin. Not at all a pleasant sensation, but she let it develop. It would be to her disadvantage to wait any longer; and since the psis weren't around themselves, this was as good a place as any for the encounter. The Cloudsplitter was drifting up a wide valley into the higher ranges of the park. There was a chill in the breeze and few tourists about. At the moment she saw only three aircars, far ahead.

The energy pattern grew denser, became a shuddering thunder. She gathered it in, held it aimed like a gun, let it build up until she was trembling almost unbearably with its violence, then abruptly released her shield.

Almost at once, seeing the dark shape plunge at her through the nothing-space of psi, she knew that on this beast it wasn't going to work. Energy smashed about it but found no entry point; it wasn't being touched. She expended the bolt's fury as the shape rushed up, snapped the shield shut before it reached her—immediately found herself slewing the Cloudsplitter around in a sharp turn as if to avoid a physical collision. There was a sound then, a deep bubbling howl, which chilled her through and through.

Glancing around, she saw it for an instant twenty feet behind the car—no mind image, but a thick powerful animal body, plunging head downward, stretched out as if it were diving, through the air of Melna Park. Then it vanished.

It was a psi creature whose natural prey were other psi creatures, she thought; that was why she hadn't been able to touch it. Its species had a developed immunity to such defensive blasts and could ignore them. It had a sense through which it traced out and approached the minds of prospective victims, and it had the psi ability to flick itself across space when it knew by the mind contact where they were to be found. For the kill it needed only physical weapons—the strength of its massive body, its great teeth and the broad flat nails of the reaching beast hands which had seemed only inches from her when the shield shut them from view. If she hadn't swerved aside in that instant, the thing would have crashed down into the car and torn the life out of her moments later.

Her attempt to confront it had made the situation more immediately dangerous. Handling that flood of deadly energy had drained her strength; and a kind of dullness was settling on her now, composed in part of growing fatigue and in part of a puzzled wonder that she really seemed able to do nothing to get away from the thing. It was some minutes before she could push the feeling aside and get her thoughts again into some kind of order.

The creature's dip through space seemed to have confused it temporarily; at any rate, it had lost too much contact with her to materialize near her again, though she didn't doubt it was still very close mentally. There were moments when she thought she could sense its presence just beyond the shield. She'd had a respite, but no more than that. It probably wasn't even a very intelligent animal; a species with its abilities and strength wouldn't need much mental equipment to get along in its world. But she was caught in a game which was being played by the animal's rules, not hers, and there still seemed no way to get around them.

Some time past the middle of the afternoon, she edged the Cloudsplitter down into a cluster of thickets on sloping ground, brushing through the vegetation until the car was completely concealed. She shut off its engines and climbed out, stood swaying unsteadily for a moment, then turned and pushed her way out of the thickets.

If she'd remained sitting in the car, she would have

been asleep in minutes. By staying on her feet, she might gain another period of time to work out the solution. But she wasn't far from the point where she'd have to call the park rangers and ask them to get a fix on her and come to her help. Stimulants could keep her awake for several days.

At that point, she would have invited danger from a new source. A public appeal for help from someone in Melna Park could be a beacon to her enemies; she had to count on the possibility that they waited alertly for just such an indication that their hunter had the quarry pinned down. She might be identified very quickly then.

But to try to stay awake on her own for even another fifteen or twenty minutes could be fatal. The thing was *near*! A dozen times she'd been on the verge of drifting into a half-dreaming level where outside reality and the universe of psi seemed to blend, and had been jolted awake by a suddenly growing sense of the psi beast's presence.

Getting out of the car and on her feet had roused her a little. The cold of the mountain air produced a further stimulating effect. She'd come far up into a region of the park which already seemed touched by winter. It might have been almost half an hour since she'd last seen a tourist car or any other indication of humanity on the planet.

She stood looking around, rubbing her arms with her hands to warm them. She was above a rounded dip in the mountains between two adjoining ridges. Hip-high brown grass and straggling trees filled the dip. A swift narrow stream wound through it. She'd grounded the car three quarters of the way up the western side. The far side was an almost vertical rock wall, festooned with yellow cobwebs of withering vines. That half of the dip was still bathed in sunlight coming over the top of the ridge behind her. Her side was in shadow.

She shivered in the chill, shook her head to drive away another wave of drowsiness. She seemed unable to concentrate on the problem of the psi beast. Her thoughts shifted to the sun-warmed rocks she'd crossed at the top of the ridge as she turned the Cloudsplitter down into the little valley.

She pictured herself sitting there, warmed by the sun. It was a convincing picture. In imagination she felt the sun on her shoulders and back, the warm rock beneath her, saw the dry thorny fall growth about—

Her eyes flickered, widened thoughtfully. After a moment, she brought the picture back into her mind.

I'm here, she thought. I'm sitting in the sun. I'm half asleep, nodding, feeling the warmth—forgetting I'm in danger. The wind blows over the rocks, and the bushes are rustling all around me . . .

She relaxed the shield—"I'm here, Bozo!"—closed it.

She stood in the shadow of the western ridge, shivering and chilled, listening. Far above, for a moment, there'd been noises as if something plunged heavily about in the growth at the top of the ridge. Then the noises ended abruptly.

Telzey's gaze shifted down into the dip between the ridges, followed the course of the little stream up out of the shadows to a point where it ran between flat sandy banks, glittering and sparkling in the afternoon sun—held there.

And now I'm *here*, she thought, and nodded down at the little stream. I'm sitting in warm sand, in the sun again, sheltered from the wind, listening to the friendly water—

The shield opened. For an instant.

"I'm here!"

Looking down from the shaded slope, shield sealed tight, she saw, for the second time that day, Bozo the beast appear in Melna Park, half in the stream, half out. Its heavy head swung this way and that; it leaped forward, wheeled, glared about, plunged suddenly out of sight among the trees. For an instant, she heard its odd howling voice, like amplified drunken human laughter, furious with frustrated eagerness.

Telzey leaned back against the tree behind her and closed her eyes. Drowsiness rolled in immediately in sweet heavy treacherous waves. She shook her head, drove it back.

Darkness, she thought. Darkness, black and cold.

Black, black all around me—because I've fallen asleep, Bozo. Now you can get me—

Blackness closed in on her mind like a rush of wind. The shield slipped open.

*"Bozo! I'm HERE!"*

In the blackness, Bozo's image flashed up before her, jaws wide, red eyes blazing, great arms sweeping out to seize her.

The shield snapped shut.

Eyes still closed, Telzey swayed against the tree, listening to the echoes of the second explosion she'd heard today. This one had been short and sharp, monstrously loud, like a thunderbolt slamming into the earth a hundred feet from her.

She shook her head, opened her eyes, and looked across the dip. The cliff face on the eastern side had changed its appearance. A jagged dark fissure showed in it, beginning at the top, extending halfway down to the valley. Puffs of mineral dust still drifted out of the fissure into the open air.

She'd wondered what would happen if something more than five hundred pounds of solid animal materialized, suddenly deep inside solid rock. She'd expected it might be something like this. This time, Bozo hadn't been able to flick back into no-space again.

"Goodbye, Bozo!" she said aloud, across the dip. "I won't miss you at all!"

That had been one part of it, she thought.

And now the other.

The shield thinned again, opened out. And stayed open—one minute, two minutes, three—as her perceptions spread, searching for impressions of the psi mind that had cursed her with Bozo, long, long hours ago, at Robane's house. That mind, or any mind like it.

And there was nothing. Nowhere around here, for many miles at least, was anyone thinking of her at the moment, giving her any attention at all.

Then you've lost me for now, she told them. She turned, stumbling, her balance not too good at the moment on the rocky ground, and pushed back through the bushes to the point where she'd left the Cloudsplitter. A minute later, she'd lifted the car above the ridges, swung it around to the south. Its canopy was closed and she was luxuriously soaking in the warmth of the heaters. She wanted to go to sleep very badly now, but there was one thing still to be done. It was nearly finished.

One section, a tiny section, of her mind was forming itself into an alarm system. It would remain permanently on guard against psis of the kind who'd nearly trapped her, for good. At the slightest, most distant indication that minds like that were about, long before she became consciously aware of them, her screens would lock into a shield and she would know why.

It was necessary. There was no reason to believe she was done with them. They'd relied on their trap; and it had failed. But they could go back now to the night Robane's spook had been killed and try to find out who'd been involved in that. She'd covered herself as well as she could. It would involve a great deal of probing around in the minds of park personnel, a detailed checking of visitors' registers at the entrance stations; but eventually they could work out a line on the psi who'd trespassed on their operation and locate her. If she were doing it herself, it shouldn't take more than two weeks. She had to assume it would take them no longer.

Telzey felt her new alarm system complete itself, reached over and set the Cloudsplitter on the automatic controls which would guide it back down through the mountains into the warm southern plains of Melna Park to drift along with other tourist cars. Later, she thought, she'd decide what she'd have to be doing about the psis within the next two weeks. Later—

She slumped back gently in the seat and was instantly asleep.

# VI: The Lion Game

## Chapter 1

Telzey was about to sit down for a snack in her bungalow before evening classes when the ring she'd worn on her left forefinger for the past week gave her a sting.

It was a fairly emphatic sting. Emphatic enough to have brought her out of a sound sleep if she'd happened to be sleeping. She grimaced, pulled off the ring, rubbed her finger, slipped the ring back on, went to the ComWeb and tapped a button.

Elsewhere on the grounds of Pehanron College several other ComWebs started burring a special signal. One or the other of them would now be switched on, and somebody would listen to what she had to say. She'd become used to that; the realization didn't disturb her.

What she said to her course computer was, "This is Telzey Amberdon. Cancel me for both classes tonight."

The computer acknowledged. Winter rains had been pounding against Pehanron's weather shields throughout the day. Telzey got into boots, long coat and gloves, wrapped a scarf around her head, and went out to the carport at the back of the bungalow. A few minutes later, her car slid out of Pehanron's main gate, switched on its fog beams and arrowed up into a howling storm.

Somebody would be following her through the dark sky. She'd got used to that, too.

She went into a public ComWeb booth not long after leaving the college and dialed a number. The screen lit up and a face appeared.

"Hello, Klayung," she said. "I got your signal. I'm calling from Beale."

"I know," said Klayung. He was an executive of the Psychology Service, old, stringy, mild-mannered. "Leave the booth, turn left, walk down to the corner. There's a car waiting."

"All right," Telzey said. "Anything else?"

"Not till I see you."

It was raining as hard on Beale as on Pehanron, and this section of the town had no weather shielding. Head bent, Telzey ran down the street to the corner. The door to the back compartment of a big aircar standing there opened as she came up. She slipped inside. The door closed.

Clouds blotted out the lights of Beale below as she was fishing tissues from her purse to dry her face. The big car was a space job though it didn't look like one. She could see the driver silhouetted beyond the partition. They were alone in the car.

She directed a mental tap at the driver, touched a mind shield, standard Psychology Service type. There was no flicker of response or recognition, so he was no psi-operator.

Telzey settled back on the seat. Life had become

a rather complicated business these days. She'd reported her experiences in Melna Park to the Psychology Service, which, among other things, handled problems connected with psi and did it quietly to avoid disturbing the public. The Service people went to work on the information she could give them. While she waited for results from that quarter, she had some matters to take care of herself.

Until now, her psi armament had seemed adequate. She should be able to wind up her law studies at Pehanron in another year, and she'd intended to wait till then before giving serious attention to psi and what could be done with it—or, at any rate, to what she could do with it.

Clearly, that idea had better be dropped at once! Half a psi talent could turn into a dangerous gift when it drew the attention of others who didn't stick to halfway measures. She'd made a few modifications immediately. When she locked her screens into a shield now, they stayed locked without further attention, whether she was drowsy, wide awake or sound asleep, until she decided to open them again. *That* particular problem wouldn't recur! What she needed, however, was a general crash course in dealing with unfriendly mentalities of more than average capability. The Service might be willing to train her, but not necessarily along the lines she wanted. Besides, she preferred not to become too obligated to them.

There was a psi she knew, an independent like herself, who should have the required experience, if she could get him to share it. Sams Larking wasn't exactly a friend. He was, in fact, untrustworthy, unethical, underhanded and sneaky. The point nevertheless was that he was psi-sneaky in a highly accomplished manner, and packed a heavy mind clout. Telzey looked him up.

"Why should I help make you any tougher than you are?" Sams inquired.

She explained that Service operators had been giving her too much attention lately. She didn't like the idea of having somebody prying around her like that.

Sams grunted. He hated the Psychology Service.

"Been up to something they don't approve of, eh?" he said. "All right. Let's see if we can't have a few surprises ready for them the next time. You want to be able to spot them without letting them spot you, or send them home with lumps—that kind of thing?"

"That kind of thing," Telzey agreed. "I particularly want to learn how to work through my own screens. I've noticed you're very good at that. . . . The lumps could be sort of permanent, too!"

Sams looked briefly startled. "Getting rather ferocious, aren't you?" He studied her. "Well, we'll see how much you can handle. It can't be done in an hour or two, you know. Drop in at the ranch first thing this weekend, and we'll give it a couple of days. The house is psi-blocked, in case somebody comes snooping."

He added, "I'll behave. Word of honor! This will be business—if I can sharpen you up enough, you might be useful to me some day. Get a good night's rest before you come. I'll work you till you're begging to quit."

Work her relentlessly he did. Telzey didn't ask for time out. She was being drilled through techniques it might have taken her months to develop by herself. They discovered she could handle them. Then something went wrong.

She didn't know immediately what it was. She looked over at Sams.

He was smiling, a bit unpleasantly.

"Controlled, aren't you?"

Telzey felt a touch of apprehension. She considered. "Yes," she said, "I am. I must be! But—"

She hesitated. Sams nodded.

"You've been under control for the past half-hour. You wouldn't know it now if I hadn't let you know it—and you still don't understand how it's being done, so there's nothing you can do about it, is there?" He grinned suddenly, and Telzey felt the psi controls she hadn't been able to sense till then release her.

"Just a demonstration, this time!" Sams said. "Don't let yourself get caught again. Get a few hours' sleep, and we'll go on. You're a good student."

Around the middle of the second day, he said, "You've done fine! There really isn't much more I can do for you. But now a special gimmick. I never expected to show it to anyone, but let's see if you can work it. It takes plenty of coordination. Screens tight, both sides. You scan. If I spot you, you get jolted so hard your teeth rattle!"

After a few seconds, she said, "I'm there."

Sams nodded.

"Good! I can't tell it. Now I'll leave you an opening, just a flash. You're to try to catch it and slam me at the same instant."

"Well, wait a moment!" Telzey said. "Supposing I don't just try—I *do* it?"

"Don't worry. I'll block. Watch out for the counter!"

Sams's screen opening flicked through her awareness five seconds later. She slammed. But, squeamishly perhaps, she held back somewhat on the bolt.

It took her an hour to bring Sams around. He sat up groggily at last.

"How do you feel?" she asked.

He shook his head. "Never mind. Goodbye! Go home. You've graduated. I'm a little sorry for the Service."

Telzey knew she hadn't given the Service much to work on, but there were a few possible lines of general investigation. Since the Melna Park psis apparently had set Robane the task of developing psi machines

for them, they should be interested in psi machines
generally. They might, or might not, be connected with
the criminal ring with which he'd had contacts; if they
were, they presumably controlled it. And, of course,
they definitely did make use of a teleporting creature,
of which there seemed to be no record otherwise, to
kill people.

She'd been able to add one other thing about them
which could be significant. They might be a mutant
strain of humanity. The impressions of the thought
forms she'd retained seemed to have a distinctive
quality she'd never sensed in human minds before.

A machine copied the impressions from her
memory. They were analyzed, checked against Service files. They did have a distinctive quality, and it
was one which wasn't on record. Special investigators with back-up teams began to scan Orado system-
atically, trying to pick up mental traces which might
match the impressions, while outfits involved in psi
technology, along with assorted criminal organizations,
were scrutinized for indications of telepathic control.
Neither approach produced results.

The Service went on giving Orado primary attention but extended its investigations next to the Hub
worlds in general. There the sheer size of the Hub's
populations raised immense difficulties. Psi machines
were regarded by many as a coming thing; on a
thousand worlds, great numbers of people currently
were trying to develop effective designs. Another
multitude, of course, was involved in organized crime.
Eccentric forms of murder, including a variety which
conceivably could have been carried out by Telzey's
psi beasts, were hardly uncommon. Against such a
background, the secretive psis might remain invisible
indefinitely.

"Nevertheless," Klayung, who was in charge of the
Service operation, told Telzey, "we may be getting a
pattern! It's not too substantial, but it's consistent. If

it indicates what it seems to, the people you became involved with are neither a local group nor a small one. In fact, they appear to be distributed rather evenly about the more heavily populated Federation worlds."

She didn't like that. "What kind of pattern is it?"

"Violent death, without witnesses and of recurring specific types—types which could be explained by your teleporting animal. The beast kills but not in obvious beast manner. It remains under restraint. If, for example, it had been able to reach you in Melna Park, it might have broken your neck, dropped you out of your aircar, and vanished. Elsewhere it might have smothered or strangled you, suggesting a human assailant. There are a number of variations repetitive enough to be included in the pattern. We're trying to establish connections among the victims. So far we don't have any. You remain our best lead."

Telzey already had concluded that. There were no detectable signs, but she was closely watched, carefully guarded. If another creature like Bozo the Beast should materialize suddenly in her college bungalow while she was alone, it would be dead before it touched her. That was reassuring at present. But it didn't solve the problem.

Evidence that the psis had found her developed within ten days. As Klayung described it, there was now a new kind of awareness of Telzey about Pehanron College, of her coming and going. Not among friends and acquaintances but among people she barely knew by sight, who, between them, were in a good position to tell approximately where she was, what she did, much of the time. Then there was the matter of the ComWebs. No attempt had been made to tamper with the instrument in her bungalow. But a number of other ComWebs responded whenever it was switched on; and her conversations were monitored.

"These people aren't controlled in the ordinary

sense," Klayung remarked. "They've been given a very few specific instructions, carry them out, and don't know they're doing it. They have no conscious interest in you. And they haven't been touched in any other way. All have wide-open minds. Somebody presumably scans those minds periodically for information. He hasn't been caught at it. Whoever arranged this is a highly skilled operator. It's an interesting contrast to that first, rather crude, trap prepared for you."

"That one nearly worked," Telzey said thoughtfully. "Nobody's tried to probe me here—I've been waiting for it. They know who I am, and they must be pretty sure I'm the one who did away with Bozo. You think they suspect I'm being watched?"

"I'd suspect it in their place," Klayung said. "They know who you are—not what you are. Possibly a highly talented junior Service operator. We're covered, I think. But I'd smell a trap. We have to assume that whoever is handling the matter on their side also smells a trap."

"Then what's going to happen?"

Klayung shrugged.

"I know it isn't pleasant, Telzey, but it's a waiting game here—unless they make a move. They may not do it. They may simply fade away again."

She made a small grimace. "That's what I'm afraid of!"

"I know. But we're working on other approaches. They've been able to keep out of our way so far. But we're aware of them now—we'll be watching for slips, and sooner or later we'll pick up a line to them."

Sooner or later! She didn't like it at all! She'd become a pawn. A well-protected one—but one with no scrap of privacy left, under scrutiny from two directions. She didn't blame Klayung or the Service. For them, this was one problem among very many they had to handle, always short of sufficiently skilled personnel, always trying to recruit any psi of the slightest usable ability who was willing to be recruited.

She was one of those who hadn't been willing, not wanting the restrictions it would place on her. She couldn't complain.

But she couldn't accept the situation either. It had to be resolved.

Somehow. . . .

## Chapter 2

"What do you know about Tinokti?" Klayung asked.

"Tinokti?" Telzey had been transferred from the car that picked her up in Beale to a small space cruiser standing off Orado. She, Klayung, and the car driver seemed to be the only people aboard. "I haven't been there, and I haven't made a special study of it." She reflected. "Nineteen hours liner time from Orado. Rather dense population. High living standards. Worldwide portal circuit system—the most involved in the Federation. A social caste system that's also pretty involved. Government by syndicate—a scientific body, the Tongi Phon. Corrupt, but they have plenty of popular support. As scientists they're supposed to be outstanding in a number of fields." She shrugged. "That's it, mainly. Is it enough?"

Klayung nodded. "For now. I'll fill you in. The Tongi Phon's not partial to the Service. They've been working hard at developing a psi technology of their own. They've got farther than most, but still not very far. Their approach is much too conservative— paradoxes disturb them. But they've learned enough to be aware of a number of possibilities. That's made them suspicious of us."

"Well, they might have a good deal to hide," Telzey said.

"Definitely. They do what they can to limit our activities. A majority of the commercial and private circuits are psi-blocked, as a result of a carefully underplayed campaign of psi and psi machine scares. The Tongi Phon Institute is blocked, of course; the Phons wear mind shields. Tinokti in general presents extraordinary operational difficulties. So it was something of a surprise when we got a request for help today from the Tongi Phon."

"Help in what?" Telzey asked.

"Four high-ranking Phons," Klayung explained, "were found dead together in a locked and guarded vault area at the Institute. Their necks had been broken and the backs of the skulls caved in—in each case apparently by a single violent blow. The bodies showed bruises but no other significant damage."

She said after a moment, "Did the Institute find out anything?"

"Yes. The investigators assumed at first a temporary portal had been set up secretly to the vault. But there should have been residual portal energy detectable, and there wasn't. They did establish then that a life form of unknown type had been present at the time of the killings. Estimated body weight close to ten hundred pounds."

Telzey nodded. "That was one of Bozo's relatives, all right!"

"We can assume it. The vault area was psi-blocked. So that's no obstacle to them. The Phons are badly frightened. Political assassinations are no novelty at the Institute, but here all factions lost leading members. Nobody feels safe. They don't know the source of the threat or the reason for it, but they've decided psi may have been involved. Within limits, they're willing to cooperate with the Service."

He added, "As it happens, we'd already been giving Tinokti special attention. It's one of perhaps a dozen Hub worlds where a secret psi organization would find almost ideal conditions. Since they've demonstrated an interest in psi machines, the Institute's intensive work in the area should be a further attraction. Mind shields or not, it wouldn't be surprising to discover the psis have been following that project for some time. So the Service will move to Tinokti in strength. If we can trap a sizable nest, it might be a long step toward rounding up the lot wherever they're hiding."

He regarded Telzey a moment. She responded by saying, "I assume you're telling me all this because you want me to go to Tinokti?"

"Yes. We should be able to make very good use of you. The fact that you're sensitized to the psis' mind type gives you an advantage over our operators. And your sudden interest in Tinokti after what's occurred might stimulate some reaction from the local group."

"I'll be bait?" Telzey said.

"In part. Our moment to moment tactics will depend on developments, of course."

She nodded. "Well, I'm bait here, and I want them off my neck. What will the arrangement be?"

"You're making the arrangement," Klayung told her. "A psi arrangement, to keep you in character— the junior Service operator who's maintaining her well-established cover as a law student. You'll have Pehanron assign you to a field trip to Tinokti to do a paper on the legalistic aspects of the Tongi Phon government."

"It'll have to be cleared with the Institute," Telzey said.

"We'll take care of that."

"All right." She considered. "I may have to work on three or four minds. When do I leave?"

"A week from today."

Telzey nodded. "That's no problem then. There's one thing. . . ."

"Yes?"

"The psis have been so careful not to give themselves away here. Why should they create an obvious mystery on Tinokti?"

Klayung said, "I'm wondering. There may be something the Phons haven't told us. However, the sup-
position at present is that the beast failed to follow
its instructions exactly—as the creatures may, in fact,
have done on other occasions with less revealing
results. You had the impression that Bozo wasn't too
intelligent."

"Yes, I did," Telzey said. "But it doesn't seem very
intelligent either to use an animal like that where
something could go seriously wrong, as it certainly
might in a place like the Institute. Particularly when
they still haven't found out what happened to their
other psi beast on Orado."

What were they?

Telzey had fed questions to information centers.
Reports about psi mutant strains weren't uncommon,
but one had to go a long way back to find something
like confirming evidence. She condensed the information she obtained, gave it, combined with her own
recent experiences, to Pehanron's probability computer
to digest. The machine stated that she was dealing
with descendants of the historical mind masters of
Nalakia, the Elaigar.

She mentioned it to Klayung. He wasn't surprised.
The Service's probability computers concurred.

"But that's impossible!" Telzey said, startled. The
information centers had provided her with a great deal
of material on the Elaigar. "If the records are right,
they averaged out at more than five hundred pounds.
Besides, they looked like ogres! How could someone
like that be moving around in a Hub city without
being noticed?"

Klayung said they wouldn't necessarily have to let
themselves be seen, at least not by people who could

talk about them. If they'd returned to the Hub from some other galactic section, they might have set up bases on unused nonoxygen worlds a few hours from their points of operation, almost safe from detection so long as their presence wasn't suspected. He wasn't discounting the possibility.

Telzey, going over the material again later, found that she didn't much care for the possibility. The Elaigar belonged to the Hub's early colonial period. They'd been physical giants with psi minds, a bio-structure believed to be of human origin, developed by a science-based cult called the Grisands, which had moved out from the Old Territory not long before and established itself in a stronghold on Nalakia. In the Grisand idiom, Elaigar meant the Lion People. It suggested what the Grisands intended to achieve—a controlled formidable strain through which they could dominate the other humans on Nalakia and on neighboring colony worlds. But they lost command of their creation. The Elaigar turned on them, and the Grisands died in the ruins of their stronghold. Then the Elaigar set out on conquests of their own.

Apparently they'd been the terrors of that area of space for a number of years, taking over one colony after another. The humans they met and didn't kill were mentally enslaved and thereafter lived to serve them. Eventually, war fleets were assembled in other parts of the Hub; and the prowess of the Elaigar proved to be no match for superior space firepower. The survivors among them fled in ships crewed by their slaves and hadn't been heard from again.

Visual reproductions of a few of the slain mutants were included in the data Telzey had gathered. There hadn't been many available. The Hub's War Centuries lay between that time and her own; most of the colonial period's records had been destroyed or lost. Even dead and seen in the faded recordings, the Elaigar appeared as alarming as their reputation had been. There were a variety of giant strains in the Hub, but most of them looked reasonably human. The Elaigar seemed a different species. The massive bodies were like those of powerful animals, and the broad hairless faces brought to mind the faces of great cats.

But human the prototype must have been, Telzey thought—if it *was* Elaigar she'd met briefly on the psi level in Orado's Melna Park. The basic human mental patterns were discernible in the thought forms she'd registered. What was different might fit these images of the Nalakian mind masters and their brief, bloody Hub history. Klayung could be right.

"Well, just be sure," Jessamine Amberdon commented when Telzey informed her parents by Com-Web one evening that she'd be off on a field assignment to Tinokti next day, "that you're back ten days from now."

"Why?" asked Telzey.

"For the celebration, of course."

"Eh?"

Jessamine sighed. "Oh, Telzey! You've become the most absent-minded dear lately! That's your birthday, remember? You'll be sixteen."

# Chapter 3

Citizens of Tinokti tended to regard the megacities of other Federation worlds as overgrown primitive villages. They, or some seventy percent of them, lived and worked in the enclosed portal systems called circuits. For most it was a comfortable existence; for many a luxurious one.

A portal, for practical purposes, was two points in space clamped together to form one. It was a method of moving in a step from here to there, within a limited but considerable range. Portal circuits could be found on many Hub worlds. On Tinokti they were everywhere. Varying widely in extent and complexity, serving many purposes, they formed the framework of the planet's culture.

On disembarking at the spaceport, Telzey had checked in at a great commercial circuit called the Luerral Hotel. It had been selected for her because it was free of the psi blocks in rather general use here otherwise. The Luerral catered to the interstellar trade; and the force patterns which created the blocks were likely to give people unaccustomed to them a mildly oppressive feeling of being enclosed. For Telzey's purpose, of course, they were more serious obstacles.

While registering, she was equipped with a guest key. The Luerral Hotel was exclusive; its portals passed only those who carried a Luerral key or were in the immediate company of somebody who did. The keys were accessories of the Luerral's central computer and on request gave verbal directions and other information. The one Telzey selected had the form of a slender ring. She let it guide her to her room, found her luggage had preceded her there, and made a call to the Tongi Phon Institute. Tinokti ran on Institute time; the official workday wouldn't begin for another three hours. But she was connected with someone who knew of her application to do legal research, and was told a guide would come to take her to the Institute when it opened.

She set out then on a stroll about the hotel and circled Tinokti twice in an hour's unhurried walk, passing through portals which might open on shopping malls, tropical parks or snowy mountain resorts, as the circuit dipped in and out of the more attractive parts of the planet. She was already at work for Klayung, playing the role of a psi operator who was playing the role of an innocent student tourist. She wore a tracer which pinpointed her for a net of spacecraft deployed about the planet. The bracelet on her left wrist was a Service communicator; and she was in wispy but uninterrupted mind contact with a Service telepath whose specialty it was to keep such contacts undetectable for other minds. She also had armed company unobtrusively preceding and following her. They were probing Tinokti carefully in many ways; she was now one of the probes.

Her thoughts searched through each circuit section and the open areas surrounding it as she moved along. She picked up no conscious impressions of the Service's quarry. But twice during that hour's walk, the screens enclosing her mind like a flexing bubble tightened abruptly into a solid shield. Her automatic detectors, more sensitive than conscious probes, had responded to a passing touch of the type of mental patterns they'd been designed to warn her against. The psis were here—and evidently less cautious than they'd been on Orado after her first encounter with them.

When she'd come back to the hotel's Great Lobby, Gudast, her Service contact, inquired mentally, "Mind doing a little more walking?"

Telzey checked her watch. "Just so I'm not late for the Phons."

"We'll get you back in time."

"All right. Where do I go?"

Gudast said, "Those mind touches you reported came at points where the Luerral Hotel passes through major city complexes. We'd like you to go back to them, leave the circuit and see if you can pick up something outside."

She got short-cut directions from the Luerral computer, set out again. The larger sections had assorted transportation aids, but, on the whole, circuit dwellers seemed to do a healthy amount of walking. Almost all of the traffic she saw was pedestrian.

She took an exit presently, found herself in one of the city complexes mentioned by Gudast. Her Luerral ring key informed her the hotel had turned her over to the guidance of an area computer and that the key remained at her service if she needed information. Directed by Gudast, she took a seat on a slideway, let it carry her along a main street. Superficially, the appearance of things here was not unlike that of some large city on Orado. The differences were functional. Psi blocks were all about, sensed as a gradually shifting pattern of barriers to probes as the slideway moved on with her. Probably less than a fifth of the space of the great buildings was locally open; everything else was taken up by circuit sections connected to other points of the planet, ranging in size from a few residential or storage rooms to several building levels. Milkily gleaming horizontal streaks along the sides of the buildings showed that many of the sections were protected by force fields. Tinokti's citizens placed a high value on privacy.

Telzey stiffened suddenly. "Defense reaction!" she told Gudast.

"Caught it," his thought whispered.

"It's continuing." She passed her tongue over her lips.

"See a good place to get off the slideway?"

Telzey glanced along the street, stood up. "Yes! Big display windows just ahead. Quite a few people."

"Sounds right."

She stepped off the slideway as it came up to the window fronts, walked over, started along the gleaming windows, then stopped, looking in at the displayed merchandise. "I'm there," she told Gudast. "Reaction stopped a moment ago."

"See what you can do. We're set up."

Her psi sensors reached out. She brought up the

thought patterns she'd recorded in Melna Park and stored in memory, blurred them, projected them briefly as something carelessly let slip from an otherwise guarded mind. She waited.

Her screens tried to tighten again. She kept them as they were, overriding the automatic reaction. Then something moved faintly into awareness—a mind behind shielding, alert, questioning, perhaps suspicious. Still barely discernible.

"Easy—easy!" whispered Gudast. "I'm getting it. We're getting it. Don't push at all! Give us fifteen seconds . . . ten . . ."

Psi-block!

The impression had vanished.

Somewhere the being producing it had moved into a psi-blocked section of this city complex. Perhaps deliberately, choosing mental concealment. Perhaps simply because that was where it happened to be going when its attention was caught for a moment by Telzey's broadcast pattern. The impression hadn't been sufficiently strong to say anything about it except that this had been a mind of the type Telzey had encountered on Orado. They'd all caught for an instant the specific qualities she'd recorded.

The instant hadn't been enough. Klayung had brought a number of living psi compasses to Tinokti, operators who could have pinpointed the position of the body housing that elusive mentality, given a few more seconds in which to work.

They hadn't been given those seconds, and the mentality wasn't contacted again. Telzey went on presently to the other place where she'd sensed a sudden warning, and prowled about here and there outside the Luerral Circuit, while Klayung's pack waited for renewed indications. This time they drew a blank.

But it had been confirmed that the psis—some of them—were on Tinokti.

The problem would be how to dig them out of the

planet-wide maze of force-screened and psi-blocked circuit sections.

Telzey's Institute guide, a young man named Phon Hajugan, appeared punctually with the beginning of Tinokti's workday. He informed Telzey he held the lowest Tongi Phon rank. The lower echelons evidently hadn't been informed of the recent killings in the Institute vault and their superiors' apprehensions— Phon Hajugan was in a cheery and talkative mood. Telzey's probe disclosed that he was equipped with a chemical mind shield.

There was no portal connection between the Luerral Hotel's circuit and that of the Institute. Telzey and her guide walked along a block of what appeared to be a sizable residential town before reaching an entry portal of the Tongi Phon Circuit, where she was provided with another portal key. She'd been making note of the route; in future she didn't intend to be distracted by the presence of a guide. The office to which Phon Hajugan conducted her was that of a senior Phon named Trondbarg. It was clear that Phon Trondbarg did know what was going on. He discussed Telzey's Pehanron project in polite detail but with an air of nervous detachment. It had been indicated to the Institute that she was a special agent of the Service, and that her research here was for form's sake only.

The interview didn't take long. Her credentials would be processed, and she was to return in four hours. She would have access then to normally restricted materials and be able to obtain other information as required. In effect, she was being given a nearly free run of the Institute, which was the purpose. Unless there were other developments, much of the Service's immediate attention would be focused on the areas and personnel associated with the Tongi Phon's psi technology projects. The Phon leadership didn't like it but had no choice. They would have liked it less if they'd suspected that mind shields now would start coming quietly undone. The Service wanted to find out who around here was controlled and in what manner.

Some form of counteraction by the concealed opposition might be expected. Preparations were being made for it, and Telzey's personal warning system was one part of the preparations.

She returned to the Luerral Circuit and her hotel room alone except for her unnoticeable Service escorts, spent the next two hours asleep to get herself shifted over to the local time system, then dressed in a Tinokti fashion item, a sky-blue belted jacket of military cut and matching skirt, and had a belated breakfast in a stratosphere restaurant of the hotel. Back in the Great Lobby, she began to retrace the route to the Tongi Phon Institute she'd followed with Phon Hajugan some five hours ago. A series of drop shafts took her to a scenic link with swift-moving slideways; then there was a three-portal shift to the southern hemisphere where the Institute's major structures were located. She moved on through changing patterns of human traffic until she reached the ninth portal from the Great Lobby. On the far side of that portal, she stopped with a catch in her breath, spun about, found herself looking at a blank wall, and turned again.

Her mental contact with Gudast was gone. The portal had shifted her into a big, long, high-ceilinged room, empty and silent. She hadn't passed through any such room with Phon Hajugan. She should have exited here instead into the main passage of a shopping center.

She touched the wall through which she'd stepped an instant ago—as solid now as it looked. A one-way portal. The room held the peculiar air of blankness, a cave of stillness about the mind, which said it was psi-blocked and that the blocking fields were close by.

Watching a large closed door at the other end of the room, Telzey clicked on the bracelet communicator. No response from the Service. . . . No response either, a moment later, from the Luerral ring key!

She'd heard that in the complexities of major portal systems, it could happen that a shift became temporarily distorted and one emerged somewhere else than one had intended to go. But that hadn't happened here. There'd been people directly ahead of her, others not many yards behind, her Service escorts among them, and no one else had portaled into this big room which was no part of the Luerral Circuit.

So it must be a trap—and a trap set up specifically for her along her route from the hotel room to the Tongi Phon Institute. As she reached the portal some observer had tripped the mechanisms which flicked in another exit for the instant needed to bring her to the room. If the Service still had a fix on the tracking device they'd given her, they would have recognized what had happened and be zeroing in on her now, but she had an unpleasantly strong conviction that whoever had cut her off so effectively from psi and communicator contacts also had considered the possibility of a tracking device and made sure it wouldn't act as one here.

The room remained quiet. A strip of window just below the ceiling ran along the wall on her left, showing patches of blue sky and tree greenery outside. It was far out of her reach, and if she found something that let her climb up to it, there was no reason to think it would be possible to get through that window. But she started cautiously forward. The room was L-shaped; on her right, the wall extended not much more than two thirds of its length before it cornered.

She could sense nothing, but wasn't sure no one was waiting behind the corner for her until she got there. No one was. That part of the room was as bare

as the other. At the end of it was a second closed
door, a smaller one.

She turned back toward the first door, checked,
skin crawling. Mind screens had contracted abruptly
into a hard shield. One of *them* had come into this
psi-blocked structure.

One or more of them. . . .

The larger door opened seconds later. Three tall
people came into the room.

# Chapter 4

Telzey's continuing automatic reaction told her the
three were psis of the type she'd conditioned herself
to detect and recognize. Whatever they were, they
had nothing resembling the bulk and massive structure of the Elaigar mind masters she'd studied in the
old Nalakian records. They might be nearly as tall.
The smallest, in the rich blue cloak and hood of a
Sparan woman, must measure at least seven feet, and
came barely up to the shoulders of her companions
who wore the corresponding gray cloaks of Sparan
men. Veils, golden for the woman, white for the men,
concealed their faces below the eyes and fell to their
chests.

But, of course, they weren't Sparans. Telzey had
looked into Sparan minds. They probably were the
Hub's most widespread giant strain, should have the
average sprinkling of psi ability. They weren't an
organization of psis. Their familiar standardized dressing practices simply provided these three with an
effective form of concealment.

Telzey, heart racing, smiled at them.

"I hope I'm not trespassing!" she told them. "I was

in the Luerral Hotel just a minute ago and have no idea how I got here! Can you tell me how to get back?"

The woman said in an impersonal voice, "I'm sure you're quite aware you're not here by accident. We'll take you presently to some people who want to see you. Now stand still while I search you."

She'd come up as she spoke, removing her golden gloves. Telzey stood still. The men had turned to the left along the wall, and a recess was suddenly in sight there . . . some portal arrangement. The recess seemed to be a large, half-filled storage closet. The men began bringing items out of it, while the woman searched Telzey quickly. The communicator and the Service's tracking device disappeared under the blue cloak. The woman took nothing else. She straightened again, said, "Stay where you are," and turned to join her companions who now were packing selected pieces of equipment into two carrier cases they'd taken from the closet. They worked methodically but with some haste, occasionally exchanging a few words in a language Telzey didn't know. Finally they snapped the cases shut, began to remove their Sparan veils and cloaks.

Telzey watched them warily. Her first sight of their faces was jarring. They were strong handsome faces with a breed similarity between them. But there was more than a suggestion there of the cruel cat masks of Nalakia. They'd needed the cover of the Sparan veil to avoid drawing attention to themselves.

The bodies were as distinctive. The woman, now in trunks, boots and short-sleeved shirt, as were the men, a gun belt fastened about her, looked slender with her height and length of limb, but layers of well-defined muscle shifted along her arms and legs as she moved. Her neck was a round strong column, the sloping shoulders correspondingly heavy, and there was a great depth of rib cage, drawing in sharply to the flat waist. She differed from the human standard as a strain of animals bred for speed or fighting might differ from other strains of the same species. Her companions were male counterparts, larger, more heavily muscled.

There'd been no trace of a mental or emotional impression from any of them; they were closely screened. The door at the end of the room opened now, and a third man of the same type came in. He was dressed almost as the others were, but everything he wore was dark green; and instead of a gun, a broad knife swung in its scabbard from his belt. He glanced at Telzey, said something in their language. The woman looked over at Telzey.

"Who are you?" Telzey asked her.

The woman said, "My name is Kolki Ming. I'm afraid there's no time for questions. We have work to do." She indicated the third man. "Tscharen will be in charge of you at present."

"We'll leave now," Tscharen told Telzey.

They were in a portal circuit. Once out of the room where Telzey had been trapped, they used no more doors. The portal sections through which they passed were small ones, dingy by contrast with the Luerral's luxuries, windowless interiors where people once had lived. Lighting and other automatic equipment still functioned; furnishings stood about. But there was a general air of long disuse. Psi blocks tangibly enclosed each section.

The portals weren't marked in any way, but Tscharen moved on without hesitation. They'd reach a wall and the wall would seem to dissolve about and before them; and they'd be through it, somewhere else—a somewhere else which didn't look very different from the section they'd just left. After the sixth portal shift, Tscharen turned into a room and unlocked and opened a wall cabinet.

A viewscreen had been installed in the cabinet. He manipulated the settings, and a brightly lit and richly furnished area, which might have been the reception room of some great house, appeared in the screen. There was no one in sight; the screen was silent. Tscharen studied the room for perhaps a minute, then switched off the screen, closed and locked the cabinet, motioned to Telzey and turned to leave. She followed.

They passed through two more portals. The second one took them into the big room of the viewscreen. They'd moved on a few steps across thick carpeting when Tscharen whirled abruptly. Telzey had a glimpse of a gun in his hand, saw him drop sideways. Someone landed with a harsh yell on the floor behind her, and a great hand gripped the back of her jacket below the collar. For a moment, a face stared down into hers. Then she was tossed aside with careless violence, and when she looked up from the carpeting, the giants were coming in through a doorspace at the far end of the room.

They moved like swift animals. She had barely time to scramble to her feet before they were there. One of them caught her arm, held her in a rock-hard grip, but the immediate attention of the group was on Tscharen. They crouched about him, shifting quickly back and forth. He'd recovered from whatever had knocked him out, was struggling violently. There were short angry shouts. Gusts of savage emotion boiled up, a battering of psi energies. Telzey's gaze flicked to the wall through which they'd stepped. Grips were fastened to it above the point where the portal had opened briefly. That was where Tscharen's attacker had clung, waiting. So these others had known he was coming along that route, or that someone was coming, and had laid an ambush.

The psi tumult ebbed out. They began to separate, get to their feet. She saw Tscharen lying face down, hands fastened behind his back, trussed up generally and motionless. Two remained beside him. The others turned toward Telzey, spreading out in a semicircle.

She swallowed carefully. More than a dozen stared at her, faces showing little expression at the moment. They were dressed in the same sort of dark green outfit as Tscharen, belted with guns and knives. The majority were of his type. Two of them, slighter, smaller-boned, were females.

But four in the group were not at all of the same type. They stood not many inches taller than the rest but were much more hugely designed throughout. They were, in fact, unmistakably what the old records had told about and shown—the psi ogres of Nalakia, the Elaigar.

One of these rumbled something to the lesser giant holding Telzey's arm. Thought patterns flickered for a moment through her awareness. She had the impression they didn't quite know what to make of the fact that she'd been in Tscharen's company.

She glanced toward the ogre who'd spoken. His brooding eyes narrowed. A mind probe stabbed at her.

Her shield blocked it.

Interest flared in the broad face. The others stirred, went quiet again.

So now they knew she was a psi.

Another probe came from the Elaigar, heavy and hard, testing the shield in earnest. It held. Some of the others began to grin. He grunted, in annoyance now, returned with a ramming thrust. Telzey slammed a bolt back at him, struck heavy shielding; and his eyes went wide with surprise. There was a roar of laughter. As psi mentalities, the great Elaigar seemed the same as Tscharen's kind; she could make out no difference between them.

The noise ended abruptly. Faces turned toward the doorspace and the group shifted position, hands moving toward guns and knife hilts. Telzey followed their gaze. Hot fright jolted through her.

An animal stood in the room thirty feet away, small red eyes fixed on her. Thick-bodied, with massive head and forelimbs—one of their teleporting killers. It didn't move, but its appearance and stare were infinitely menacing. The giants themselves clearly weren't at ease in its presence.

It vanished.

Simultaneously, a voice spoke harshly from the doorway and another huge Elaigar strode into the room, followed by a humanoid creature in green uniform. It was a moment before Telzey realized the newcomer was female. There was little to distinguish her physically from the males of her type here. But something did distinguish her—something like a blaze of furious energy which enlivened the brutal features in their frame of shaggy black hair. Through her shield, Telzey felt a powerful mind sweep toward her, then abruptly withdraw. The giantess glanced at her as she approached, said something to the attendant humanoid, then turned toward Tscharen and addressed the others in a hard deep voice. The attitude of the group indicated she held authority among them.

The humanoid stopped before Telzey, took an instrument from one of his uniform pockets, thumbed open the cover, held the instrument to his mouth, pronounced a few high-pitched sentences, closed the device and replaced it. He looked up at the giant holding Telzey by the arm, and the giant growled a few words and moved off. The humanoid looked at Telzey. She looked at him.

Except for the fact that he wasn't much taller than she, his appearance was no more reassuring than that of the giants. The large round head and the hands were covered by skin like plum-colored velvet. The two eyes set wide apart in the head were white circles with black dots as pupils. There were no indications of ears, nostrils, or other sense organs. The mouth was a long straight lipless line. A variety of weapons and less readily definable devices were attached to the broad belt about the flat body.

The creature unclipped two of the belt gadgets now, stepped up to Telzey and began running them over her clothes. She realized she was being searched again and stood still. Plum-face was methodical and thorough. Everything he found he looked over briefly and stuffed into one of his pockets, winding up by pulling the Luerral ring key from Telzey's finger and adding it to the other items. Then he returned the search devices to his belt and spoke to somebody who was now standing behind Telzey. The somebody moved around into view.

Another kind of alien. This one was also about Telzey's size, wore clothing, walked upright on two legs. Any physical resemblance to humanity ended there. It had a head like that of a soft-shelled green bug, jaws hinged side to side. A curved band of yellow circles across the upper part of the face seemed to be eyes. What was visible of arms and legs, ending in the bony hands and narrow, shod feet, was reedy and knob-jointed, the same shade of green as the head.

This creature didn't look at Telzey but simply stood there. Telzey guessed Plum-face had summoned it to the room with his communicator. Two of the group had picked up Tscharen now and were carrying him from the room. The giantess snapped out some command. The rest started toward the doorspace. She watched them leave, then turned abruptly. Telzey felt a thrill of alarm as the monster came up. The Elaigar spoke, a few short words.

The green alien at once told Telzey softly, in perfect translingue, "You are in the presence of Stiltik, who is a High Commander of the Elaigar. I'm to translate her instructions to you—and I advise you most urgently to do whatever she says, with no hesitation."

The jaws hadn't moved, but a short tube protruded

from the front of the stalk-like neck. The voice had
come from there. The end of the tube was split,
forming flexible lips with a fleshy blue tongue tip
between them.

The harsh voice of Stiltik, High Commander of the
Elaigar, broke in. The green alien resumed quickly.
"You must open your mind to Stiltik. Do it imme-
diately!"

But that was the last thing she should do. Telzey
said unsteadily, "Open my mind? I don't know what
she means."

Bug-face translated. Stiltik, eyes fixed hard on
Telzey, growled a brief response. The green creature,
seeming almost in distress, said, "Stiltik says you're
lying. Please don't defy her! She's very quick to anger."

Telzey shook her head helplessly.

"But it's impossible! I—"

She broke off. This time, Stiltik hadn't waited for
translation. Psi pressure clamped about Telzey's shield,
tightened like a great fist. She gave a startled gasp.
There was no need to pretend being frightened; she
was afraid enough of Stiltik. But not of this form of
attack. Her shield had stood up under the crushing
onslaught of a great psi machine. As far as she knew,
no living mind could produce similar forces.

And in not too many seconds, Stiltik appeared to
understand she would accomplish nothing in that
manner. The pressure ended abruptly. She stared
down at Telzey, made a snorting sound, leaned forward. The mouth smiled in murderous anger; and the
huge hands reached out with blurring speed, gripped
Telzey, went knowingly to work.

Telzey was reminded in an instant then that when
pain is excruciating enough there is no outcry, because
lungs and throat seem paralyzed. She could have
blocked out most of it, but Stiltik might be in a killing fury, and pain now offered a means of escape. It
flowed through her like bursts of fire leaping up and

combining. Her mind dimmed in shock, and she found herself lying on the floor, shaking, shield tight-locked. Stiltik roared out something high above her. Then there were footsteps, moving off. Then darkness, rolling in.

## Chapter 5

She decided presently that she hadn't been unconscious very long, though she hurt a great deal less than she'd expected to be hurting when she woke up. She kept her eyes shut; she wasn't alone. She was lying on her side, with something like a hard cot underneath. The area was psi-blocked, and evidently it was a large structure because she had no feeling of blocking fields close by. Her warning mechanisms indicated one or more minds of the Elaigar type around.

Something touched her lightly in an area which was still sufficiently painful. Around the touch pain began to diminish, as if a slow wave of coolness were spreading out and absorbing it. So she was being treated for the mauling she'd had from Stiltik—very effectively treated, to judge by the way she felt.

Now to determine who was in the vicinity.

Telzey canceled the alerting mechanisms, lightened her shielding, reached out cautiously. After a minute or two, vague thought configurations touched her awareness. Nonpsi and alien they were—she could develop that contact readily.

Next, sense of a psi shield. Whoever used it wasn't far away. . . .

The device which had been draining pain from her withdrew, leaving a barely noticeable residual discomfort where it had been. It touched another sore spot, resumed its ministrations. A mingling of the alien thoughts accompanied the transfer. They were beginning to seem comprehensible—a language half understood. The xenotelepathic quality of her mind was at work.

Her screens abruptly drew tight. There'd been a momentary wash of Elaigar thought. Gone now. But—

Fury swirled about her, surging unshielded, nakedly open. An Elaigar mind. The rage, whatever caused it, had nothing to do with Telzey. The giant didn't appear aware that she was in the area.

The impression faded again, didn't return. Telzey waited a minute, slid a light probe toward the psi shield she'd touched. She picked up no indication of anything there. It was a good tight shield, and that was all. Psi shield installed over a nonpsi mind? It should be that.

She left a watch thought there, a trace of awareness. If the shield opened or softened, she'd know, be back for a further look. She returned to the alien nonpsi thought patterns. By now, it was obvious that they were being produced by two minds of the same species.

It was a gentle, unsuspicious species. Telzey moved easily into both minds. One was Stiltik's green-bug interpreter, named Couse; a female. Couse's race called themselves the Tanvens. Her companion was Sasar, male; a physician. Kind Bug-faces! They had problems enough of their own, no happy future ahead. But at the moment, they were feeling sorry for the human who had been mishandled by Stiltik and were doing what they could to help her.

They might help more than they realized. Telzey put taps on their memory banks which would feed general information to hers without further attention, began dropping specific questions into the nonresisting awarenesses.

Responses came automatically.

After she lost consciousness, she'd been brought here by Essu. Essu was Plum-face, the uniformed humanoid. He was a Tolant, chief of Stiltik's company of Tolants. Stiltik had ordered Couse to summon

Sasar, the most skilled physician in her command, to
tend to the human's injuries and revive her. She was
a valuable captive who was to remain in Essu's charge
then, until Stiltik sent for her. The Tanvens didn't
know when that would be. But it might be a considerable while, because Stiltik was interrogating the
other captive now.

Essu was waiting in the passage outside this room.
So he was the wearer of the psi shield, though the
Tanvens knew nothing of that. Stiltik presumably had
equipped him with one to safeguard her secrets from
other psi minds. Essu acted as her general assistant,
frequently as her executioner and torturer. A cruel,
cunning creature! The Tanvens feared him almost as
much as they feared Stiltik.

They didn't know there was an Elaigar in the
vicinity. As far as they were aware, they were alone
in this circuit section with Essu and Telzey. It had
been a hospital facility once, but was now rarely used.
The bad-tempered giant might be a good distance
away from them.

Telzey shifted her line of questioning. The Elaigar
had enslaved members of many races besides Tanvens
and Tolants. Giants of Stiltik's kind were called
Sattarams and supplied almost all the leaders. The
lesser Elaigar were Otessans. Tscharen belonged to
a third variety called Alattas, who looked like Otessans
and now and then were caught masquerading as them,
as Tscharen had been. The Alattas were enemies of
the Sattarams and Otessans, and Couse and Sasar had
heard rumors that an Alatta force was at present trying
to invade the circuit.

At that point, Telzey drew back from the Tanven
minds, leaving only the memory taps in place. For
immediate practical purposes, Couse and Sasar had
a limited usefulness. They were unable to think about
the Elaigar in any real detail. When she tried to pin

them down, their thought simply blurred. They knew only as much about their masters as they needed to know to perform their duties.

Similarly, they had a frustratingly vague picture of the portal circuit the Elaigar had occupied on Tinokti. It appeared to be an extensive system. They were familiar with a limited part of it and had been supplied with key packs which permitted them to move about within that area. They had no curiosity about what lay beyond. In particular, they'd never wondered about the location of exits from the circuit to the world outside. Escape was something they didn't think about; it was a meaningless concept. The Elaigar had done a thorough job of conditioning them.

She could control the Tanvens easily, but it wouldn't gain her anything.

Plum-face was the logical one to get under control. He was in charge of her, and the fact that he was Stiltik's assistant could make him the most useful sort of confederate. However, the psi shield presented a problem. Telzey thought she could work through it, given time enough. But Stiltik might show up and discover what she was doing. Stiltik would make very sure then that she didn't get a chance to try other tricks.

She decided to wait a little with Essu. The shield might be less inflexible than it seemed at present. Meanwhile, there was a fourth mind around. The Elaigar mind.

She considered, not liking that notion too well. There'd been occasional impressions which indicated this particular Elaigar remained careless about his shielding. He didn't seem to be aware of any of them here. But if he suspected he was being probed, he'd start hunting around the limited psi-blocked area for the prober.

She thought finally she should take the chance—he was preoccupied and angry.

She reached out gradually toward the Elaigar awareness. Her concern lessened then. There was a screen there but so loosely held it might as well have been nonexistent. The thought currents behind it shifted in fluctuating disorder over a quivering under-current of anger. Insane, she realized. A sick old male sunk deep in derangement, staring at problems for which there was no real solution, rousing himself periodically to futile fury.

Telzey eased in a memory tap, paused—

*Stiltik!* She slipped out of the Elaigar mind, flicked her watch thought away from Essu's shield. Tight went her own shield then.

Stiltik was present, after a fashion. Somewhere in this psi-blocked structure, a portal had opened and she'd stepped through. A signal now touched Essu's shield, and the shield went soft. Not many seconds later, it hardened again. Some instruction had been given the Tolant.

But Stiltik wasn't yet gone. Telzey sensed a search thought about. She could hide from it by ceasing all psi activity, but that simply would tell Stiltik she was conscious. She allowed a normal trickle of psi energy to drift out, let Stiltik's mind find her behind her shield.

Something touched the shield, tested it with a slow pressure probe, which got nowhere, withdrew. A hard, dizzying bolt slammed suddenly at her then; another. That sort of thing shouldn't help an unconscious patient make a faster recovery, Telzey thought. Perhaps Stiltik had the same reflection; she let it go at that. When Telzey made a cautious scan of the area a minute or two later, there was no trace of the giantess in the structure.

Essu appeared in the entrance to the room and wanted to know how much longer it was going to take

Sasar to get the human awake and in good enough shape so she could walk. Telzey followed the talk through Couse's mind. Couse was acting as interpreter again. Essu didn't understand the Tanven tongue, nor Sasar that of the Tolants or Elaigar. The physician was alarmed by Essu's indications of impatience, but replied bravely enough. Couse had given him Stiltik's instructions: he was to make sure the patient retained no dangerous injuries before he released her to Essu, and he couldn't be sure of it yet. She appeared to be healing well and rapidly, but her continuing unconsciousness was not a good sign. Essu pronounced a few imprecations in his high sharp voice, resumed his post in the passage.

The signal which caused Essu's shield to relax presently reached it again. Essu wasn't aware of it, but the shield softened in mechanical obedience. This time, it was Telzey's probe which slipped through. She'd reproduced the signal as carefully as she could, but hadn't been too sure it was an exact copy. Evidently she'd come close enough—and now for some quick and nervous work! If Stiltik happened to return before she got organized here, it wasn't likely she could escape discovery.

That part of it then turned out to be easier than she'd expected. Essu's mind already was well organized for her purpose. She flicked through installed telepathic channels to indicated control points. By the time she'd scanned the system, knew she understood it, most of the Tolant's concepts were becoming comprehensible to her. She checked on the immediately important point. What was he to do with her after she came awake and Sasar pronounced her condition to be satisfactory?

Response came promptly. Essu would take her to Stiltik's private lockup, inform Stiltik of the fact, and stay with Telzey until Stiltik wanted her. The lockup was a small sealed circuit section known only to Stiltik and Essu. Stiltik believed the human psi would be an important catch. She didn't want her enemies to hear about it until she'd finished squeezing the truth from the Alatta, and had searched through Telzey's mind for information she could turn to political advantage. It appeared Stiltik was engaged in a power struggle with Boragost, the other High Commander in the Elaigar circuit.

Essu's shield hardened again until it appeared solidly locked, though a really close investigation would have revealed that contact remained now between his mind and Telzey's. Telzey didn't want to break that contact unless she had to. The Tolant should turn out to be as useful as she'd thought, and she had to do a good deal of work on him before he'd be ready for use—which made it time to be restored officially to consciousness and health. Once Stiltik was informed the prisoner was safely in the lockup, she should be satisfied to leave it to Essu to see Telzey stayed there.

And that would be essential for a while.

A thought whispered, "I know you're planning to escape from the Elaigar! Would you permit me to accompany you?"

For an instant Telzey froze in shock. That had been a human thought. Otherwise there hadn't been—and still wasn't—the slightest indication of another human being around. She flicked back a question. "Where are you?"

"Not far away. I could be with you in a minute."

Now she'd noticed something. "You're human?" she asked.

"Of course. My name is Thrakell Dees."

"It seems to me," Telzey remarked, "there's something here that could be part of the two Tanven minds I've been in contact with—or perhaps a third Tanven mind. But if you look closely, it's only the impression of a Tanven mind."

Silence for a moment. "A projected form of concealment," Thrakell Dees's thought said then. "One of the means I've developed to stay alive in this cave of devils."

"How do you happen to be in the circuit?"

"I was trapped here over six years ago when the Elaigar suddenly appeared. I've never found a way to get out."

Telzey gave Essu's mind a questioning prod. "You mean you don't know where the exits to Tinokti are?" she asked Thrakell Dees.

"I have an approximate idea of where they should be. However, they're very securely guarded."

Yes, wild humans, Essu was thinking. Quite a number of humans had managed to hide out in the circuit in the early period. Hunting them had been good sport for a while. There were occasional indications that a few still survived, skulking about in unused sections.

"What happened to the other human beings in the circuit?" Telzey asked Thrakell Dees.

"The Elaigar and their serfs killed most of them at once. I myself was nearly caught often enough in those days. Only my psi abilities saved me. Later I learned other methods of avoiding the creatures. The circuit is very large, and only a part of it is occupied by them."

"Is anyone left besides you?"

"No, I'm the last. A year ago I encountered another survivor, but he was killed soon afterwards. The Elaigar have brought in captured humans from time to time, but none ever escaped and few lived long. Today I learned from a serf mind that Stiltik had trapped a human psi. I began looking for you, thinking I might be of help. But it seems you have your own plans. I suggest we cooperate. I can be very useful."

"What do you know about my plans?" Telzey asked.

"Nothing directly. Your thoughts were too closely screened. But I've been following the responses you drew from the Tanvens. They indicate you intend to attempt an escape."

"All right," Telzey said. "I will try to escape. If you want to come along, fine. We should be able to help each other. But keep out of the way now, because I'll be busy. The Tolant will be taking me somewhere else soon. Can you follow without letting him see you?"

"I'm rarely seen unless I want to be." His reply seemed to hold a momentary odd note of amusement. "I can follow you easily in the general circuit. I have keys for some sealed areas, too. Not, of course, for all of them."

"We'll be in a sealed area for a while, but we'll come back out," Telzey told him. "Let's not talk any more now. I'm going to wake up."

She dissolved the memory taps in the Tanven minds and that of the old Elaigar, stirred about on the cot, then opened her eyes, looked up into Couse's green face and glanced over at Sasar who had drawn back a trifle when she began to move.

"What's happened?" Telzey asked. She looked at Couse again, blinked. "You're the interpreter. . . ."

"Yes, I am," said Couse.

Sasar said in the Tanven tongue, "What is the human saying? Ask her how she feels," the thoughts carrying through the meaningless sound. Essu, hearing the voices, had appeared in the entrance again and was watching the group.

Couse relayed the question, adding that Sasar had been acting as Telzey's physician after she had been injured. Telzey shifted her shoulders, twisted her neck, touched herself cautiously.

"He's a very good physician!" she told Couse. "I'm still aching a little here and there, but that's all."

Couse translated that twice, first for Sasar, and then for Essu, who had some understanding of translingue but not enough to be certain of what Telzey was saying.

"The human aches a little!" Essu repeated. "It's

awake and it can walk, so it's healthy enough. Tell your healer he's relieved of his responsibility, and be on your way, both of you!"

The Tanvens left quickly and quietly. There was a belt of woven metal fastened around Telzey's waist, with a strap of the same material attached to the belt. The other end of the strap was locked to the wall beyond the cot. Essu unfastened it now and brought Telzey flopping off the cot to the floor with a sudden haul on the strap. A short green rod appeared in Essu's free hand then. He pointed it at Telzey's legs, and she felt two sharp insect stings.

"Get *hup!*" said Essu, practicing his translingue.

She got up. He shoved her hands through loops in the back of the belt, and tightened the loops on her wrists. Then he took the end of the strap and left the room with the prisoner in tow. The Tanvens had turned right along the passage. Essu turned left. A closed door blocked the end, and as they approached it, he took something from his pocket, touched the device to the doorlock. The door swung open. They went through into an extension of the passage, and the door swung shut on its lock behind them.

There was a sudden heavy stirring in Telzey's mind. . . . Elaigar thoughts. The old male was coming alert. She realized suddenly he could hear them. This seemed to be his area—and Essu was unaware it had an occupant. There was a heavily curtained doorspace in the wall just ahead—

As they came up to it, the curtains were swept aside and a huge Sattaram loomed above them. She felt Essu's shock of alarm. Then the Elaigar's hand flicked out with the same startling speed Stiltik had shown. Telzey was struck across the side of the head, went stumbling back against the wall. With her hands fastened behind her, she couldn't get her balance back quickly enough and sat down.

It hadn't been too hard a blow—from the giant's

point of view no more than a peevish cuff. But he wasn't
finished. He'd whipped a heavy knife from his belt, and
was looking down at her. A human! He'd had no sport
for too long a time. His lip curled, drawing up

Telzey felt dismay rather than fright. Fast-moving
they were—but this Elaigar's mind was open to her
and he wasn't aware of the fact. She could slash
psi-death into it through the sloppily held screens
before the knife touched her skin.

But that could cost her too much—Essu, for one
thing. He knew she was a psi, and if a Sattaram
died in the act of attacking her, he wasn't likely to
consider it a coincidence. He'd try to get the information to Stiltik at once. She was beginning to
develop some degree of control over Essu but was
unsure of its effect on the unfamiliar Tolant mind.
In any case, she couldn't control him enough at
present to override any sudden strong motivation.
She might have to kill him in the same manner.

It was Essu who saved matters then.

He'd hung on to the end of the strap when Telzey
fell, but he stood as far from her and the Elaigar as
he possibly could, arm stretched out, eyes averted
from both, as if detaching himself completely from
this unpleasant situation. When he spoke in the
Elaigar language, he appeared to be addressing the
wall before him.

"Glorious One—is it your intention to deprive
*Stiltik* of prey?"

Slow surge of alarm in the old Sattaram. Stiltik? The
hate-filled eyes grew vague. He swung his ponderous
head toward the Tolant, stared a long moment, then
turned and lumbered back through the doorspace. The
curtains swung shut behind him.

Essu was beside Telzey, jerking her up to her
feet.

"Come! Come!" he hissed in translingue.

They hurried quietly on along the passage.

# Chapter 6

Essu, though a bold being, had been shaken by the encounter, and it continued to preoccupy him. As a rule, the green uniform of Stiltik's servants was safeguard enough against mistreatment by other Elaigar even when they weren't aware that he was her valued assistant. But when age came on them, they grew morose and became more savage and unpredictable than ever. The great knife might have turned swiftly on him after it finished Telzey; and to use one of the weapons on his belt then would have been almost as dangerous for Essu as not using them. Self-defense was no excuse for killing or injuring one of the masters.

Much greater, however, had been his fear of facing Stiltik after letting her prisoner get killed. He blamed Telzey for putting him in such a terrible predicament, and was simmering with vengeful notions. But he didn't let that distract him from choosing the rest of their route with great care.

Telzey, aware of Essu's angry spite, was too busy to give it much consideration. Being involved in Stiltik's business, the Tolant knew a great deal more about the circuit and what went on in it than the Tanvens; she was getting additional information now. The four Alattas involved in bringing her into the circuit had been operating here as Otessans—Tscharen and the woman Kolki Ming in Stiltik's command, the other two in Boragost's. Tscharen was permanently stationed in the circuit; the others were frequently given outside assignments. Stiltik had been watching Tscharen for some time; her spy system indicated he was occasionally engaged in off-duty activities in unused sealed areas, and she had her scientists set up traps. His secret meeting with the other three and the human they'd brought into the circuit with them was observed on a scanner. Knowing now that she dealt with Alatta infiltrators, Stiltik sprang her traps. But so far only Tscharen and the human had been caught. The others had withdrawn into sealed sections, and a search force of Elaigar and Tolants sent to dig them out had run into difficulties and returned empty-handed.

This obviously was a vast portal system which might almost rival the Luerral in its ramifications. Essu had seen a good deal of it on Stiltik's business, but by no means every part; and he was no more aware of exits to the planet or able to consider the possibility of making use of them than the Tanvens. How the Elaigar could have taken over such a complex, and killed off the humans living there, without creating a stir on Tinokti, was something else he didn't know. The answer might be found in the material Telzey's memory tap had drawn from the old Elaigar, but she couldn't spare time to start sorting through that at present.

None of the sections along their route seemed to be in use by the Elaigar. It was like moving about parts of a deserted city through which a marauding army had swept, stripping all removable equipment from some points while others remained overlooked. Where maintenance machinery still functioned completely, it often appeared that the former occupants might have left only the day before.

But all was silent; all was psi-blocked. Even where daylight or starshine filled empty courtyards or flowering gardens, impenetrable energy screens lay between them and the unaware world outside.

The arrangements of Stiltik's lockup were much like those in the series of sections through which Tscharen had taken Telzey. It lay well within a sealed area, and its connecting portals showed no betraying gleam,

remained barely visible for the moment it took Essu
and Telzey to pass them. The Tolant shoved her
eventually into a small room, slammed and locked the
door. She stayed with him mentally as he went off
down a passage to report by communicator to Stiltik,
who might be on the far side of Tinokti now.

He returned presently. The Elaigar commander had
indicated it still could be several hours before she
sent for them. When he opened the door, the prisoner was leaning against the wall. Essu went over to
the single large cot the room contained, sat down on
it, and fixed his round white eyes on the human.

Telzey looked at him. Torture and killing were the
high points of Essu's existence. She didn't particularly
blame him. Tolants regarded warfare as the natural
way of life, and when a group found itself temporarily out of neighbors, it relieved the monotony by
internal blood feuds. Under such circumstances, the
exercise of cruelty, the antidote to fear, became a
practical virtue. Elaigar service had done nothing to
diminish the tendency in Essu.

If he hadn't been required to take on responsibility
for the human captive, he would have been assist-
ing Stiltik now in her interrogation of Tscharen. That
pleasure was denied him. The human, in addition,
very nearly had placed him in the position of becoming a candidate for Stiltik's lingering attentions himself.
Clearly, she owed him something! He couldn't do
much to her, but Stiltik wouldn't begrudge him some
minor amusements to help while away the waiting
period.

Very deliberately then, Essu brought out the green
device with which he'd jabbed Telzey before, and let
her look at it.

Telzey sighed. She was now supposed to display
fear. Then, after she'd cringed sufficiently at the threat
of the prod, the hot stings would begin. If necessary,
she could shut out most of the pain and put up with

that kind of treatment for quite a while. Essu wouldn't risk carrying it far enough to incapacitate her. But it seemed a good time to find out whether it was still necessary to put up with anything at all from him.

She sent a series of impulses through one of the control centers she'd secured in Essu's mind. Essu carefully turned the green rod down, pointed it at his foot. One of his fingers pressed a button. He jerked his foot aside and uttered a shrill yelp. Then he quietly returned the rod to his pocket.

It was a good indication of solid control. However, she didn't feel quite sure of the Tolant. An unshielded telepathic mind which wasn't resisting might be taken over almost in moments by another psi, particularly if the other psi was of the same species. All required channels were wide open. A nontelepathic mind, even that of another human, could require considerable work. In Essu's mind, nontelepathic and nonhuman, there were many patterns which closely paralleled human ones. Others were quite dissimilar. Stiltik had left a kind of blueprint in there for Telzey to follow, but she didn't know whether she'd interpreted all the details of the blueprint correctly.

She put in some ten minutes of testing before she was certain. Essu performed perfectly. There was no reason to think he wouldn't continue to perform perfectly when he was no longer under direct control.

They left the sealed area together, moved on quickly. Stiltik wasn't likely to come looking for them soon, but as a start, Telzey wanted to put considerable distance between herself and the lockup. Some while later, she was on a narrow gallery overlooking a huge hall, watching Essu cross the hall almost two hundred yards below. He knew where he could pick up a set of circuit maps without drawing attention to himself, was on his way to get them. Dependable maps of the portal system were one of the things she was going to need. She'd kept one of Essu's weapons, a small gun which didn't demand too much experience with guns to be used effectively at close range. She also was keeping his key pack, except for the keys he needed for his present mission.

She followed him mentally. Essu knew what he was doing and it wouldn't occur to him to wonder why he was doing it. He'd simply serve her with mechanical loyalty, incapable of acting in any other way. As he reached the portal toward which he'd been headed and passed through it, his thought patterns vanished. But here, within the psi blocks enclosing the great hall and part of the structure behind Telzey, something else remained. The vague impression of a Tolant mentality.

So that veteran wild human Thrakell Dees had managed to follow them, as he'd said he would, and was now trying to remain unobtrusive! Telzey considered. Shortly after the encounter with the old Elaigar, she'd become aware of Thrakell's light, stealthy probe at her screens. She'd jabbed back irritatedly with psi and drawn a startled reaction. After that, Thrakell refrained from manifesting himself. She hadn't been sure until now that he was around.

He might, she thought, turn out to be more of a problem than a help. In any case, they'd have to have a definite understanding if they were to work together to reach a portal exit. He'd soon realize that Essu had left the area. Telzey decided to wait and see what he would do.

She settled herself on the gallery floor behind the balustrade, from where she could keep watch on the portal where Essu presently would reappear, and began bringing up information she'd tapped from the old Elaigar's mind and hadn't filtered through her awareness yet. She could spend some time on that now. Part of her attention remained on Thrakell's dimly shifting Tolant cover impressions.

The hodgepodge of information started to acquire some order as she let herself become conscious of it. The Elaigar's name was Korm. He'd been Suan Uwin once, a High Commander, who'd fallen into disgrace. . . .

She made some unexpected discoveries next.

They seemed a stranger variation of the human race than she'd thought, these Elaigar! Their individual life span was short—perhaps too short to have let them develop the intricate skills of civilization if they'd wanted to. As they considered it, however, mental and physical toil were equally unworthy of an Elaigar. They prided themselves on being the masters of those who'd acquired advanced civilized skills and were putting that knowledge now to Elaigar use.

She couldn't make out clearly what Korm's measurement of time came to in Federation units, but by normal human standards, he wasn't more than middle-aged, if that. As an Elaigar, he was very old. That limitation was a race secret, kept concealed from serfs. Essu and the Tanvens assumed Sattarams and Otessans were two distinct Elaigar strains. But one was simply the mature adult, the other the juvenile form, which apparently made a rather abrupt transition presently to adulthood.

The Alattas? A debased subrace. It had lost the ability to develop into Sattarams, and it worked like serfs because it had no serfs. Beyond that, the Alattas were enemies who might threaten the entire Elaigar campaign in the human Federation

Telzey broke off her review of Korm's muddled angry mind content.

Had there been some change in those fake Tolant impressions put out by Thrakell Dees? . . . Yes, there had! She came fully alert.

"Thrakell?"

No response. The impressions shifted slowly.

"You might as well start talking," she told him. "I know you're there!"

After a moment, his reply came sulkily. "You weren't very friendly a while ago!"

He didn't seem far away. Telzey glanced along the gallery, then over at the door through which she'd come out on it. Behind the door, a passage ran parallel to the gallery. Thrakell Dees probably was there.

She said, "I didn't think it was friendly of you either to try to get to my mind when you thought I might be too busy to notice! If we're going to work together, there can't be any more tricks like that."

A lengthy pause. The screening alien patterns blurred, reformed, blurred again.

"Where did you send the Tolant?" Thrakell Dees asked suddenly.

"He's getting something for me."

"What kind of thing?"

This time it was Telzey who didn't reply. Stalling, she thought. Her skin began to prickle. What was he up to?

She glanced uneasily up and down the gallery. He wasn't there. But—

Her breath caught softly.

It was as if she'd blinked away a blur on her vision.

She took Essu's gun from her jacket pocket, turned, pointed the gun toward the gallery wall on her right.

And there Thrakell Dees, moving very quietly toward her, barely twenty feet away, came to an abrupt halt, eyes widening in consternation.

"Yes, I see you now!" Telzey said between her teeth, cheeks hot with anger. "I know that not-there trick! And it won't work on me when I suspect it's being used."

Thrakell moistened his lips. He was a bony man of less than average height, who might be forty years of age. He wore shirt and trousers of mottled brown shades, a round white belt encircling his waist in two tight loops. He had small intent blue eyes, set deep under thick brows, and a high bulging forehead. His long hair was pulled sharply to the back of his head and tied there. A ragged beard framed the lower face.

"No need to point the gun at me," he said. He smiled, showing bad teeth. "I'm afraid I was trying to impress you with my abilities. I admit it was a thoughtless thing to do."

Telzey didn't lower the gun. She felt quite certain there'd been nothing thoughtless about that stealthy approach. He'd had a purpose; and whatever it had been, it wasn't simply to impress her with his abilities.

"Thrakell," she said, "just keep your hands in sight and sit down over there by the balustrade. You can help me watch the hall while I watch you. There're some things I want you to tell me about—but better not do anything at all to make me nervous before Essu gets back!"

He shrugged and complied. When he was settled on the floor to Telzey's satisfaction, she laid the gun down before her. Thrakell might be useful, but he was going to take watching, at least until she knew more about him.

He seemed anxious to make amends, answering her questions promptly and refraining from asking questions himself after she'd told him once there was no time for that now.

The picture she got of the Elaigar circuit was rather startling. What the Service was confronted with on Tinokti was a huge and virtually invisible fortress. The circuit had no official existence; there never had been a record of it in Tongi Phon files. Its individual sections were scattered about the planet, most of them buried among thousands of sections of other circuits, outwardly indistinguishable from them. If a section did happen to be identified and its force screens were overpowered, which could be no simple matter in populated areas, it would be cut automatically out of the circuit from a central control section, leaving searchers no farther than before. The control section itself lay deep underground. They'd have to start digging up Tinokti to locate it.

Then there was a device called the Vingarran, connected with the control section. Telzey had found impressions of it in the material drawn from Korm's mind. Korm knew how the Vingarran was used and hadn't been interested in knowing more. Thrakell couldn't add much. It was a development of alien technology, constructed by the Elaigar's serf scientists. It was like a superportal with a minimum range which made it unusable within the limited extent of a planet. Its original purpose might have been to provide interplanetary transportation. The Elaigar used it to connect the Tinokti circuit with spaceships at the fringes of the system. They came and went customarily by that method, though there were a number of portal exits to the planetary surface. They were in no way trapped here by the Service's investment of Tinokti.

"How could a circuit like that get set up in the first place?" Telzey asked.

Thrakell bared his teeth in an unpleasant grimace.

"Phons of the Institute planned it and had it done. Who else could have arranged it secretly?"

"Why did they do it?"

He shrugged. "It was their private kingdom. Whoever was brought into it, as I was one day, became their slave. Escape was impossible. Our Phon lords were responsible to no one and did as they pleased—until the Elaigar came. Then they were no more than their slaves and died with them."

Telzey reflected. "You've been able to tap Elaigar minds without getting caught at it?" she asked.

"I've done it on occasion," Thrakell said, "but I

haven't tried it for some time. I made a nearly disastrous slip with a relatively inexperienced Otessan, and decided to discontinue the practice. An Elaigar mind is always dangerous—the creatures are suspicious of one another and alert for attempted probes and controls. Instead I maintain an information network of unshielded serfs. I can pick up almost anything I want to know from one or the other of them, without running risks." He added, "Of course, old Korm can be probed rather safely, as I imagine you discovered."

"Yes, I did," Telzey said. "Then you've never tried to control one of them?"

Thrakell looked startled. "That would be most inadvisable!"

"It might be." Telzey said, "By our standards, Korm isn't really old, is he?"

"Not at all!" Thrakell Dees seemed amused. "Twenty-four Federation years, at most."

"They don't live any longer than *that*?" Telzey said.

"Few live even that long! One recurring satisfaction I've had here is to watch my enemies go lumbering down to death, one after the other, these past six years. Stiltik, at seventeen, is in her prime. Boragost, now twenty, is past his. And Korm exists only as an object lesson."

Telzey had seen that part vividly in Korm's jumbled recalls. Sattarams, male or female, weren't expected to outlive their vigor. When they began to weaken noticeably, they challenged younger and stronger Sattarams and died fighting. Those who appeared hesitant about it were taken to see Korm. He'd held back too long on issuing his final challenge, and had been shut away, left to deteriorate, his condition a warning to others who risked falling into the same error.

She learned that the Elaigar changed from the Otessan form to the adult one in their fourteenth year. That sudden drastic metamorphosis was also a racial

secret. Otessans approaching the point left the circuit; those who returned as Sattarams weren't recognized by the serfs. Thrakell could add nothing to
the information about the Alattas Telzey already had
gathered. He knew Alatta spies had been captured
in the circuit before this; they'd died by torture or
in ritual combat with Sattaram leaders. There was a
deadly enmity between the two obviously related
strains.

On the subject of the location of the Elaigar home
territories, he could offer only that they must be
several months' travel from the Hub clusters. And
Korm evidently knew no more. Space navigation was
serf work, its details below an Elaigar's notice.

"Have they caught the three Alattas who got away
from Stiltik yet?" Telzey asked.

There Thrakell was informed. He'd been listening
around among his mental contacts before following
Telzey to the hospital area. The three still had been
at large at that time, and there seemed to be no
immediate prospect of catching up with them. They'd
proved to be expert portal technicians who'd sealed
off sizable circuit areas by distorting portal patterns
and substituting their own. Stiltik's portal specialists
hadn't been able to handle the problem. The armed
party sent after the three was equipped with copies
of a key pack taken from Tscharen but had no better luck. The matter wasn't being discussed, and
Thrakell Dees suspected not all of the hunters had
returned.

"Stiltik would very much like to be able to
announce that she's rounded up the infiltrators," he
said. "It would add to her prestige which is high at
present."

"Apparently Stiltik and Boragost—the Suan Uwin—
don't get along very well?" Telzey said.

He laughed. "One of them will kill the other! Stiltik

doesn't intend to wait much longer to become senior Suan Uwin, and she's generally rated now as the deadliest fighter in the circuit. The Elaigar make few of our nice distinctions between the sexes."

Boragost's qualities as a leader, it appeared, were in question. Stiltik had been pushing for a unified drive to clear the Alattas out of the Federation. She'd gained a large following. Boragost blocked the move, on the grounds that a major operation of the kind couldn't be carried out without alerting the Federation's humans to the presence of aliens. And now Boragost had committed a blunder which might have accomplished just that. "You know what dagens are?" Thrakell asked.

"Yes. The mind hounds. I saw Stiltik's when they caught me."

He shifted uncomfortably. "Horrible creatures! Fortunately, there're only three in the circuit at present because few Elaigar are capable of controlling them. A short while ago, Boragost fumbled a dagen kill outside the circuit."

Telzey nodded. "Four Phons in the Institute. That wasn't planned then?"

"Far from it! Only one of the Phons was to die, and that neither in the Institute nor in the presence of witnesses. But Boragost failed to verify the victim's exact whereabouts at the moment he released the mind hound, and the mind hound, of course, went where the Phon was. When it found him among others, it killed them, too. Stiltik's followers claim that was what brought the Psychology Service to Tinokti."

"It was," Telzey said. "How will they settle it?"

"Almost certainly through Stiltik's challenge to Boragost. The other high-ranking Sattarams in the Hub have been coming in with their staffs through the Vingarran Gate throughout the week. They'll decide whether Boragost's conduct under their codes entitles Stiltik to challenge. If it does, he must accept. If it doesn't, she'll be deprived of rank and returned to their home territories. The codes these creatures bind themselves by are iron rules. It's the only way they have to avoid major butcheries among the factions."

Telzey was silent a moment, blinking reflectively at him.

"Thrakell," she said, "when we met, you told me you were the last human left alive in the circuit."

His eyes went wary. "That's right."

"There's been someone besides us with a human mind in this section for some little while now," Telzey told him. "The name is Neto. Neto Nayne-Mel."

# Chapter 7

Thrakell Dees said quickly, "Have nothing to do with that creature! She's dangerously unbalanced! I didn't tell you about her because I was afraid you might think of letting her join us."

"I am letting her join us," Telzey said.

Thrakell shook his head violently. "I advise you strongly against it! Neto Nayne-Mel is unpredictable. I know that she has ambushed and killed two Elaigar. She could endanger us all with her hatreds!"

Telzey said, "I understand she was a servant of the Elaigar in the circuit for a couple of years before she managed to get away from them. I suppose that might leave someone a little unbalanced. She's got something for me. I told her to bring it here to the gallery."

Thrakell grimaced nervously. "Neto's threatened to shoot me if she finds me within two hundred yards of her!"

"Well, Thrakell," Telzey said, "she may have caught you trying to sneak up on her, like I did. But that won't count now. We're going to need one another's help to get out. Neto understands that."

Thrakell argued no further. He still looked badly upset, due in part perhaps to the fact that there'd been a mental exchange between Neto and Telzey of which he'd remained unaware.

A human being who was to stay alive and at large for any length of time in the Elaigar circuit would need either an unreasonable amount of luck or rather special qualities. Thrakell, along with the ability to project a negation of his physical presence, had mental camouflage, and xenotelepathy which enabled him to draw information from unsuspecting alien mentalities around him.

Neto was otherwise equipped. Her mind didn't shield itself, but its patterns could be perceived only by a degree of psi sensitivity which Thrakell Dees lacked, and the Elaigar evidently also lacked. She'd devised a form of physical concealment almost as effective as Thrakell's. Her other resources were quick physical reactions and a natural accuracy with a gun which she'd discovered after escaping from her masters. She'd killed four Elaigar since then, not two. Her experiences had, in fact, left her somewhat unbalanced, but not in a way Telzey felt at all concerned about.

A few minutes later, Neto stepped out suddenly on the gallery a hundred feet away and started toward them. The figure they saw was that of a Fossily mechanic, one of the serf people in the circuit—a body of slim human type enclosed by a fitted yellow coverall which left only the face exposed. The face was a mask of vivid black and yellow lines. Neto was almost within speaking distance before the human features concealed by the Fossily face pattern began to be discernible.

That was the disguise Neto had adopted for herself. Fossily mechanics, with their tool kits hung knapsack-

wise behind their shoulders, were employed almost
everywhere in the circuit and drew no attention in
chance encounters. Moreover, they had a species odor
profoundly offensive to Elaigar nostrils. Their coverall suits were chemically impregnated to hide it; and
the resulting sour but tolerable smell also covered the
human scent. A second yellow tool bag swung by its
straps from Neto's gloved left hand. In it was a Fossily
suit for Telzey, and black and yellow face paint.

Essu returned not long afterwards. Telzey touched
his mind as he appeared in the portal down in the
great hall, and knew he'd carried out his assignment.
A pack of circuit diagram maps was concealed under
his uniform jacket. He hadn't let himself be seen.

He joined them on the gallery, blandly accepting
the presence of two wild humans and the fact that
Telzey and Neto were disguised as Fossily mechanics. Telzey looked at Thrakell Dees.

Thrakell could be a valuable confederate. Could
be. She wasn't sure what else he might be. Neto
suspected he was a murderer, that he'd done away
with other circuit survivors. There was no proof of
it, but Telzey hadn't taken her attention off him
since she'd caught him stalking her in his uncanny
manner on the gallery, and there'd been an occasional shimmer of human thought through the cover
pattern, which he'd changed meanwhile to that of
a Fossily mechanic. She'd made out nothing clearly,
but what she seemed to sense at those moments
hadn't reduced her uneasiness about Thrakell.

"Thrakell," she said, "before we get down to business, I'm giving you a choice."

He frowned. "A choice?"

"Yes. What I'd like you to do is to give up that
Fossily cover and open your screens for a minute,
so I can see what you're thinking. That would be
simplest."

Thrakell shook his head. "I don't understand."

Neto chuckled softly.

"Oh, you understand," Telzey said. "You wanted to come along when I try to get out of the circuit, so you are coming along. But we didn't get off to a good start, and I don't feel I can take you on trust now. You could prove I can by letting me look at your mind. Just the surface stuff—I want to know what made you decide to contact me, that's all."

Thrakell's small eyes glittered with angry apprehension. But his voice was even. "What if I refuse?"

"Then Essu will take your weapons and circuit key pack."

Thrakell looked shocked. "That's completely unfair! If we became separated, I'd be confined to whatever section I happened to be in. I'd be helpless!"

"Well, that will make you see to it we *don't* get separated," Telzey said. "I don't think we should now. Which will it be?"

Thrakell jerked his head sullenly at Neto. "What about her?"

"She's sure of me," Neto told him. "Quite, quite sure! She's already been all through my mind, that's why!" She laughed.

Essu, round white eyes fixed on Thrakell, reached for a gun on his belt, and Thrakell said hastily, "Let the Tolant have the articles then! I rarely use a weapon, in any case. I detest violence."

Essu began going over him with his search devices. Telzey and Neto looked on.

Telzey could, in fact, be very sure of Neto. Neto had known no hope of escape from the circuit. She'd lived by careful planning and constant alertness for the past two years, a vengeful, desperate ghost slipping about the fringe areas which would open to the portal keys she'd obtained, as wary of the few wild humans who'd still been around at first as of the Elaigar and their alien servants. There were periods when she no longer believed there was a world outside the circuit and seemed unable to remember what she had done before she met the Elaigar. At other times, she was aware of what was happening to her and knew there could be only one end to that.

Then, once more trailing the murderer who could slip up on you invisibly if you weren't careful, trying to determine what sort of mischief he was involved in, she'd touched a new mind.

In moments, Neto knew something like adoration. She'd found a protector, and gave herself over willingly and completely. Let this other one decide what should happen now, let her take control, as she began doing at once.

Neto's stresses dissolved in blind trust. Telzey saw to it that they did.

"Two problems," Telzey remarked presently. "The diagrams don't show exits to Tinokti, and they seem to add up to an incomplete map anyway. Then the keys we have between us apparently won't let us into more than about a fourth of the areas that look worth checking out. We could be one portal step away from an exit, know it's there, and still not be able to reach it."

Thrakell said sourly, "I see no way to remedy that! Many sections have a specialized or secret use, and only certain Elaigar leaders have access to them. That might well be the case with sections containing planetary exits. Then there's the fact that the Alatta intruders have altered the portal patterns of large complexes. I'm beginning to suspect you'll find yourself no more able to leave the circuit than we've been!" He glanced briefly over at Neto.

"Well," Telzey said, "let's try to get the second problem worked out first. Essu knows where he can get pretty complete sets of portal packs. But he will need help."

"What place is that?" asked Thrakell suspiciously. "As far as I know, only the Suan Uwin possess omnipacks."

"That's what Essu thinks. These are in a safe in one of Stiltik's offices. He can open the safe."

Thrakell shook his head.

"Impossible! Suicidal! The headquarters of the Suan Uwin are closely guarded against moves by political enemies. Even if we could get into Stiltik's compound, we'd never get out again alive!"

Neto said boredly to Telzey, "Why don't you lock this thing up somewhere? We can pick him up afterwards, if you feel like taking him along."

That ended Thrakell's protests. It wasn't, in fact, an impossible undertaking. Stiltik used Essu regularly to carry out special assignments which she preferred not to entrust even to close followers. There was a portal, unmarked and unguarded, to which only she and the Tolant had a key. If they were careful, they could get into the headquarters compound.

They did presently. They were then in a small room behind a locked door. To that door again only Stiltik and Essu had keys. Unless Stiltik happened to come in while they were there, they should be safe from detection.

Telzey scanned while her companions remained behind cover. It took time because she went about it very carefully, touching minds here and there with gossamer lightness. Details gradually developed. At last she thought she'd gathered a sufficiently complete picture.

Elaigar minds were about—some two dozen. There was no trace of Stiltik. The Suan Uwin appeared to be in an interrogation complex with the captured Alatta; and that understandably was a psi-blocked unit. There were Tolant minds and two unfamiliar alien mind types here. The serfs didn't count, and the only Elaigar in the central offices were two bored Otessan females, keeping an eye on the working staff. They might notice Essu going into Stiltik's offices presently, but there was nothing unusual about that. They weren't likely to be aware he was supposed to be somewhere else.

Another of the minds around here might count for a great deal. It was that of Stiltik's dagen.

The work she'd put in improving her psi techniques with Sams Larking and by herself was making all the difference now, Telzey thought. When Bozo was tracking her, she'd felt and been nearly helpless. She'd better remain very wary around this psi beast, but she wasn't in the least helpless, and knew it. Her screens hid her mind from it, and she'd learned how to reach through the screens with delicately sensing probes.

A probe reached toward the dagen mind—the barest touch. There was no reaction. Cautiously then, Telzey began to trace out what she could discern.

The creature was in an enclosure without physical exits. It needed none, of course. On Stiltik's order, it could flick itself into the enclosure and out again.

It could do very little that wasn't done on Stiltik's mental orders. Stiltik had clamped heavy and rigid controls on her monster. A human mind placed under similar controls would have been effectively paralyzed. The dagen's rugged psyche was in no sense paralyzed. It simply was unable to act except as its handler permitted it to act.

It wasn't very intelligent, but it knew who kept it chained.

Telzey studied the controls until she was satisfied she understood them. Then she told Essu to go after the omnipacks in Stiltik's office. She accompanied him mentally, alert for developing problems. Essu encountered none and was back with the packs five minutes later. He'd been seen but disregarded. Nothing seemed to have changed in the headquarters compound.

They left by the secret portal, and Essu handed Telzey its key. She said to the others, "Wait for me here! When I come out, we'll go back along the route we came—and for the first few sections we'll be running."

Thrakell Dees whispered agitatedly, "What are—"

She stepped through the portal into the room. Her mind returned gently to the dagen mind. The beast seemed half asleep now.

Psi sheared abruptly through Stiltik's control patterns. As abruptly, the dagen came awake. Telzey slipped out through the portal.

"Now *run!*"

Essu's haul of portal key packs had been eminently satisfactory. One of them had been taken from Tscharen after his capture. Essu interlocked it with an omnipack, gave the combination to Telzey. She slipped it into a pocket of the Fossily suit. It was small, weighed half as much as Essu's gun which was in another pocket of the suit. But it would open most of the significant sections of the circuit to her. Essu assembled a duplicate for himself with a copy of Tscharen's pack, clamped the other keys together at random, and pocketed both sets. Thrakell Dees looked bitter, but said nothing. The arrangement was that he would stay close enough to Essu to pass through any portal they came to with the Tolant. Neto would stay similarly close to Telzey.

"And now?" Thrakell asked.

"Now we'll pick a route to the hospital area where the Tanvens put me back in shape," Telzey said. "We still want a guide."

# Chapter 8

The Third Planetary Exit control room was quiet. Telzey was at the instrument stand, watching the viewscreen. Thrakell Dees sat on the floor off to her left, with his back to the wall. He was getting some of her attention. A Sattaram giant was near the door behind her. He needed no attention—he was lying on his back and very dead.

In a room on the level below them, Neto and Korm, one-time Suan Uwin of the Elaigar, waited behind a locked door. Some attention from Telzey was required there from moment to moment, mainly to make sure Korm kept his mind shield tight. He'd been out of practice too long in that matter. Otherwise, he seemed ready to go. Neto was completely ready to go.

The viewscreen showed the circuit exit area on the other side of the locked door. The portal which opened on Tinokti was within a shielded vault-like recess of a massive square structure a hundred yards across—mainly, it seemed, as a precaution against an Alatta attempt to invade the circuit at this point. The controls of the shielding and of the portal itself were on the instrument stand, and Telzey was ready to use them. She was also ready to unlock the door for Neto and Korm.

She couldn't do it at the moment. Something like a dozen Elaigar stood or moved around the exit structure. They were never all in sight at the same time, so she wasn't sure of the number. It was approximately a dozen. Most of them were Otessans; but at least three Sattarams were among them. Technically, they were on guard duty. Telzey had gathered from occasional washes of Elaigar thought that the duty was chiefly a disciplinary measure; these were members of visiting teams who'd got into trouble in the circuit. They weren't taking the assignment very seriously, but all wore guns. About half of them might be in view along the front of the structure at any one time. At present, only four were there.

Four were still too many. Essu would have been useful now, but Essu was dead. Korm had been leading them through a section like a giant greenhouse, long untended, when they spotted a Boragost patrol coming toward them and realized an encounter couldn't be avoided. The troops handled it well. Telzey and Thrakell didn't take part in the action, and weren't needed. The patrol—a Sattaram, an Otessan, six or seven Tolants—was ambushed in dense vegetation, wiped out in moments. Korm gained a Sattaram uniform in Boragost's black and silver, which was better cover for him than what he was wearing. And Telzey lost Essu.

She spared a momentary glance for Thrakell Dees. He was watching her, face expressionless.

When they'd taken the control room, looked at the situation in the exit area, she'd said to him, "You realize we can only get Neto through here. You and I'll have to get away and do something else."

Korm wouldn't accompany them—that was understood by everyone in the room but Korm.

Thrakell hadn't argued, and Telzey wasn't surprised. She'd been studying him as she'd studied Korm on the way, trying to draw in as much last-minute information on a number of matters as she could. It had seemed to her presently that Thrakell Dees didn't really intend to leave the Elaigar circuit. Why he'd approached her originally remained unclear. What he mainly wanted now was one of the portal omnipacks she carried, the one Essu had assembled for her, or the one she'd taken from Essu after he was killed.

Thrakell had mentioned it, as a practical matter, after Korm and Neto took up their stations on the lower level, and they were alone in the control room.

"Thrakell," she'd said, "I need *you* as a guide now. There's a place I want to go to next, and it seems to be about as far from this part of the circuit as one can get. I might find it by myself with the maps, but it'll be faster with you. We've already spent too much time. I want to be there before anyone starts hunting for me."

Thrakell blinked slowly.

"What's the significance of the place?"

"The Alattas switched me into the circuit by a portal," Telzey said. "It may still be there and operational. If it is, you can get back to Tinokti, if you like. Or you can have one of the omnipacks—after you've let me look into your mind. That's still a condition. We can split up at that point. Not yet."

Thrakell stared at her a moment.

"I had the curious impression," he remarked, "that you'd decided before we got here you wouldn't be using this exit yourself to leave the circuit. The degree of control you've been exercising over Korm and Neto Nayne-Mel shows you could have arranged to do it, of course. I'm wondering about your motivation."

She smiled. "That makes us even. I've wondered a bit about yours."

But it had startled her. So he'd been studying her, too. She'd tried to be careful, but tensions were heavy now and she'd been preoccupied. She wasn't sure how much she might have revealed.

It was true she couldn't afford to leave yet. There were possibilities in the overall situation no one could have suspected, and her information wasn't definite enough. A faulty or incomplete report might do more harm than none; she simply wasn't sure. Through Neto she could see to it that the Service would at least know everything she was able to guess at present. So Neto would be maneuvered safely out of the circuit here. If possible.

But Neto wouldn't report immediately. The planetary exit opened into an old unused Phon villa. Neto would find money and aircars there. She'd get out of her Fossily disguise, move on and lie low in one of Tinokti's cities for the next ten days. If Telzey hadn't showed up by that time, Neto would contact the Psychology Service.

Telzey leaned forward suddenly, hands shifting

toward the controls she'd marked. Thrakell stirred in his corner.

"Stay where you are!" she told him, without taking her eyes from the screen. Essu's gun lay on the stand beside her. With neither Essu nor Neto to watch him, Thrakell was going to take careful handling.

She nudged Neto, Korm. *Alert!* Neto responded. Korm didn't. He hadn't felt the nudge consciously, but he was now aware that the action might be about to begin. He was eager for it. Telzey had spent forty minutes working on him before he led them out of the hospital area. It was a patchwork job, but it would hold up as long as it had to. Korm's fears and hesitancies had been blocked away; in his mind, he was the lordly Suan Uwin of a few years ago. Insult had been offered him, and there was a raging thirst for vengeance simmering just below the surface, ready to be triggered. His great knife hung from his belt along with two Elaigar guns.

Two of the four Otessans who'd been in view in the screen still stood near the shielded portal recess. The other pair had moved toward the corner of the structure, and a Sattaram now had appeared there and was speaking to them. Telzey's finger rested on the door's lock switch. She watched the three, biting her lip.

The Sattaram turned, went around the side of the structure. The two Otessans followed. As they vanished, she unlocked the door in the room below. Whisper of acknowledgment from Neto.

And now to keep Korm's shield tight—tight—

He came into view below. The two remaining Otessans turned to look at him. He strode toward them, the fake Fossily mechanic trotting nimbly at his heels, keeping Korm between herself and the Otessans. Korm was huge, even among Sattarams. He was in the uniform of an officer of Boragost's command, and his age-ravaged face was half hidden by

black rank markings which identified him as one of
Boragost's temporary deputies. The two might be
curious about what special duty brought him here,
but no more than that.

He came up to them. His knife was abruptly deep
in an Otessan chest.

They had flash reactions. The other had leaped
sideways and back, and his gun was in his hand. It
wasn't Korm but the gun already waiting in Neto's
hand which brought that one down. She darted past
him as the recess shield opened and the exit portal
woke into gleaming life behind it. Through recess and
portal—gone! The recess shield closed.

Korm's guns and his fury erupted together. Turning from the screen, Telzey had a glimpse of Elaigar
shapes appearing at the side of the structure, of two
or three going down. Korm roared in savage triumph.
He wouldn't last long, but she'd locked the door on
the lower level again. Survivors couldn't get out until
someone came to let them out. . . .

That, however, might happen at any time.


She was seen twice on the way to the brightly lit
big room where she and Tscharen had been captured,
but nobody paid the purposefully moving mechanic
any attention; and, of course, nobody saw Thrakell
Dees. Another time they spotted an approaching
Fossily work party led by a pair of Otessans, and got
out of sight. They had to stay out of sight a while
then—the mechanics were busy not at all far from
their hiding place. Telzey drifted mentally about the
Otessans, presently was following much of their talk.

There were interesting rumors going around about
the accident in the headquarters compound of Stiltik's
command. The two had heard different versions. It was
clear that the Suan Uwin's mind hound had slipped
its controls and made a shambles of the place. Stiltik's
carelessness . . . or could wily old Boragost have had

a hand in that slipping? They argued the point. The
mind hound was dead; so were an unspecified number of Stiltik's top officers. Neither fact would *hurt*
Boragost! But how could he have gone about it?

Stiltik, unfortunately, wasn't among the casualties.
She'd killed the dagen herself. Telzey thought it might
at least keep her mind off the human psi for a while,
though that wasn't certain. The ambushed Boragost
patrol apparently hadn't been missed yet; nor was there
mention of a maniac Sattaram who'd tried to wipe out
the guards at Planetary Exit Three. The circuit should
be simmering with rumors and speculations presently.

They reached the big room at last. Telzey motioned
Thrakell to stand off to one side, then went toward
the paneled wall through which she'd stepped with
Tscharen, trying to remember the exact location of
the portal. Not far from the centerline of the
room. . . . She came to that point, and no dim portal outline appeared in the wall. She turned right,
moved along the wall, left hand sliding across the
panels. Eight steps on, her hand dipped into the wall.
Now the portal was there in ghostly semivisibility.

She turned, beckoned to Thrakell Dees.

She'd memorized the route along which Tscharen
had taken her, almost automatically, but thinking even
then it wasn't impossible she'd be returning over it by
herself. She found now she had very little searching
to do. It helped that these were small circuit sections,
a few rooms cut here and there out of Tinokti's buildings. It helped, too, that Thrakell remained on his best
behavior. When they passed through the glimmering
of a portal into another dim hall or room, he was closer
to her than she liked, but that couldn't be avoided.
Essu's gun was in a pocket on the side she kept turned
away from him. Between portals he walked ahead of
her without waiting to be told.

He knew they'd entered a sealed area and should
know they were getting close to the place where she'd

been brought into the circuit. Neither of them mentioned it. Telzey felt sure he didn't have the slightest intention of letting her look into his mind, couldn't afford to do it. What he did intend, beyond getting one of the key packs, remained obscure. Not a trickle of comprehensible thought had come through the blur of reproduced alien patterns, which now seemed to change from moment to moment as if Thrakell were mimicking first one species, then another. He might be trying to distract her. She had no further need of him as a guide; in fact, he soon could become a liability. The question was what to do with him.

She located the eight portals along the route in twice as many minutes. Then, at the end of a passage, there was a door. She motioned Thrakell aside again, tried the handle, drew the door back, and was looking down one side of the L-shaped room into which she'd been transported from the Luerral Circuit. The other door, the one by which the three Alattas had entered, stood open. The big wall closet they'd used for storage was also open. A stink of burned materials came from it. So Stiltik's searchers had been here.

She glanced at Thrakell. His intent little eyes met hers for an instant. She indicated the room. "Stand over there against the wall! I want to look around. And keep quiet—Stiltik had gadgets installed here. They just might still be operating."

He nodded, entered the room and stopped by the wall. Telzey went past him, to the corner of the ell. There were no signs of damage in the other part of the room. The portal which had brought her into the circuit might still be there, undetected, and one of the keys Tscharen had carried might activate it.

She'd wanted to find out about that. In an emergency, it could be the last remaining way of escape.

There was an abrupt crashing sound high above her, to her left. Startled, she spun around, looking up.

Something whipped about her ankles and drew her legs together in a sudden violent jerk, throwing her off balance.

# Chapter 9

She went down, turning, as the metal ring Thrakell had pitched against the overhead window strip to deflect her attention clattered to the floor. The Fossily bag on her back padded her fall. Thrakell, plunging toward her, came to an abrupt stop five feet away.

"You almost made it!" Telzey said softly. "But don't you dare move now!"

He looked at the gun pointed at his middle. His face whitened. "I meant no harm! I—"

"Don't talk either, Thrakell. You know I may have to kill you. So be careful!"

Thrakell was silent then. Telzey got into a sitting position, drew her legs up, looked at her ankles and back at Thrakell. The thing that clamped her legs together, held them locked tightly enough to be painful, was the round white cord which had been wrapped about his waist as a belt. No belt—a weapon, and one which had fooled Essu and his search instruments.

"How do you make it stop squeezing and come loose?" she asked.

It seemed there were controls installed in each tapered end of the slick white rope. Telzey told Thrakell to get down on hands and knees, stretched her legs out toward him, and had him crawl up until he could reach her ankles and free her. Then she edged back, got to her feet. The gun had remained pointed at Thrakell throughout. "Show me how to work it," she said.

Thrakell looked glum, but showed her. It was simple enough. Hold the thing by one end, press the setting that prepared it to coil with the degree of force desired. Whatever it touched next was instantly wrapped up.

Telzey put the information to use, and the device soon held Thrakell's wrists pinned together behind him.

"Now let me explain," he said. He cleared his throat. "I realized the circuit exit of which you spoke must be somewhere nearby—probably in this room! I was afraid you might have decided to use it and leave me here. I only wanted to be certain you didn't. Surely, you understand, that?"

"Just stay where you are," Telzey said.

The key packs she carried evoked no portal glimmer anywhere in the big room. The one which had transported her here probably had been destructured immediately afterwards. So there'd be no emergency escape open to her now by that route. Part of one of the walls of the adjoining room had been blasted away, down to the point where its materials were turned into unyielding slickness by the force field net pressing against them.

Telzey looked at the spot a moment. There had been a portal there, the one by which the three Alattas had entered. But Stiltik's search party had located it, and made sure it wouldn't be used again. No other portal led away from the room.

She went back into the big room, told Thrakell, "Go stand against the wall over there, facing me."

"Why?" he said warily.

"Go ahead. We have to settle something."

Thrakell moved over to the wall with obvious reluctance. "You haven't accepted my explanation?"

"No," Telzey said.

"If I'd wanted to hurt you, I could have set the cord as easily to break your legs!"

"Or my neck," Telzey agreed. "I know you weren't

trying to do that. But I have to find out what you were trying to do. So get rid of that blur over your mind, and open your screens."

"I'm afraid that's impossible," Thrakell said.

"You won't do it?"

"I'm unable to do it. I can dispel one pattern only by forming another." Thrakell shrugged, smiled. "I have no psi screen otherwise, and my mind evidently refuses to expose itself! I can do nothing about it consciously."

"That's about what I told Stiltik when she wanted me to open my screens," Telzey said thoughtfully. "She didn't believe me. I don't believe you either." She took Essu's gun from her pocket.

Thrakell looked at the gun, at her face. He shook his head.

"No," he said. "You might have killed me after I tripped you up. You felt threatened. But you won't kill someone who's helpless and can't endanger you."

"Don't count on it," Telzey said. "Right now, I'll be trying not to kill you—but I probably will, anyway."

Alarm showed in Thrakell's face. "What do you mean?"

"I'm going to shoot as close to you as I can without hitting you," Telzey explained. "But I'm not really that good a shot. Sooner or later, you'll get hit."

"That's—"

She lifted the gun, pointed it, pressed the trigger button. There was a thudding sound, and a blazing patch twice the size of her palm appeared on the wall four inches from Thrakell's left ear. He cried out in fright, jerked away from it.

Telzey said, somewhat shakily, "That wasn't where I was aiming! And you'd better not move again because I'll be shooting on both sides . . . like this!"

She didn't come quite as close to him this time, but Thrakell yelled and dropped to his knees.

"Above your head!" Telzey told him.

The concealing blur of mind patterns vanished. Thrakell was making harsh sobbing noises. Telzey placed the gun back in her pocket. Her hands were trembling. She drew in a slow breath.

"Keep it open," she said.

Presently, she added, "I've got what I wanted—and I see you're somebody I can't control. You can blur up again. And stand up. We're leaving. How long have you been working for Boragost?"

Thrakell swallowed. "Two years. I had no choice. I faced torture and death!"

"I saw that," Telzey said. "Come along."

She led the way from the room toward the portaled sections. She'd seen more than that. Thrakell Dees, as she'd suspected, hadn't joined her with the intention of getting out of the Elaigar circuit. He couldn't afford being investigated on Tinokti, particularly not by the Psychology Service; and if the Service learned about him from Neto or Telzey, he'd have no chance of avoiding an investigation. Besides, he'd made a rather good thing out of being a secret operator for Boragost. As he judged it, the Elaigar would remain securely entrenched on Tinokti and elsewhere in the Hub for a considerable time. There was no immediate reason to think of changing his way of life. However, he should be prepared to shift allegiance in case the showdown between Boragost and Stiltik left Stiltik on top, as it probably would. The return of Telzey alive was an offering which would smooth his way with Stiltik. He'd hoped to be able to add to it the report of an undiscovered portal used by Alattas.

Under its blurring patterns, Thrakell's mind was wide open and unprotected. But Telzey couldn't simply take control of him as she'd intended. She'd heard there were psi minds like that. Thrakell's was the first she'd encountered. There seemed to be none of the standard control points by which a mind could be secured, and she didn't have time for experimentation. Boragost hadn't found a way to control Thrakell directly. It wasn't likely she would.

She said over her shoulder, "I'm taking you along because the only other thing I can do at the moment is kill you, and I'd still rather not. Don't ask questions—I'm not telling you anything. You'll just be there. Don't interfere or try to get away! If I shoot at you again, I won't be trying to miss."

There were portals in the string of sections she'd come through which led deeper into the circuit's sealed areas. At least, there had to be one such portal. The three Alattas had used it in effecting their withdrawal; so had Stiltik's hunters in following them. It should open to one of the keys that had been part of Tscharen's pack.

Telzey found the portal in the second section up from the big room, passed through it with Thrakell Dees into another nondescript place, dingy and windowless. A portal presently awoke to glimmering life in one of the walls. They went on.

The next section was very dimly lit and apparently extensive. Telzey stationed Thrakell in the main passage, went into a room, checked it and an adjoining room out, returned to the passage, started along it

Slight creak of the neglected flooring—and abrupt blazing awareness of something overlooked! She dropped to her knees, bent forward, clawing out Essu's gun.

Thrakell's strangle rope slapped against the passage wall above her. She rolled away from it as it fell, and Thrakell pounced on her, pinning her to the floor on her side, the gun beneath her. She forced it out, twisted the muzzle up, pressed the trigger blindly. There was the thudding sound of the charge, and a yell of alarm from Thrakell. Something ripped at the Fossily suit. Then his weight was abruptly off her. She

rolled over, saw him darting along the passage toward
the portal through which they'd come, knew he'd got
one or both of her key packs.

She pointed the gun at the moving figure, pressed
the trigger five or six times as quickly as she could.
She missed Thrakell. But the charges formed a sudden blazing pattern on the portal wall ahead of him,
and he veered aside out of the line of fire and vanished through a doorspace that opened on the
passage.

Breathing hard, Telzey came up on her knees, saw
one of the key packs lying beside her, picked it up,
looked at it and put it in her left suit pocket. The
pocket on the right side had been almost torn off, and
Thrakell had got away with the other pack. Something
stirred behind her. She glanced around, saw the white
rope lying against the wall a few feet away—stretched
out, shifting, turning with stiff springy motions, unable
to grip what it had touched. She stood up on shaky
legs, reached down until the gun almost touched the
thing, and blasted it apart. Thrakell wasn't going to be
able to use that device against her again—this time it
*had* been aimed at her neck.

She started quietly down the passage toward the
doorspace, gun held ready to fire. No sounds came
tion, and she could pick up no trace of Thrakell's
camouflage patterns. She didn't like that—she wasn't
sure now he mightn't have tricks he hadn't revealed
so far.

She stepped out before the doorspace, gun pointing
into the room behind it.

It was a rather small room, as dimly lit as the rest
of the section, and empty. Not-there effect or not,
Thrakell wasn't in it; after a moment, Telzey felt sure
of that. There was another doorway on one side. She
couldn't see what lay beyond it. But if it was a dead
end, if it didn't lead to a portal, she had Thrakell
boxed in.

She started cautiously into the room.

Her foot went on down through the floor as if nothing were there. She caught at the doorjamb with her free hand, discovered it had become as insubstantial as the floor. Falling, she twisted backward, landed on her back in the passage, legs dangling from the knees down through the nothingness of the room's floor . . . through a portal.

She discovered then that she'd hung on to the gun. She let go of it, squirmed back from the trap, completely unnerved.

# Chapter 10

No need to look farther for Thrakell Dees! When Telzey felt steady enough to stand up, she went back to the two rooms she'd checked. A partly disassembled piece of machinery stood in one of them. She looked it over, discovered a twelve-foot section of thin, light piping she could remove, detached it and straightened it out. She took that to the room with the portal flooring, reached down through the portal with it. The tip didn't touch anything even when she knelt in the doorway, her hand a few inches above the floor, and when she twisted the piping about horizontally, she didn't reach the sides of whatever was below there either.

She drew the piping out again. It was cold to the touch now, showed spots of frosting. The portal trap extended about twelve feet into the room. It had been activated by her key pack, as it had been activated by the pack Thrakell had taken from her. Wherever he'd gone, he wasn't likely to be back.

Essu and Thrakell had heard that the group Stiltik

sent into the sealed areas after the Alattas had run into difficulties and returned. If this was a sample of the difficulties they'd run into, it wasn't surprising that Stiltik seemed to have been in no great hurry to continue her efforts to dig the three out of hiding.

When Telzey started off again to look for the portal which would take her on to the next section, her key pack was fastened to the tip of the piping, and she didn't put her foot anywhere the pack hadn't touched and found solid first. Her diagram maps didn't tell her at all definitely where she was, but did indicate that she'd moved beyond the possibility of being picked up in scanning systems installed by Stiltik's technicians. What lay ahead was, temporarily at least, Alatta territory. And the Alattas had set up their own scan systems. Presently she should be registering in them.

She uncovered a number of other portal traps. One of them, rather shockingly, was a wall portal indistinguishable from all the others she'd passed through. If she hadn't been put on guard, there would have been no reason to assume it wasn't the section exit she was trying to find. But a probe with the piping revealed there was a sheer drop beyond. The actual exit was a few yards farther on along the wall. She passed through a few larger sections of the type she'd had in mind as a place to get rid of Thrakell Dees, stocked with provisions sufficient to have kept him going for years, or until someone came to get him out. She stopped in one of them long enough to wash the Fossily tiger striping from her face.

And then she was in a section where it seemed she couldn't go on. She'd been around the walls and come back to the portal by which she'd entered. She stood still, reflecting. She'd expected to reach a place like this eventually. What it would mean was that she had come to the limit of the area made open to Tscharen's portal keys. There should be a second portal here— one newly provided with settings which could be activated only by keys carried now by the other three Alattas.

But she hadn't expected to get to that point so soon.

Her gaze shifted to an area of flooring thirty feet away. There was a portal there. A trap. An invisible rectangle some eight feet long by six wide, lying almost against the wall. She'd discovered it as she moved along the wall, established its contours, gone around it.

She went back there now, tapping the floor ahead of her with the key pack until it sank out of sight. She drew it back, defined the outline of the portal with it again, moved up to the edge. She hadn't stopped to probe the trap before; there'd been no reason for it. Now she reversed the piping, gripped it by the pack, let the other end down through the portal.

There was a pull on the piping. She allowed it to follow the pull. It swung to her left as if drawn by a magnet on the far side of the portal, until its unseen tip touched a solid surface. It stayed there. Telzey's eyelids flickered. She moved quickly around to that end of the portal, knelt down beside it, already sure of what she'd found.

She pulled out the piping, reached through the portal with her arm, touched a smooth solid surface seemingly set at right angles to the one on which she knelt. She patted it probingly, lifted her hand away and let it drop back—pulled by gravity which also seemed set at right angles to the pull of gravity on this side of the portal. She shoved the piping through then, bent forward and came crawling out of the lower end of a wall portal into a new section.

Something like two hours after setting out from the big room with Thrakell Dees, she knew she'd reached the end of her route. She was now on the perimeter of the area the Alattas had made inaccessible to all others. She'd checked the section carefully. The only portal she could use here was the one by which she'd entered. Her key pack would take her no farther.

There was nothing to indicate what purpose this section originally had served. It was a sizable complex with a large central area, smaller rooms and passages along the sides. It was completely empty, a blank, lifeless place in which her footsteps raised hollow echoes. She laid the piping down by a wall of the central area, got her Tinokti street clothes out of the Fossily tool bag, changed to them, and sat down with her back to the wall.

A waiting game now. She leaned her head against the wall, closed her eyes. Mind screens thinned almost to the point of nonexistence, permitting ultimate sensitivity of perception. Meanwhile she rested physically.

Time passed. At last, her screens tightened in abrupt warning. She thinned them again, waited again.

Somewhere something stirred.

It was the least, most momentary of stirrings. As if ears had pricked quietly, or sharp eyes had turned to peer in her direction, not seeing her yet but aware there was something to be seen.

A thought touched her suddenly, like a thin cold whisper:

"If you move, make a sound, or think a warning, you'll die."

There was a shivering in the air. Then a great dagen crouched on the floor fifteen feet away, squatted back on its haunches, staring at Telzey. Swift electric thrills ran up and down her spine. This was a huge beast, bigger and heavier than the other two she'd seen, lighter in color. The small red eyes in the massive head had murder in them.

Her screens had locked instantly into a defensive shield. She made no physical motion at all.

The mind hound vanished.

Telzey's gaze shifted to the left. A tall figure stood in a passage entrance, the Alatta woman Kolki Ming. For a moment, she studied Telzey, the Fossily bag, the length of piping with the attached key pack.

"This is a surprise!" she said. "We didn't expect you here, though there was some reason to believe you were no longer Stiltik's captive. You came alone?"

"Yes."

The Alatta nodded. "We'll see."

She remained silent a minute or two, eyes fixed expressionlessly on Telzey. Telzey guessed the dagen was scouting through adjoining sections.

Kolki Ming said suddenly, "It seems you did come alone. How did you escape?"

"Stiltik put a Tolant in charge of me. Essu. We were off by ourselves."

"And you took Essu under control?"

"Yes."

"Where is he now?"

"He got killed. We ran into some of Boragost's people."

"A patrol in the ninety-sixth sector?"

"A big greenhouse."

"You've been busy today!" Kolki Ming remarked. "That patrol was reported wiped out by gunfire. Tell me the rest of it."

Neto Nayne-Mel wouldn't be mentioned. Telzey gave a brief and fairly truthful account of her activities otherwise. She'd planned to get back to Tinokti at once, had realized by the time she reached the planetary exit why she couldn't—that she didn't know enough about the role the Alattas were playing in connection with the Tinokti circuit and in the Hub. She found then she'd worked Korm up too far to restrain him sufficiently. She and Thrakell Dees left for the sealed areas, while Korm went after the exit guards.

"Where is Boragost's strangler now?" the Alatta asked.

"We had a disagreement. He fell through one of your portal traps."

Kolki Ming shook her head slightly.

"And you're here to find out what we're doing," she said. "The Elaigar have one dagen less at their disposal, which is no small advantage to us. We might seem to owe you the information. But we can't let you take it to the Psychology Service. Essu's body, incidentally, wasn't found with the dead of the patrol."

"We took him along and hid him somewhere else," Telzey said. "I thought Stiltik mightn't know yet that I'd got away."

"She may not." The Alatta considered. "We're involved in an operation of extreme importance. Tscharen's capture has forced us to modify it and made it much more difficult than it should have been. It will have to be concluded quickly if it's to succeed. I'm not sure we can fit you in, but for the moment, at least, you're coming with me. Let me have your gun."

They emerged from a portal into a dark narrow street a few minutes later. The only light came from dim overhead globes. Looking back as they walked on, Telzey saw a dilapidated wall looming behind them. They'd stepped out of that. To right and left were small shabby houses, pressed close together. The cracked pavement was covered here and there by piles of litter. There was a stale smell in the air, and from somewhere arose a vague rumbling, so indistinct it seemed a tactile sensation rather than something heard.

"This section was some Phon's private experimental project," Kolki Ming said. "It doesn't appear on any regular circuit map and the Elaigar never found it, so we're using it as a temporary operations base." She glanced about. "Some two hundred people were trapped here when the Elaigar came. They escaped the general killing but were unable to leave the section and died when their supplies gave out."

She broke off. Something flicked abruptly through Telzey's awareness—a brief savage flash of psi. There was a gurgling howl, and the dagen materialized across the street from them.

"Scag was waiting for us, hoping to remain unnoticed," Kolki Ming said.

"He was going to attack?"

"If he got the chance. When he's under light working controls, as at present, he needs careful watching." They'd turned into another street, somewhat wider than the first, otherwise no different from it. On either side was the same ugly huddle of houses, lightless and silent. The mind hound was striding soundlessly along with them now, thirty feet away. The Alatta turned in toward one of the larger houses. "Here's my watchpost."

The ground floor of the house had been cleared of whatever it might have contained. Two portal outlines flickered on the walls, and a variety of instruments stood about, apparently hastily assembled. Kolki Ming said, "Ellorad and Sartes won't be back for a while. Sit down while I check on my duties."

"There's one thing I'd like to know," Telzey said.

"Yes?"

"How old are you?"

The Alatta glanced over at her.

"So you learned about that," she said. "I'm twenty-seven of your standard years. As for the rest of it, there may be time to talk later."

Telzey sat down on an empty instrument case, while Kolki Ming spoke briefly into a communicator. She seemed to listen then to a reply which remained inaudible to Telzey, and turned to a panel of scanning devices.

Presently they had time to talk.

✧   ✧   ✧

The Elaigar's transition to the Sattaram form at maturity was connected with a death gene the Grisand cult on Nalakia had designed to help keep the mutation under control. The Elaigar didn't know it. After they destroyed the Grisands, they developed no biological science of their own, and to allow serf scientists to experiment physically with the masters was unthinkable under their code system.

But an early group had broken that rule. They set alien researchers the task of finding a method of prolonging their lives. They were told that for them as individuals there was no method, but that the gene could be deleted for their offspring. They settled for that—the Alattas came into existence. They remained Otessans in physical structure and had regained a normal human life span. With it, they presently regained lost interests and goals. They had time to learn, and learned very quickly because they could draw in the Elaigar manner on alien science and technology. Now they began making both their own.

Most of the Elaigar despised them equally for having abandoned the majestic structure of the mature Lion People and for degrading themselves with serf labor. They did their best to wipe out the new strain, but the Alattas drew ahead from the start.

"That was centuries ago, of course," said Kolki Ming. "We have our own civilization now and no longer need to borrow from others—though the Federation of the Hub was still one of our teachers on occasion as little as eighty years ago. The Elaigar remain dependent on their slave people and are no longer a match for us. And their codes limit them mentally. Some join us of their own accord, and while we can do nothing for them, their children acquire our life span. Otherwise, we collect the Elaigar at every opportunity, and whether they want it or not, any children of those we collect are also born as

Alattas. They hate us for that, but they've become divided among themselves. In part, that's what led them to risk everything on this operation in the Hub. Bringing the old human enemy under control seemed a project great enough to unite them again. When we discovered what they were doing, we came back to the Federation ourselves."

Telzey said, "You've been trying to get them out of the Federation before we found out they were around?"

"That was the plan. We want no revival of that ancient trouble. It hasn't been a simple undertaking, but we've worked very carefully, and our preparations are complete. We three had the assignment to secure the central control section of the Tinokti circuit at a given moment. If we can do it now, most of the Sattaram leadership in the Hub will be trapped. We've waited months for the opportunity. We're prepared to move simultaneously against all other Elaigar positions in the Federation. So there's a great deal at stake. If we can't get the Elaigar out unnoticed before human forces contact them, it may become disastrous enough for all sides. To expect Federation warships to distinguish neatly between Alattas and Elaigar after the shooting begins would be expecting too much. And it would be no one-sided matter. We have heavy armament, as do the Elaigar."

She added, "The Elaigar are essentially our problem, not that of the Federation. We're still too close to them to regard them as enemies. My parents were of their kind and didn't elect to have their gene patterns modified. If they hadn't been captured and forced to it, I might have fought for Suan Uwin rank in my time as ruthlessly as Boragost or Stiltik—and, as I judge you now, so might you if your ancestors had happened to be Grisand research subjects on Nalakia. But we're gaining control of the Elaigar everywhere. If we succeed here, the last Sattaram will be dead less than thirty years from now."

She broke off, studied a set of indicators for a moment, picked up the communicator. Voice murmuring reached Telzey. It went on for perhaps two minutes. Kolki Ming set the communicator aside without replying. One of the other Alattas evidently had recorded a message for her.

She stood up, face thoughtful, fastened on a gun belt.

"We've been trying to force Boragost and Stiltik to open the Lion Game with us," she said. "It'll be the quickest way to accomplish our purpose. Perhaps the only way left at present! It seems we've succeeded." She indicated the street door. "We'll go outside. The first move should be made shortly. I must call in Scag."

Telzey came to her feet. "What's the Lion Game?"

"The one you're playing, I think," said Kolki Ming. "I don't believe you've been entirely candid with me. But whether it was your purpose or not, it seems you're involved in the Game now."

## Chapter 11

Kolki Ming had set up a light outside the house which brought full visibility to a hundred yard stretch of the dismal street and its house fronts. She and Telzey remained near the entrance. Scag now appeared abruptly in the illuminated area, stared coldly at them, glanced back bristling over his shoulder and was gone again.

Telzey had done the Alattas a greater favor than she knew in eliminating Stiltik's dagen. When they learned of it, they'd been able to go about their work more freely. A situation involving the possible use of dagens became so dangerously complicated that those threatened by them had to direct their primary efforts to getting the beasts out of the way. Scag had killed several of Stiltik's people during their surprise attack in the sealed areas; so it was known the three Alattas had brought a mind hound in with them.

There were two other dagens at present in the circuit, Boragost's and one whose handler was a Sattaram leader who had arrived with his beast during the week. Predictably, if Boragost was to take action against the Alattas, as it now seemed he would, his first step would be to use the pair to get rid of Scag. If the Elaigar dagens could be finished off at the same time, it would be worth the loss of Scag to the Alattas. They could go ahead immediately then with their plans.

That was the part of the game being played at present. Scag came and went. His kind could sense and track each other—he knew he was being sought by hunters as savage as he was. He wasn't trying to evade them. His role simply was to make sure the encounter took place here. The gun Kolki Ming held had been designed for use against dagens, who weren't easy creatures to kill.

Now Scag was back, and remained, half crouched, great head turning from side to side.

"They're coming!" Kolki Ming started forward. "Stay here and don't move!"

Abruptly, two other dagens appeared, to right and left of Scag. He hurled himself on the nearest one.

It became a wild blur of noise and motion. The street filled with the deep howling voices of the mind hounds, sounding like peals of insane laughter. They grappled and slashed, flicked in and out of sight, seeking advantage. Yellow blood smears began to appear on the paving behind them. Scag seemed not at all daunted by the fact that he was fighting two; they were lesser beasts, though one wasn't much smaller than he. For moments, it looked to Telzey as if he might kill them unaided. But he was getting help. Kolki Ming shifted this way and that about that spinning tangle, gun in sporadic action, perilously close to the struggle. But the dagens ignored her.

Then one of Scag's opponents lay on the paving, neck twisted back, unmoving. Scag and the other rolled, locked together, across the street toward Telzey; she watched yellow blood pumping from the side of Scag's neck and through his jaws. The Alatta followed, gun muzzle now almost touching the back of the other dagen. The beast jerked around toward her, jaws gaping. Scag came to his feet, stood swaying a moment, head lowered, made a gurgling noise, fell.

The other, braced up on its forelegs, paralyzed hindquarters dragging, was trying to reach Kolki Ming. She stepped aside from its lunge. The gun blazed again at its flank. It howled and vanished.

She waited perhaps a minute, gun half lifted. Then she lowered it, turned back to Telzey.

"Gone back to its handler!" She was breathing deeply but easily. "They won't use that one again! But they'll learn from its mind before they destroy it that Scag and the other are dead. Now the codes take over!"

Both in practice and theory, the maximum range of portal shift was considered definitely established. The security of the Elaigar circuits control center was based on that. Sections within potential shift range of the center were heavily guarded; a threat to them would bring overall defense systems into instant action.

Alatta scientists had managed to extend the shift range. For ordinary purposes the increase was insignificant. But here specifically, it could allow Alatta agents to bypass guarded sections and reach the control center without alerting defenders. The four agents planted in the center had set up a series of camouflaged portal contacts which led for the most part through sealed areas and ended at the center. The chief responsibility for this part of the operation had been Tscharen's.

After the work was completed, it became a matter of waiting for the next of the periodic gatherings of Elaigar leaders. Tscharen's duties as a member of Stiltik's staff kept him in the circuit; the other three were sent off presently on various assignments. Tscharen evidently decided to add to his security measures and was observed at it. As a result, he and Telzey were picked up by Stiltik when his associates returned to the circuit to carry out the planned operation, and the others were revealed as Alatta agents.

The original scheme had to be abandoned. Stiltik had forced Tscharen to face her in formal combat and outmatched him easily. That made him her personal captive; she could use any information she was able to wring from him to her own advantage. It wasn't an immediate threat; it should be many hours before she broke down his defenses. But the Elaigar in general had been alerted. A direct approach to the control center section would almost certainly be detected.

The Alattas decided to play on the tensions between the Suan Uwin, considerably heightened at the moment because no one was sure of the significance of the events for which Telzey and her group were responsible. Ellorad and Sartes, the other two agents, controlled a number of minds in Boragost's command. Through them, the feeling spread among both Boragost's supporters and opponents that since Stiltik had walked the Lion Way in allowing the captured Alatta his chance in ritual combat, Boragost could do no less. He must give personal challenge to the three trapped in the sealed areas—which in turn would draw Stiltik back into the matter.

"You *want* to fight those monsters?" Telzey had said, somewhat incredulously.

"I'd sooner not have to face either of them," said Kolki Ming. "Stiltik, in particular. But that won't be my part here. With Sartes and Ellorad openly committed, it will seem we've accepted defeat and are seeking combat death in preference to capture. That should draw the attention of the Elaigar temporarily off me and give me a chance to get to the control center unnoticed."

She added, "The fighting will be less uneven than you think. Tscharen had no special combat skills, but we others were trained to be collectors of the Elaigar and are as practiced in the weapon types allowed under their codes as any of them. Boragost might prefer to hunt us down with a sufficient force of Elaigar and Tolants, but his prestige is at stake. He's issued his challenge by sending his dagens in against ours, and that part is now concluded, with neither side retaining an advantage. We'll accept the challenge shortly by showing ourselves. Boragost is bound then by the codes."

She'd cut an opening in the heel of one of Telzey's shoes and was assembling a miniature pack of portal keys to fit into it. Each of the Alattas carried such a concealed set, and, in case of accidents, a more obvious but less complete pack of standard size such as the one taken from Tscharen. That was what had enabled them to withdraw so quickly from Stiltik's initial attack.

Telzey said, "It was the Alattas who were watching me on Orado, wasn't it?"

"I was," said Kolki Ming.

"Why? After you switched me into the circuit, you said there were people who wanted to see me."

"There are. We haven't as much information as we want about the type of psis currently in the Federation. We've avoided contact with them here, and even the Elaigar have had the sense to keep away from the institutions of the Psychology Service. But some now believe that the power of the Psychology Service is based chiefly on its use of psi machines rather than on its members' ability as psis—in fact, that psis of the original human strain simply don't develop a degree of ability that can compare with our own. And that can become dangerous thinking. We have our fools, as you do. Some of them might begin to assume that the Federation could be challenged with impunity."

"You don't think so then?" Telzey said.

"I happen to know better. But we wanted to be able to establish the fact beyond question. I learned on Orado that a Sattaram handler had set his dagen on a prying human psi and that the dagen then had inexplicably disappeared. That psi seemed worth further study, particularly after I'd identified you and discovered you hadn't yet attained your physical maturity. There also seemed to be a connection between you and the Psychology Service. It was decided to pick you up for analysis by experts, if it could be done safely. Then the Tinokti matter came up and you transferred here. That gave me the opportunity to bring you into the circuit. We expected to conclude our operation quickly, and take you along."

She added, "A lifetime of exile among us wasn't planned for you. You'd have remained unconscious throughout most of the analysis and presently have found yourself on Orado again, with nothing of significance concerning us to relate. I don't know what the arrangement will be now, assuming we survive the next hour or two."

Ellorad and Sartes arrived soon afterwards. They'd been checking on developments through their mind contacts. Boragost had expressed doubts publicly that the Alatta agents would choose combat. However, if they did, he'd be pleased to meet them in the Hall of Challenge and add their heads to his minor trophies. Stiltik wouldn't involve herself until Boragost had fought at least once.

"Boragost will have a witness?" Kolki Ming asked.

"Yes. Lishon, the Adjutant, as usual," said Sartes. "Stiltik, also as usual, will fight without witness—a hunt in the Kaht Chasm."

Ellorad added, "Sartes will face Boragost. I'll be his witness there. We don't want to bring Stiltik into it too quickly." He glanced at Telzey. "When we show ourselves, she may learn for the first time that she's lost her human captive and grow hungry for action. But a Chasm hunt can be extended, and I'll make it thoroughly extensive. You should have the time to do what's necessary."

Kolki Ming nodded. "Yes, I should."

"Then let's determine our route! When we're seen, we should be within a few minutes of the Hall of Challenge, then out of sight again until Sartes and I actually enter the Hall. That will leave Stiltik no time to interfere with the present arrangement."

When they set off, the Alattas wore the short-sleeved shirts, trunks and boots which had been concealed by their Sparan garments. Long knives hung from their belts next to guns. Combat under code conditions allowed only weapons depending on physical dexterity and strength, and the weapons of psi. Guns were worn by witnesses as a formal guarantee that the codes would be observed. Principals didn't carry them.

Ellorad and Sartes strode ahead, moving with relaxed ease. They looked formidable enough, and if, to Telzey, even those long powerful bodies appeared no real match for the Sattaram giants, they should know what they were attempting—which might be only to give Kolki Ming time to conclude the operation.

Boragost's technicians had been at work in fringe sections of the sealed areas they'd been able to penetrate, setting up a scanning system. Kolki Ming had followed their progress on her instruments. The route she'd outlined would take them through such a section. Telzey didn't know they'd reached it until a Sattaram voice abruptly addressed them in the Elaigar language. They stopped.

The deep harsh voice went on, speaking slowly and with emphasis. When it finished, Ellorad replied, then started toward the end of the section. The others followed; and as soon as they'd left the section, they moved quickly. Kolki Ming said to Telzey, "That was Boragost's witness. The challenge has been acknowledged by both sides, and we've been told to select the one who is to face Boragost first and have him come at once with his witness to the Hall. It's the situation we wanted!"

They hurried after the men, came after another three sections into a room where the two had turned on a viewscreen. The screen showed a wide hall with black and silver walls. Two Sattarams stood there unmoving. The one farthest from the screen wore a gun belt. The other balanced a huge axe on his shoulder.

"They entered just now," Ellorad said. "Sartes is pleased to see Boragost has selected the long axe. He thinks he can spin out that fight until the Suan Uwin is falling over his own feet!"

The two left immediately. Sartes had removed his gun, but Ellorad retained his.

# Chapter 12

Kolki Ming said, "That hall is only two portals from here, but the Elaigar haven't been able to establish access to these sections. Boragost doesn't know we

can see him. We'll wait till the combat begins, then
be off on our route at once."

Telzey nodded mutely. Boragost looked almost as
huge as Korm and seemed to her to show no indications of aging. The handle of the axe he held must
be at least five feet long.

Ellorad and Sartes appeared suddenly in the screen,
moving toward the center of the hall. Sartes walked
ahead; Ellorad followed a dozen steps behind him and
to the right. The two Sattarams stood motionless,
watching them. A third of the way down the hall,
Sartes and Ellorad stopped. Ellorad spoke briefly.
Lishon rumbled a reply. Then Sartes drew his knife,
and Boragost grinned, took the axe in both hands and
started unhurriedly forward—

Kolki Ming sucked in her breath, sprang back from
the screen, darted from the room. Telzey sprinted
after her, mind in a whirl, not quite sure of what she'd
seen. There'd been the plum-colored shapes of Tolants
suddenly on either side of the great hall. Three, it
seemed, on each side—yes, six in all! As she saw
them, each had an arm drawn back, was swinging it
forward, down. They appeared to be holding short
sticks. She'd had a blurred glimpse of Ellorad snatch-
ing his gun from its holster, then falling forward, of
Sartes already on the floor—

Kolki Ming was thirty feet ahead of her, racing
down a passage, then disappeared through a portal
at the end. Telzey passed through the portal moments
later, saw the Alatta had nearly doubled the distance
between them, was holding her gun. Kolki Ming
checked suddenly, then vanished through the wall on
her right.

That portal brought Telzey out into the great hall
they'd been watching.

There, Kolki Ming's gun snarled and snarled.

Lishon was on his side, kicking, bellowing. Boragost
had dropped to hands and knees, his great head

covered with blood, shaking it slowly as if dazed.
Smaller plum-colored bodies lay and rolled here and
there on the floor. Two still darted squealing along
the right side of the hall. The gun found one, flung
him twisting through the air. The other turned
abruptly, disappeared through the wall—

Portals. The Tolant troop had received some signal, stepped simultaneously into the hall through a
string of concealed portals lining its sides. . . .

Boragost collapsed forward on his face, lay still.

Kolki Ming glanced around at Telzey, eyes glaring
from a dead-white face, then hurried past Boragost
toward Lishon. Telzey ran after her, skirting Sartes
on the floor, saw something small, black and bushy
planted in Sartes's shoulder. . . . Throwing sticks,
poisoned darts.

Kolki Ming's gun spoke again. Lishon roared, in
pain or rage. The Alatta reached him, bent over him,
straightened, and now his gun was in her other hand.
She thrust it under her belt, started back to Boragost,
Telzey trailing her, stood looking down at the giant,
prodded his ribs with her boot. "Dead," she said in
a flat voice.

She looked about the hall, wiped the back of her
hand across her forehead. "All dead but Lishon, who
shares Boragost's dishonor, and a frightened Tolant.
Now we wait. Not long, I think! The Tolant will run
in his panic to the Elaigar." She glanced down at
Telzey. "Tolant poison—our two died as they fell.
Three darts in each. Boragost didn't like the look of
the Lion Way today! If we hadn't been watching, his
scheme would have worked. The Tolants and their
darts would have been gone, the punctures covered
by axe strokes. We—"

She broke off.

A wide flight of stairs rose up to the rear of the hall
beyond the point where Lishon lay. It had appeared
to end against a blank wall. Now a great slab in that

wall was sliding sideways—an opening door linked to an opening portal. A storm of deep voices and furious emotion burst through it simultaneously; then, as the opening widened, the Elaigar poured through in a crowd. The ones in the front ranks checked as they caught sight of Kolki Ming and Telzey and turned, outbellowing the others. The motion slowed; abruptly there was silence.

Kolki Ming, eyes blazing, flung up her arms, knife in one hand, gun in the other, shouted a dozen words at them.

One of the Sattarams roared back, tossing his head. The pack poured down the steps into the hall. The first to reach Sartes's body bent, plucked the dart from Sartes's shoulder, another from his side, held them up.

At that, there was stillness again. The faces showed shocked fury. The Sattaram who had replied to Kolki Ming growled something. A minor disturbance in the dense ranks followed. An Otessan emerged, holding a Tolant by the neck. The Tolant began to squeal. The Elaigar lifted him, clamped the Tolant's ankles together in one hand, swung the squirming creature around and up in a long single-armed sweep, down again. The squeals stopped as the body slapped against the flooring and broke.

The Sattaram looked over at Lishon, rumbled again. Three others moved quickly toward Lishon. His eyes were wide and staring as two hauled him to his feet, held him upright by the arms. The third drew a short knife, shoved Lishon's chin back with the heel of his hand, sank the knife deep into Lishon's throat, drew it sideways.

Dead Boragost didn't feel it, but he got his throat cut next.

They were elsewhere then in a room, Kolki Ming and Telzey, with something more than a dozen Sattarams. They didn't appear to be exactly prisoners at present. Their key packs had been taken from them—the obvious ones—but Kolki Ming retained her weapons. The Elaigar codes were involved; and from the loud and heated exchange going on, it appeared the codes rarely had been called upon to deal with so complicated a situation. Shields were tight all around. Telzey could pick up no specific impressions, but the general trend of the talk was obvious. Kolki Ming spoke incisively now and then. When she did, the giants listened—with black scowls, most of them; but they listened. She was an enemy, but her ancestors had been Elaigar, and she and her associates had shown they would abide by the codes. Whereupon a Suan Uwin of the Lion People, aided by his witness, shamefully broke the codes to avoid facing Alattas in combat!

A damnable state of affairs! There was much scratching of shaggy scalps. Then Kolki Ming spoke again, now at some length. The group began turning their heads to stare at Telzey, standing off by the wall with a Sattaram who seemed to have put himself in charge of her. This monster addressed Telzey when Kolki Ming stopped speaking.

"The Alatta," he rumbled, "says you're an agent of the Psychology Service. Is that true?"

Telzey looked up at him, startled by his fluent use of translingue. She reminded herself then that in spite of his appearance he might be barely older than she— could, not much more than a year ago, have been an Otessan moving about among the people of the Hub in something like Sparan disguise.

"Yes, it's true," she said carefully.

There was muttering among the others. Apparently more than a few knew translingue.

"The Alatta further says," Telzey's Sattaram resumed, "that it was you who turned Stiltik's dagen on her in the headquarters, that you also stole her omnipacks and made yourself mind master of her chief Tolant as well as of Korm Nyokee, the disgraced one. And that it was you and your slaves who drew Boragost's patrol into ambush and killed them. Finally, that you chose to restore to Korm Nyokee the honor he'd lost by letting him seek combat death. Are all these things true?"

"Yes."

"Ho!" His tangled eyebrows lifted. "You then joined the Alatta agents to help them against us?"

"Yes."

"Ho-ho!" The broad ogre face split in a slow grin. He dug at his chin with a thumbnail, staring down at her. Grunts came from the group where one of them was speaking, apparently repeating what had been said for nonlinguists. Telzey collected more stares. Her guard clamped a crushing hand on her shoulder.

"I've told them before this," he remarked, "that there are humans who must be called codeworthy!" His face darkened. "More so certainly than Boragost and Lishon! No one believes now that was the first treachery committed by those two." He shook his great head glumly. "These are sorry times!"

The general discussion had resumed meanwhile, soon grew as heated as before. One of the Sattarams abruptly left the room. Telzey's giant told her, "He's to find out what Stiltik wants, since she alone is now Suan Uwin. But whatever she wants, we are the chiefs who will determine what the codes demand."

The Elaigar who'd left came back shortly, made his report. More talk, Kolki Ming joining in. The guard said to Telzey, "Stiltik claims it's her right to have the Alatta who was of her command face her in the Kaht Chasm. It's agreed this is proper under the codes, and Kolki Ming has accepted. Stiltik also says, however, that you should be returned to her at once as her prisoner. I think she feels you've brought ridicule on her, as you have. This is now being discussed."

Telzey didn't reply. She felt chilled. The talk went on. Her Sattaram broke in several times, presently began to grin. One of the giants in the group addressed her in translingue.

"Is it your choice," he asked, "to face Stiltik in the Kaht Chasm beside the Alatta Kolki Ming?"

Telzey didn't hesitate. "Yes, it is."

He translated. Nods from the group. Telzey's Sattaram said something in their language. A few of them laughed. He said to Telzey, holding out his huge hand, "Give me your belt!"

She looked up at him, took off her jacket belt and gave it to him. He reached inside his vest-like upper garment, brought out a knife in a narrow metal sheath, fastened the sheath on the belt, handed the belt back. "You were Stiltik's prisoner and freed yourself fairly!" he rumbled. "I say you're codeworthy and have told them so. You won't face Stiltik in the Kaht Chasm unarmed!" His toothy grin reappeared. "Who knows? You may claim Suan Uwin rank among us before you're done!"

He translated that for the group. There was a roar of laughter. Telzey's giant laughed with the others, but then looked down at her and shook his head.

"No," he said. "Stiltik will eat your heart and that of Kolki Ming. But if we find then that you were able to redden your knife before it happened, I shall be pleased!"

# Chapter 13

The portal to which Kolki Ming and Telzey were taken let them out into a sloping mountain area. When Telzey glanced back, a sheer cliff towered

behind them. Tinokti's sun shone through invisible
circuit barriers overhead.

Kolki Ming turned toward a small building a
hundred yards away. "Come quickly! Stiltik may not
wait long before following."

Telzey hurried after her. Behind the building, the
rock-studded slope curved down out of sight. Perhaps
half a mile away was another steep cliff face. Dark
narrow lines of trees climbed along it; some sections
were covered by tangles of vines. The great wall
curved in to left and right until it nearly met the
mountain front out of which they'd stepped. On the
right, at the point where the two rock masses came
closest, water streamed through, dropping in long
cascades toward the hidden floor of the Kaht Chasm.
Far to the left, the stream foamed away through
another break in the mountains.

*If water—*

Telzey brushed the thought aside. Whatever appli-
cations of portal technology were involved, the fact
that water appeared to flow freely through the force
barriers about this vast section didn't mean there were
possible exit or entry points there.

She followed Kolki Ming into the building. The
interior was a single large room. Mountaineering
equipment, geared to Elaigar proportions, hung from
walls and posts. Ropes, clamps, hooks . . . Kolki Ming
selected a coil of transparent rope, stripped hooks from
it, attached it to her belt beside the long knife which
was now her only weapon. Outside the building, she
stooped, legs bent. "Up on my back; hang on! We want
to put distance between ourselves and this place."

Telzey scrambled up, clamped her legs around the
Alatta's waist, locked her hands on the tough shirt
material. Kolki Ming started down the slope.

"This is an exercise area for general use when it
isn't serving as Stiltik's hunting ground," she said. "As
a rule, the Suan Uwin likes a long chase, but today

she may be impatient. She's tireless, almost as fast as I am, twice as strong, and as skilled a fighter on the rocks as in the water below. The only exit is at the end of the Chasm near the foot of the falls, and it will open now only to Stiltik's key. Beyond it is her Hall of Triumph where the Elaigar will wait to see her display her new trophies to them."

The slope suddenly dropped off. Kolki Ming turned her face to the rock, climbed on down, using hands and feet and moving almost as quickly as before. Telzey tightened her grip. She'd done some rockwork for sport, but that had been a different matter from this wild, swaying ride along what was turning into a precipitous cliff.

A minute or two later, Kolki Ming glanced sideways and down, said, "Hold on hard!" and pushed away from the rock. They dropped. Telzey clutched convulsively. The drop ended not much more than twelve feet below, almost without a jar. Kolki Ming went on along a path some three feet wide, leading around a curve of the cliff.

Telzey swallowed. "How will Stiltik find us?" she asked.

"By following our scent trail until she has us in sight. She's a mind hunter, too, so keep your screens locked." Kolki Ming's breathing still seemed relaxed and unhurried. "This may look like an uneven game to the Elaigar, but since there always was a chance I would have to face Stiltik here some day, I've made the Chasm my exercise area whenever I was in the circuit . . . and they don't know that of the three of us I was the dagen handler."

The rumble of rushing water was audible now, and growing louder. The stream must pass almost directly beneath them, some three hundred yards down. They moved into shadow. The path narrowed, narrowed further. There came a place where the Alatta turned sideways and edged along where Telzey could barely make out footholds, never seeming to give a thought to the long drop below. Very gradually, the path began to widen again as the curve of the cliff reversed itself, leading them back into sunlight. And presently back into shadow.

Then, as they rounded another bulge, Telzey saw a point ahead where the path forked, one arm leading up through a narrow crevice, the other descending along the cliff. An instant later, a thought tendril touched her screens, coldly alert, searching. It lingered, faded.

"Yes, Stiltik's in the Chasm," Kolki Ming said. "She'll be on our trail in moments."

She took the downward fork. It curved in and out, dipped steeply, rose again. Kolki Ming checked at an opening in the rock, a narrow high cave mouth. Dirt had collected within it, and cliff vines had taken root and grown, forming a tangle which almost filled the opening.

Kolki Ming glanced back, parted the tangle, edged inside. "You can get down."

Telzey slid to the ground, stood on unsteady legs, drew a long breath. "And now?" she asked.

"Now," said Kolki Ming, voice and face expressionless, "I leave you. Don't think of me. Wait here behind the vines. You'll see Stiltik coming long before she sees you. Then be ready to do whatever seems required."

She turned, moved back into the dimness of the cave, seemed to vanish behind a corner. Completely disconcerted for the moment, Telzey stared after her. There came faint sounds, a scraping, the clattering of a dislodged rock. Then silence.

Telzey went to the cave opening, looked back along the path that wound in and out along the curves of the cliff. Stiltik would be in sight on it minutes before she got this far—and surely she couldn't be very close yet! Telzey moved into the cave, came to the corner around which Kolki Ming had disappeared. Almost pitch-darkness there. After a dozen groping steps, she came to a stop. There was a rock before her. On either side, not much more than two and a half feet apart, was also rock. Water trickled slowly down the wall on the right, seeping into the dust about her shoes.

She looked up into darkness, reached on tiptoe, arms stretching, touched nothing. A draft moved past her face. So here the cave turned upward, became a narrow tunnel; and up that black hole Kolki Ming had gone. Telzey wondered whether she would be able to follow, stood a moment reflecting, then returned to the cave opening. She sat down where she could watch their trail, drew the vines into a thicker tangle before her. Pieces of rock lay around, and her hands went out, began gathering them into a pile, while her eyes remained fastened on the path.

On the path, presently, Stiltik appeared, coming around a distant turn. Telzey's breath caught. Stiltik's bulk looked misshapen and awkward at that range, but she moved with swift assurance, like a creature born to mountain heights, along a thread of shelf almost indiscernible from the cave. She went out of sight behind the thrust of the mountain, emerged again, closer.

Telzey let a trickle of fear escape through her screens, then drew them into a tight shield. She saw Stiltik lift her head without checking her stride. Thought probed alertly about, slid away. But not entirely. She sensed a waiting watchfulness now as Stiltik continued to vanish and reappear along the winding path.

Presently Telzey could begin to distinguish the features of the heavy-jawed face. A short-handled double-headed hatchet hung from Stiltik's belt, along with a knife and a coil of rope. She came to the point where the path forked, paused, measuring the branch which led up through the crevice, stooped abruptly, half crouched, bringing her head close to the ground, face shifting back and forth, almost nosing the path like a dog. Telzey saw the bunching of heavy back muscles through the material of the sleeveless shirt. For a moment, it seemed wholly the posture of an animal. The giantess straightened, again looked up along the crevice. Telzey's hand moved forward. The pile of rocks she'd gathered rattled through the vines to the path below the cave opening. A brief hot gust of terror burst from the shield.

Stiltik's head turned. Then, swiftly, she started along the path toward the cave.

Telzey sat still, breathing so shallow it might almost have stopped. Stiltik's mouth hung open; her eyes stared, seeming to probe through the vines. Around a curve she came, loosening the hatchet at her belt, cold mind impulses searching.

A psi bolt slammed, hard, heavy, fast, jarring Telzey through her shield. It hadn't been directed at her.

Stiltik swayed on the path, gave a grunting exhalation of surprise, and something flicked down out of the air above her like a thin glassy snake. The looped end of Kolki Ming's rope dropped around her neck, jerked tight.

One of her great hands caught at the rope, the other struck up with the hatchet. But she was stumbling backward, being hauled off the path. Two minds slashed at each other, indistinguishable in fury. Then Stiltik's massive body plunged down along the side of the cliff with a clatter of rocks, dropped below Telzey's line of sight. The rope jerked tight again; there was a crack like the snapping of a thick tree branch. The end of the rope flicked down past the path, following the falling body. From above came a yell, savage and triumphant. From below, seconds later, came the sound of impact.

Abruptly, there was stillness. Telzey drew a deep,

sighing breath, stood up, pushed her way out through the vine tangles to the cave opening. She waited there a minute or two. Then Kolki Ming, smeared with the dark slime of the winding tunnel through which she'd crept to the cliff top, came down along the crevice to the fork of the path, and turned back toward the cave.

They reached the floor of the Kaht Chasm presently, found Stiltik's broken body. Kolki Ming drew her knife and was busy for a time, while Telzey sat on a rock and looked up the Chasm to the point where the foaming stream tumbled through a narrow break in the mountain. She thought she could make out a pale shimmer on the rocks. It should be the Chasm's exit portal, not far from the falls, and not very far from them now. Tinokti's sun had moved beyond the crest of the cliff. All the lower part of the Chasm lay in deep shadow.

Then Kolki Ming finished, came to Telzey and held up dripping hands. "Blood of a Suan Uwin!" she said. "The Elaigar will see your knife reddened. I wonder if they'll be pleased! Didn't you know I sensed you draw Stiltik's attention toward you when her suspicions awoke? If you hadn't, I'm not at all sure the matter could have ended well for either of us." She drew the knife from Telzey's belt, ran fingers over blade, hilt and sheath, replaced the knife. A knuckle tilted Telzey's chin up; a hand smeared wetness across her face. "Don't be too dainty!" Kolki Ming told her. "They're to see you took a full share of their Suan Uwin's defeat."

They walked along the floor of the Chasm, beside the cold rush of water, toward the portal shimmer, Stiltik's blood painting them, Stiltik's severed head swinging by its hair from Kolki Ming's right hand. The portal brightened as they reached it, and they went through.

The Elaigar stood waiting, filling the long hall.

They walked forward, toward those nearest the portal. The giants stared, jaws dropping. A rumble of voices began here and there, ended quickly. The Elaigar standing before them started to move aside, clearing the way. The motion spread, and a wide lane opened through the ranks as they came on. Beyond, Telzey saw a ramp leading to a raised section at the end of the hall. They reached the ramp, went up it, and at the top Kolki Ming turned. Telzey turned with her.

Below stood the Lion People, unmoving, silent, broad faces lifted and watching. Kolki Ming's arm swung far back, came forward. She hurled Stiltik's head back at them. It bounced and rolled along the ramp, black hair whipping about, blood spattering. It rolled on into the hall, the giants giving way before it. Then a roar of voices arose.

"This way!" said Kolki Ming.

They were at the wall, passed through a portal, the noise cutting off behind them.

"Now quickly!"

They ran. None of the sections they went through in the next minutes looked familiar to Telzey, but Kolki Ming didn't hesitate. Telzey realized suddenly they were back in sealed areas again; the portals here were of the disguised variety. She was gasping for breath, vision blurring with exhaustion. The Alatta was setting a pace she couldn't possibly keep up with much longer.

Then they were in a room with a viewscreen stand in one corner. Here Kolki Ming stopped. "Get your breath back," she told Telzey. "One more move only, and we have time for that—though perhaps no more time than it takes Stiltik's blood to dry on us." She was activating the screen as she spoke, spinning dials. Stiltik's Hall of Triumph swam into view, with a burst of Elaigar voices. Churning groups of the giants filled the hall; more had come in since they left, and others were still arriving. Most of them appeared to be talking at once; and much of the talk seemed furious argument.

"Now they debate!" said Kolki Ming. "What do the codes demand? Whatever conclusion they come to, it will involve our death. That's necessary. But first they must decide how to kill us with honor—to us and themselves. Then they'll start asking where we've gone."

She turned away. Telzey watched the screen a moment longer, her breathing beginning to ease. When she looked around, Kolki Ming had opened a closet in the wall, was fastening a gun she'd taken from it to her belt. She removed two small flat slabs of plastic and metal from a closet shelf, closed the closet, laid the slabs on a table. She came back to the screen, dialed to another view.

"The control section," she said. "Our goal now!"

The control section was a large place. Telzey looked out at a curving wall crowded with instrument stands. On the right was a great black square in the wall— a blackness which seemed to draw the mind down into vast depths. "The Vingarran Gate," said Kolki Ming. Two Sattarams stood at one end of the section, watching the technicians. They wore guns. The technicians, perhaps two dozen in all, represented three life forms, two of which suggested the humanoid type, though no more so than Couse's people. The third was a lumpy disk covered with yellow scales and equipped with a variety of flexible limbs.

"Those two must die," Kolki Ming said, indicating the Sattarams. "They're controlled servants of the Suan Uwin, jointly conditioned by Boragost and Stiltik as safeguard against surprises by either. The instrument handlers are conditioned, too, but they'll be no problem." She switched off the screen. "Now come." She took the two slabs from the table.

There was no more running, though Kolki Ming still

moved swiftly. Five sections on, she stopped before a
blank wall. "There's a portal here, left incomplete to
prevent discovery," she said. "The section's on one of
the potential approaches to the control area, so it's
inspected frequently and thoroughly. Now I'll close the
field!"

She searched along the wall, placed one of the
slabs carefully against it. It adhered. She opened the
back of the slab, adjusted settings, pressed the cover
shut. "Come through immediately behind me," she
told Telzey. "And be very quiet! On these last fifty
steps, things might still go wrong."

They came out into semidarkness, went down a
flight of stairs. Below, Kolki Ming halted, head turned.
Telzey listened from behind her. There were faint
distant sounds, which might be voices but not Elaigar
voices. After some moments they faded. Kolki Ming
moved on silently, Telzey following.

The remaining slab went against a wall. Peering
through the dark, Kolki Ming made final adjustments.
She paused then, stepped back. Her face turned
toward Telzey.

"We weren't able to test this one," she whispered.
"When I close the last switch, it will trigger alarms—
here, in an adjoining guarded section, and in the
control area. Be ready!"

Her left hand reached out to the slab. Sound
blared in the darkness about them, and Kolki Ming
had vanished through the portal. Telzey followed at
once.

The two Sattarams on guard had no chance. Kolki
Ming had emerged from the wall behind them, gun
blazing. By then, there were guns in their hands, too;
but they died before they saw her. She ran past the
bodies toward the technicians at the instrument banks,
shouting Elaigar orders above the clanging alarm din
in the air. The technicians didn't hesitate. For a

moment, there was a wild scramble of variously shaped bodies at an exit at the far end of the big room. Then the last of them disappeared.

Kolki Ming was at the instrument stands, gun back in its holster, hands flicking about. Series of buttons stabbed down. Two massive switches above her swung over, snapped shut. The alarm signal ended.

In the sudden silence, she looked at Telzey who had followed her across the room.

"And now," she said, drawing a deep breath, "it's done! Every section in the circuit has been sealed. No portal can open until it's released from this room. Wherever the Elaigar were a moment ago, there they'll stay." She smiled without mirth. "How they'll rage! But not for long. Now I'll reset the Vingarran, and the Gate will open and my people will come through to remove our captives from section after section, and take them and their servants to our transports."

She went to another instrument console, unlocked it, bent over it. Telzey stood watching. The Alatta's hand moved to a group of controls, hesitated. She frowned. The hand shifted uncertainly.

Kolki Ming stiffened. Her hand jerked toward the gun at her belt. The motion wasn't completed.

She straightened then, turned to stare at Telzey. And Telzey felt the Alatta's mind turning also, wonderingly, incredulously, seeking a way to escape the intangible web of holds that had fastened on it, and realizing there was no way—that it was unable now even to understand how it was held.

"You?" Kolki Ming said heavily at last. "How could—"

"When you killed Stiltik."

A mind blazingly open, telepathically vulnerable, powers and attention wholly committed. Only for instants; but in those instants, Telzey, waiting and watching, had flowed inside.

"I sensed nothing." Kolki Ming shook her head. "Of course—that was the first awareness you blocked."

"Yes," Telzey said. "It was. I had plenty of time afterwards for the rest of it."

The Alatta's eyes were bleak. "And now?"

"Now we're going to a planetary exit." Telzey touched a point in the captive mind. "That hidden one you people installed. . . . Set up a route through empty sections, and unseal that series of portals."

The planetary exit portal opened on an enclosed courtyard. Four aircars stood in a row along one wall. Telzey paused at the exit beside Kolki Ming, looking around. It appeared to be early morning in that part of Tinokti. They were on the fringes of a city; buildings stretched away in the distance. There were city sounds, vague and remote.

She glanced down at herself. She'd washed hands, face and hair on the way, but hadn't been able to get her clothing clean. It didn't show; she'd fastened a wide shawl of bright-colored fabric around herself, a strip they'd cut from tapestry in one of the circuit sections. It concealed the blood and dirt stains on her clothes, and the Elaigar knife at her belt.

She adjusted the shawl, looked up at the immensely formidable creature beside her. The Alatta's eyes returned her gaze without expression. Telzey started forward toward the cars. Kolki Ming stayed where she was. Telzey climbed into the nearest of the cars, checked the controls. The interior was designed to Sparan proportions, otherwise this was standard equipment. She could handle it. She unlocked the engine, turned it on. A red alert light appeared, then faded as the invisible energy field above the court dissolved to let her through.

She swung the car about, lifted it from the ground, moved up out of the court. Two hundred yards away, she spun the viewscreen dial to focus on the motionless figure by the portal. The car drove up and on in a straight line. When the figure began to dwindle in the screen, Telzey abruptly withdrew her holds from Kolki Ming's mind, slammed her own shield tight, remembering their lightning reflexes.

But nothing happened. Kolki Ming remained where she was for a moment, seemed to be looking after her. Then she turned aside, disappeared through the portal.

Five minutes later, Telzey brought the car down in a public parking area, left it there with locked engine and doors. The entrance to a general transportation circuit fronted on the parking space. She went inside, oriented herself on the circuit maps, and set out. Not long afterwards, she exited near a large freight spaceport.

# Chapter 14

The freight port adjoined a run-down city area with a population which lived in the main on Tongi Phon handouts. It had few attractions and an oversupply of predators. Otherwise, it was a good place for somebody who wanted to drop out of sight.

Telzey let a thoroughly vicious pair of predators, one of them a young woman of about her size, trail her along the main streets for a while. They were uncomplicated mentalities, readily accessible. She turned at last into a narrow alley, and when they caught up with her there, they were her robots. She exchanged street clothes with the woman in a deserted backyard, left the alley with the Elaigar knife wrapped in a cloth she'd taken from a trash pile. The two went on in the opposite direction, the woman carrying the folded length of tapestry she'd coveted. Their minds had been provided with a grim but plausible account of how she'd come by it and the bloodstained expensive clothing she now wore.

Telzey stopped at a nearby store she'd learned about from them. The store paid cash for anything salable; and when she left it a few minutes later, it had the Elaigar knife and she had a pocketful of Tinokti coins. It wasn't much money but enough for her immediate needs. An hour later, she'd rented a room above a small store for a week, locked the door, and unpacked the few items she'd picked up. One of them was a recorder. She turned it on, stretched out on the narrow bed.

It was high time. Part of her mind had been called upon to do more than was healthy for it in these hours, and it was now under noticeable strain. There were flickerings of distorted thought, emotional surges, impulses born in other minds and reproduced in her own. She'd been keeping it under control because she had to. Tolant and Tanven, Elaigar and Alatta, Thrakell Dees—Phon Dees once, a lord of the circuit, and, in the end, its last human survivor—they'd all been packed in under her recent personal experiences which were crammed and jolting enough. She'd lived something of the life of each in their memories, and she had to get untangled from that before there were permanent effects.

She let the stream of borrowed impressions start boiling through into consciousness, sorting them over as they came, drained off emotional poisons. Now and then, she spoke into the recorder. That was for the Psychology Service; there were things they should know. Other things might be useful for her to remember privately. They went back now into mental storage, turned into neat, neutral facts—knowledge. Much of the rest was valueless, had been picked up incidentally. It could be sponged from her mind at once, and was, became nonexistent.

The process continued; pressures began to reduce. The first two days she had nightmares when she slept, felt depressed while awake. Then her mood lightened. She ate when hungry; exercised when she felt like it, went on putting her mental house back in order. By the sixth day, as recorded by the little calendar watch she'd bought, she was done. Her experiences with the Elaigar, from the first contact in Melna Park on, were put in perspective, had become a thing of the past, no longer to concern her.

Back to normal. . . .

She spent the last few hours of the day working over her report to the Psychology Service, and had her first night of unbroken sleep in a week. Early next morning, she slipped the recorder into her pocket, unlocked the door, went whistling softly down to the store. The storekeeper, who had just opened up, gave her a puzzled look and scratched his chin. He was wondering how it could have completely slipped his mind all week that he had a renter upstairs. Telzey smiled amiably at him, went out into the street. He stared after her a moment, then turned away and forgot the renter again, this time for good.

Telzey walked on half a block, relaxed her screens and sent an identification thought to her Service contacts. A Service squad was there four minutes later to pick her up.

"There's somebody else," Klayung told her eventually, "who'd like to speak to you about your report." This was two days later, and they were in a Service ship standing off Tinokti.

"Who is it this time?" Telzey inquired warily. She'd had a number of talks with Klayung and a few other Service people about her experiences in the Elaigar circuit. Within limits, she hadn't minded giving them more detailed information than the report provided, but she was beginning to feel that for the moment she'd been pumped enough.

"He's a ranking official of a department which had a supporting role in the operation," Klayung said. "For security reasons, he doesn't want his identity to be known."

"I see. What about my identity?" Klayung had been very careful to keep Telzey unidentified so far. The role she'd played on Tinokti was known, in varying degrees, only to a few dozen members of the Service, to Neto Nayne-Mel who was at present in Service therapy, and to the Alattas, who no longer mattered.

"We'll have you well camouflaged during the discussion," Klayung said. "You'll talk by viewscreen."

"I suppose he isn't satisfied with the report?" Telzey said.

"No. He feels it doesn't go far enough and suspects you're holding things back deliberately. He's also unhappy about your timing."

She considered. It made no difference now. "He doesn't know about the part with Neto, does he?"

"No. Except for you and the therapists and a few others like myself, there was no Neto Nayne-Mel in the circuit."

"Shall I be frank with him otherwise?"

"Within reason," said Klayung.

She found herself sitting shortly before a viewscreen, with Klayung in the room behind her. The official at the other screen wore a full facemask. He might as well have left it off. She knew who he was as soon as he started to speak. They'd met on Orado.

She wasn't wearing a mask. Klayung's make-up people had put in half an hour preparing her for the meeting. What the official saw and heard was an undersized middle-aged man with a twang to his voice.

The discussion began on a polite if cool note.

Telzey was informed that the circuit she'd described had been located that morning. The force fields about the individual sections had all cut off simultaneously. After an entry into one of the sections was effected, it was discovered there was no need for the special portal keys with which she'd provided the Service. The entire system was now as open as any general circuit on Tinokti. Exploration remained cautious until it became obvious that the portal traps of which she'd spoken had been destructured. Nor was anything left which might have provided a clue to the device referred to in the report as the Vingarran Gate. "And, needless to say," said the official, "no one was found in the circuit."

Telzey nodded. "They've been gone for a week now. They set the force fields to shut off after it was safe, so you could stop looking for them."

"Meanwhile," the official went on, "we've had verification enough for your statement that groups of these aliens, both the Alattas and the Elaigar, were masquerading as human giants throughout the Federation. They've even owned considerable property. One well-known shipping line ostensibly was bought up by a Sparan organization three years ago and thereafter operated exclusively by Sparans. We know now that's not what they were. All these groups have vanished. Every positive lead we've traced reveals the same story. They disappeared within less than a standard day of one another, leaving nothing behind to indicate where they came from or where they've gone."

"That was the Alatta plan," Telzey acknowledged. "They wanted it to be a fast, clean break and a complete one.

"It seems," the official said, "you had this information in your possession a week before you chose to reveal it. I'm wondering, of course, what made you assume the responsibility of allowing the aliens to escape."

"For one thing, there wasn't much time," Telzey said. "If the Alatta operation was delayed, the situation would change—they wouldn't be able to carry out their plan as they'd intended. For another, I wasn't sure everyone here would understand what the situation was. I wanted them to be out of the Hub with the Elaigar before somebody made the wrong decision."

"And what makes you sure you made the right one?" the official demanded. "You may have saved us trouble at the moment while setting us up for much more serious trouble in the future."

She shook her head.

"They're not coming back," she said. "If they did, we'd spot them, now that we know about them. But the Elaigar won't be able to come back, and the Alattas don't want to. They think it will be better if there's no further contact at all between them and the Federation for a good long time to come."

"How do you know?"

"I looked through the mind of one of them," Telzey said. "That was one of the things I had to know, of course."

The official regarded her a moment.

"In looking through that Alatta's mind, you must have picked up some impression of their galactic location. . . ."

"No, I didn't," Telzey said. "I was careful not to. I didn't want to know that."

"Why not?" There was an edge of exasperation to his voice.

"Because *I* think it will be much better if there's no further contact, between us for a good long time. From either side."

The facemask shifted slightly, turning in Klayung's direction.

"Dr. Klayung," said the official, "with all the devices at the Service's disposal, there must be some way of determining whether this man has told us the full truth!"

Klayung scratched his chin.

"Knowing him as I do," he said, "I'm sure that if he felt he might be forced to reveal something he didn't wish to reveal, he'd simply wipe the matter from his mind. And we'd get nothing. So we might as well accept his statement. The Service is quite willing to do it."

"In that case," the official said, "there seems to be no point in continuing this talk."

"I had the impression," Klayung remarked, as he left the communication room with Telzey, "that you knew who he was."

Telzey nodded. "I do. Ramadoon. How'd he get involved in this? I thought he was only a Council Deputy."

"He fills a number of roles, depending on circumstances," Klayung told her. "A valuable man. Excellent organizer, highly intelligent, with a total loyalty to the Federation."

"And very stubborn," Telzey added. "I think he plans to put in a lot of effort now to get that psi in the Tinokti circuit identified."

"No doubt," said Klayung. "But it won't be long before that slips from his mind again."

"It will? Well, good! Then I won't have to worry about it. I can see why he might feel I've put the Federation at a disadvantage."

"Haven't you?"

"You didn't believe I don't know where the Alatta territories are, did you?"

"No," Klayung said. "We assumed you'd bring up that subject eventually."

"Well, I'm telling the Service, of course. But I thought we'd wait until things settle down again all around. I got a good general impression, but it will take mapping specialists and plenty of time to pinpoint it. They must be way off our charts. And that," Telzey added, "technically will put the Alattas at a disadvantage then."

"I'm not sure I follow you," Klayung said.

"The way the Alattas have worked it out, the human psis of the time, and especially the variations in them, had a good deal to do with defeating the Elaigar at Nalakia."

"Hmmm!" Klayung rubbed his jaw. "We've no record of that—but there would be none on our side, of course. An interesting speculation!"

"They don't think it's speculation. They're all psis, but they're all the same general kind of psi. They're born that way; it's part of the mutation. They don't change. They know we vary a lot and that we do change. That's why they wanted to take me along and analyze me. I'm pretty close to the Elaigar type of psi myself at present, but they figured there was more to it than that."

"Well," Klayung said, "you may have proved the point to their satisfaction now. The disadvantage, incidentally, will remain a technical one. The Service also feels contacts between the Federation and the Alattas would be quite undesirable in any foreseeable future."

They were passing a reflecting bulkhead as he spoke, and Telzey caught a sudden glimpse of herself. The middle-aged little man in the bulkhead grimaced distastefully at her. Her gaze shifted to a big wall clock at the end of the passageway, showing Tongi Phon and standard time and dates.

She calculated a moment.

"Klayung," she said, "does the Service owe me a favor?"

Klayung's expression became a trifle cautious. "Why, I'd say we're under considerable obligation to you. What favor did you have in mind?"

"Will you have Make-up turn me back like I was right away?"

"Of course. And?"

"Can you put me on a ship that's fast enough to get me to Orado City this evening, local time?"

Klayung glanced at the clock, calculated briefly in turn.

"I'm sure that can be arranged," he said then. He looked curiously at her. "Is there some special significance to the time you arrive there?"

"Not to me so much," Telzey said. "But I just remembered—today's my birthday. I'm sixteen, and the family wants me to be home for the party."

# BLOOD OF NALAKIA

*[Editor's note: This story is not part of the Telzey cycle, since it is set in a much earlier period of Hub history. It gives some of the background of the Elaigar who figure as Telzey's opponents in the "Lion Game" sequence.]*

It was an added bitterness to Lane Rawlings to discover that in the face of sudden disaster the Nachief of Frome could react with the same unshakable, almost contemptuous, self-confidence which he showed toward her and his other human slaves. That the lonely station of the Terrestrial Bureau of Agriculture and the nameless world far below them was both alert and heavily armed enough to ward off the attack of a spaceship should have come as a stunning surprise to him—and Lane would have exchanged her own very slim chances of survival at that point for the satisfaction of seeing the Nachief show fear.

Instead, he did instantly what had to be done to avoid complete defeat.

Lane's mind did not attempt to keep up with the Nachief's actions. The ship was still rocking from the first blow of the unseen guns beneath, when she, Grant, and Sean were being flung into the central escape bubble. When a lock snapped shut behind them and the bubble lit up inside, she saw that the Nachief had followed them in and was crouched over the controls. Tenths of a second later came another explosion, triggered by the Nachief himself— an explosion that simultaneously ripped out the side of the ship and flung the bubble free . . .

Lane found herself staring out of the bubble's telescopic ports at the sunlit, green and brown strip of land toward which they were falling. It was framed on two sides by a great blue sweep of sea. Behind them, to the left, was the glassy dome of the station, twin trails of white smoke marking the mile-long parallel scars the ship's guns had cut into the soil in the instant of the Nachief's savage, wanton attack. The trails stopped just short of the dome. Whoever was down there also had reacted in the nick of time.

The scene tilted violently outside, and Lane went sprawling back on the forms of Sean and Grant. The two colonists gave no indication even of being conscious. They had sat about like terrorized children for the past several days; they lay there now like stunned animals. Regaining her balance, Lane realized the bubble was falling much too fast, and for an instant she had the fierce hope that it was out of control.

Then she understood: he wants to get us down near that station—near a food supply! A wave of sick, helpless fury washed over her.

The Nachief looked around, grinning briefly, almost as if he had caught the thought.

"Pot-shooting at us, Lane! But we'll make it."

The deep voice; the friendly, authoritative, easily amused voice she'd been in love with for over a year. The voice that had told her, quite casually, less than thirty-six hours ago, that she and Sean and Grant would have to die, because she had found out something she wasn't supposed to know—and because she had made the additional mistake of telling the other two. The voice had gone on as casually to describe the grotesque indecency of the kind of death the Nachief was planning for them—

She stared at the back of his massive blond head, weak with her terror and hatred, until the bubble lurched violently again, flinging her back. This time, when she scrambled up on hands and knees, they were dropping with a headlong, rushing finality that told her the bubble had been hit and was going to crash. But they were still a mile above ground.

She offered no resistance when the Nachief picked her up and hauled her out of the lock with him.

Ribbon-chutes were unfolding in a coordinated pattern of minor jolts above them. Though it was only the Nachief's arm that held her clamped hard against his side, Lane felt quite insanely calm. They had dropped below the point where the station's gunners could target on them. He was going to get her down alive. He had no intention of giving up his prey merely because his own life was in danger. Something struck against her legs—the barrel of the big hunting gun he held in his other hand. A sudden cunning thought came to her, and she went completely limp, waiting.

The ground was less than a hundred feet below, turning, tilting, expanding and rushing up at them, before she flung herself into a spasm of furious

activity. She heard the Nachief's angry shout, felt them
sway and jerk as his arm tightened with punishing,
rib-cracking intensity about her. Then they struck.

Lane stood up presently, looked about dazedly and
went limping over to the Nachief. He lay face down
two hundred feet away. The chutes were entangled
in a cluster of stubby trees, but they had dragged
him that far first. He was breathing. He wasn't dead;
but he was unconscious. She stared down at him
incredulously, briefly close to hysterical laughter. She
couldn't have done it intentionally; the Nachief kept
his slaves under a repression to attempt no physical harm against him. She was free, for the moment
anyway, only because she had tried to kill herself.
Her glance went to a rock near his head, but a
sense of weakness, a heavy dread, swept through her
instantly.

The thing to do was to get out of the vicinity
immediately. If she could reach the station before he
did, she might warn its occupants what they were up
against—provided they didn't kill her first. The
Nachief's hunting gun lay almost at the point where
she had fallen. It was too heavy for her use, or even
to carry. But she paused long enough to thrust it
hurriedly into a tangle of dry brush which should hide
it from him for a while. Then she set off in the
general direction of the station.

Only five hundred yards away, she had an unexpected glimpse of the crashed bubble in open ground
far below her and stopped to stare at it with a sensation of horrified remorse. Grant and Sean hadn't
had a chance after she had told them what she knew
about the Nachief; in a way, she was responsible for
their deaths. Hurrying on, she dismissed the thought
with an effort, because it was more important just now
that somebody might be coming out from the station
to investigate the crash. But she couldn't risk waiting here. The station must be more than three miles

away, and her fear of the Nachief actually still seemed to be growing. Out of sight and sound, the illusion of humanity he presented was dropping away. What remained was an almost featureless awareness of a creature as coldly and savagely alien as a monstrous spider—

Suddenly breathless and shaking, Lane stopped long enough to fight down that feeling. When she set off again, it was at a pace designed to carry her all the way to the station, if nobody came to meet her.

Ten minutes later, she heard the sharp crack of a missile-gun and a whistling overhead, followed by a distant shout. It wasn't the Nachief's gun. She turned to look for her challenger, a vast relief flooding through her.

The tall, brown-skinned man who stepped out of a little gravity-rider a few dozen feet away held a gun in his hands, but looked at Lane with no particular indication of anything but self-confident wariness and some curiosity. A sharp-snouted, sinuous, streamlined animal, something like a heavy, short-legged dog, flowed out of the rider's door behind him, sat up on muscular haunches and regarded Lane with gleaming black eyes. The man said, "Unh-uh, Sally!" warningly.

"Any other survivors?" His voice was not loud but carried the same self-assurance as his attitude.

"Only one." Lane hadn't missed the by-play. That animal, whatever it was, needed only a gesture to launch itself at her throat. Its lean brown form was that of a natural killer, and the command could easily be given. "Look," she hurried on, "will you just listen to me for thirty seconds, without interrupting—without any questions?"

"Thirty seconds?" He almost smiled. "Why not?"

"This other survivor—he's armed and dangerous! He's the one who tried to destroy your station—"

She hesitated and swallowed, realizing for the first

time how preposterous her story would sound. "He's not a human being," she said flatly, almost sullenly.

The man's eyes might have become a trifle more wary, but he only nodded. And suddenly something seemed to break in Lane. She heard herself babbling it out—how Frome was a small human colony on a franchised world; how they had gone out there in a group from the Hub Systems a year before. That the Nachief, Bruce Sinclair Frome, had organized the emigration, the trip, everything. She'd been his secretary—

The station man kept on nodding and listening, noncommittally.

"I found out a few days ago that he's a man-eater! A blood-drinker—like a vampire—that was why he had set up the colony of Frome. He had eight hundred people under hypnotic control, and he was using ultrasonic signals to keep the controls in force. He's got instruments for that!" Lane said, her voice going shrill suddenly. "And he's been living on our blood all along, and nobody knew, and—"

"Take it easy!" It was a crisp though level-toned interruption, and it checked her effectively. She was sweating and shivering.

"You don't believe me, of course. He'll—"

"I might believe you," the man said amazingly. "You think he's after you now?"

"Of course, he's after me! He'll want to keep me from telling anyone. He brought us out here to kill us, the three who knew. The other two crashed in the bubble . . ."

He studied her another moment and motioned toward the gravity rider. "Better get in there."

The brown animal he'd called Sally slipped into the back of the rider ahead of Lane. It had a pungent, catty odor—the smell of a wild thing. The man came in last, and the rider rose from the ground. Seconds later, it was tracing a swift, erratic course at a twenty-foot height among the trees, soundless as a shadow.

"We're retreating a bit until we get this straightened out," the station man explained. "My name's Frazer. Yours?"

"Lane. Lane Rawlings."

"Well, Lane, we've a problem here. You see, I'm manning the station alone at present—unless you count Sally. There's a mining outfit five space-days away; they're the closest I know of. But they're not too cooperative. They might send an armed party over if I gave them an urgent enough call; and they might not. Five days is too long to wait anyway. We'll have to handle this ourselves."

"Oh, no!" she cried, stunned. "He—you don't realize how dangerous he is!"

"There'll be less risk," Frazer continued bluntly, "in going after him now, before he gets his bearings, so to speak, than to wait till he comes after us. We're on an island here, and it's not even a very big island. If he's—well, a sort of ogre, as you describe him— he'll find precious little to live on. The Bureau cleaned the animal life off the island quite a while ago. We're using it as an experimental ranch."

"Why can't we lock ourselves up in the station?" Fear was pounding in her again, a quick, hot tide.

Frazer brought the rider around in a slowing turn, halting it in mid-air.

"There's some sixty years of experimental work involved," he explained patiently. "And some of our cultures, some of the stuff we're growing here, becomes impossibly dangerous if it's not constantly controlled. The Bureau could get out a relief crew within two weeks, but we'd be obliged to raze the island from one end to the other by that time. That's getting rid of your Nachief of Frome the hard way."

Lane realized in abrupt dismay that she wouldn't be able to shake this man's hard self-confidence. And recalling suddenly the speed and effectiveness with which he had countered the Nachief's space-attack, she admitted that he might have some justification for it.

"He's got a long-range hunting gun," she warned shakily. "I suppose you know what you're doing—"

"Sure I know." Frazer smiled down at her. "Now, I'll drop you off at the station; and then Sally and I will go after your friend—"

"No!" she interrupted, terrified again at the prospect of being trapped alone on an island with the Nachief of Frome if Frazer failed. "I'll go with you. I can help."

Frazer seemed surprised but pleased. "You could be a help at that," he admitted. "Particularly since you know all his little ways. And we've got the rider— that should give us about the advantage we need . . ."

"What makes you so sure," Lane inquired a while later, "that he'll come to the bubble? He may suspect it's being watched."

They sat side by side hidden by shrubbery, a half mile from the wreck of the escape bubble, on somewhat higher ground. The gravity rider stood among bushes thirty feet behind them. A few hundred yards behind that was a great, rugged cliff face, bare of vegetation. It curved away to their left until, in the hazy distance, it dipped toward the sea.

"I imagine he does suspect it," Frazer conceded. "If he's anywhere around, he may even have seen us touch ground here." They had lifted high into the air to scan the area but had made sure of only one thing: that the Nachief of Frome was no longer where Lane had left him. On the other hand, there were a great many places where he could be by now. This part of the island was haphazardly forested. Thickets of trees alternated with stretches of rocky soil which seemed to support only a straw-colored reed. Zigzagging dense lines of hedgelike growths, almost black, seemed to follow concealed watercourses. Except for the towering cliff front, it was a place without distinguishing features of any kind where one could get lost very easily. It also provided, Lane realized uncomfortably, an ideal sort of background for the deadly game of hide-and-seek in which she was involved.

"He hasn't much choice though," Frazer was saying. "As I told you, the island's bare of all sizable animal life. He'll get hungry eventually."

Staring at the bubble, Lane felt herself whitening. Frazer went on, unaware of the effect he'd produced or unconcerned about it. "The other thing he might try is to get into the station, but his gun won't help him there. So he'll be back." His eyes shifted past Lane to the wide spread of scrub growth beyond her. "Just Sally," he said in a low voice, as if reassuring himself.

Sally came gliding into view a moment later, raised her head to gaze at them impersonally and vanished again with an undulating smoothness of motion that reminded Lane of a snake. It was as if the creature had slipped without a ripple into a gray-green sea.

"Trapped Sally on the mainland four years ago," Frazer remarked conversationally, still in low tones. "She's an elaig—seventy-pounds of killer and more brains than you'd believe. In bush like this, the average armed man wouldn't stand a chance against Sally. She knows pretty well what we're here for by now."

Lane shivered. Something about the cool, unhurried manner of Frazer as he talked and acted gave her, for minutes at a time, a sense of security she knew was false and highly dangerous. He seemed actually incapable of understanding the uncanny deadliness of this situation. She felt almost sorry for Frazer.

"You're wondering why I'm so afraid of him, aren't you?" she said slowly.

Frazer didn't answer immediately. Gun across his knees, a small knapsack he'd taken out of the rider strapped to his hip, he was studying her. Pleasantly enough, but not without an obvious appreciation of what he saw, even a touch of calculation. A tall, sun-darkened, competent man who felt capable of handling this or any other problem that might come his way to his complete satisfaction.

"Irrational fear of him could have been part of that hypnotic treatment he gave you," he told her, almost absently.

Lane shrugged, aware of a wave of sharp irritation. In the year since she'd known Bruce Sinclair Frome, she had almost forgotten the attraction the strong, clean lines of her body had for other men. She was being reminded of it now. And, perhaps because of that, she was realizing that part of her hatred for the Nachief was based in the complete shattering of her vanity in being discarded by him. She had a moment of unpleasant speculation as to what her reaction would have been if she had found out the truth about him—but had found out also that he still wanted her nevertheless . . .

She drove the thought away. The Nachief would die, if she could abet it. But the chances were that he regarded her and this overgrown boy scout beside her as not much more of a menace than Sean and Grant had been. She sat silent, fingering the small Deen nerve-gun Frazer had given her to pocket—"just in case." She'd warned him she probably wouldn't be able to force herself to use it—

"I just had the pleasant notion," Frazer remarked, "that your Nachief might ramble into one of our less hospitable cultures around here. That's what happened to the last two assistants they gave me, less than six months ago—and it would settle the problem, all right." He paused, thinking. "But I suppose any reasonably alert outworlder would be able to spot most of those things."

"I'm afraid," Lane agreed coolly, "that he'll be quite alert."

He looked at her again, digesting that in silence. "You really believe he isn't human, don't you?"

"I know he isn't human! He's different biologically. He actually needs blood to live on."

"Frome was his farm, and you colonists were his livestock, eh?"

"Something like that," she said, displeased at a description that was accurate enough to jolt her.

"The three of you he brought out here—what was his purpose in that?"

"To turn us loose, hunt us down, and eat us!" Lane said, all in a breath. And there was a momentary, tremendous relief at having been able to put it into so many words, finally.

Frazer blinked at her in thoughtful silence. "That gives us a sort of special advantage," he grinned then. "There's a group of primitive little humanoids along the mainland coast the Nachief could live on, if he got over there. But he doesn't know about them. So he'll be pretty careful not to blast us to pieces with that big gun you told me about."

Lane twisted her hands hard together. "He'd prefer that . . ." she agreed tonelessly.

"Then there's the gravity rider." Frazer turned a glance in the direction of the half-hidden vehicle behind them. "It gives us the greater mobility. If I were the Nachief, I'd wreck the rider before I tried to close in."

"And what do we do then?"

"Why, then we'll have a few tricks to play." He gave her his quick grin. "The rider's our bait. Until the Nachief takes it—or shows himself at the bubble— we can't do much about him. But after he's taken it, he'll try to move in on us."

Lane shook her head resignedly. She didn't particularly like Frazer. But she had a feeling now that he wasn't bluffing. He was decidedly of a different and more dangerous breed than the colonists of Frome. "You're in charge," she said.

"Still afraid of him?" he challenged.

"Plenty! But in a way this is better than I'd hoped for. I thought if I told anyone here about the Nachief, they'd think I was crazy—until it was too late."

Frazer scratched his chin, squinting at the distant bubble, as if studying some motion she couldn't see. "If he isn't human," he said, "what do you think he is?"

"I don't know," she admitted, with the surge of superstitious terror that speculation always aroused in her.

"I might have thought you were crazy," Frazer went on, smiling at her, "except—it seems you've never heard of the Nalakians?"

She shook her head.

"It was a colony of Earth people. Not too far from the Hub Systems, but not much of a colony either—everybody seems to have forgotten about it for about eight generations after it was started. When it was rediscovered, the descendants of the original colonists had changed into something more or less like you describe your Nachief. There were internal physiological modifications—I forget the details. Those new Nalakians showed a cannibalistic interest in other human beings, which may have been mainly psychological. And they're supposed to have been muscled like lions, with a lion's reactions. In short, a perfect human carnivore type."

He had her interest now—because it fitted! She sat up excitedly. "What happened to them?"

Frazer grinned. "What a lion can expect to happen when he draws too much attention to himself. They raided colonies in nearby systems, got tracked back to their own planet, and were pretty thoroughly exterminated. All that was about eighty years ago. But there may have been survivors in space at the time, you see. And those survivors may have had descendants who were clever enough to camouflage themselves as ordinary human beings. I thought of that when you first told me about your Nachief."

It gave her a curious sense of relief. The Nachief of Frome had become somewhat less terrifying, seemed much more on a par with themselves. "It could be."

"It could very much be," Frazer nodded. "Aside from wanting to play cat-and-mouse with you, he didn't tell you of any special motive for bringing you to this particular world, did he?"

"No," Lane said puzzled. "He was taking us away from Frome, so he could make it look like an accident. What other special motive should he have?"

"Probably not a very sane one," Frazer said, "but it checks, all right. I was born on this station, you see, and I know the area pretty well. This planet *is* Nalakia, and the original Nalakian colony was on the mainland, only eight hundred miles from here. They even used animals like Sally there in their hunting."

They stared at each other in speculative silence; and Lane shivered.

"They're not here now," Frazer said positively. "Not one of them—or I would have spotted their traces. But what was his purpose? A sort of blood-sacrifice to his lamented ancestors, or to planetary gods? I almost wish we could take him alive, to find out—"

He stopped suddenly. Lane stiffened, wondering what he'd seen or heard. He made a tiny gesture with one hand, motioning her to silence. In the stillness, she became aware of something moving into her range of vision to the left and becoming quiet again. She realized Sally had joined them.

Then there were long seconds filled with nothing but the wild beating of her heart.

The period ended in a brief, not-very-loud

thudding sound behind them, which was nevertheless the complete and final shattering of the gravity rider.

The Nachief of Frome had grounded them.

More than a mile off, Frazer was flattened on the rocky ground beside her, pulling her backward. "He's got me outgunned, all right. Now, just keep crawling back till you reach the gully that's twenty feet behind us. When you get there, keep low and let yourself slide down into it."

Lane tried to answer and shook her head instead.

"Is he using one of those ultrasonic gadgets you were telling me about? Sally feels something she doesn't like."

"I—I don't know. He never used one on me before."

"Well, how do you feel?"

"It's crazy!" she bleated. "I want to run back there! I want to run back to him!" Her legs were beginning to jerk uncontrollably.

"Close your eyes a moment, Lane."

She didn't question him . . . he was going to do something to help her. She closed her eyes.

Very gradually, Lane Rawlings became aware of the fact that she and Frazer and Sally were in a different sort of place now. It began to shape itself in her consciousness as a deeply shaded place with tall trees all around. To the right, a wall of gray rock rose steeply to a point where it vanished above the tops of the trees. The nearby area was dotted with boulders and grown with straggling gray grass. It was enclosed by solid ranks of gray-green thickets which rose up to a height of twenty feet or more between the trees.

Lane had a vague feeling next that a considerable amount of time had passed. Only then did she realize that her eyes were open—and that she was suspended somehow in mid-air, her feet free of the ground. The next thing she noticed was that her hands were fastened together before her. Jolted fully awake by that, she discovered finally the harness of straps around her by which she swung from a thick tree-branch overhead.

Frazer was standing beside her. He looked both apologetic and grimly amused.

"Sorry I had to tie you up. You were being very active." His voice was low and careful.

"What happened?" Becoming aware of assorted aches and discomforts in her body, she squirmed futilely. "Can't you let me down?"

"Not so loud." He made a gesture of silence. "Afraid not. Your friend isn't so far off, though I don't think he's actually located us as yet."

She swallowed and was still.

"He keeps trying to get a reaction out of you," Frazer went on, in the same careful tone. "It's some kind of signal. Sally can sense it, and it makes her furious; though I don't feel anything myself. You must be conditioned to it—and the effect is to make you want to run toward the source of the vibrations."

"I didn't know he'd brought any instruments with him," Lane said dully.

"He may not have intended to use them, unless the game took a turn he didn't like. Which I expect it has now. I gave you a hypo shot back at the gully that knocked you out, an hour ago," he added mildly. "The reason you're tied up is that, conscious or not, you keep trying to run back to the Nachief. It's rather fantastic to watch, but running in the air won't get you any closer to him . . ."

He turned suddenly. Sally, upright on her haunches twenty feet away, had made a soft, snarling sound. Her head was pointing at the thickets to their left, and the black eyes glittered with excitement.

"Better not talk any more," Frazer cautioned. "He's fairly close, though he's taking his time. He's a good hunter." he added with a curious air of approval. "Now I'm giving you another shot to keep you quiet while he closes in, or he might be able to force you to do something that would spoil the play." He was reaching for her arm as he spoke.

Lane started to protest but didn't quite make it. Something jolted through her body like an electric shock. Her legs jerked violently—and Frazer's face, and the trees and rocks behind him, started vanishing in a swirling blackness. In the blackness, she felt herself running; and at its other end, the Nachief's smiling face looked at her, waiting. She thought she was screaming and became briefly aware of the hard, sweaty pads of Frazer's palm clasped about her mouth.

Frazer stood beside Lane's slowly twisting and jerking body a few seconds longer, watching her anxiously. He couldn't very well load her down with any more drug than she was carrying right now. Satisfied then that she was incapable of making any disturbance for the time, he moved quietly back to Sally, gun ready in his hands.

"Getting close, eh?" he murmured. Sally twitched both ears impatiently and thereafter ignored him.

Frazer, almost immediately, became as oblivious of his companion. In a less clearly defined way, he was also quite conscious of the gradual approach of the Nachief of Frome, though the fierce little animal beside him was using more direct channels of awareness. He knew that the approach was following the winding path through the thickets he had taken thirty minutes earlier with Lane slung across his shoulder. And he didn't need the bristling of the hair at the back of his neck or the steady thumping of his heart to tell him that an entirely new sort of death was walking on his trail.

If the Nachief of Frome followed that path to the end, he told himself calculatingly, it was going to be a very close thing—probably not even the fifty-fifty chance he'd previously considered to be the worst he need expect. He had selected the spot where they and their guns would settle it, if it came to that. But it would be the Nachief then who could select the exact instant in time for the meeting. And Frazer knew by now, with a sure, impersonal judgment of himself and of the creature gliding up the path, that he was outmatched. The Nachief simply had turned out to be a little more than he'd counted on.

For a long minute or two, it seemed the stalker had stopped and was waiting. Lane hung quietly in her harness. Frazer decided the Nachief had given up trying to prod her into action. So he knew also, now, that it was between the two of them. Frazer grinned whitely in the shadows.

But what happened next took him completely by surprise. A sense of something almost tangible but invisible, a shadow that wasn't a shadow, coming toward him. Sally, Frazer realized, wasn't aware of it; and he reassured himself by thinking that whatever Sally couldn't detect could not be very damaging, physically. Nevertheless, he discovered in himself, in the next few seconds, an unexpected capacity for horror. The mind of the Nachief of Frome was speaking to him, demandingly, a momentary indecision overlying its dark, icy purpose of destruction. Frazer, refusing the answer, felt his own mind shudder away from that contact.

Almost immediately, the contact was broken; the shadow had vanished. He had no time to wonder about it; because now the final meeting, if it came, would be only seconds away . . .

Then, as if she had received a signal, Sally made a soft, breathing sound and settled slowly back to the ground on all fours, relaxing. She glanced up at Frazer for a moment, before shifting her gaze to a point in the bushes before her.

Frazer, a little less certain of his senses, did not relax just yet. But he, too, turned his eyes cautiously from the point where the path came into the glade to study the thickets ahead of them.

Those twenty-foot bushes were an unusual sort of growth. Not precisely a native of Nalakia, but one of the genetic experiments left by the colonists, that couldn't have been tolerated on any less isolated world. The tops of a group of the shrubs dead ahead, near one of the turns of the hidden path, were shivering slightly. The Nachief, having decided to make his final approach through the thickets, was a sufficiently expert stalker not to disturb the growth to that extent.

The growth was disturbing itself . . .

Aware of the warm-blooded life moving through below it, it was gently shaking out the fluffy pods at its tips to send near-microscopic enzyme crystals floating down on the intruding life form. Coating it with a fine, dissolving dust—

Dissolving through the pores of the skin; entering more swiftly through breathing nostrils into the lungs. Seeping through mouth, and ears, and eyes—

A thrashing commotion began suddenly in the thickets. It shook a new cloud of dust out of the pods, which made a visible haze in the air, even from where Frazer stood. He watched it a trifle worriedly, though the crystals did not travel far, even on a good breeze. The growth preferred to contact and keep other life forms where they would do it the most good, immediately above its roots.

The thrashing became frenzied. There was a sudden gurgling screech.

"That's fine," Frazer said softly between his teeth. "A few good breaths of the stuff now. It'll be over quicker."

More screeches, which merged within seconds into a wet, rapid yapping. The thrashing motions had weakened but they went on for another half minute or so, before they and the yapping stopped together, abruptly. The Nachief of Frome was giving up life very reluctantly; but he gave it up.

And now, gradually, Frazer relaxed. Oddly enough, watching the tops of the monstrous growth that had done his killing for him continue to quiver in a gentle, satisfied agitation, he was aware of a feeling of sharp physical letdown. Almost of disappointment—

But that, he realized, was scarcely a rational feeling. Frazer was, by and large, a very practical man.

Some time later, he removed from his knapsack one of the tools an employee of the Bureau's lonely outworld stations was likely to require at any time. Carefully, without moving from his tracks, he burned his vegetable ally out of existence. With another tool, he presently smothered the spreading flames again.

After a little rummaging, he discovered what must be the ultrasonic transmitter—a beautifully compact little gadget, which the fire had not damaged beyond the point of repair. Frazer cleaned it off carefully and pocketed it.

It was near nightfall when he put Lane Rawlings down on his bed in the station's living area. She had not regained consciousness on the long hike back to the station. He was a little worried, since he had never been obliged to use that type of drug in so massive a dose on a human being before. However, he decided that Lane was sleeping naturally now. Her sleep might be due as much to emotional exhaustion as to the effects of the drug. She should wake up presently, very hungry and with very sore muscles, but otherwise none the worse.

Straightening up, he found Sally beside him with her forepaws on the bed, peering at the girl's face. Sally looked up at him briefly, with an obvious question. The same hungry question she had asked when they first met Lane.

He shook his head, a gesture Sally understood very well. "Unh-uh," he said softly. "This one's our friend— if you can get that kind of idea into your ugly little head. Outside, Sally!"

He shut the door to the room behind him, because one couldn't be quite sure of Sally, though the chances were she would simply ignore the girl's existence from now on. A decision involving Lane Rawlings had been shaping itself in his mind throughout the day; but he had kept pushing it back out of sight. There was no point in getting excited about it before he found out whether or not it was practicable.

Sally padded silently after him as he made his customary nightfall round of the station's control areas. A little later, checking one of the Bureau's star-maps, he found the world of Frome indicated there. That was exceptionally good luck, since he wouldn't have to rely now on the spotty kind of information regarding its location he could expect to get from Lane. And, considering his plans, the location couldn't have been improved on—almost but not quite beyond the range of the little stellar flier waiting to serve in emergencies in its bombproof hangar beneath the station. He intended to leave the Bureau's investigators no reason to suspect anything but a destructive space-raid had occurred here. But even if he slipped up, they wouldn't think of looking for Frazer as far away as Frome.

What had been no more than a notion in his mind not many hours before suddenly looked not only practicable, but foolproof. Or very nearly—

Whistling gently, he settled down in the central room of his living area, to think out the details. Now he could afford to let the excitement grow up in him.

"Know what, Sally?" he addressed his silent companion genially. "That might, just possibly, have been my old man we bumped off today!"

It was a point Sally wasn't interested in. She had

jumped up on a table and was thumping its surface gently with her tapered, muscular tail, watching him— waiting to be fed. Frazer brought a container that held a day's rations for Sally out of a wall cabinet. and emptied its liquid contents into a bowl for her. Sally began to lap. Frazer hesitated a moment, took out a second container and partly filled another bowl for himself. Looking from it to the animal with an expression of sardonic amusement, he raised the second bowl to his lips. Presently be set it down empty. Sally was still lapping.

It wasn't too likely, he knew, that the late Nachief of Frome actually had been his father. But it was far from being an impossibility. Frazer had known since he was twelve years old that he had been fathered by a Nalakian living in the Hub Systems. His mother had told him, when an incident involving one of the humanoids of the mainland had revealed Frazer's developing Nalakian inclinations. She had made a fumbling, hysterical attempt to kill him immediately afterward, but had died herself instead. Even at that age, Frazer had been very quick. It had taught him, however, that to be quick wasn't enough—even living on the fringes of the unaware herds of civilization as he usually was, there remained always for one of the Nalakian breed the disagreeable necessity of being very cautious.

Until today—

At this point in his existence, he could afford to drop caution. Pure, ruthless boldness should make him sole lord and owner of the colony and the world of Frome within a week. Frazer was comfortably certain that he had enough and to spare of that quality to take over his heritage in style.

He studied the Nachief's ultrasonic transmitter a while.

"Have to learn how to use this gadget," he informed Sally idly. "But it's not very complicated. And if he has them already conditioned—"

Otherwise, he decided, he was quite capable now of doing it himself. An attempt to assume hypnotic control of his two latest station assistants had turned out unsatisfactorily half a year before, so that he'd been obliged to dispose of them. The possibility of reinforcing controls by mechanical means hadn't occurred to him at the time. His admiration for the Nachief of Frome's ingenuity was high. But it was mingled with a sort of impersonal contempt.

"Sally, if he hadn't overplayed it like a fool, he would have had all he could want for life. But a pure carnivore's bound to have a one-track mind, I suppose—"

He completed the thought to himself: That he had a very desirable advantage over the Nachief there. Biologically, he could get by comfortably on a humanly acceptable diet. Aside from the necessity of indoctrinating Lane Rawlings with a suitable set of memories, he might even decide to refrain from the use of hypnotic conditioning, until an emergency might call for it. His Nalakian qualities, sensibly restrained, would make him a natural leader in any frontier colony. There was something intriguing now about the notion of giving up the lonely delights of the predator to assume that role on Frome. In another generation, the genetically engineered biological pattern should be diluted beyond the danger point in his strain. No one need ever know.

Frazer chuckled, somewhat surprised by the sudden emergence of the social-human side of him—and also aware of the fact that he probably wouldn't take the notion too seriously in the end. But that was something he could decide on later . . .

He sat there a while, thinking pleasurably of Lane's strong young body. To play the human role completely should have undeniable compensations. Finally he became aware of Sally again, watching him with quiet black eyes. She had finished her bowl.

"Have some more?" he invited good-humoredly. "It's a celebration!"

Sally licked her lips.

He poured the balance of his container into her bowl and stood beside her, scratching her gently back of the ears, while she lapped swiftly at the thick, red liquid, shivering in the ecstasy of gorging. Frazer waited until she had finished the last drop before shooting her carefully through the back of the skull. Sally sank forward without a quiver and lay still.

"Hated to do it, Sally," he apologized gravely. "But I just couldn't take you along. We carnivores can't ever really be trusted."

Which was, he decided somewhat wryly, the simple truth. He might accept the human role, at that; but, depending on the circumstances, never quite without qualification.

It was almost his last coherent thought. The very brief one that followed was a shocked realization that the sudden, terrible, thudding sensation in his spine and skull meant that a Deen gun was being used on him.

Lane Rawlings remained motionless in the doorframe behind Frazer, leaning against it as if for support, for a good three minutes after he had dropped to the floor and stopped kicking. It wasn't that she was afraid of fainting. She only wanted to make very sure, at this distance, that Frazer was going to stay dead. She agreed thoroughly with his last remark.

The thought passed through her mind in that time that she could be grateful to the Nachief of Frome for one thing, at any rate—it had amused him to train his secretary to be a very precise shot.

After a while, she triggered the Deen gun once more, experimentally. Frazer produced no reactions now; he was as dead as Sally. Lane gave both of them a brief inspection before she pocketed the little gun and turned her attention to the food containers in the wall cabinet. With some reluctance, she opened one and found exactly what she expected to find. Now, the mainland humanoids Frazer had talked about might have a less harried existence in the future.

She looked down at Frazer's long, muscular body once more, with almost clinical curiosity. Then left the room and locked it behind her. She had no intention of entering it again, but there was evidence here that would be of interest to others—provided she found herself capable of operating the type of communicators used by the station.

Thirty minutes later, with no particular difficulty, she had contacted the area headquarters of the Bureau of Agriculture. She gave them her story coherently. Even if they didn't believe her, it was obvious they would waste no time in getting a relief crew to the station. Which was all Lane was interested in. After the Bureau concluded its investigations, somebody might do something about providing psychological treatment for the Frome colonists. But she wasn't concerned about that. She was returning to the Hub Systems.

She remained seated in the dim light of the communications cell for a time. She watched her dark reflection in the polished surfaces of its walls and listened to the intermittent whirring of a ventilator in the next office, which was all that broke the silence of the station now. She wondered whether she would have become suspicious of Frazer soon enough to do her any good, if she hadn't known for the past few weeks that she was carrying a child of the Nachief of Frome. For the past three days, she had been wondering also whether saving her life, at least for a while, by informing the Nachief of the fact, would be worthwhile. It was easy to imagine what a child of his might grow up to be.

Unaware, detail by detail since their meeting,

Frazer had filled out her mental picture of that. So she had known enough to survive the two feral creatures in the end . . .

As soon as she returned to the easy-going anonymity of the Hub Systems, this other one of their strain would die unborn. The terrible insistence on life on their own terms which Frazer and the Nachief had shown was warning enough against repetition of the nightmare.

Lane caught herself thinking, though, that there had been something basically pitiful about that inward-staring, alien blindness to human values, which forced all other life into subservience to itself because it could see only itself. She stirred uneasily.

The ventilator in the next office shut off with a sudden click.

"Of course, it will die!" she heard herself say aloud in the silence of the station. *Perhaps a little too loudly . . .*

After that, the silence remained undisturbed. A new contemplation grew in Lane as she sat there wondering about *Frazer's* mother.

# THE STAR HYACINTHS

[Editor's note: Although Telzey herself does not appear in this story, the hero is the same Wellan Dasinger who figures so prominently in her various adventures.]

The two wrecked spaceships rested almost side by side near the tip of a narrow, deep arm of a great lake.

The only man on the planet sat on a rocky ledge three miles uphill from the two ships, gazing broodingly down at them. He was a big fellow in neatly patched shipboard clothing. His hands were clean, his face carefully shaved. He had two of the castaway's traditional possessions with him: a massive hunting bow rested against the rocks, and a minor representative of the class of life which was this world's equivalent of birds was hopping about near his feet. This was a thrush-sized creature with a jaunty bearing and bright yellow eyes. From the front of its round face protruded a short, narrow tube tipped with small, sharp teeth. Round, horny knobs at the ends of its long toes protected retractile claws as it bounded back and forth between the bow and the man, giving a quick flutter of its wings on each bound. Finally it stopped before the man, stretching its neck to stare up at him, trying to catch his attention.

He roused from his musing, glanced irritably down at it.

"Not now, Birdie," he said. "Keep quiet!"

The man's gaze returned to the two ships, then passed briefly along a towering range of volcanoes on the other side of the lake, and lifted to the cloudless blue sky. His eyes probed on, searching the sunlit, empty vault above him. If a ship ever came again, it would come from there, the two wrecks by the lake arm already fixed in its detectors; it would not come gliding along the surface of the planet.

Birdie produced a sharp, plaintive whistle. The man looked at it.

"Shut up, stupid!" he told it.

He reached into the inner pocket of his coat, took out a small object wrapped in a piece of leather, and unfolded the leather.

Then it lay in his cupped palm, and blazed with the brilliance of twenty diamonds, seeming to flash the fires of the spectrum furiously from every faceted surface, without ever quite subduing the pure violet luminance which made a star hyacinth impossible to imitate or, once seen, to forget. The most beautiful of gems, the rarest, the most valuable. The man who was a castaway stared at it for long seconds, his breath quickening and his hand beginning to tremble. Finally he folded the chip of incredible mineral back into the leather, replaced it carefully in his pocket.

When he looked about again, the sunlit air seemed brighter, the coloring of lake and land more vivid and

alive. Once during each of this world's short days, but
no oftener, he permitted himself to look at the star
hyacinth. It was a ritual adhered to with almost
religious strictness, and it had kept him as sane as
he was ever likely to be again, for over six years.

It might, he sometimes thought, keep him sane
until a third ship presently came along to this place.
And then . . .

The third ship was coming along at that moment,
still some five hours' flight out from the system. She
was a small ship with lean, rakish lines, a hot little
speedster, gliding placidly through subspace just now,
her engines throttled down.

Aboard her, things were less peaceful.

The girl was putting up a pretty good fight but
getting nowhere with it against the bull-necked
Fleetman who had her pinned back against the wall.

Wellan Dasinger paused in momentary indecision
at the entrance to the half-darkened control section
of the speedboat. The scuffle in there very probably
was none of his business. The people of the roving
Independent Fleets had their own practices and mores
and resented interference from uninformed planet
dwellers. For all Dasinger knew, their blue-eyed lady
pilot enjoyed roughhousing with the burly members
of her crew. If the thing wasn't serious. . . .

He heard the man rap out something in the Willata
Fleet tongue, following the words up with a solid
thump of his fist into the girl's side. The thump hadn't
been playful, and her sharp gasp of pain indicated
no enjoyment whatever. Dasinger stepped quickly into
the room.

He saw the girl turn startled eyes toward him as he
came up behind the man. The man was Liu Taunus,
the bigger of the two crew members . . . too big and
too well muscled by a good deal, in fact, to make a
sportsmanlike suggestion to divert his thumpings to

Dasinger look like a sensible approach. Besides, Dasinger didn't know the Willata Fleet's language. The edge of his hand slashed twice from behind along the thick neck; then his fist brought the breath whistling from Taunus' lungs before the Fleetman had time to turn fully towards him.

It gave Dasinger a considerable starting advantage. During the next twenty seconds or so the advantage seemed to diminish rapidly. Taunus's fists and boots had scored only near misses so far, but he began to look like the hardest big man to chop down Dasinger had yet run into. And then the Fleetman was suddenly sprawling on the floor, face down, arms flung out limply, a tough boy with a thoroughly bludgeoned nervous system.

Dasinger was straightening up when he heard the *thunk* of the wrench. He turned sharply, discovered first the girl standing ten feet away with the wrench in her raised hand, next their second crew member lying on the carpet between them, finally the long, thin knife lying near the man's hand.

"Thanks, Miss Mines!" he said, somewhat out of breath. "I really should have remembered Calat might be somewhere around."

Duomart Mines gestured with her head at the adjoining control cabin. "He was in there," she said, also breathlessly. She was a long-legged blonde with a limber way of moving, pleasing to look at in her shaped Fleet uniform, though with somewhat aloof and calculating eyes. In the dim light of the room she seemed to be studying Dasinger now with an expression somewhere between wariness and surprised speculation. Then, as he took a step forward to check on Calat's condition, she backed off slightly, half lifting the wrench again.

Dasinger stopped and looked at her. "Well," he said, "make up your mind! Whose side are you on here?"

Miss Mines hesitated, let the wrench down. "Yours,

I guess," she acknowledged. "I'd better be, now! They'd murder me for helping a planeteer."

Dasinger went down on one knee beside Calat, rather cautiously though the Fleetman wasn't stirring, and picked up the knife. Miss Mines turned up the room's lights. Dasinger asked, "What was this . . . a mutiny? You're technically in charge of the ship, aren't you?"

"Technically," she agreed, added, "We were arguing about a Fleet matter."

"I see. We'll call it mutiny." Dasinger checked to be sure Calat wasn't faking unconsciousness. He inquired, "Do you really need these boys to help you?"

Duomart Mines shook her blond head. "Not at all. Flying the *Mooncat* is a one-man job."

"I did have a feeling," Dasinger admitted, "that Willata's Fleet was doing a little featherbedding when they said I'd have to hire a crew of three to go along with their speedboat."

"Uh-huh." Her tone was noncommittal. "They were. What are you going to do with them?"

"Anywhere they can be locked up safely?"

"Not safely. Their own cabin's as good as anything. They can batter their way out of here if they try hard enough. Of course we'd hear them doing it."

"Well, we can fix that." Dasinger stood up, fished his cabin key out of a pocket and gave it to her. "Tan suitcase standing at the head of my bunk," he said. "Mind bringing that and the little crane from the storeroom up here?"

Neither of the Fleetman had begun to stir when Duomart Mines came riding a gravity crane back in through the door a couple of minutes later, the suitcase dangling in front of her. She halted the crane in the center of the room, slid out of its saddle with a supple twist of her body, and handed Dasinger his cabin key.

"Thanks." Dasinger took the suitcase from the crane, unlocked and opened it. He brought out a pair of plastic handcuffs, aware that Miss Mines stood behind him making an intent scrutiny of what could be seen of the suitcase's contents. He didn't blame her for feeling curious; she was looking at a variety of devices which might have delighted the eyes of both a professional burglar and military spy. She offered no comment.

Neither did Dasinger. He hauled Liu Taunus over on his back, fastened handcuffs about the Fleetman's wrists, then rolled him over on his face again. He did the same for Calat, hung the suitcase back in the crane, slung a leg across the crane's saddle and settled into it.

Miss Mines remarked, "I'd look their cabin over pretty closely for guns and so on before leaving them there."

"I intend to. By the way, has Dr. Egavine mentioned how close we are to our destination?" Dasinger maneuvered the crane over to Taunus, lowered a beam to the small of the Fleetman's back and hoisted him up carefully, arms, head and legs dangling.

The blond girl checked her watch. "He didn't tell me exactly," she said, "but there's what seems to be a terraprox in the G-2 system ahead. If that's it, we'll get there in around five hours depending on what subspace conditions in the system are. Dr. Egavine's due up here in thirty minutes to give me the final figures." She paused, added curiously, "Don't you know yourself just where we're going?"

"No," Dasinger said. "I'm financing the trip. The doctor is the man with the maps and other pertinent information."

"I thought you were partners."

"We are. Dr. Egavine is taciturn about some things. I'll bring him back here with me as soon as I have these two locked away." Dasinger finished picking up Calat, swung the crane slowly towards the door, the unconscious Fleetmen suspended ahead of him.

❖     ❖     ❖

Dr. Egavine stood at the open door to his stateroom as Dasinger came walking back up the passage from the crew quarters and the storage. Quist, the doctor's manservant, peered out of the stateroom behind him.

"What in heaven's name were you doing with those two men?" Egavine inquired, twitching his eyebrows disapprovingly up and down. The doctor was a tall, thin man in his forties, dressed habitually in undertaker black, with bony features and intense dark eyes. He added, "They appeared to be unconscious . . . and fettered!"

"They were both," Dasinger admitted. "I've confined them to their cabin."

"Why?"

"We had a little slugfest in the control section a few minutes ago. One of the boys was beating around on our pilot, so I laid him out, and she laid out the other one when he tried to get into the act with a knife. She says the original dispute was a Fleet matter . . . in other words, none of our business. However, I don't know. There's something decidedly fishy about the situation."

"In what way?" Egavine asked.

Dasinger said, "I checked over the crew quarters for weapons just now and found something which suggests that Willata's Fleet is much more interested in what we're doing out here than we thought."

Egavine looked startled, peered quickly along the passage to the control section. "I feel," he said, lowering his voice, "that we should continue this discussion behind closed doors. . . ."

"All right." Quist, a bandy-legged, wiry little man with a large bulb of a nose and close-set, small, eyes, moved back from the door. Dasinger went inside. Egavine pulled the door shut behind them and drew a chair out from the cabin table. Dasinger sat down opposite him.

"What did you find?" Dr. Egavine asked.

Dasinger said, "You know Miss Mines is supposed to be the only Fleet member on board who speaks the Federation's translingue. However, there was a listening device attached to the inside of the cabin communicator in the crew quarters. Its setting show that the Willata Fleet people have bugged each of the *Mooncat*'s other cabins, and also—which I think is an interesting point—the control section. Have you and Quist discussed our project in any detail since coming aboard?"

"I believe we did, on several occasions," Egavine said hesitantly.

"Then we'd better assume Taunus and Calat knew that we're looking for the wreck of the Dosey Asteroids raider, and . . ."

Egavine put a cautioning finger to his lips. "Should we . . . ?"

"Oh, no harm in talking now," Dasinger assured him. "I pulled the instrument out and dropped it in my cabin. Actually, the thing needn't be too serious if we stay on guard. But of course we shouldn't go back to the Fleet station after we have the stuff. Gadgetry of that kind suggests bad intentions . . . also a rather sophisticated level of criminality for an I-Fleet. We'll return directly to the Hub. We might have to go on short rations for a few weeks, but we'll make it. And we'll keep those two so-called crew members locked up."

The doctor cleared his throat. "Miss Mines . . ."

"She doesn't appear to be personally involved in any piratical schemes," Dasinger said. "Otherwise they wouldn't have bugged her cabin and the control rooms. If we dangle a few star hyacinths before her eyes, she should be willing to fly us back. If she balks, I think I can handle the *Mooncat* well enough to get us there."

Dr. Egavine tugged pensively at his ear lobe. "I see." His hand moved on toward his right coat lapel. "What do you think of . . ."

"Mind watching this for a moment, doctor?" Dasinger interrupted. He nodded at his own hand lying on the table before him.

"Watch . . . ?" Egavine began questioningly. Then his eyes went wide with alarm.

Dasinger's hand had turned suddenly sideways from the wrist, turned up again. There was a small gun in the hand now, its stubby muzzle pointing up steadily at Egavine's chest.

"Dasinger! What does . . ."

"Neat trick, eh?" Dasinger commented. "Sleeve gun. Now keep quiet and hold everything just as it is. If you move or Quist over there moves before I tell you to, you've had it, doctor!"

He reached across the table with his left hand, slipped it beneath Egavine's right coat lapel, tugged sharply at something in there, and brought out a flat black pouch with a tiny spray needle projecting from it. He dropped the pouch in his pocket, said, "Keep your seat, doctor," stood up and went over to Quist. Quist darted an anxious glance at his employer, and made a whimpering sound in his throat.

"You're not getting hurt," Dasinger told him. "Just put your hands on top of your head and stand still. Now let's take a look at the thing you started to pull from your pocket a moment ago . . . Electric stunsap, eh? That wasn't very nice of you, Quist! Let's see what else—"

"Good Lord, Egavine," he announced presently, "your boy's a regular armory! Two blasters, a pencil-beam, a knife, and the sap . . . All right, Quist. Go over and sit down with the doctor." He watched the little man move dejectedly to the table, then fitted the assorted lethal devices carefully into one of his coat pockets, brought the pouch he had taken from Egavine out of the other pocket.

"Now, doctor," he said, "let's talk. I'm unhappy

about this. I discovered you were carrying this thing around before we left Mezmiali, and I had a sample of its contents analyzed. I was told it's a hypnotic with an almost instantaneous effect both at skin contact and when inhaled. Care to comment?"

"I do indeed!" Egavine said frigidly. "I have no intention of denying that the instrument is a hypnotic spray. As you know, I dislike guns and similar weapons, and we are engaged in a matter in which the need to defend myself against a personal attack might arise. Your assumption, however, that I intended to employ the spray on you just now is simply ridiculous!"

"I might be chuckling myself," Dasinger said, "if Quist hadn't had the sap halfway out of his pocket as soon as you reached for your lapel. If I'd ducked from the spray, I'd have backed into the sap, right? There's a little too much at stake here, doctor. You may be telling the truth, but just in case you're nourishing unfriendly ideas—and that's what it looks like to me—I'm taking a few precautions."

Dr. Egavine stared at him, his mouth set in a thin, bitter line. Then he asked, "What kind of precautions?"

Dasinger said, "I'll keep the hypnotic and Quist's bag of dirty tricks until we land. You might need those things on the planet but you don't need them on shipboard. You and I'll go up to the control section now to give Miss Mines her final flight directions. After that, you and Quist stay in this cabin with the door locked until the ship has set down. I don't want to have anything else to worry about while we're making the approach. If my suspicions turn out to be unjustified, I'll apologize . . . after we're all safely back in the Hub."

"What was your partner looking so sour about?" Duomart Mines inquired a little later, her eyes on the flight screens. "Have a quarrel with him?"

Dasinger, standing in the entry to the little control cabin across from her, shrugged his shoulders.

"Not exactly," he said. "Egavine tried to use a hypno spray on me."

"Hypno spray?" the young woman asked.

"A chemical which induces an instantaneous hypnotic trance in people. Leaves them wide open to suggestion. Medical hypnotists make a lot of use of it. So do criminals."

She turned away from the control console to look at him. "Why would your partner want to hypnotize you?"

"I don't know," Dasinger said. "He hasn't admitted that he intended to do it."

"Is he a criminal?"

"I wouldn't say he isn't," Dasinger observed judiciously, "but I couldn't prove it."

Duomart puckered her lips, staring at him thoughtfully. "What about yourself?" she asked.

"No, Miss Mines, I have a very high regard for the law. I'm a simple businessman."

"A simple businessman who flies his own cruiser four weeks out from the Hub into I-Fleet territory?"

"That's the kind of business I'm in," Dasinger explained. "I own a charter ship company."

"I see," she said. "Well, you two make an odd pair of partners. . . ."

"I suppose we do. Incidentally, has there been any occasion when you and Dr. Egavine—or you and Dr. Egavine and his servant—were alone somewhere in the ship together? For example, except when we came up here to give you further flight instructions, did he ever enter the control room?"

She shook her blond head. "No. Those are the only times I've seen him."

"Certain of that?" he asked.

Duomart nodded without hesitation. "Quite certain!"

Dasinger took an ointment tube from his pocket, removed its cap, squeezed a drop of black, oily substance out on a fingertip. "Mind rolling up your sleeve a moment?" he asked. "Just above the elbow . . ."

"What for?"

"It's because of the way those hypno sprays work," Dasinger said. "Give your victim a dose of the stuff, tell him what to do, and it usually gets done. And if you're being illegal about it, one of the first things you tell him to do is to forget he's ever been sprayed. This goop is designed for the specific purpose of knocking out hypnotic commands. Just roll up your sleeve like a good girl now, and I'll rub a little of it on your arm."

"You're not rubbing anything on my arm, mister!" Duomart told him coldly.

Dasinger shrugged resignedly, recapped the tube, and dropped it in his pocket. "Have it your way then," he remarked. "I was only . . ."

He lunged suddenly towards her.

Duomart gave him quite a struggle. A minute or two later, he had her down on the floor, her body and one arm clamped between his knees, while he unzipped the cuff on the sleeve of the other arm and pulled the sleeve up. He brought out the tube of antihypno ointment and rubbed a few drops of the ointment into the hollow of Duomart's elbow, put the tube back in his pocket, then went on holding her down for nearly another minute. She was gasping for breath, blue eyes furious, muscles tensed.

Suddenly he felt her relax. An expression of stunned surprise appeared on her face. "Why," she began incredulously, "he *did* . . ."

"Gave you the spray treatment, eh?" Dasinger said, satisfied. "I was pretty sure he had."

"Why, that— At his beck and call, he says! Well, we'll just see about . . . let me up, Dasinger! Just wait till I get my hands on that bony partner of yours!'"

"Now take it easy."

"Take it easy! Why should I? I . . ."

"It would be better," Dasinger explained, "if Egavine believes you're still under the influence."

She scowled up at him; then her face turned thoughtful. "Ho! You feel it isn't that he's a depraved old goat, that he's got something more sinister in mind?"

"It's a definite possibility. Why not wait and find out? The ointment will immunize you against further tricks."

Miss Mines regarded him consideringly for a few seconds, then nodded. "All right! You can let me up now. What do you think he's planning?"

"Not easy to say with Dr. Egavine. He's a devious man." Dasinger got himself disentangled, came to his feet, and reached down to help her scramble up.

"They certainly wrap you up with that hypno stuff, don't they?" she observed wonderingly.

Dasinger nodded. "They certainly do." Then he added, "I'm keeping the doctor and his little side-kick locked up, too, until we get to the planet. That leaves you and me with the run of the ship."

Duomart looked at him. "So it does," she agreed.

"Know how to use a gun?"

"Of course. But I'm not allow—don't have one with me on this trip."

He reached into his coat, took out a small gun in a fabric holster. Duomart glanced at it, then her eyes went back to his face.

"Might clip it to your belt," Dasinger said. "It's a good little shocker, fifty-foot range, safe for shipboard use. It's got a full load, eighty shots. We may or may not run into emergencies. If we don't, you'll still be more comfortable carrying it."

Duomart holstered the gun and attached the holster to her belt. She slid the tip of her tongue reflectively out between her lips, drew it back, blinked at the flight screens for a few seconds, then looked across at Dasinger and tapped the holster at her side.

"That sort of changes things, too," she said.

"Changes what?"

"Tell you in a minute. Sit down, Dasinger. Manual course corrections coming up . . ." She slid into the pilot seat, moved her hands out over the controls, and appeared to forget about him.

Dasinger settled into a chair to her left and watched her, glancing occasionally at the screens. She was jockeying the *Mooncat* deftly in and out of the fringes of a gravitic stress knot, presently brought it into the clear, slapped over a direction lever and slid the palm of her right hand along a row of speed control buttons depressing them in turn.

"Nice piece of piloting," Dasinger observed.

Duomart lifted one shoulder in a slight shrug. "That's my job." Her face remained serious. "Are you wondering why I edged us through that thing instead of going around it?"

"Uh-huh, a little," Dasinger admitted.

"It knocked half an hour off the time it should take us to get to your planet," she said. "That is, *if* you'll still want to go there. We're being followed, you see."

"By whom?"

"They call her the *Spy*. After the *Mooncat* she's the fastest job in the Fleet. She's got guns, and her normal complement is twenty armed men."

"The idea being to have us lead them to what we're after, and then take it away from us?" Dasinger asked.

"That's right. I'm not supposed to know about it. You know what a Gray Fleet is?"

Dasinger nodded. "An Independent that's turned criminal."

"Yes. Willata's Fleet was a legitimate outfit up to four years ago. Then Liu Taunus and Calat and their

gang took over. That happened to be the two Fleet
bosses you slapped handcuffs on, Dasinger. We're a
Gray Fleet now. So I had some plans of my own for
this trip. If I can get to some other I-Fleet or to the
Hub I might be able to do something about Taunus.
After we were down on the planet, I was going to
steal the *Mooncat* and take off by myself."

"Why are you telling me?"

Miss Mines colored a little. "Well, you gave me
the gun," she said. "And you clobbered Taunus, and
got me out of that hypno thing . . . I mean, I'd have
to be pretty much of a jerk to ditch you now, wouldn't
I? Anyway, now that I've told you, you won't be going
back to Willata's Fleet, whatever you do. I'll still get
to the Hub." She paused. "So what do you want to
do now? Beat it until the coast's clear, or make a quick
try for your loot before the *Spy* gets there?"

"How far is she behind us?" Dasinger asked.

Duomart said, "I don't know exactly. Here's what
happened. When we started out, Taunus told me not
to let the *Mooncat* travel at more than three-quarters
speed for any reason. I figured then the *Spy* was
involved in whatever he was planning; she can keep
up with us at that rate, and she has considerably better
detector reach than the *Cat*. She's stayed far enough
back not to register on our plates throughout the trip.

"Late yesterday we hit some extensive turbulence
areas, and I started playing games. There was this
little cluster of three sun systems ahead. One of them
was our target, though Dr. Egavine hadn't yet said
which. I ducked around a few twisters, doubled back,
and there was the *Spy* coming the other way. I beat
it then—top velocity. The *Spy* dropped off our detectors two hours later, and she can't have kept us on
for more than another hour herself.

"So they'll assume we're headed for one of those
three systems, but they don't know which one.
They'll have to look for us. There's only one

terraprox in the system we're going to. There may be none in the others, or maybe four or five. But the terraprox worlds is where they'll look because the salvage suits you're carrying are designed for ordinary underwater work. After the way I ran from them, they'll figure something's gone wrong with Taunus's plans, of course."

Dasinger rubbed his chin. "and if they're lucky and follow us straight in to the planet?"

"Then," Miss Mines said, "you might still have up to six or seven hours to locate the stuff you want, load it aboard and be gone again."

"Might have?"

She shrugged. "We've got a lead on them, but just how big a lead we finally wind up with depends to a considerable extent on the flight conditions they run into behind us. They might get a break there, too. Then there's another very unfortunate thing. The system Dr. Egavine's directed us to now is the one we were closest to when I broke out of detection range. They'll probably decide to look there first. You see?"

"Yes," Dasinger said. "Not so good, is it?" He knuckled his jaw again reflectively. "Why was Taunus pounding around on you when I came forward?"

"Oh, those two runches caught me flying the ship at top speed. Taunus was furious. He couldn't know whether the *Spy* still had a fix on us or not. Of course he didn't tell me that. The lumps he was preparing to hand out were to be for disregarding his instructions. He does things like that." She paused. "Well, are you going to make a try for the planet?"

"Yes," Dasinger said. "If we wait, there's entirely too good a chance the *Spy* will run across what we're after while she's snooping around for us there. We'll try to arrange things for a quick getaway in case our luck doesn't hold up."

Duomart nodded. "Mind telling me what you're after?"

"Not at all. Under the circumstances you should be told . . .

"Of course," Dasinger concluded a minute or two later, "all we'll have a legal claim to is the salvage fee."

Miss Mines glanced over at him, looking somewhat shaken. "You *are* playing this legally?"

"Definitely."

"Even so," she said, "if that really is the wreck of the Dosey Asteroids raider, and the stones are still on board . . . you two will collect something like ten million credits between you!"

"Roughly," Dasinger agreed. "Dr. Egavine learned about the matter from one of your Willata Fleetmen."

Her eyes widened. "He what!"

"The Fleet lost a unit called *Handing's Scout* about four years ago, didn't it?"

"Three and a half," she said. She paused. "*Handing's Scout* is the other wreck down there?"

"Yes. There was one survivor . . . as far as we know. You may recall his name. Leed Farous."

Duomart nodded. "The little kwil hound. He was assistant navigator. How did Dr. Egavine . . . ?"

Dasinger said, "Farous died in a Federation hospital on Mezmiali two years ago, apparently of the accumulative effects of kwil addiction. He'd been picked up in Hub space in a lifeboat which we now know was one of the two on *Handing's Scout*."

"In Hub space? Why, it must have taken him almost a year to get that far in one of those tubs!"

"From what Dr. Egavine learned," Dasinger said, "it did take that long. The lifeboat couldn't be identified at the time. Neither could Farous. He was completely addled with kwil . . . quite incoherent, in fact already apparently in the terminal stages of the addiction. Strenuous efforts were made to identify him because a single large star hyacinth had been found in the lifeboat . . . there was the possibility it was one of the stones the Dosey Asteroids Company had lost. But Farous died some months later without regaining his senses sufficiently to offer any information.

"Dr. Egavine was the physician in charge of the case, and eventually also the man who signed the death certificate. The doctor stayed on at the hospital for another year, then resigned, announcing that he intended to go into private research. Before Farous died, Egavine had of course obtained his story from him."

Miss Mines looked puzzled. "If Farous never regained his senses . . ."

"Dr. Egavine is a hypnotherapist of exceptional ability," Dasinger said. "Leed Farous wasn't so far gone that the information couldn't be pried out of him with an understanding use of drug hypnosis."

"Then why didn't others . . ."

"Oh, it was attempted. But you'll remember," Dasinger said, "that I had a little trouble getting close to you with an antihypnotic. The good doctor got to Farous first, that's all. Instead of the few minutes he spent on you, he could put in hour after hour conditioning Farous. Later comers simply didn't stand a chance of getting through to him."

Duomart Mines was silent a moment, then asked, "Why did you two come out to the Willata Fleet station and hire one of our ships? Your cruiser's a lot slower than the *Mooncat* but it would have got you here."

Dasinger said, "Dr. Egavine slipped up on one point. One can hardly blame him for it since interstellar navigation isn't in his line. The reference points on the maps he had Farous make up for him turned out to be meaningless when compared with

Federation star charts. We needed the opportunity
to check them against your Fleet maps. They make
sense then."

"I see." Duomart gave him a sideways glance,
remarked, "You know, the way you've put it, the
thing's still pretty fishy."

"In what manner?"

"Dr. Egavine finished off old Farous, didn't he?"

"He may have," Dasinger conceded. "It would be
impossible to prove it now. You can't force a man to
testify against himself. It's true, of course, that Farous
died at a very convenient moment, from Dr. Egavine's
point of view."

"Well," she said, "a man like that wouldn't be
satisfied with half a salvage fee when he saw the
chance to quietly make away with the entire Dosey
Asteroids haul."

"That could be," Dasinger said thoughtfully. "On
the other hand, a man who had committed an unprov-
able murder to obtain a legal claim to six million
credits might very well decide not to push his luck
any farther. You know the space salvage ruling that
when a criminal act or criminal intent can be shown
in connection with an operation like this, the guilty
person automatically forfeits any claim he has to the
fee."

"Yes, I know . . . and of course," Miss Mines said,
"you aren't necessarily so lily white either. That's
another possibility. And there's still another one. You
don't happen to be a Federation detective, do you?"

Dasinger blinked. After a moment he said, "Not
a bad guess. However, I don't work for the Federation."

"Oh? For whom do you work?"

"At the moment, and indirectly, for the Dosey
Asteroids Company."

"Insurance?"

"No. After Farous died, Dosey Asteroids employed

a detective agency to investigate the matter. I represent the agency."

"The agency collects on the salvage?"

"That's the agreement. We deliver the goods or get nothing."

"And Dr. Egavine?"

Dasinger shrugged. "If the doctor keeps his nose clean, he stays entitled to half the salvage fee."

"What about the way he got the information from Farous?" she asked.

"From any professional viewpoint, that was highly unethical procedure. But there's no evidence Egavine broke any laws."

Miss Mines studied him, her eyes bright and quizzical. "I had a feeling about you," she said. "I . . ."

A warning burr came from the tolerance indicator; the girl turned her head quickly, said, "*Cat's* complaining . . . looks like we're hitting the first system stresses!" She slid back into the pilot seat. "Be with you again in a while . . ."

When Dasinger returned presently to the control section Duomart sat at ease in the pilot seat with coffee and a sandwich before her.

"How are the mutineers doing?" she asked.

"They ate with a good appetite, said nothing, and gave me no trouble," Dasinger said; "They still pretend they don't understand Federation translingue. Dr. Egavine's a bit sulky. He wanted to be up front during the prelanding period. I told him he could watch things through his cabin communicator screen."

Miss Mines finished her sandwich, her eyes thoughtful. "I've been wondering, you know . . . how can you be sure Dr. Egavine told you the truth about what he got from Leed Farous?"

Dasinger said, "I studied the recordings Dr. Egavine made of his sessions with Farous in the hospital. He may have held back on a few details, but the recordings were genuine enough."

"So Farous passes out on a kwil jag," she said, "and he doesn't even know they're making a landing. When he comes to, the scout's parked, the Number Three drive is smashed, the lock is open, and not another soul is aboard or in sight.

"Then he notices another wreck with its lock open, wanders over, sees a few bones and stuff lying around inside, picks up a star hyacinth, and learns from the ship's records that down in the hold under sixty feet of water is a sealed compartment with a whole little crateful of the stones . . ."

"That's the story," Dasinger agreed.

"In the Fleets," she remarked, "if we heard of a place where a couple of ship's crews seemed to have vanished into thin air, we'd call it a spooked world. And usually we'd keep away from it." She clamped her lower lip lightly between her teeth for a moment. "Do you think Dr. Egavine has considered the kwil angle?"

Dasinger nodded. "I'm sure of it. Of course it's only a guess that the kwil made a difference for Farous. The stuff has no known medical value of any kind. But when the only known survivor of two crews happens to be a kwil-eater, the point has to be considered."

"Nobody else on *Handing's Scout* took kwil," Duomart said. "I know that. There aren't many in the Fleet who do." She hesitated. "You know, Dasinger, perhaps I should try it again! Maybe if I took it straight from the injector this time . . ."

Dasinger shook his head. "If the little flake you nibbled made you feel drowsy, even a quarter of a standard shot would put you out cold for an hour or two. Kwil has that effect on a lot of people. Which is one reason it isn't a very popular drug."

"What effect does it have on you?" she asked.

"Depends to some extent on the size of the dose. Sometimes it slows me down physically and mentally. At other times there were no effects that I could tell until the kwil wore off. Then I'd have hallucinations for a while—that can be very distracting, of course, when there's something you have to do. Those hang-over hallucinations seem to be another fairly common reaction."

He concluded, "Since you can't take the drug and stay awake, you'll simply remain inside the locked ship. It will be better anyway to keep the *Mooncat* well up in the air and ready to move most of the time we're on the planet."

"What about Taunus and Calat?" she asked.

"They come out with us, of course. If kwil is what it takes to stay healthy down there, I've enough to go around. And if it knocks them out, it will keep them out of trouble."

"Looks like there's a firemaker down there!" Duomart's slim forefinger indicated a point on the ground-view plate. "Column of smoke starting to come up next to that big patch of trees! ... Two point nine miles due north and uphill of the wrecks."

From a wall screen Dr. Egavine's voice repeated sharply "Smoke? Then Leed Farous was not the only survivor!"

Duomart gave him a cool glance. "Might be a native animal that knows how to make fire. They're not so unusual." She went on to Dasinger. "It would take a hand detector to spot us where we are, but it does look like a distress signal. If it's men from one of the wrecks, why haven't they used the scout's other lifeboat?"

"Would the lifeboat still be intact?" Dasinger asked.

Duomart spun the ground-view plate back to the scout. "Look for yourself," she said. "It *couldn't* have been damaged in as light a crash as that one was.

Those tubs are built to stand a really solid shaking up! And what else could have harmed it?"

"Farous may have put it out of commission before he left," Dasinger said. "He wanted to come back from the Hub with an expedition to get the hyacinths, so he wouldn't have cared for the idea of anyone else getting away from the planet meanwhile." He looked over at the screen. "How about it, doctor? Did Farous make any mention of that?"

Dr. Egavine seemed to hesitate an instant. "As a matter of fact, he did. Farous was approximately a third of the way to the Hub when he realized he might have made a mistake in not rendering the second lifeboat unusable. But by then it was too late to turn back, and of course he was almost certain there were no other survivors."

"So that lifeboat should still be in good condition?"

"It was in good condition when Farous left here."

"Well, whoever's down there simply may not know how to handle it."

Duomart shook her blond head decidedly. "That's out too!" she said. "Our Fleet lifeboats all came off an old Grand Commerce liner which was up for scrap eighty, ninety years ago. They're designed so any fool can tell what to do, and the navigational settings are completely automatic. Of course if it *is* a native firemaker—with mighty keen eyesight—down there, that could be different! A creature like that mightn't think of going near the scout. Should I start easing the *Cat* in towards the smoke, Dasinger?"

"Yes. We'll have to find out what the signal means before we try to approach the wrecks. Doctor, are you satisfied now that Miss Mines's outworld biotic check was correct?"

"The analysis appears to be fairly accurate," Dr. Egavine acknowledged, "and all detectable trouble sources are covered by the selected Fleet serum."

✧        ✧        ✧

Dasinger said, "We'll prepare for an immediate landing then. There'll be less than an hour of daylight left on the ground, but the night's so short we'll disregard that factor." He switched off the connection to Egavine's cabin, turned to Duomart. "Now our communicators, you say, have a five mile range?"

"A little over five."

"Then," Dasinger said, "we'll keep you and the *Cat* stationed at an exact five mile altitude ninety-five per cent of the time we spend on the planet. If the *Spy* arrives while you're up there, how much time will we have to clear out?"

She shrugged. "That depends of course on how they arrive. My detectors can pick the *Spy* up in space before their detectors can make out the *Cat* against the planet. If we spot them as they're heading in, we'll have around fifteen minutes.

"But if they show up on the horizon in atmosphere, or surface her out of subspace, that's something else. If I don't move instantly then, they'll have me bracketed . . . and *BLOOIE*!"

Dasinger said, "Then those are the possibilities you'll have to watch for. Think you could draw the *Spy* far enough away in a chase to be able to come back for us?"

"They wouldn't follow me that far," Duomart said. "They know the *Cat* can outrun them easily once she's really stretched out, so if they can't nail her in the first few minutes they'll come back to look around for what we were interested in here." She added, "And if I *don't* let the *Cat* go all out but just keep a little ahead of them, they'll know that I'm trying to draw them away from something."

Dasinger nodded. "In that case we'll each be on our own, and your job will be to keep right on going and get the information as quickly as possible to the Kyth detective agency in Orado. The agency will take the matter from there."

✧        ✧        ✧

Miss Mines looked at him. "Aren't you sort of likely to be dead before the agency can do anything about the situation?"

"I'll try to avoid it," Dasinger said. "Now, we've assumed the worst as far as the *Spy* is concerned. But things might also go wrong downstairs. Say I lose control of the group, or we all get hit down there by whatever hit the previous landing parties and it turns out that kwil's no good for it. It's understood that in any such event you again head the *Cat* immediately for the Hub and get the word to the agency. Right?"

Duomart nodded.

He brought a flat case of medical injectors out of his pocket, and opened it.

"Going to take your shot of kwil before we land?" Miss Mines asked.

"No. I want you to keep one of these injectors on hand, at least until we find out what the problem is. It'll knock you out if you have to take it, but it might also keep you alive. I'm waiting myself to see if it's necessary to go on kwil. The hallucinations I get from stuff afterwards could hit me while we're in the middle of some critical activity or other, and that mightn't be so good." He closed the case again, put it away. "I think we've covered everything. If you'll check the view plate, something—or somebody—has come out from under the trees near the column of smoke. And unless I'm mistaken it's a human being."

Duomart slipped the kwil injectors he'd given her into a drawer of the instrument console. "I don't think you're mistaken," she said. "I've been watching him for the last thirty seconds."

"It is a man?"

"Pretty sure of it. He moves like one."

Dasinger stood up. "I'll go talk with Egavine then. I had a job in mind for him and his hypno sprays if we happened to run into human survivors."

"Shall I put the ship down next to this one?"

"No. Land around five hundred yards to the north, in the middle of that big stretch of open ground. That should keep us out of ambushes. Better keep clear of the airspace immediately around the wrecks as you go down."

Duomart looked at him. "Darn right I'll keep clear of that area!"

Dasinger grinned. "Something about the scout?"

"Sure. No visible reason at all why the scout should have settled hard enough to buckle a drive. Handing was a good pilot."

"Hm-m-m." Dasinger rubbed his chin. "Well, I've been wondering. The Dosey Asteroids raiders are supposed to have used an unknown type of antipersonnel weapon in their attack on the station. All of the people killed in the raid had gunshot wounds. But a study of their bodies showed that for the most part the wounds had been inflicted on corpses."

Duomart looked startled. "You mean—you think someone was trying to hide the fact that they were killed some other way? An unknown way?"

Dasinger nodded. "'Unknown way' is right. The raiders left very few clues. It appeared that the attack on the station had been carried out by a single ship, and that the locks to the dome had been opened from within. That implies an insider involved, of course. But the only thing that's known for sure is that in a manner never clearly explained, the Dosey Asteroids Company lost six months' production of gem-quality cut star hyacinths valued at nearly a hundred million credits. That was six years ago—and the great Dosey Asteroids robbery is still an unsolved mystery."

He shook his head. "But let's stick to the present. There's nothing in sight on their wreck that might be, say, an automatic gun but . . . well, just move in carefully and stay ready to haul away very fast at the first hint of trouble!"

❖ ❖ ❖

The *Mooncat* slid slowly down through the air near the point where the man stood in open ground, a hundred yards from the clump of trees out of which smoke still billowed thickly upwards. The man watched the speedboat's descent quietly, making no further attempt to attract the attention of those on board to himself.

Duomart had said that the man was not a member of Handing's lost crew but a stranger. He was therefore one of the Dosey Asteroid raiders.

Putting down her two land legs, the *Mooncat* touched the open hillside a little over a quarter of a mile from the woods, stood straddled and rakish, nose high. The storeroom lock opened, and a slender ramp slid out. Quist showed in the lock, dumped two portable shelters to the ground, came scrambling nimbly down the ramp. Dr. Egavine followed, more cautiously, the two handcuffed Fleetmen behind him. Dasinger came out last, glancing over at the castaway who had started across the slope towards the ship.

"Everyone's out," he told his wrist communicator. "Take her up."

The ramp snaked soundlessly back into the lock, the lock snapped shut and the *Mooncat* lifted smoothly and quickly from the ground. Liu Taunus glanced after the rising speedboat, looked at Calat, and spoke loudly and emphatically in Fleetlingue for a few seconds, his broad face without expression. Dasinger said, "All right, Quist, break out the shelter."

When the shelter was assembled, Dasinger motioned the Fleetmen towards the door with his thumb. "Inside, boys!" he said. "Quist, lock the shelter behind them and stay on guard here. Come on, doctor. We'll meet our friend halfway . . ."

The castaway approached unhurriedly, walking with a long, easy stride, the bird thing on his shoulder craning its neck to peer at the strangers with round yellow eyes. The man was big and rangy, probably less heavy by thirty pounds than Liu Taunus, but in perfect physical condition. The face was strong and intelligent, smiling elatedly now.

"I'd nearly stopped hoping this day would arrive!" he said in translingue. "May I ask who you are?"

"An exploration group." Dasinger gripped the extended hand, shook it, as Dr. Egavine's right hand went casually to his coat lapel. "We noticed the two wrecked ships down by the lake," Dasinger explained, "then saw your smoke signal. Your name?"

"Graylock. Once chief engineer of the *Antares*, out of Vanadia on Aruaque." Graylock turned, still smiling, towards Egavine.

Egavine smiled as pleasantly.

"Graylock," he observed, "you feel, and will continue to feel, that this is the conversation you planned to conduct with us, that everything is going exactly in accordance with your wishes." He turned his head to Dasinger, inquired, "Would you prefer to question him yourself, Dasinger?"

Dasinger hesitated, startled; but Graylock's expression did not change. Dasinger shook his head. "Very smooth, doctor!" he commented. "No, go ahead. You're obviously the expert here."

"Very well . . . Graylock," Dr. Egavine resumed, "you will cooperate with me fully and to the best of your ability now, knowing that I am both your master and friend. Are any of the other men who came here on those two ships down by the water still alive?"

There was complete stillness for a second or two. Then Graylock's face began to work unpleasantly, all color draining from it. He said harshly, "No. But I . . . I don't . . ." He stammered incomprehensibly, went silent again, his expression wooden and set.

"Graylock," Egavine continued to probe, "you can

remember everything now, and you are not afraid. Tell me what happened to the other men."

Sweat covered the castaway's ashen face. His mouth twisted in agonized, silent grimaces again. The bird thing leaped from his shoulder with a small purring sound, fluttered softly away.

Dr. Egavine repeated, "You are not afraid. You can remember. What happened to them? How did they die?"

And abruptly the big man's face smoothed out. He looked from Egavine to Dasinger and back with an air of brief puzzlement, then explained conversationally, "Why, Hovig's generator killed many of us as we ran away from the *Antares*. Some reached the edges of the circle with me, and I killed them later."

Dr. Egavine flicked another glance towards Dasinger but did not pause.

"And the crew of the second ship?" he asked.

"Those two. They had things I needed, and naturally I didn't want them alive here."

"Is Hovig's generator still on the *Antares*?"

"Yes."

"How does the generator kill?"

Sweat suddenly started out on Graylock's face again, but now he seemed unaware of any accompanying emotions. He said, "It kills by fear, of course. . . ."

The story of the Dosey Asteroids raider and of Hovig's fear generators unfolded quickly from there. Hovig had developed his machines for the single purpose of robbing the Dosey Asteroids Shipping Station. The plan then had been to have the *Antares* cruise in uncharted space with the looted star hyacinths for at least two years, finally to approach the area of the Federation from a sector far removed from the Dosey system. That precaution resulted in disaster for Hovig. Chief Engineer Graylock had time to consider that his share in the profits of the raid would be relatively insignificant, and that there was a possibility of increasing it.

Graylock and his friends attacked their shipmates as the raider was touching down to the surface of an uncharted world to replenish its water supply. The attack succeeded but Hovig, fatally wounded, took a terrible revenge on the mutineers. He contrived to set off one of his grisly devices, and to all intents and purposes everyone still alive on board the *Antares* immediately went insane with fear. The ship crashed out of control at the edge of a lake. Somebody had opened a lock and a number of the frantic crew plunged from the ramp and fell to their death on the rocks below. Those who reached the foot of the ramp fled frenziedly from the wreck, the effects of Hovig's machine pursuing them but weakening gradually as they widened the distance between themselves and the *Antares*. Finally, almost three miles away, the fear impulses faded out completely. . . .

But thereafter the wreck was unapproachable. The fear generator did not run out of power, might not run out of power for years.

Dasinger said, "Doctor, let's hurry this up! Ask him why they weren't affected by their murder machines when they robbed Dosey Asteroids. Do the generators have a beam-operated shutoff, or what?"

Graylock listened to the question, said, "We had taken kwil. The effects were still very unpleasant, but they could be tolerated."

There was a pause of a few seconds. Dr. Egavine cleared his throat. "It appears, Dasinger," he remarked, "that we have failed to consider a very important clue!"

Dasinger nodded. "And an obvious one," he said dryly. "Keep it moving along, doctor. How much kwil did they take? How long had they been taking it before the raid?"

Dr. Egavine glanced over at him, repeated the questions.

Graylock said Hovig had begun conditioning the
crew to kwil a week or two before the *Antares* slipped
out of Aruaque for the strike on the station. In each
case the dosage had been built up gradually to the
quantity the man in question required to remain
immune to the generators. Individual variations had
been wide and unpredictable.

Dasinger passed his tongue over his lips, nodded.
"Ask him . . ."

He checked himself at a soft, purring noise, a
shadowy fluttering in the air. Graylock's animal flew
past him, settled on its master's shoulder, turned to
stare at Dasinger and Egavine. Dasinger looked at the
yellow owl-eyes, the odd little tube of a mouth,
continued to Egavine, "Ask him where the haul was
stored in the ship."

Graylock confirmed Leed Farous's statement of what
he had seen in the *Antares*'s records. All but a few of
the star hyacinths had been placed in a vault-like compartment in the storage, and the compartment was
sealed. Explosives would be required to open it. Hovig
kept out half a dozen of the larger stones, perhaps as
an antidote to boredom during the long voyage ahead.
Graylock had found one of them just before Hovig's
infernal instrument went into action.

"And where is that one now?" Dr. Egavine asked.

"I still have it."

"On your person?"

"Yes."

Dr. Egavine held out his hand, palm upward. "You
no longer want it, Graylock. Give it to me."

Graylock looked bewildered; for a moment he
appeared about to weep. Then he brought a knotted piece of leather from his pocket, unwrapped it,
took out the gem and placed it in Egavine's hand.
Egavine picked it up between thumb and forefinger
of his other hand, held it out before him.

There was silence for some seconds while the star hyacinth burned in the evening air and the three men and the small winged animal stared at it. Then Dr. Egavine exhaled slowly.

"Ah, now!" he said, his voice a trifle unsteady. "Men might kill and kill for that one beauty alone, that is true! . . . Will you keep it for now, Dasinger? Or shall I?"

Dasinger looked at him thoughtfully.

"You keep it, doctor," he said.

"Dasinger," Dr. Egavine observed a few minutes later, "I have been thinking. . . ."

"Yes?"

"Graylock's attempted description of his experience indicates that the machine on the *Antares* does not actually broadcast the emotion of terror, as he believes. The picture presented is that of a mind in which both the natural and the acquired barriers of compartmentalization are temporarily nullified, resulting in an explosion of compounded insanity to an extent which would be inconceivable without such an outside agent. As we saw in Graylock, the condition is in fact impossible to describe or imagine! A diabolical device . . ."

He frowned. "Why the drug kwil counteracts such an effect remains unclear. But since we now know that it does, I may have a solution to the problem confronting us."

Dasinger nodded. "Let's hear it."

"Have Miss Mines bring the ship down immediately," Egavine instructed him. "There is a definite probability that among my medical supplies will be an effective substitute for kwil, for this particular purpose. A few hours of experimentation, and . . ."

"Doctor," Dasinger interrupted, "hold it right there! So far there's been no real harm in sparring around. But we're in a different situation now . . . we may be running out of time very quickly. Let's quit playing games."

Dr. Egavine glanced sharply across at him. "What do you mean?"

"I mean that we both have kwil, of course. There's no reason to experiment. But the fact that we have it is no guarantee that we'll be able to get near that generator. Leed Farous's tissues were soaked with the drug. Graylock's outfit had weeks to determine how much each of them needed to be able to operate within range of the machines and stay sane. We're likely to have trouble enough without trying to jockey each other."

Dr. Egavine cleared his throat. "But I . . ."

Dasinger interrupted again. "Your reluctance to tell me everything you knew or had guessed is understandable. You had no more reason to trust me completely than I had to trust you. So before you say anything else I'd like you to look at these credentials. You're familiar with the Federation seal, I think."

Dr. Egavine took the proffered identification case, glanced at Dasinger again, then opened the case.

"So," he said presently. "You're a detective working for the Dosey Asteroids Company . . ." His voice was even. "That alters the situation, of course. Why didn't you tell me this?"

"That should be obvious," Dasinger said. "If you're an honest man, the fact can make no difference. The company remains legally bound to pay out the salvage fee for the star hyacinths. They have no objection to that. What they didn't like was the possibility of having the gems stolen for the second time. If that's what you had in mind, you wouldn't, of course, have led an agent of the company here. In other words, doctor, in cooperating with me you're running no risk of being cheated out of your half of the salvage rights."

Dasinger patted the gun in his coat pocket. "And

of course," he added, "if I happened to be a bandit in spite of the credentials, I'd be eliminating you from the partnership right now instead of talking to you! The fact that I'm not doing it should be a sufficient guarantee that I don't intend to do it."

Dr. Egavine nodded. "I'm aware of the point."

"Then let's get on with the salvage," Dasinger said. "For your further information, there's an armed Fleet ship hunting for us with piratical intentions, and the probability is that it will find us in a matter of hours. . . ."

He described the situation briefly, concluded, "You've carried out your part of the contract by directing us here. You can, if you wish, minimize further personal risks by using the Fleet scout's lifeboat to get yourself and Quist off the planet, providing kwil will get you to the scout. Set a normspace course for Orado then, and we'll pick you up after we've finished the job."

Dr. Egavine shook his head. "Thank you, but I'm staying. It's in my interest to give you what assistance I can . . . and, as you've surmised, I do have a supply of kwil. What is your plan?"

"Getting Hovig's generator shut off is the first step," Dasinger said. "And since we don't know what dosage of the drug is required for each of us, we'd be asking for trouble by approaching the *Antares* in the ship. Miss Mines happens to be a kwil sensitive, in any case. So it's going to take hiking, and I'll start down immediately now. Would Graylock and the Fleetmen obey hypnotic orders to the extent of helping out dependably in the salvage work?"

Egavine nodded. "There is no question of that."

"Then you might start conditioning them to the idea now. From the outer appearance of the *Antares*, it may be a real job to cut through inside her to get to the star hyacinths. We have the three salvage suits.

If I can make it to the generator, shut it off, and it turns out then that I need some hypnotized brawn down there, Miss Mines will fly over the shelter as a signal to start marching the men down."

"Why march? At that point, Miss Mines could take us to the wreck within seconds."

Dasinger shook his head. "Sorry, doctor. Nobody but Miss Mines or myself goes aboard the *Mooncat* until we either wind up the job or are forced to clear out and run. I'm afraid that's one precaution I'll have to take. When you get to the *Antares* we'll give each of the boys a full shot of kwil. The ones that don't go limp on it can start helping."

Dr. Egavine said reflectively, "You feel the drug would still be a requirement?"

"Well," Dasinger said, "Hovig appears to have been a man who took precautions, too. We know he had three generators and that he set off one of them. The question is where the other two are. It wouldn't be so very surprising, would it, if one or both of them turned out to be waiting for intruders in the vault where he sealed away the loot?"

The night was cool. Wind rustled in the ground vegetation and the occasional patches of trees. Otherwise the slopes were quiet. The sky was covered with cloud layers through which the *Mooncat* drifted invisibly. In the infrared glasses Dasinger had slipped on when he started, the rocky hillside showed clear for two hundred yards, tinted green as though bathed by a strange moonlight; beyond was murky darkness.

"Still all right?" Duomart's voice inquired from the wrist communicator.

"Uh-huh!" Dasinger said. "A little nervous, but I'd be feeling that way in any case, under the circumstances."

"I'm not so sure," she said. "You've gone past the

two and a half mile line from the generator. From
what that Graylock monster said, you should have
started to pick up its effects. Why not take your shot,
and play safe?"

"No," Dasinger said. "If I wait until I feel something that can be definitely attributed to the machine,
I can keep the kwil dose down to what I need. I don't
want to load myself up with the drug any more than
I have to."

A stand of tall trees with furry trunks moved presently into range of the glasses, thick undergrowth
beneath. Dasinger picked his way through the thickets
with some caution. The indications so far had been
that local animals had as much good reason to avoid
the vicinity of Hovig's machine as human beings, but
if there was any venomous vermin in the area this
would be a good place for it to be lurking. Which
seemed a fairly reasonable apprehension. Other,
equally definite, apprehensions looked less reasonable
when considered objectively. If he stumbled on a
stone, it produced a surge of sharp alarm which lingered for seconds; and his breathing had quickened
much more than could be accounted for by the
exertions of the downhill climb.

Five minutes beyond the wood Dasinger emerged
from the mouth of a narrow gorge, and stopped short
with a startled exclamation. His hand dug hurriedly
into his pocket for the case of kwil injectors.

"What's the matter?" Duomart inquired sharply.

Dasinger produced a somewhat breathless laugh.
"I've decided to take the kwil. At once!"

"You're feeling . . . things?" Her voice was also
shaky.

"I'll say! Not just a matter of feeling it, either. For
example, a couple of old friends are walking towards
me at the moment. Dead ones, as it happens."

"Ugh!" she said faintly. "Hurry up!"

Dasinger pressed the kwil injector against the inside of his elbow and held down the button for a measured second. He stood still for some seconds more, filled his lungs with the cool night air, and let it out in a long sigh.

"That did it!" he announced, his voice steadying again. "The stuff works fast. A quarter dose . . ."

"Why did you wait so long?"

"It wasn't too bad till just now. Then suddenly . . . that generator can't be putting out evenly! Anyway, it hit me like a rock. I doubt you'd be interested in details."

"I wouldn't," Duomart agreed. "I'm crawly enough as it is up here. I wish we were through with this!"

"With just a little luck we should be off the planet in an hour."

By the time he could hear the lapping of the lake water on the wind, he was aware of the growing pulse of Hovig's generator ahead of him, alive and malignant in the night. Then the Fleet scout came into the glasses, a squat, dark ship, its base concealed in the growth that had sprung up around it after it piled up on the slope. Dasinger moved past the scout, pushing through bushy aromatic shrubbery which thickened as he neared the water. He felt physically sick and sluggish now, was aware, too, of an increasing reluctance to go on. He would need more of the drug before attempting to enter the *Antares*.

To the west, the sky was partly clear, and presently he saw the wreck of the Dosey Asteroid raider loom up over the edge of the lake arm, blotting out a section of stars. Still beyond the field of the glasses, it looked like an armored water animal about to crawl up on the slopes. Dasinger approached slowly, in foggy unwillingness, emerged from the bushes into open ground, and saw a broad ramp furred with a thick coat of mold-like growth rise steeply towards an open lock in the upper part of the *Antares*. The pulse of the generator might have been the beating of the maimed ship's heart, angry and threatening. It seemed to be growing stronger. And had something moved in the lock? Dasinger stood, senses swimming sickly, dreaming that something huge rose slowly, towered over him like a giant wave, leaned forwards. . . .

"Still all right?" Duomart inquired.

The wave broke.

"*Dasinger! What's happened?*"

"Nothing," Dasinger said, his voice raw. He looked at the empty injector in his hand, dropped it. "But something nearly did! The kwil I took wasn't enough. I was standing here waiting to let that damned machine swamp me when you spoke."

"You should have heard what you sounded like over the communicator! I thought you were . . ." her voice stopped for an instant, began again. "Anyway," she said briskly, "you're loaded with kwil now, I hope?"

"More than I should be, probably." Dasinger rubbed both hands slowly down along his face. "Well, it couldn't be helped. That was pretty close, I guess! I don't even remember getting the injector out of the case."

He looked back up at the looming bow of the *Antares*, unbeautiful enough but prosaically devoid of menace and mystery now, though the pulsing beat still came from there. A mechanical obstacle and nothing else. "I'm going on in now."

From the darkness within the lock came the smell of stagnant water, of old decay. The mold that proliferated over the ramp did not extend into the wreck. But other things grew inside, pale and oily tendrils festooning the walls. Dasinger removed his night glasses, brought out a pencil light, let the beam fan out, and moved through the lock.

The crash which had crumpled the ship's lower

shell had thrust up the flooring of the lock compartment, turned it into what was nearly level footing now. On the right, a twenty-foot black gap showed between the ragged edge of the deck and the far bulkhead from which it had been torn. The oily plant life spread over the edges of the flooring and on down into the flooded lower sections of the *Antares*. The pulse of Hovig's generator came from above and the left where a passage slanted steeply up into the ship's nose. Dasinger turned towards the passage, began clambering up.

There was no guesswork involved in determining which of the doors along the passage hid the machine in what, if Graylock's story was correct, had been Hovig's personal stateroom. As Dasinger approached that point, it was like climbing into silent thunder. The door was locked, and though the walls beside it were warped and cracked, the cracks were too narrow to permit entry. Dasinger dug out a tool which had once been the prized property of one of Orado's more eminent safecrackers, and went to work on the lock. A minute or two later he forced the door partly back in its tilted frame, scrambled through into the cabin.

Not enough was left of Hovig after this span of time to be particularly offensive. The generator lay in a lower corner, half buried under other molded and unrecognizable debris. Dasinger uncovered it, feeling as if he were drowning in the invisible torrent pouring out from it, knelt down and placed the light against the wall beside him.

The machine matched Graylock's description. A pancake-shaped heavy plastic casing eighteen inches across, two thick studs set into its edge, one stud depressed and flush with the surface, the other extended. Dasinger thumbed experimentally at the extended stud, found it apparently immovable, took out his gun.

"How is it going, Dasinger?" Miss Mines asked.

"All right," Dasinger said. He realized he was speaking with difficulty. "I've found the thing! Trying to get it shut off now. Tell you in a minute . . ."

He tapped the extended stud twice with the butt of the gun, then slashed heavily down. The stud flattened back into the machine. Its counterpart didn't move. The drowning sensations continued.

Dasinger licked his lips, dropped the gun into his pocket, brought out the lock opener. He had the generator's cover plate pried partway back when it shattered. With that, the thunder that wasn't sound ebbed swiftly from the cabin. Dasinger reached into the generator, wrenched out a power battery, snapping half a dozen leads.

He sat back on his heels, momentarily dizzy with relief, then climbed to his feet with the smashed components of Hovig's machine, and turned to the door. Something in the debris along the wall flashed dazzlingly in the beam of his light.

Dasinger stared at the star hyacinth for an instant, then picked it up. It was slightly larger than the one Graylock had carried out of the *Antares* with him, perfectly cut. He found four others of similar quality within the next minute, started back down to the lock compartment with what might amount to two million credits in honest money, around half that in the Hub's underworld gem trade, in one of his pockets.

"Yes?"

"Got the thing's teeth pulled now."

"Thank God! Coming right down. . . ."

The *Mooncat* was sliding in from the south as Dasinger stepped out on the head of the ramp. "Lock's open," Duomart's voice informed him. "I'll come aft and help."

It took four trips with the gravity crane to transfer the salvage equipment into the *Antares*'s lock compartment. Then Miss Mines sealed the *Mooncat* and went back upstairs. Dasinger climbed into one of the three salvage suits, hung the communicator inside the helmet, snapped on the suit's lights and went over to the edge of the compartment deck. Black water reflected the lights thirty feet below. He checked the assortment of tools attached to his belt, nudged the suit's gravity cutoff to the right, energized magnetic pads on knees, boot tips and wrists, then fly-walked rapidly down a bulkhead and dropped into the water.

"No go, Duomart!" he informed the girl ten minutes later, his voice heavy with disappointment. "It's an ungodly twisted mess down here . . . worse than I thought it might be! Looks as if we'll have to cut all the way through to that vault. Give Egavine the signal to start herding the boys down."

Approximately an hour afterwards, Miss Mines reported urgently through the communicator, "They'll reach the lock in less than four minutes now, Dasinger! Better drop it and come up!"

"I'm on my way." Dasinger reluctantly switched off the beam-saw he was working with, fastened it to the belt of the salvage suit, turned in the murky water and started back towards the upper sections of the wreck. The job of getting through the tangled jungle of metal and plastic to the gem vault appeared no more than half completed, and the prospect of being delayed over it until the *Spy* discovered them here began to look like a disagreeably definite possibility. He clambered and floated hurriedly up through the almost vertical passage he'd cleared, found daylight flooding the lock compartment, the system's yellow sun well above the horizon. Peeling off the salvage suit, he restored the communicator to his wrist and went over to the head of the ramp.

The five men came filing down the last slopes in the morning light, Taunus and Calat in the lead,

Graylock behind them, the winged animal riding his shoulder and lifting occasionally into the air to flutter about the group. Quist and Egavine brought up the rear. Dasinger took the gun from his pocket.

"I'll clip my gun to the suit belt when I go back down in the water with the boys," he told the communicator. "If the doctor's turning any tricks over in his mind, that should give him food for thought. I'll relieve Quist of his weapon as he comes in."

"What about the guns in Graylock's hut?" Duomart asked.

"No charge left in them. If I'm reasonably careful, I really don't see what Dr. Egavine can do. He knows he loses his half-interest in the salvage the moment he pulls any illegal stunts."

A minute or two later, he called out, "Hold it there, doctor?"

The group shuffled to a stop near the foot of the ramp, staring up at him.

"Yes, Dasinger?" Dr. Egavine called back, sounding a trifle winded.

"Have Quist come up first and alone, please." Dasinger disarmed the little man at the entrance to the lock, motioned him on to the center of the compartment. The others arrived then in a line, filed past Dasinger and joined Quist.

"You've explained the situation to everybody?" Dasinger asked Egavine. There was an air of tenseness about the little group he didn't like, though tension might be understandable enough under the circumstances.

"Yes," Dr. Egavine said. "They feel entirely willing to assist us, of course." He smiled significantly.

"Fine." Dasinger nodded. "Line them up and let's get going! Taunus first. Get . . ."

There was a momentary stirring of the air back of his head. He turned sharply, jerking up the gun, felt twin needles drive into either side of his neck.

His body instantly went insensate. The lock appeared to circle about him, then he was on his back and Graylock's pet was alighting with a flutter of wings on his chest. It craned its head forward to peer into his face, the tip of its mouth tube open, showing a ring of tiny teeth. Vision and awareness left Dasinger together.

The other men hadn't moved. Now Dr. Egavine, his face a little pale, came over to Dasinger, the birdlike creature bounding back to the edge of the lock as he approached. Egavine knelt down, said quietly, his mouth near the wrist communicator, "Duomart Mines, you will obey me."

There was silence for a second or two. Then the communicator whispered, "Yes."

Dr. Egavine drew in a long, slow breath.

"You feel no question, no concern, no doubt about this situation," he went on. "You will bring the ship down now and land it safely beside the *Antares*. Then come up into the lock of the *Antares* for further instructions." Egavine stood up, his eyes bright with triumph.

In the *Mooncat* three miles overhead, Duomart switched off her communicator, sat white-faced, staring at the image of the *Antares* in the ground-view plate.

"Sweet Jana!" she whispered. "How did he . . . now what do I . . ."

She hesitated an instant, then opened a console drawer, took out the kwil injector Dasinger had left with her and slipped it into a pocket, clipped the holstered shocker back to her belt, and reached for the controls. A vast whistling shriek smote the *Antares* and the ears of those within as the *Mooncat* ripped down through atmosphere at an unatmospheric speed, leveled out smoothly and floated to the ground beside the wreck.

There was no one in sight in the lock of the *Antares* as Duomart came out and sealed the *Mooncat's* entry behind her. She went quickly up the broad, mold-covered ramp. The lock remained empty. From beyond it came the sound of some metallic object being pulled about, a murmur of voices. Twelve steps from the top, she took out the little gun, ran up to the lock and into it, bringing the gun up. She had a glimpse of Dr. Egavine and Quist standing near a rusty bench in the compartment, of Graylock half into a salvage suit, Dasinger on the floor . . . then a flick of motion to right and left.

The tips of two space lines lashed about her simultaneously, one pinning her arms to her sides, the other clamping about her ankles and twitching her legs out from beneath her. She fired twice blindly to the left as the lines snapped her face down to the floor of the compartment.

The gun was clamped beneath her stretched-out body and useless.

"What made that animal attack me anyway?" Dasinger asked wearily. He had just regained consciousness and been ordered by Calat to join the others on a rusted metal bench in the center of the lock compartment; Duomart to his left, Egavine on his right, Quist on the other side of Egavine. Calat stood watching them fifteen feet away, holding Dasinger's gun in one hand while he jiggled a few of Hovig's star hyacinths gently about in the other.

Calat's expression was cheerful, which made him the exception here. Liu Taunus and Graylock were down in the hold of the ship, working sturdily with cutter beams and power hoists to get to the sealed vault and blow it open. How long they'd been at it, Dasinger didn't know.

"You can thank your double-crossing partner for what happened!" Duomart informed him. She looked

pretty thoroughly mussed up though still unsubdued.
"Graylock's been using the bird-thing to hunt with,"
she said. "It's a bloodsucker . . . nicks some animal with
its claws and the animal stays knocked out while the
little beast fills its tummy. So the intellectual over
there had Graylock point you out to his pet, and it
waited until your back was turned . . ." She hesitated,
went on less vehemently, "Sorry about not carrying
out orders, Dasinger. I assumed Egavine really was
in control here, and I could have handled him. I
walked into a trap." She fished the shards of a
smashed kwil injector out of her pocket, looked at
them, and dropped them on the floor before her. "I
got slammed around a little," she explained.

Calat laughed, said something in the Fleet tongue,
grinning at her. She ignored him.

Egavine said, "My effects were secretly inspected
while we were at the Fleet station, Dasinger, and the
Fleetmen have been taking drugs to immunize themselves against my hypnotic agents. They disclosed this
when Miss Mines brought the speedboat down. There
was nothing I could do. I regret to say that they
intend to murder us. They are waiting only to assure
themselves that the star hyacinths actually are in the
indicated compartment."

"Great!" Dasinger groaned. He put his hands back
in a groping gesture to support himself on the bench.

"Still pretty feeble, I suppose?" Miss Mines
inquired, gentle sympathy in her voice.

"I'm poisoned," he muttered brokenly. "The thing's
left me paralyzed. . . ." He sagged side ways a little,
his hand moving behind Duomart. He pinched her
then in a markedly unparalyzed and vigorous manner.

Duomart's right eyelid flickered for an instant.

"Somebody wrung the little monster's neck before
I got here," she remarked. "But there're other necks

I'd sooner wring! Your partner's, for instance. Not that he's necessarily the biggest louse around at the moment." She nodded at Calat. "The two runches who call themselves Fleetmen don't intend to share the star hyacinths even with their own gang! They're rushing the job through so they can be on their way to the Hub before the *Spy* arrives. And don't think Liu Taunus trusts that muscle-bound foogal standing there, either! He's hanging on to the key of the *Mooncat*'s console until he comes back up."

Calat smiled with a suggestion of strain, then said something in a flat, expressionless voice, staring at her.

"Oh, sure," she returned. "With Taunus holding me, I suppose?" She looked at Dasinger. "They're not shooting me right off, you know," she told him. "They're annoyed with me, so they're taking me along for something a little more special. But they'll have to skip the fun if the *Spy* shows up, or I'll be telling twenty armed Fleetmen exactly what kind of thieving cheats they have leading them!" She looked back at Calat, smiled, placed the tip of her tongue lightly between her lips for an instant, then pronounced a few dozen Fleet words in a clear, precise voice.

It must have been an extraordinarily unflattering comment. Calat went white, then red. Half-smart tough had been Duomart's earlier description of him. It began to look like an accurate one . . . Dasinger felt a surge of pleased anticipation. His legs already were drawn well back beneath the bench; he shifted his weight slowly forwards now, keeping an expression of anxious concern on his face. Calat spoke in Fleet-lingue again, voice thickening with rage.

Miss Mines replied sweetly, stood up. The challenge direct.

The Fleetman's face worked in incredulous fury. He shifted the gun to his left hand and came striding purposefully towards Miss Mines, right fist cocked. Then, as Dasinger tensed his legs happily, a muffled thump from deep within the wreck announced the opening of the star hyacinth vault.

The sound was followed by instant proof that Hovig had trapped the vault.

Duomart and Calat screamed together. Dasinger drove himself forward off the bench, aiming for the Fleetman's legs, checked and turned for the gun which Calat, staggering and shrieking, his face distorted with lunatic terror, had flung aside. Dr. Egavine, alert for this contingency, already was stooping for the gun, hand outstretched, when Dasinger lunged against him, bowling him over.

Dasinger came up with the gun, Quist pounding at his shoulders, flung the little man aside, turned back in a frenzy of urgency. Duomart twisted about on the floor near the far end of the compartment, arms covering her face. The noises that bubbled out from behind her arms set Dasinger's teeth on edge. She rolled over convulsively twice, stopped dangerously close to the edge of the jagged break in the deck, was turning again as Dasinger dropped beside her and caught her.

Immediately there was a heavy, painful blow on his shoulder. He glanced up, saw Quist running toward him, a rusted chunk of metal like the one he had thrown in his raised hand, and Egavine peering at both of them from the other side of the compartment. Dasinger flung a leg across Duomart, pinning her down, pulled out the gun, fired without aiming. Quist reversed his direction almost in mid-stride.

Dasinger fired again, saw Egavine dart towards the lock, hesitate there an instant, then disappear down the ramp, Quist sprinting out frantically after him.

A moment later he injected a full dose of kwil right through the cloth of Duomart's uniform.

The drug hit hard and promptly. Between one

instant and the next, the plunging and screaming ended;
she drew in a long, shuddering breath, went limp, her
eyes closing slowly. Dasinger was lifting her attention.
He looked around. Calat was not in sight. And only
then did he become aware of a familiar sensation . . . a
Hovig generator's pulsing, savage storm of seeming
nothingness, nullified by the drug in his blood.

He laid the unconscious girl on the bench, went
on to the lock.

Dr. Egavine and Quist had vanished; the thick
shrubbery along the lake bank stirred uneasily at
twenty different points but he wasn't looking for the
pair. With the *Mooncat* inaccessible to them, there
was only one place they could go. Calat's body lay
doubled up in the rocks below the ramp, almost sixty
feet down, where other human bodies had lain six
years earlier. Dasinger glanced over at the Fleet scout,
went back into the compartment.

He was buckling himself into the third salvage suit
when he heard the scout's lifeboat take off. At a guess
Hovig's little private collection of star hyacinths was
taking off with it. Dasinger decided he couldn't care
less.

He snapped on the headpiece, then hesitated at
the edge of the deck, looking down. A bubble of foggy
white light was rising slowly through the water of the
hold, and in a moment the headpiece of one of the
other suits broke the oily surface, stayed there, bob-
bing gently about. Dasinger climbed down, brought
Liu Taunus' body back up to the lock compartment,
and recovered the *Mooncat*'s master key.

He found Graylock floating in his suit against a
bulkhead not far from the shattered vault where
Hovig's two remaining generators thundered. Dasinger
silenced the machines, fastened them and a small steel
case containing nearly a hundred million credits' worth
of star hyacinths to the salvage carrier, and towed it
all up to the lock compartment.

A very few minutes later, the *Mooncat* lifted in somewhat jerky, erratic fashion from the planet's surface. As Dasinger had suspected, he lacked, and by a good deal, Miss Mines's trained sensitivity with the speedboat's controls; but he succeeded in wrestling the little ship up to a five-mile altitude where a subspace dive might be carried out in relative safety.

He was attempting then to get the *Mooncat's* nose turned away from the distant volcano ranges towards which she seemed determined to point when the detector needles slapped flat against their pins and the alarm bell sounded. A strange ship stood outlined in the *Mooncat's* stern screen.

The image vanished as Dasinger hit the dive button, simultaneously flattening the speed controls with a slam of his hand. The semisolid subspace turbulence representing the mountain ranges beyond the lake flashed instantly past below him . . . within yards, it seemed. Another second put them beyond the planet's atmosphere. Then the *Spy* reappeared in subspace, following hard. A hammering series of explosions showed suddenly in the screens, kept up for a few hair-raising moments, began to drop back. Five minutes later, with the distance between them widening rapidly, the *Spy* gave up the chase, swung around and headed back towards the planet.

Dasinger shakily reduced his ship's speed to a relatively sane level, kept her moving along another twenty minutes, then surfaced into normspace and set a general course for the Hub. He was a very fair yachtsman for a planeteer. But after riding the *Mooncat* for the short time he'd turned her loose to keep ahead of the *Spy* through the G2's stress zone, he didn't have to be told that in Fleet territory he was outclassed. He mopped his forehead, climbed gratefully out of the pilot seat and went to the cot he had hauled into the control room, to check on Duomart Mines.

She was still unconscious, of course; the dose he'd given her was enough to knock a kwil-sensitive out for at least a dozen hours. Dasinger looked down at the filth-smudged, pale face, the bruised cheeks and blackened left eye for a few seconds, then opened Dr. Egavine's medical kit to do what he could about getting Miss Mines patched up again.

Fifteen hours later she was still asleep, though to all outer appearances back in good repair. Dasinger happened to be bemusedly studying her face once more when she opened her eyes and gazed up at him.

"We made it! You . . ." She smiled, tried to sit up, looked startled, then indignant. "What's the idea of tying me down to this thing?"

Dasinger nodded. "I guess you're all there!" He reached down to unfasten her from the cot. "After what happened, I wasn't so sure you'd be entirely rational when the kwil wore off and you woke up."

Duomart paled a little. "I hadn't imagined . . ." She shook her blond head. "Well, let's skip that! I'll have nightmares for years. . . . What happened to the others?"

Dasinger told her, concluded, "Egavine may have run into the *Spy*, but I doubt it. He'll probably show up in the Hub eventually with the gems he took from Calat, and if he doesn't get caught peddling them he may wind up with around a million credits . . . about the sixth part of what he would have collected if he'd stopped playing crooked and trying to get everything. I doubt the doctor will ever quit kicking himself for that!"

"Your agency gets the whole salvage fee now, eh?"

"Not exactly," Dasinger said. "Considering everything that's happened, the Kyth Interstellar Detective Agency would have to be extremely ungrateful if it didn't feel you'd earned the same split we were going to give Dr. Egavine."

Miss Mines gazed at him in startled silence, flushed excitedly. "Think you can talk the Kyth people into *that*, Dasinger?"

"I imagine so," Dasinger said, "since I own the agency. That should finance your Willata Fleet operation very comfortably and still leave a couple of million credits over for your old age. I doubt we'll clear anything on Hovig's generators . . ."

Miss Mines looked uncomfortable. "Do you have those things aboard?"

"At the moment. Disassembled of course. Primarily I didn't want the Fleet gang to get their hands on them. We might lose them in space somewhere or take them back to the Federation for the scientists to poke over. We'll discuss that on the way. Now, do you feel perky enough to want a look at the stuff that's cost around a hundred and fifty lives before it ever hit the Hub's markets?"

"Couldn't feel perkier!" She straightened up expectantly. "Let's see them . . ."

Dasinger turned away towards the wall where he had put down the little steel case with the loot of the Dosey Asteroids robbery.

Behind him, Duomart screamed. He spun back to her, his face white. "What's the matter?"

Duomart was staring wide-eyed past him towards the instrument console, the back of one hand to her mouth. "That . . . the thing!"

"Thing?"

"Big . . . yellow . . . wet . . . ugh! It's ducked behind the console, Dasinger! It's lurking there!"

"Oh!" Dasinger said, relaxing. He smiled. "That's all right. Don't worry about it."

"*Don't worry about* . . . are you crazy?"

"Not in the least. I thought you were for a second, but it's very simple. You've worked off the kwil and now you're in the hangover period. You get hallucinations then, just as I usually do. For the next eight or nine hours, you'll be seeing odd things around from time to time. So what? They're not real."

"All right, they're not real, but they seem real enough while they're around," Duomart said. "I don't want to see them." She caught her breath and her hand flew up to her mouth again. "Dasinger, please, don't you have something that will put me back to sleep till I'm past the hangover too?"

Dasinger reflected. "One of Doc Egavine's hypno sprays will do it. I know enough of the mumbo jumbo to send you to dreamland for another ten hours." He smiled evilly. "Of course, you realize that means you're putting yourself completely in my power."

Duomart's eyes narrowed for an instant. She considered him, grinned. "I'll risk it," she said.

# AFTERWORD

## by Eric Flint

In James H. Schmitz's heyday, he was one of science fiction's best known and loved authors. But that heyday was brief—not much more than a decade. Although Schmitz published his first science fiction story in 1943—"Greenface," which appeared in the August issue of *Unknown*—his SF writing career was desultory for the next many years.

1961 was the turning point of Schmitz's career. The previous eighteen years had produced exactly that number of stories—most of them (with the notable exceptions of "Grandpa" and the four Agent of Vega stories) of rather mediocre quality. Then, in the dozen years which followed, the same man wrote and publish over fifty. And these stories included his best writing: his four novels—*Legacy, The Witches of Karres, The Demon Breed, The Eternal Frontiers*— as well almost the entirety of his Federation of the Hub tales. Every one of the Telzey Amberdon stories,

which, along with *The Witches of Karres*, were
Schmitz's most popular works, were written in that
period.

There has rarely been anything comparable in the
history of any SF writer. Throughout the sixties, especially in the first half of the decade before he
turned to novels, not more than a couple of months
would go by without a Schmitz story appearing in one
of the premier SF magazines of the day. And those
stories were, with few if any exceptions, invariably the
lead story of that month's issue.

That was the period in which I first encountered
James H. Schmitz, as a teenager newly introduced to
science fiction. To me, he loomed as large in the
pantheon of science fiction's great writers as such
figures as Heinlein, Clarke and Asimov. I would have
been shocked to discover, had someone told me at
the time, that he would eventually fade into near
oblivion.

Yet, fade away he did. Schmitz's writing career was
effectively over by the end of 1974, and he died in
1981. Many of the Telzey stories were reissued in
paperback in the early eighties, along with a new edition of *The Witches of Karres*, but those went out of
print after a time. Since then, except for the New
England Science Fiction Association's 1990 one-
volume hardcover edition of some of his stories, there
has been nothing.

Why? It's not because his reputation has declined,
that's for sure. My own allegiance to Schmitz is by
no means uncommon among longtime SF readers. I
have met many others who, like me, would never go
into a bookstore without checking to see if there
might, hopefully, be a new reissue of something by
him.

I think, more than anything, that Schmitz fell
victim to a profound shift in the science fiction
market. Because of the nature of the market in his

time, and his own natural talent and inclination, Schmitz was basically a writer of short fiction. He wrote only four novels, and, except for *The Witches of Karres*, none of them are the length associated in today's world with the term "novel." *The Demon Breed*, for instance, may well be a perfect short novel—SF's equivalent of Joseph Conrad's *Heart of Darkness*. But, although its length (50,000 words) officially qualifies it as a "novel," there isn't a commercial publisher today outside of the young adult market who would accept that short a manuscript.

Today's world is the world of the Novellus Giganticus. It is a science fiction market dominated by thick novels—more often than not, massive multi-volume series. In that new land of behemoths, the supple charm of Schmitz's multitude of short stories, novelettes, novellas and short novels quickly gets trampled underfoot.

The one exception, of course, is *The Witches of Karres*. But that novel, although it is respectably long even by modern standards and is generally considered his masterpiece, is not enough to keep Schmitz afloat. With rare exceptions, "one-work" authors do not stay in print.

As it happens, however—this is my opinion, at least—*The Witches of Karres* is *not* James H. Schmitz's masterpiece. As delightful as it is—and *Witches* is perhaps the greatest example of a successful picaresque novel in all of science fiction—it takes second place to something else.

That "something else" is Schmitz's universe of the Federation of the Hub, taken as a whole. Depending on exactly where you draw the boundary, that universe includes approximately thirty stories of varying length. Ranging from two novels—*Legacy* and *The Demon Breed*—through a multitude of novellas, novelettes and short stories, the entirety of Schmitz's works centered in his Hub universe comprises the majority of his total output and comes to well over half a million words of print. More than enough, even in this modern world of literary dinosaurs, to hold its place.

This edition is the first time—*ever*—that the Federation of the Hub has been presented that way to science fiction readers. Not in bits and pieces, some Telzey here and the occasional Trigger over there, but *as a whole*. All of it. For the first time, through four volumes, readers will be able to follow the adventures of Schmitz's characters as they continually intersect, interact, and cross each other paths. Telzey Amberdon occupies pride of place, of course, but you will also find all of Trigger Argee (my personal favorite), the roguish Heslet Quillan, Holati Tate, Pilch, Professor Mantelish, Wellan Dasinger—each and every one.

The end result, for all its length, is not another "series." It is something much rarer, and more precious. It is one immensely talented writer's kaleidoscopic vision of a future universe, painted like an impressionist master might portray the teeming life in a field. It is James H. Schmitz's principal legacy to science fiction.

We will be presenting that universe in four volumes, centered on the three most important characters in Schmitz's Hub universe: Telzey Amberdon, Trigger Argee and Nile Etland. Volumes One and Two present the Telzey saga, with Trigger making her first appearance as Telzey's companion in Volume Two. Volume Three revolves around Trigger. Volume Four will focus on Nile Etland.

This series is the culmination of what, for me, was a daydream for a quarter of a century. For that, I have many people to thank.

First and foremost is my publisher, Jim Baen. Without his support from the outset, this project would have been quite impossible.

Then, I want to make special mention of my

co-editor, Guy Gordon. I did not know Guy when I began editing this project. I encountered him purely by accident, as I was surfing the web looking for anything related to James H. Schmitz. Quite to my surprise, I discovered that there was an entire site devoted to JHS—and an excellent one. (It's still there, too—www.white-crane.com/Schmitz/index.htm, or do a web search for the words "Schmitz Encyclopedia"—and I urge anyone with an interest in James Schmitz to investigate it.)

With the collaboration of a number of other devoted fans, Guy set up the site and has spent the past several years assembling Schmitz's complete writings and a host of secondary material. By now, he is quite probably the world's expert on the life and work of James H. Schmitz. Guy and his colleagues generously offered to put those resources at my disposal, an offer which I eagerly accepted. In the months that followed, as we worked together preparing this volume, Guy's role came to be the one which is formally recognized on the title page: co-editor of the series. It has been a genuine pleasure to work with him, and one of the unexpected benefits of this project.

I can't mention by name all of the people who have been involved in the "Schmitz Mailing List"—there have literally been dozens—but the key figures require public acknowledgment for their work: Harry Erwin, Gharlane of Eddore, George Phillies, and Ken Uecker. And thanks also to Arnold Bailey, Patrick Campbell and Sharon Custer for their help along the way. Finally, I'd like to give a bow to all the many people in Baen Books' web page (www.baen.com—then select "Hang Out at Baen's Bar") who cheered the project on from the moment I first tossed it out as an idle thought and Jim responded with an offer to throw his support behind the idea. Let it never be said that a chat room is simply a pleasant waste of time. In a very real sense, this series was born there.

# THE FEDERATION
# OF THE HUB:
## An Overview

## by Guy Gordon

James H. Schmitz knew one of the cardinal rules of writing science fiction adventure: *don't inflict the reader with irrelevant background material—get on with the story!* And so Schmitz seldom comes right out and tells us any facts about the Hub. (After all, when was the last time world geography came up in your casual conversation?) Part of the fun of reading Schmitz is piecing together the clues dropped here and there, because the Hub is an amazing place to visit.

Still, readers new to Schmitz might benefit from an overview of what the Hub is, and how it got there.

In Schmitz's future, humanity moved out from Earth slowly. In the first thousand years or so of

431

interstellar travel only sporadic colonies were founded in what he refers to as the "Old Territories." Terratype planets were rare and hard to find. In "The Symbiotes" we learn that "Old Territory people thought it had been proved there'd be a permanent shortage of habitable planets around. So that sets it back about eleven hundred years, when they'd begun to get range but didn't yet know where and how to look."

By the time of "Blood of Nalakia," humanity has discovered a dense cluster of Terratype worlds known as "the Hub Systems." It is there that most colonies are formed. The Hub (as opposed to the Federation as a political organization) is a star cluster—most likely a global cluster with fairly distinct boundaries.

But "Blood of Nalakia" is the *only* Hub story that mentions both Earth and the Hub. After that there is a huge break in human history known as "The War Centuries."

Though he never wrote any War Centuries stories, Schmitz had some very concrete ideas about what happened then. "Humans fought one another for many star periods throughout [the Hub] with a sustained fury rarely observed in other species." In one story he even lets drop the reason for the wars: psychological control of planetary populations. There are hints that entire planets died. One of them may have been the Earth.

The Earth—or, at least, its historical significance—is known to the inhabitants of the Hub, but they have no contact with it. There are references to species of monkeys, otters, horses, and sequoia trees that were "preserved in the Life Banks on Maccadon"—but there is no definitive word as to just *what* they were preserved from.

Out of this centuries-long, vicious war was founded the Federation of the Hub.

❖   ❖   ❖

The Federation is big. We learn in *Legacy* that there are twelve hundred and fifty-eight member worlds (including two hundred and fourteen restricted worlds), with a combined population of over six hundred billion. This provides Schmitz the room needed for all sorts of disparate cultures and adventures. If that weren't enough, there are worlds outside the Hub like Precolonial worlds, I-Fleet territories, and the domains of various nonhuman intelligent species.

Although the sheer size of the Hub is mentioned several times, Schmitz never tells us its precise dimensions. Instead we are given the more relevant measure of how long it takes to travel from world to world. Some Hub planets are mere hours apart by "subspace" FTL flight. The frontiers are much farther. Manon is two weeks' travel from the Hub, and Nandy Cline is three.

Neither are we given a timeline for all this. Unlike most science fiction writers who have written a large number of stories set in a single future universe, Schmitz organized his stories "horizontally" rather than chronologically. The majority of the stories, including all of the ones involving Telzey Amberdon and Trigger Argee, take place within a very short time span— not more than three years. We are given a cross-section of life in the Hub, rather than a linear series of adventures taking place one after the other.

Almost all the Hub stories take place 200 years after the founding of the Federation. But there are only two clues as to how far this is in our future. One is Trigger's statement about the Old Territories being explored "eleven hundred years ago." The other is that the dust jacket of the rare collection *A Nice Day for Screaming, and Other Tales of the Hub* states that the date is 3500 A.D. But we don't know if that date came from Schmitz or the publisher.

The physical facts about the Hub are less interesting than the political facts. But, again, the picture we get from Schmitz is impressionistic rather than precise.

The Federation is sometimes referred to as the Overgovernment—indicating that it is indeed a Federation in the political sense, and not just in name. Planetary governments take care of such things as taxes, police, courts, etc. To outward appearances, the Federation simply handles defense, colonization, and relations with alien species.

But appearances are deceiving. There's a lot more going on behind the scenes. Because of our vantage point, we get to see more than the average citizen of the Hub. Schmitz has some exciting tales to tell, and exciting events tend to draw in the Federation.

The Federation has several major worries. Number one is preventing the return of the War Centuries. Second, is protecting the Hub from hostile aliens. And number three is advancing humanity as a species.

The Federation is ruled by the Council—and the Council rules by sending out members or deputies to direct the activity of the Departments. Telzey's mother, Federation Councilwoman Jessamine Amberdon, is one, and is a member of the powerful Hace Committee. (It's very interesting that this is an *ethics* committee.)

Often, these officials only pop up after the action is over, and seem mostly concerned with judging the performance of the actors. As one alien observes: "The Federation Council, though popularly regarded as the central seat of authority, frequently appears to be acting more as moderator among numerous powerful departments."

These Departments include the Psychology Service, the Federation Navy, Precolonization (or Precol), Conservation, and Outposts. Despite that fact that Schmitz flew for the Army Air Force in WWII, he has little to say about the armed forces of the Hub. Heslet Quillan works for Intelligence, but we never see the organization. Trigger and Tate both work for Precol, but we see little of that. We never learn much about any of the other Departments of the Hub except, to a certain degree, the Psychology Service.

The pattern appears to be that each of the Departments goes about its business as it sees fit, reporting to the Council as needed. When the Council thinks something is important enough, they send a Deputy, or even a Council Member to take charge, investigate, or overrule the Department.

The overall impression which Schmitz gives us is of a powerful but loosely organized government. Except for the complete absence of any form of hereditary privilege, the internal structure of the Federation seems almost quasifeudal. The Departments rule their "fiefdoms" with great latitude, with the Overgovernment serving as a court of last resort and occasional overseer—much as did the medieval monarchs.

The danger of political abuse in such a system is obvious, but seems to be counteracted by the Overgovernment's determination to leave the basic workings of Hub society in a state of semianarchy. Even such institutions as "private wars" are allowed, apparently in the belief that to suppress such violence by police action would run the risk of placing a political straitjacket on the Hub. Thus, if the various Departments of the Federation wield immense power, so too do the various nongovernmental institutions and agencies of Hub society.

But here we are verging on sheer guesswork. The simple fact is that Schmitz never had much to say about the political structure of the Hub in the abstract. Unlike some science fiction writers who have created complex future universes portrayed in many stories, Schmitz was not a "theoretical synthesizer." He was always content to let the reader get mere glimpses of the various powerful forces behind the scenes, as his

# ERIC FLINT
## ONE OF THE BEST ALTERNATE-HISTORY AUTHORS OF TODAY!

# DAVID DRAKE RULES!

### Hammer's Slammers:

| | | |
|---|---|---|
| The Tank Lords | 87794-1 ◆ $6.99 | ☐ |
| Caught in the Crossfire | 87882-4 ◆ $6.99 | ☐ |
| The Butcher's Bill | 57773-5 ◆ $6.99 | ☐ |
| The Sharp End | 87632-5 ◆ $7.99 | ☐ |
| Cross the Stars | 57821-9 ◆ $6.99 | ☐ |

### RCN series:

| | | |
|---|---|---|
| With the Lightnings | 57818-9 ◆ $6.99 | ☐ |
| Lt. Leary, Commanding (HC) | 57875-8 ◆ $24.00 | ☐ |
| Lt. Leary, Commanding (PB) | 31992-2 ◆ $7.99 | ☐ |

## The Belisarius series with Eric Flint:

| | | |
|---|---|---|
| An Oblique Approach | 87865-4 ◆ $6.99 | ☐ |
| In the Heart of Darkness | 87885-9 ◆ $6.99 | ☐ |
| Destiny's Shield | 57872-3 ◆ $6.99 | ☐ |
| Fortune's Stroke (HC) | 57871-5 ◆ $24.00 | ☐ |
| Fortune's Stroke (PB) | 31998-1 ◆ $7.99 | ☐ |
| The Tide of Victory (HC) | 31996-5 ◆ $22.00 | ☐ |

## The General series with S.M. Stirling:

| | | |
|---|---|---|
| The Forge | 72037-6 ◆ $5.99 | ☐ |
| The Chosen | 87724-0 ◆ $6.99 | ☐ |
| The Reformer | 57860-X ◆ $6.99 | ☐ |

## Independent Novels and Collections:

| | | |
|---|---|---|
| The Dragon Lord (fantasy) | 87890-5 ◆ $6.99 | ☐ |
| Birds of Prey | 57790-5 ◆ $6.99 | ☐ |
| Northworld Trilogy | 57787-5 ◆ $6.99 | ☐ |

# CLASSIC MASTERS OF SCIENCE FICTION BACK IN PRINT!

⸻∞⸻

## James Schmitz's stories
### edited by Eric Flint

| | | |
|---|---|---|
| *Telzey Amberdon* | 57851-0 ✦ $7.99 | ___ |
| *T'NT: Telzey & Trigger* | 57879-0 ✦ $6.99 | ___ |
| *Trigger & Friends* | 31966-3 ✦ $6.99 | ___ |
| *The Hub: Dangerous Territory* | | |
| | 31984-1 ✦ $6.99 | ___ |
| *Agent of Vega & Other Stories* | | |
| | 31847-0 ✦ $7.99 | ___ |

## Keith Laumer's writing
### edited by Eric Flint

| | | |
|---|---|---|
| *Retief!* | 31857-8 ✦ $6.99 | ___ |
| *Odyssey* (Mar 2002) | 0-7434-3527-3 ✦ $6.99 | ___ |

⸻∞⸻

for more books by the masters of science fiction and fantasy,
ask for our free catalog or go to www.baen.com

---

If not available through your local bookstore send this coupon and a check or money order for the cover price(s) + $1.50 s/h to Baen Books, Dept. BA, P.O. Box 1403, Riverdale, NY 10471. Delivery can take up to eight weeks.

NAME: _____

ADDRESS: _____

_____

I have enclosed a check or money order in the amount of  $ _____